Marked by Ash
Cadence Connor

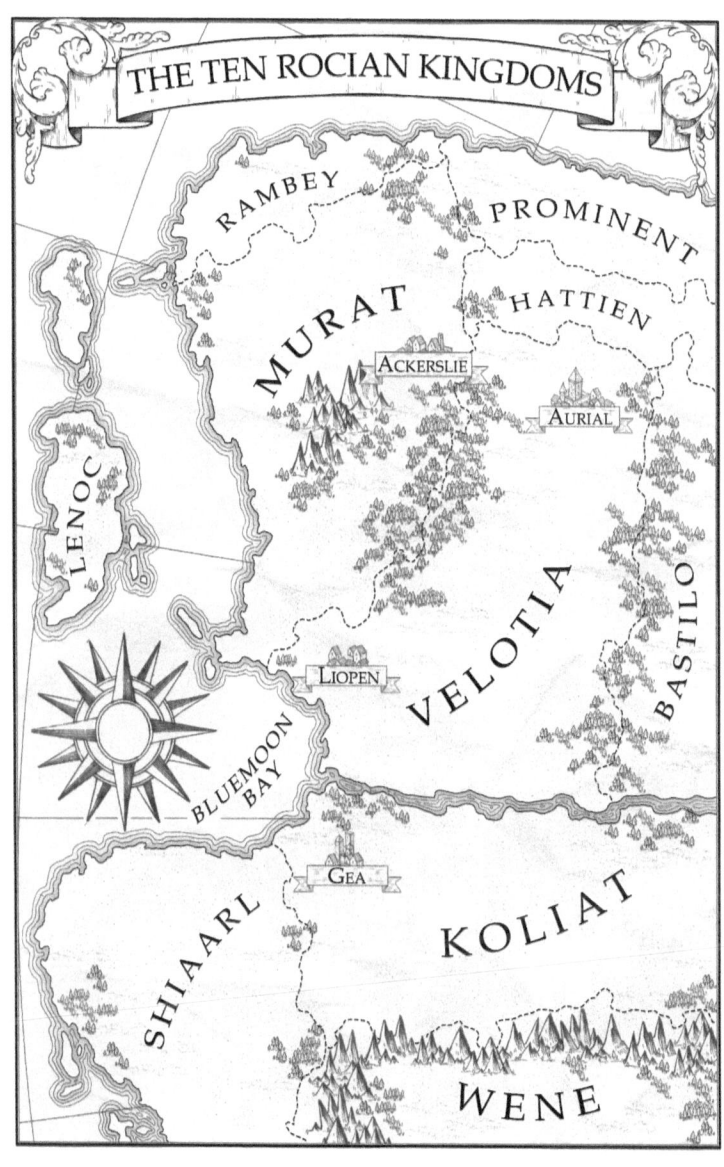

THE TEN ROCIAN KINGDOMS

RAMBEY

PROMINENT

MURAT

HATTIEN

ACKERSLIE

AURIAL

LENOC

BASTILO

VELOTIA

LIOPEN

BLUEMOON BAY

GEA

KOLIAT

SHIAARL

WENE

One
The Captain

The trickster goddess was determined to drag out his torture. Assigning him the worst punishment known to every soldier in this cursed camp was the latest from her basket of twisted gifts. No one else had been tasked with guarding the princess for this long.

No one.

Even the commander had it out for him. Why else assign him the absurdly painful duty of tailing the useless, monarchical brat?

The answer was clear, even if he refused to admit it out loud. It was the same reason he was always last to receive his rations, why his tent looked like it was regularly used for archery practice, and why he'd been scraping his way up from the bottom regiments for the past two years.

Atonement.

Commander Skallen was intent on dragging out his punishment, and *she* topped the list of anything thrown his way so far. Surely, Skallen couldn't have known how exhausting the girl was when he threw her care into the hands of his least favorite Pedite soldier.

The Princess of Velotia stood before him as the picture of absolute arrogance against the backdrop of luscious forest behind her. The way she shoved her hands on her hips and screwed her face into a frown told him exactly how much trouble he would be in if he didn't comply. If he wasn't certain he'd be thrown out of this camp before uttering the last syllable, he'd tell her exactly where she could stick her request.

The princess would have been considered stunning by all standards, if it hadn't been for that constant scowl stuck to her face. The audacity she had to act as if she were the one inconvenienced by this trip and not the other way around. She wore travel leathers—a sturdier material than his frayed uniform—with white furs to help against the forest chills, which she constantly complained about. A simple, gold circlet rested on thick brown hair that was tied back in a manner far too flashy for their journey, but then again, she had a contingent of ladies to help her dress every morning, even in the midst of a moving military camp.

She easily stuck out from the scores of black-and-silver-clad soldiers, likely by design, and squirmed with discomfort every time a branch creaked in the thick woods behind them or a harmless insect whizzed by on the way to its nest.

And, once again, she refused to listen to logic or reason. "I don't see any danger," she said. "There are no Muratians around. We haven't heard reports of them for days." She gestured around the camp, where soldiers lounged in small groups against the backs of giant redwoods, some sat next to hastily built firepits, already eating their mid-day rations—hare, judging from the smell of it. "Unless you expect one to pop out from behind a tent pole, can I have five minutes of peace without someone constantly trailing me?"

He pinched the bridge of his nose and sent a silent prayer to the goddess for patience. "As I've told you before, it's not—"

"I'm merely going for a walk in the forest," she snapped in that annoyingly airy voice that made his skin crawl. She pointed at the thick wall of vibrant greenery behind him. "I need to get away from this disgusting camp stench before I grow faint. There are men patrolling all around, and there's nothing but birds in the trees. I highly doubt a raven is going to hop out of its nest and peck my eyes out. There's nothing out here that can harm me."

Still, the commander would have his head if she so much as tripped over a loose root or ran into a wayward branch. He ground his feet into the dirt and reminded himself of his duty—his infuriating duty. "As long as it's my job to keep you safe—then no. I cannot leave your side."

Princess Isla's brown eyes, filled with layers of disdain and barely veiled anger, traveled the length of him. She took in his uniform—once black, now a faded gray, with silver stitching and matching rows of buttons—and lingered, with a smirk, on the dark spot where his Pedite crest had once been stitched.

"Out of my way, imbecile." With surprising force for one who looked so delicate, she pushed past him and skirted out of the way before he could grab her, storming off into the thickness of the woods—where she could be swallowed by a sinking mud pit as far as he was concerned.

No, wait. If that happened then *he'd* be the one to pay.

Laughter came from the nearest group of Divite soldiers, huddled in a circle over a pair of dice while finishing the last of their generous rations. One of the big stupid ones, Aniel, sneered and whispered to the hooded wielder at his side. The wielder's unwavering eyes must be on him, judging by the way the hair at the back of his neck stuck up.

It was a blessing from the goddess that the Pedite camp was usually set up far from theirs. He never could stand their withering stares, and at least nighttime brought a welcome reprieve from the stares.

There were four branches of the Velotian military: the hooded Agicae, filled with magic wielders blessed by the goddesses—or cursed, depending on who you talked to—and identified by their badge of a sword overtop a flame; the cavalry forces of the Divites, who came from influential families that chose to enlist and wore pristine uniforms adorned with dual sword badges; his infantry, the Pedites, was made up of conscripted soldiers like himself.

The Pedite captain's badge he'd once worn was decorated with an overlaid sword and hammer. The least desirable duties in the camp always fell to the Pedites, and the worst of those terrible duties––like guarding the princess––had fallen to him.

The last branch was the Siicas—special forces he'd only seen once, wearing uniforms of pure silver with badges of onyx. They usually guarded the king. Though why he didn't send them to escort his only daughter halfway across the Velotian kingdom was still a mystery—and the very reason he'd been assigned to this dreadful task instead.

A bitter laugh came from his left, and he recognized those double-looped braids instantly. *Freya.* His old friend barely glanced his way as she sat under the shade of a towering willow, sharpening the blade of her double-edged axe, Bone Breaker, with a smirk on her freckled face. "You'd better follow your charge or Commander Skallen will make your life miserable."

"Even more than now," one of the Divite soldiers called out. "If that's possible."

Laughter erupted again.

It took every ounce of strength not to turn around, grab his pack from where it still lay discarded by a broken cart, hand in his commissions to the commander, and leave this place for good. Surely, this was meant to break him. They wanted to push him over the edge and force his premature departure. He had half a mind to give them what they wanted.

Except there was nowhere else to go. And he had only one option.

One dreadful, vexing option.

Cursing to himself, he stormed after the source of his irritation. He strode past the group of laughing soldiers that circled the game, ignoring the twist in his stomach, and around a row of snacking horses, kicking rocks out of his path as he followed his charge into the canopy of green. A soldier sneered "Captain Cordrai" as he passed.

Stupid assignment.

Stupid punishment.

Stupid fucking princess.

They've reduced him to nothing more than a chaperone, traipsing off into the forest with his princess charge instead of the royal soldier he ought to be.

Why they veered this far off course into the Ashenwoods with the princess and two full battalions was beyond him. But they had a mission to complete, as simplistic as it seemed, and a package to ensure safely delivered to the Koliats. Not that there was much of a threat around here.

The Velotian military was the best throughout the ten Rocian kingdoms. Only the Muratians came close to their power—though they always lusted for more. They had already invaded the farmlands of Prominent and most of the Hattien swamplands, setting up work camps to mine for resources. They were searching for a power to overtake all the kingdoms and keep themselves at the top of it all. They'd amassed an army of wielders, mindweavers, and more magic bearers to help their cause.

But no Muratians had been spotted around here for months... and yet the commander still insisted that the princess needed protection at all times, since open war was declared two years ago. His heart thundered against his ribs at the reminder.

Naturally, princess watch had fallen straight to him. He ducked under a series of low-hanging branches and prayed to the goddess that he would make it through this in one piece.

Tracking his quarry was easy. She stomped around like a wildebeest with no care for the roots she broke or any predators she could have disturbed. While the Ashenwoods were relatively safe, vicious beasts could be lurking anywhere... and if one of those creatures happened to take a chunk out of her—as satisfying as that would be to witness—then it would mean handing in his uniform for good—or worse.

So, he followed the rampaging princess past a thorny bush, which her fur vest nearly got snagged on, through a thicket of long grass filled with ankle-breaking holes, past a particularly bristle-filled set of shrubs, and around the base of a rotting redwood. After ten minutes, she stopped outside a horrendous smelling bog that made his eyes water, which, thank the goddess, it seemed like she didn't want to soak her boots in.

A stream curled into the northern tip of the bog. Its clear water mixed with the mud and grass, battling for dominance before being consumed by the dirt and clouding over. Drooping branches tilted over the damp banks, and a canopy of green sent sparkling streams of sunlight onto the rippling water.

When he made it ten feet behind the princess, he stopped to catch his breath. He shifted from foot to foot, feeling the squish of wet moss beneath his worn boots.

All that fuss to merely stare at the bubbling brooks and reaching branches. He chuckled and asked, "Don't want to get dirty?"

At first, he thought she didn't hear, as she continued to stare at the moving water as if stuck in a trance.

He sighed.

They had to get back before anyone reported their absence to the commander. Unfortunately, with his multitude of experience with this royal terrorist, he knew he had a better chance at wrestling a red-clawed viper before convincing her to do something she didn't want to.

Perhaps he should return to the camp and pretend he never saw her storm off. Let her stumble her way back through the vines and dirt on her own.

It was a lovely thought that warmed his heart. For some reason, though, he asked, "Are you finished here?"

It was hard to see her face from this angle, but it was certainly set in that usual scowl she wore. She must be formulating her complaint to the commander and brainstorming a new way to ruin his life.

The princess shifted back, balancing on the balls of her feet. "If you must know, I'm trying to decide the best way to drown myself, so I don't have to set another foot in that atrocious camp ever again."

Dramatic, as usual. If it weren't the star-year of the goddess Slin right now, he'd think she was bluffing. But you never knew what could happen the year the stars favored the trickster goddess. Slin hated when things were in proper order and constantly hunted for new ways to torment the mortals that walked this land.

"If you need assistance throwing yourself in," he said, flexing his fingers. "Then you merely have to say the word. I'm at your service."

Her shoulders shifted as she released a quiet chuckle. An unusual sign of emotion from the taciturn princess.

A trio of blackbirds crowed loudly, skipping to the end of a long branch and angling their heads as if they watched the exchange with great interest. The leaves had started to turn blood red, an ill omen in these parts. Another reason they should return to camp immediately.

"We should really get back," he said, a hint of desperation slipping from his lips. "It'll be an early day tomorrow and Commander Skallen wishes to leave as soon as—"

"I don't care what your idiotic commander wants to do," she cut across in sharp tones, still refusing to look at him. "He can wait."

Perfect.

Short of picking her up and carrying her struggling body back, he burrowed through the recesses of his brain to figure out how to get the princess back peacefully before she could cause another delay to their progress––which the commander would inevitably blame on him again.

Perhaps a different approach would yield more success. "We need to make it to the edge of Bluemoon Bay before nightfall to set up camp so we can meet with the delegates from—"

The princess whipped around so fast that he stumbled back a step. Her eyes blazed with unrelenting fury. "I said that it can wait, *soldier.*" He refused to wince at the derogatory emphasis she placed on that word. "And if you don't stop with this incessant pestering, I'll have a word with your commander to finally remove you from your post."

He recoiled and bit out, "It's my job to make sure you get there in one piece, and I'd rather we didn't linger."

A toad croaked, and several leaves fell off their branches, landing at the base of a blooming maple. The hair on his arms bristled.

The birds had stopped their crowing and the insects' hum fell silent. The brook continued to bubble as if nothing were amiss.

The princess scoffed. "I don't take orders from a low-born simpleton that can barely manage to—"

"*Shut up,*" he hissed, holding up a hand. Every beat of his heart was amplified by the strangely quiet forest.

The princess froze with her mouth gaping, finally lost for words.

A breeze trickled through the trees and forced hair into his eyes which he quickly brushed back as he scanned the small clearing. His left hand moved to the pommel of his broadsword, one of the few possessions remaining from his father.

Princess Isla drew herself up to full height. "How dare you speak to me like—"

He threw a hand over her mouth, ignoring the weight that filled his chest. "I said be quiet," he whispered. The blood pounding against his ears drowned out nearly everything, yet he was calmly in control, as he was trained to be. "I thought I heard something."

New rustling came from a thick bush across the bog.

The princess's brown eyes grew wide and she stopped struggling. He released her mouth and moved his grip to her arm as another rustle came from behind a low clump of blossoming trees.

Princess Isla's breaths came in heavy drags, and her head whipped to the side when yet another branch creaked.

It could be nothing but a curious badger coming to investigate or a wayward doe passing by. It could have been the wind, but the wind didn't make such sounds. Could it be an elemental? The wielders from their northern neighbors, Murat, were known to bend them to their will from time to time but the likelihood of one coming this far on their own was nearly impossible.

Every fiber of his being told him this wasn't the natural swaying of the forest. It was something else. The arm beneath his grip trembled.

"Do you remember the way back to camp?" he asked, keeping his voice barely above a whisper. He never should have let her wander this far.

The princess swallowed whatever lump was in her throat and nodded.

The trees shifted as an unnatural gale swayed past, chilling his blood. He pulled his blade, Dark End, from its scabbard and released the grip on her.

"Then *run!*"

Two

The Princess

When she was little, Isla's brother replaced the jewel of her favorite necklace with a sleeping stink beetle. They were the same obsidian color and both sparkled in the sunlight, so she never noticed the difference until it was far too late. Her mother's necklace was ruined, and her maid scrubbed her in a scalding bath until her skin cracked and bled in a vain attempt to remove the smell.

All this did was goad her brother into trying new pranks that would torment her. He took the utmost pleasure in those that would bring her any form of pain, and she was never allowed to retaliate. Needless to say, she'd hated pranks since.

If this was all a trick by that paltry excuse of a Pedite soldier—Cordrai or whatever they called him—then she'd have his head removed and stuffed with a thousand stink beetles before they even arrived at that goddess-forsakened bay.

The sight must have been comical—her inept attempt to run through this weed-filled forest without losing her balance or face-planting into a redwood. Her travel leathers weren't built for such exertion, and her fur vest kept getting caught in branches determined to slow her down.

Pine-soaked air ripped through her lungs as blood pumped from her limbs into her shaking fingertips. An overhanging branch whipped across her face, clinging to the skin and drawing blood as she struggled past. The crunch of footsteps behind her was enough to tell her that she had been followed and she didn't care to find out by whom.

If she could just make it back to the camp, then the others would help her. She prayed to the goddess this was the right way.

Her foot caught on a root that had been camouflaged against the forest floor, and she flew into a pile of damp leaves, scraping off a layer of skin in the process. Her palm stung and pain worse than anything she'd experienced exploded from the side of her shoulder where she landed.

Isla never liked these forests, and now she knew why. If she burn it all down before leaving, she would.

The taste of metal coated her tongue, and the sound of dead leaves rustling was accompanied by steel unsheathing from leather. She swallowed the lump that had lodged in her throat but it wouldn't move.

Shining black boots stepped into view. She twisted her head to see a soldier with a high-collared blue leather uniform with fine gold lacings, engraved buttons, and matching knots at the shoulder. She'd been to enough war-room meetings with her father and heard enough battle depictions to recognize that uniform in an instant. It made her blood clot.

A Muratian soldier.

Noises from around the forest indicated that he was not alone.

The soldier's gloved hand tensed on the hilt of his red sword, and his boots kicked up a dirt cloud that sent her into a coughing fit. Laughter—*laughter* filled her ears before rough hands pulled her to her feet. Something hard hit her across the face and stars erupted in the back of her eyes.

If only she had a dagger or sword or—*anything*.

All she had was her fists, which she flung at the man, scraping his face with her nails as she tried to struggle free.

"You stupid bitch."

A fist hit her stomach and she doubled over gasping for breath. Before she could do more than wheeze and sputter incoherently, she was pulled upright by her hair as he shouted something at the other blue-clad soldiers.

Her heart pulsed frantically. She grabbed for his face again, rage and anger fueling her blood and threatening to spill over.

Something shiny whipped past her head, skimming the side above her ear, and momentarily stunning her. The soldier took advantage of her surprise and pinned her arms to her side. His rancid breath tickled the back of her neck and made her want to spew her lunch.

Laughter. Cold and lifeless and—female—came from a patchy area to her left.

A hooded woman slithered out of the shade of a tall pine, lithe and moving with purpose. With her were three hulking Muratian soldiers with the same crisp blue uniforms and bright gold stitching.

Where was that moody guard when she needed him? He'd followed her every step into the forest but *now* she was left on her own.

Hot tears threatened to spill out, but she refused to show any sign of weakness.

The woman spoke, and the iciness lacing every syllable sent a shudder down Isla's spine. "Why don't you make things easy and come with us, princess? We wouldn't want to mess with a pretty hair on that delicate head now, would we?"

Isla didn't need to see the woman's face to know it was twisted in a cruel sneer.

The other soldiers who joined laughed, their voices echoing all around her.

Once again, Isla stupidly reached at her side for a blade or something that would help her. She'd refused to take one on this journey as she hated carrying the extra weight, and she had no need when there were guards constantly trailing her.

All she had was the faint memories of the paltry training with her old mentor, well past his prime, who refused to instruct her in anything but the basics, under strict instructions from her father. But that was a long time ago and, to her dismay, she found nothing but dirt and leaves at her side.

The woman's cold voice rang out again. "Now, I know you don't plan on fighting us, princess?" She pulled out a hand from beneath her cloak and pointed a finger toward Isla.

Something shifted in the air, like the charge before a coming storm.

It crept along the forest bed, trailing its way to her. A wave of nausea overcame Isla when it hit her and she fell to her knees. Pain split across her bones, reaching from her insides and twisting everything until she was certain she would snap in two.

She couldn't think—couldn't scream. Pain encompassed everything she was. Blackness fogged her vision and just when she thought she would explode, it stopped.

Isla was panting on the ground, with the sounds of laughter echoing in her ears. She lifted her head and the hooded woman closed her fist.

The terrifying realization sank into her bones. That woman was a wielder... and she was not the only one.

Three

The Captain

The trickster goddess loved tormenting him, she always had.

What other explanation could there be for this happening when he was days away from finishing this assignment and getting reinstated as captain?

While his charge—his punishment—disappeared into the thick brush, headed in what he could only pray was the proper direction, a blue-clad Muratian soldier appeared out of the air and charged him.

A wielder.

They had a wielder transporting them. This one was similar to one they had when he was first conscripted, that wielder used his gifts to sneak them extra rations when the Pedites were low on supplies. He cursed his luck and flexed his grip, running his finger along the chip in Dark End's hilt.

Muscle memory from years of play-fighting using the home-made course that his father had made him and his brother run through daily came to him. They had to run up and down a steep hill littered with obstacles while keeping hold of the wooden swords he carved for them and could only come in for supper once he was satisfied with their form. All so they may survive their father's eventual *gift*—conscription into the Velotian military—and send home what little pay they received.

Whenever he was sent into battle, he liked to imagine he was back at home playing on that course. He pretended any of the soldiers he killed were nothing more than a felled tree. It helped keep the nightmares away... most nights. Thanks to those days spent on the course, he easily dodged the soldier as if he were a straw ball loftily thrown his way.

His chipped longsword was in his hand faster than the time it took the sluggish Muratian brute to turn around.

Dark End twisted in the air and flung down at the soldier's barrel chest, slicing through leather and muscle like it was water. The sight of crimson sent a tide of nausea through his gut. He didn't bother to look at his blade to know it would be covered.

Deep breaths cut across his lungs that had nothing to do with physical exertion.

A fierce wind picked up, sending branches crashing into one another and a rainfall of leaves dropping into the muddy water, which continued its bubbling, undisturbed.

Two broad-shouldered soldiers replaced the first one, appearing out of nowhere thanks to the machinations of whatever wielder they had with them.

Both wore looped knots on their shoulders, indicating their high rank in the Muratian army. The tips of their blades sparkled in the strands of light that made their way through the thick canopy overhead.

They were faster and lighter on their feet, not as poorly trained as the first soldier. It took all his years of training not to get skewered within the first five seconds.

The ring of steel against steel vibrated throughout his skull as one of the soldiers rushed him. The force of the crash sent beads of sweat flying his way. It nearly toppled him, but he dug his heel in and pushed back. If he let up for even one second then he'd be dead.

Instinct told him to use that weight against him. To use that momentum as a tool rather than allow the soldier to gain any ground.

So he countered, sliding his steel down the side of the soldier's blade until it collided with a leathered hand. The soldier yelped and dropped his hold, creating the perfect opening.

Belting a roar that sent birds scattering, he dove the end of his sword into the soldier's stomach, driving his blade until it could go in no further as he pushed him into the base of a thick redwood.

A drop of blood trickled from the corner of the soldier's mouth before the man slid to the ground, his eyes wide and lifeless.

His companion uttered a strangled cry and charged haphazardly. In his rage, he was easier to take down and tumbled to the ground in a heap of sweat and blood, joining his blue-clad companion in the dirt.

Those heavy, ragged breaths tore through his lungs, and a pair of blackbirds resumed their prior song as if nothing happened. His grip on the hilt was so tight his knuckles were turning white.

A twig snapped, and he whipped around.

He slackened his grip on Dark End when a pair of black tree mice scuttled out from under a brush.

A moment passed. Then another, in which no more soldiers appeared.

Not surprising as he was never the target of this attack. They were after *her*. He slackened the hand holding his blade but didn't slide it back into its sheath.

Why did she have to pick today to run off from camp like that? If he had stopped her like he should have, none of this mess would be happening.

The commander would surely take his uniform for this.

If he held any semblance of sanity, he should turn on his heel and run in the opposite direction until his legs gave up.

Yet he was the one handed this dreadful assignment and if he returned without the princess—in one piece—then losing his uniform would be the last thing he'd have to worry about. With a heavy sigh, he plucked a discarded Muratian dagger from the forest floor and headed in the direction of the high-pitched screams.

It was easy to find the princess. Much easier than he expected given the ruckus she'd raised on her way out, and the path she had carved into the forest from speeding off like a blind hammerboar.

She wasn't alone.

At least six soldiers surrounded her. One held her by the tangles of her hair. A quick scan told him there were at least two Muratian wielders there—judging by their blue cloaks.

His heart wilted into itself. They were outmatched.

He was a decent soldier. A gifted fighter—or so he'd been told. Still, a gifted fighter was no match against two wielders.

At least he had the element of surprise, still hidden in the shade of a thick birchwood. If he was going to go down, at least he could take a few of them with him first.

His hands dug into the belt at his side and pulled out a thin dagger that was once his father's, gifted by an old general, along with the Muratian one. They were in the air before the Muratians could register his presence.

Both met their marks and the two soldiers, including the one holding the princess, fell to the ground with a thud.

The wielder closest to him whipped around with a hand out. A rush of wind passed, before a sickening feeling overcame him, nearly sending him crashing to his knees. His vision was filled with blood and chaos and burning buildings. So many burning buildings.

A painful darkness clawed through his brain, pulling him into a never-ending abyss that would consume all. That annoying high-pitched scream cut through the shadows.

No!

His mind snapped back to the fluttering green and gold of the forest. He had an assignment to complete, and he'd be damned if anything was stopping him this time.

Sheer will and determination kept him standing, fighting against the waves of pain until it subsided. He registered a hint of surprise on what little of the wielder's face he could see, clearly not expecting him to resist the attack.

As the princess wasn't a threat and remained gasping on the ground, the remaining soldiers shifted their focus to him. Dark End was back in his hand in a swift movement, blocking the first blow.

Then the next. And the next. Inching closer to the princess with every strike. That was his focus. That was his mission.

Princess Isla somehow managed to struggle to her feet. What in Slin's name did she think she was going to do?

The first wielder—a woman—shouted orders at the others. The hard edge of her voice would have sent shivers down his spine had he not been so preoccupied with keeping his head attached to his neck.

He dodged one soldier, then blocked the next. A new one appeared out of nowhere, followed by a second.

They were still too far away from the encampment for anyone to hear. The princess was known to storm off like this regularly, and that meant nobody would come looking for them for a while. By then, it would be too late.

They had to get out of here... but how?

A shadow flew overhead. Dark and twisted. It reached into the forest with a death-like tendril trying to pull all life toward its sharp grasp.

Wielder magic.

Several of the Muratians screamed.

In what must have been a desperate attempt at ending this quickly, the second wielder dove for the princess. A surge of energy filled the air, whipping past him and sending branches falling.

His breath caught as the wielder closed the gap. He grabbed his dagger out of the unmoving body next to him and dove towards the princess, driving it into the man's chest at the same time the wielder clasped a claw-like hand around her.

The other wielder shrieked before all sound evaporated.

A burning white cloud overtook everything, heating his blood to the verge of boiling over. He tried to scream but nothing came out. Every bone, every muscle, and every inch of skin teetered on the verge of melting.

Surely, he was dying as there didn't seem to be any escape from this agony. If he wasn't already dead, he wanted to be.

Anything to stop the pain. The overwhelming, all-encompassing, bone shattering pain.

Everything stopped.

It was over as fast as it started.

He took a moment to try to get a grasp on his shaking body. It felt like a dagger had been plunged into his side, and he struggled to bring his pounding heart to a steady rhythm.

Something moved under his hand. With a start, he realized that his hand still grasped the dagger stuck in the wielder's chest. The man's eyes were wide and blank, with his mouth still open in a silent scream. He slackened his grip on the handle and let go as the wielder slumped over—directly on top of the princess.

She squealed and crumpled under the weight, landing in a tangled mess of limbs. It was difficult trying to lift the heavy, lifeless mass off her, especially when the princess wailed on him with her fists.

"I. Am. Trying. To. Help. You. Idiot," he grunted out in between blows.

At least nobody ever bothered to teach her how to properly throw a punch.

"Get off of me." She kicked his shin and shoved him hard enough to send him tripping backward over a loose stump. "I had that completely handled."

"Sure, you did." He held his hand up and caught her next punch. "It's not like you were nearly impaled at the end of a soldier's sword or about to be kidnapped to who-knows-where before I came."

The princess stared at him, then she let out a scream and stomped to the edge of the small grove—most likely to report him to the commander for insubordination and get him fully kicked off the regiment for good—when she froze.

His eyes followed hers, and the sight sent a cold punch directly to his chest.

This was all wrong.

Instead of lush, thick bases, the trees were scraggly and twisted at odd angles. The few leaves that managed to bloom were browning or already dead. There was no soft cushion of moss growing at the base of trees, and no sprouting buds on the thorny bushes. Even the smell of the forest, which was usually fresh and full of pine, was replaced with a stale, old smell—as if nothing new had grown here in years.

The sun was further down the horizon than it should have been, casting long shadows across the half-dead trees, which groaned in the wind. No birds whistled happy songs from the gnarled branches and only dirt coated the bases of the rotting trees.

His world started spinning.

No. No. No.

This could not be happening to him. Not now.

They were not in the Velotian Ashenwoods anymore.

Even though he'd never left Velotia—except for the one time which he'd expressly forbade himself from ever mentioning again—he knew this wasn't home. They had been transported to the Black Forests of Murat, right in the middle of their two capital cities, and far from where they were supposed to be. Far from where he was supposed to deliver the princess.

They were alone and in the middle of their enemy's territory.

Fuck.

At least the trickster goddess was deadly accurate in her jest this time. This princess really was going to be responsible for his total ruination and death.

Four

Mira

If the falling rocks and frequent cave-ins didn't crush her bones and crumble her spirit, then today's lumpy gruel would certainly be the end of her.

Every day down here was the same as the last. Breaking rock, digging dirt, clearing paths, avoiding slicing a hand on the sharp rock, and trying to stay as invisible as possible. That was what she did day in and day out.

It was hard to remember a time before the caves and the rocks and the digging. Her bones were constantly screaming for a break and her body felt like it could crumble at any moment. There wasn't a time when she didn't go to bed tired, hungry, and with aching muscles that dreamed of a soft mattress.

Mira had been here for what felt like forever. It had been months, maybe even years. It was hard to tell time in this place. The only benchmark she had was how long Beretta was here. She had been here for at least two years, and then Mira came sometime after. That was the only way she knew anything in this dreadful place, and her friend was the only reason she kept a slippery grip on her small semblance of sanity.

Some days stood still, seeming to never end, and others flew past before she could blink. Beretta thought the mind fog was caused by the firestone they harvested and its magical properties. It could mess with someone's mind if they were exposed to it too much.

Firestone held some of the ancient magics of the land, said to be infused by the goddesses themselves. Wielders once used the stone to advance their powers or it could be used to dull certain wielder's magic. The strongest firestone was found at the ancient portals to the godlands––several of which were hidden in these mountains centuries ago.

The stone was a powerful weapon that could reverse the tragedies of this war. At least that's what they told her and that's why they were selected to help with the harvesting. That was what they did every day besides sleeping and eating... and trying to force down the terrible gruel rations lest they waste away.

Beretta had somehow finished her entire serving and decided to lick her bowl clean. A night shift down the shaft tended to get her appetite up like this. She wiped her mouth with a dirty sleeve and peered into Mira's bowl with a wistful look in her blue eyes. "I think you got more than me."

That wasn't something to brag about. Plus, it was usually Beretta who was able to sweet talk the guards into giving her a second helping. Today they had new guards who she hadn't been able to work her charm on yet.

Mira allowed the grayish slop to tumble from her spoon into the wooden bowl without a care for the drops of gunk that splashed back on her face.

Disgusting.

She shoved the bowl in her friend's face. "If you like it so much, finish mine."

Beretta looked between her and the bowl several times, licking her lips as if the sight was somehow appetizing. She dumped the remainder of Mira's rations into her bowl, watching as the two mixed together in comical semblance of a muddy river.

Between shovelfuls of food, she managed to choke out, "I keep telling you that you need to lower your standards here. I don't know what you expect—a lavish royal spread in these conditions?" She snorted into her bowl. "Seriously, though. You need to eat more or you won't make it through the night shifts."

"I'll be fine." If she said it enough, then maybe she'd begin to think it true. That was what she clung to when it all became too much. That was all she had in a prison where they were denied anything else.

They weren't prisoners by the loosest of definitions, but they couldn't leave. It was complicated whenever Beretta explained it to her and she had to many times already. It wasn't Mira's fault that the exhaustion mixed with the firestone muddled her brain.

Beretta finished her bowl in record time. She tossed it to the side, crossed one leg over the other, and leaned back against the damp rock.

Some time remained before they would be called back so Mira crossed her arms, curled alongside her, and closed her eyes in the hopes of catching a nap. Their group had fallen behind and one of the more ruthless commanders was coming this week, so they were assigned double duty as a *favor* in order for them to catch up.

Mira didn't understand the urgency. The firestone wasn't going anywhere, it was stuck inside the mountain, so what kind of schedule could they be falling behind on?

Unless they were searching for something else.... She'd voiced her thoughts out loud before, but Beretta merely laughed her off for thinking such foolishness. Nevertheless, they continued to dig and pound away at the hard rock underneath this stubborn mountain until their callouses burst and their backs ached.

The dredger closest to them—a nickname the guards gave to the workers—threw his bowl into Beretta's discarded one. Both went clattering away and nearly hit a burly guard who stood arrogantly in his high-collared blue and gold uniform.

The guard whipped around and his eyes flashed past Mira and Beretta, who both pointedly looked away, before narrowing on the hunched-back, toothless old man who was merely flesh and bones at this point.

How long had he been down here?

Mira prayed to the one-eyed goddess Halia—goddess over the mountains and forests, whom Muratians rarely called upon—that she wouldn't be down here that long. She prayed that she'd be able to work off her debt and leave with all her teeth and limbs. Although Beretta always reminded her that she was better served to pray to the trickster goddess Slin, as surely, she had ownership over their lives now. Mira did not need any more chaos in her life and would stick to the goddess she could see and feel in the shape of this mountain.

The guard marched over to the dredger they called Ona and before anyone could utter a word, he kicked him.

The guard bent over the withering man with a dark look across his features. "Get up, you worthless dredger."

Mira sat up. A hand tightened around her elbow.

"Don't," Beretta hissed as if she could sense her intentions. "They'll make us work a triple shift... or worse."

And there was always worse. She'd seen much of it in her time here but was usually, and thankfully, spared from any of the harsher punishments herself. She stayed with Beretta, and together they kept their heads low and stayed hard at work to make that possible.

That was how they survived. It was how they made it through one horrid, never-ending day and into the next. The only hope they clung to was the thought of getting an extra-long break, being served a generous portion of food if they were friendly to the guards, and finding a good piece of firestone that may just get one of those highly sought-after daily reprieves above ground.

It happened to Mira three times since she'd been here, even though she'd found the firestone more times than that. Twice she let Beretta take the claim as her poor friend had yet to find any and desperately needed a break. One time a big miner they called Crag took the firestone from her hands after a swift punch to the gullet and claimed it as his own. He was friendly with the soldiers so there was nothing she could do about it. Several times the soldiers whom she showed the piece to had ended up taking it for themselves and promised a beating if she said anything.

Those few instances she actually claimed credit for finding that special stone were the best of times. Once, she was even allowed to take a glorious bath above ground, even if the water was cold and had probably gone through five others before she was allowed to touch it. It was the best bath she could remember having, and that was saying something.

She looked back on those times wistfully and prayed to Halia that she would find one again. The goddess knew that she needed a break.

After dumping a bucket of water on Ona, the guard decided it wasn't worth his time and stormed off, not before throwing the leftover pot of gruel against the wall. It slid down the rock in vomit-colored lumps.

Beretta groaned. Perhaps she was hoping a miracle would have afforded her another helping?

Too late for that unless she wished to eat off the ground—and they'd only ever done that once before while at their most desperate.

Strands of hair tickled her face, having fallen out of the tight braids Beretta helped weave into her *mousy hair*, as she liked to call it. She blew it out of her eye. Hopefully, Beretta would help her fix it when they had their next break—if they got one.

Not that she would complain out loud near the rest of the dredgers.

All the workers had their heads shaved a few weeks ago due to an infestation, even the poor women. All of them except for Mira and Beretta, thanks to Beretta's incessant pleading with the head guard to let them keep it, along with the promise they'd keep their hair clean and wouldn't let it get in the way. Her sweet talking and *alone time* with the guard had worked and they were the only ones spared the shears.

While Mira was glad to keep her hair, that only made the others glare at them even more than usual. Beretta wasn't as bothered by their withering stares or hate-soaked whispers. She seemed to drink in the attention and said they were just jealous.

Though she paled in comparison to her friend with her bright blue eyes and vibrant red hair that never seemed to lose its shine even when covered in dirt and dust, Mira was fond of her hair, even if Beretta told her it was dull. Not that there was anyone she wanted to impress down here... none that were down here today anyway.

Most days it was like she stood still. Unsurprising, given that she hadn't left this mountain with its low ceilings and tight tunnels, in ages.

A part of her was always waiting. Waiting for the break of dawn that lay beyond the horizon, yet the light never came. Waiting for the crash of branches against each other, and yet no sound could ever be heard.

Perhaps she'd wait forever under this mountain. Until the day it became too much.

"Come on." Beretta grabbed her arm and half-lifted her. "It's time to head back."

A groan escaped her lips. "Already? I was daydreaming of a steaming bath under the stars."

Her friend scoffed, falling in line behind a wiry dredger. "Well, if you don't get your head out of the clouds and back beneath the rocks, we're both going to get solitary punishment. Is that what you want?"

Dark memories flooded her mind.

When she first got here, Mira was subjected to days—or maybe weeks—of solitary punishment. It was hard to tell how long she was there for as time crawled in a specially tormenting kind of way. All that she knew was that it was the worst time of her life and she would do everything in her power not to go back.

If it weren't for bumping into Beretta when she got out, she may have just laid down her pickaxe and succumbed to an ever-long slumber. Thankfully, she found some semblance of a life down here, as small as that glimmer of happiness was.

This was all she had. This was all she could remember and all that she was. Her sole purpose was to dig out these magic rocks and wait for small rays of sunshine to burst through.

And so, she hoisted the heavy pick in her calloused and bruised hands and swung as hard as she could, ignoring the ache of the half-healed lashes on her knuckles from last week. It was all muscle memory now. The swing of the pickaxe through the air, the way it banged against the hard bedrock, slowly chipping away at years—at centuries—of salt, grime, and earth, all before it chipped away at her last drop of sanity.

The feel of metal crashing against the hard rock soothed her in a cathartic way. It was the one thing she had control over and the one thing she leaned into with all of her strength and every particle of her being. So, she put all her energy into every blow as if it were the last thing she would ever do, as it very well could be any day now.

They must have gone for hours into the night at least. It was hard to tell with nothing but a few small lanterns this far down.

A soldier came by with a fresh bucket of water, which was perfect as her throat had turned into a crisp desert. She was certain she'd swallowed two buckets worth of dirt that day.

"Thank the goddess," Beretta said, stopping mid swing to wipe sweat from her forehead and only succeeding in rubbing a patch of dirt across her face. Mira giggled at the sight then stopped as soon as a soldier's head snapped her way. She focused on her busted and frayed boots while nerves filled her veins, praying to the goddess that had long abandoned them that the guard hadn't noticed her laugh.

The same hunched back dredger grabbed at the bucket greedily, spilling half the water on his shoes. A second soldier, a beefy man with a wiry mustache, laughed and kicked the bucket out of Ona's frail hands, where it spilled into a puddle of mud and dirt.

The dredger dove to the ground and scooped up whatever bits of liquid he could find while the soldiers all laughed and sneered at him. Ona was always a rambler with a brain full of rocks, spewing nonsense to anyone who would listen. No wonder he didn't care about drinking muddy water.

Mira's throat constricted in protest when the last bit of water was absorbed by the rock.

"Hey!" A thick-necked dredger with a large scar across his face threw his pick into the dirt. "We didn't get any of that yet. Are you going to get more for us?"

"What did you say, scum?" The soldier marched up to him, his hand resting casually on a dagger at the side of his pressed blue and gold uniform.

Beretta looked away, pretending to adjust the hilt on her pickaxe. Try as she might not to notice, Mira couldn't help but focus on the exchange.

The dredger didn't falter in the shadow of the hulking soldier. "How do you expect us to work through the night when we haven't had a drop of water? It's impossible."

"Get back to work." The soldier gathered himself up so that he towered over the man.

"Not without some water," the dredger said.

"Don't make me say it again." A dangerous smile filled the soldier's face. He poked the man's chest with his index finger, while Mira felt the hair on her arms rise in anticipation of what happened next.

She pressed her eyes closed, holding them so tight that stars began to form. At the next sound, they snapped open of their own accord. It sounded like a boulder being cleaved in two. It wasn't a boulder but a nose breaking as a fist crashed into it.

The soldier went wheeling back into the rock.

A roar of sound rushed over them as two soldiers grabbed the dredger and dragged him, scratching and screaming, towards a protruding rock. The beefy soldier, now sporting a crooked and bleeding nose, was back on his feet and folding back the sleeves of his uniform. She'd never seen him look so happy.

A hush came over them as a new guard—a private—entered and surveyed the scene in front. Mira cast her eyes downward when they landed on her, lingering for a second longer than they should have. The private handed over a leather whip with a dozen braided ends that were designed to cause the most damage.

The soldiers didn't even bother removing the dredger's already tattered shirt before the beefy one lifted his arm. His lip curled over in pure bliss as the bicep flexed back, readying the strike.

Beretta clutched her arm, her hands shaking.

The first crack of the whip made Mira jump. She hugged her arms around herself in some pathetic form of comfort, as if anything could make this better.

This wasn't the first time this had happened, not by far.

The sound of the whip against bare flesh was familiar down here. Familiar to her. The noise haunted her dreams for as long as she could remember.

When she couldn't take that noise anymore, she clamped her hands over her ears and turned away, but Beretta held her shoulders.

"They'll see you," she said, her eyes glazed over as if she were in a land far away. That was a trick she'd taught Mira early on. Eyes on the punishment, like they wanted, but keep your mind far away. Whatever it took to stay unnoticed or they'd send you to the pits. "You have to watch or they'll punish you too."

So, Mira did the same. Her eyes traced the movement of the leather whip as it moved up and snapped down. When it made contact, she pretended it snapped against hard stone instead of tearing through weak muscle and flesh. Each time it moved into the air, she envisioned wandering through a lush forest filled with green and gold leaves, and that the sounds she heard were merely branches cracking beneath her feet. She imagined she was any place but here, and anyone but herself.

It took forever for it to be over. Two guards dragged the unmoving dredger away, leaving a bloody trail in their wake. The nearest guard yelled at them to get back to work and Mira picked up her tools with shaky hands, ignoring the prickle at the corners of her eyes.

One thing was for certain, this place was going to be the end of her if she stayed. Mira vowed to the goddess to get out before that could happen.

Five

The Captain

The hands at his side were clenched into tight balls, on the verge of cutting off all circulation. It was all he could do to stop himself from losing what small semblance of control he had in the face of Her Royal Annoyance.

"What have you done?"

"Excuse me?" If his eyebrows could have gone any higher, he was certain they'd be halfway into the tree line. His blood was at a boiling point after the slew of accusations she'd been spewing at him. "I'm the one who just saved your ass."

The tone of her voice took on a shrill pitch that would surely haunt his nightmares for weeks. It was a good thing there were no birds within earshot—he wasn't sure there was much living in this poor excuse of a forest anyway. "I'm supposed to be meeting my betrothed *tomorrow*, and you're telling me that we are weeks away from where we should be... in the middle of Muratian lands, no less."

"Yes," he said simply. Satisfaction filled him like a warm drink when all she could do was sputter while he examined the body that arrived with them.

The wielder that transported them here missed his target of the capital thanks to the dagger that slipped its way between his ribs. "I'd say we're at least five weeks' journey by foot—quicker if we can somehow find a good horse, and longer if we are forced to take any detours."

After he pulled the dagger out of the Muratian wielder, ignoring the sickening sound it made, he dug through the still-warm body's pockets, searching for anything that could help them. The sound of clinking metal caught his ear, as it always did. He pulled out a small bag of silver coins etched with the Muratian King's face and pocketed it. When he removed the man's cloak and started unbuttoning the uniform jacket underneath, the princess found her voice again.

He didn't need to see her face to know it must be twisted in some form of haughty indignation. "Are you actually robbing that dead body right now? Is a new jacket and a couple of silver coins honestly your priority? I knew you Pedite soldiers were craven but I didn't think you would stoop to this. Let the dead sleep."

This girl had to be joking. Nobody could be that stupid.

Nobody.

Then again, the idiocy of this princess surpassed anyone he'd ever known.

"Look around," he snapped, removing his jacket and pulling the blue and gold one on. It was a tight fit, but at least the blood stains mostly kept to the inside lining. "We are in the middle of Muratian lands. I'm certain half their army is out looking for you right now, and we somehow have to make our way through miles of their people and soldiers before we can get you back to safety. Do you think running around in Velotia's military colors is a good idea? Do you think they're going to let us waltz through their villages and help us out based on the goodness of their hearts? Get a grip, *Your Highness.*"

This wasn't a friendly jaunt in the forest. There were actual dangers here and she needed to realize it, or she'd get them both killed. No, he couldn't gamble on any sense of sanity pulling through with her when she had yet to display a hint of common sense since they left the capital on this cursed journey.

All she could do was stand there and glare for a moment, before spewing a stream of mixed curses and swears, calling him several colorful names—he'd been called worse by people he actually cared about.

He laughed and tossed her the cloak before grabbing a navy satchel and throwing it over his shoulder. "You'll want to wear that as not many of the plains folk over here are outfitted in fine leather or furs, and dispose of that horrid tiara. You'll give yourself away in seconds and get us both killed."

The cloak remained in her hands, limp at her side. "What do you mean?"

He stood and closed the distance between them. The princess didn't flinch this time. "If you want to survive and make it in time to your fancy wedding, then you better do what I say."

The princess's nostrils flared. At this proximity, every fleck of brown in those annoying eyes glared at him. "No... we're going to do what I say. I'm the one in charge, not some washed-up excuse of a royal soldier."

He bit down the retort simmering at the back of his throat. "You might be able to pull rank when we're in camp on *our* lands, Your Extreme Excellency, but look around." He waved his arm like a crazed person, pointing from a felled trunk to a pitiful tree that had less than ten brown leaves adorning it. "The forest is empty except for us. There's nobody else coming. It's just you and me. And the only one I trust to have the slightest chance of getting us back alive... is me!" He thrust his thumb into his chest.

That only seemed to incense her more. Perfect.

She threw her hands on her hips. "I said that *I'm* in charge and someone like you can't talk to me like that. I will make sure that you pay for this insolence when we get back. Wait! Where—where do you think you're going?"

Amid her tirade, he turned on his heel and stormed to the end of the clearing they'd landed in. "I'm going to look for a suitable place to make camp before the sun goes down and we freeze to death or get eaten alive by whatever creatures may be roaming around here."

"Camp?" she repeated, fear sneaking its way into her voice for the first time. "What do you mean by *camp*?"

He laughed uncontrollably.

The princess clenched her jaw. "I am *not* sleeping outside."

"Oh, no?" Chuckles still racked his chest no matter how hard he attempted to banish them. "Care to find us a bustling inn or comfy lodge instead? Or do you think some nearby Muratian lord will welcome us into his hearth and home? Let me know which way the nearest stronghold is and I'll gladly take you there, Your Supreme Eminence."

"Don't patronize me. I don't expect to find a castle in the middle of this—this—"

"Forest."

"In the middle of this forest," she continued, her voice growing louder with every word. He prayed to the goddess that they were alone in these cursed woods. "There must be some sort of accommodation nearby."

Clearly, they didn't teach enemy cartography in the royal palace. "Well, where's the nearest village if you're so smart?"

The princess looked from the bushes behind her to a section filled with prickly vines, then back to the brightly lit, clear path where he had been heading. She cleared her throat and adjusted the lop-sided circlet on her head.

"We're going this way." She pointed to her left, down a dark path littered with dead moss and fallen trunks. "Because I say so."

"That's a terrible idea. Why don't we just find a cliff to throw ourselves off of instead?"

She threw the wielder's cloak over her shoulder and tucked a piece of tangled hair back into the pile on top of her head. "I don't have to take this from you."

Stepping to the side in a sweeping mock-bow, he mustered the most righteous voice he could, "Go right ahead. I think I hear running water, so I'll be going that way." He pointed down the bright path.

"Fine." Her face was set, unmoving—just as his resolve was.

"Fine."

With a turn of his heel, he stormed off. Judging by the crunch of dead leaves headed in the opposite direction, so had she.

At the edge of the grove, he paused and craned his head, hoping to pick up that bubbling sound he heard earlier now that the annoyance was gone. If there was a river or stream nearby, they could follow it to a working pathway or maybe a small village where they could get some directions, and, hopefully, not end up stabbed in a hollow somewhere.

Hopefully.

Anything could happen while in Muratian territory. Deep Muratian territory if he had to guess based on the lack of any living vegetation. It would take a miracle from the star-goddess herself for him to get out of here alive. He was better off alone. There had to be a way to convince the commander none of this was his fault. Perhaps that would be easier if—

A piercing scream met his ears.

His entire body recoiled and a deep sigh rose from his chest. A small part of him begged to ignore the noise and keep going. Perhaps he could find a nice thicket full of berries to eat or some wildlife to hunt. He could try to find that fresh water source.

Anything but heading back towards that voice.

Unfortunately, the rational part of him nagged at the back of his head. It reminded him that he could never show his face back at the encampment without that godsdamned princess. He'd never get his commissions and they'd have his head for losing her. Keeping his body parts intact was the only logical option.

So, he trudged off after her, muttering angrily and shoving wayward branches out of the way as if each twig was responsible for his current situation. The path grew narrower and the roots and vines grew larger, almost grabbing at him as he stormed past.

He saw a flicker of flashing violet that was gone before he could turn around. If there were any wisps in this forest, he prayed they stayed far away from him this day.

When he finally came upon the spoiled wretch, he froze.

Once his brain caught up with his eyes, he nearly keeled over from laughter.

This *princess* had managed to ensnare herself in the middle of a sinking pit. Both legs were trapped up to her knees in mushy brown mud that only held stronger the more one struggled. She had half a spider's web stuck to the leaf-embroidered circlet and managed to get at least five trees worth of twigs attached to her within the two minutes she was on her own. One hand desperately clung to the gold circlet, as if she thought it'd save her from the grasp of the pit.

That damned circlet was probably worth enough to feed five villages for a year and yet out here, it was useless. It got in the way more than anything.

"*Are you laughing at me?*" Her shrill voice made his innards churn but did nothing to dispel the hilarity of the situation.

Another chuckle escaped his lips, which only made her turn a deep shade of red. "*Help me, you moron!*"

Helping her would be the proper thing to do. He knew that. And he would definitely do that.

Soon.

For now, he leaned against a tree and allowed a sense of joyful calm to spread through him. "Your plan didn't come through like you wanted? I don't see a village hidden in that slimy pit."

"Obviously not." She attempted to free her stuck legs and nearly toppled head-first into the mud. "Aargh."

Ever since they left the capital, this princess had made the entire journey feel like trudging past the first of Rallion's gates into the twelve hells. She may hold rank over him and had the power to make his life miserable back home, but the sight of her flapping her arms like an ailing crow in the mud, warmed his innards. In this moment, she looked the furthest thing from a royal princess, and he wished to savor the view.

This was the most he'd laughed in the past two years. He'd nearly forgotten what it felt like.

"What's wrong?" she taunted, oddly insolent as she continued pulling on her leg; half of her face was covered in mud splashes. "Didn't find your precious river?"

"No," he said, clasping his hands together. "It was hard to hear anything over the echoes of your delicate screams. I was hoping to witness you being devoured by a sharp-clawed beast, but instead, I came to find that you merely fell in some mud."

That made her freeze. Good. Perhaps she'd be easier to pull out now.

"I didn't fall," she bit out. "It's a sinking pit—and I—sunk in. Now, will you make yourself useful for once and—as you were assigned to do—*help me!*"

"Yeah. Yeah." He waved off her screams and bent at the waist, settling into another bow. "Let me help you, Your Eminence."

The princess's screech turned into a gargle when he moved from the tree.

"Here." He crouched close by, careful not to step into the sticky part of the pit. The same one his father trained him to spot since he was young. "If you're done complaining—I'm going to pull you out, if you'll let me."

The princess swallowed whatever insult was stirring and nodded. It was strange having to ask permission to save her. If she were a soldier, he'd tug her out without a care, but, again, he wanted to keep his hands and head after all of this was over.

"Grab my shoulder."

Immediately she had his arm in a tight grip, her claws digging deep. He sighed. Gently and carefully, he grabbed the leg nearest him and tugged.

Nothing budged. She was stuck damn good.

So, he shifted to his knees, ignoring the grunt of displeasure as she nearly lost her grip on him. This time, he placed one hand on her leg, just above her muddy knee, and grabbed her waist, ignoring the flush of pink that filled her face at the contact.

"What are you—"

The princess squealed when he yanked as hard as he could, pulling her out of the mud and splashing droplets everywhere. The second she was free he released his grip and she fell right onto her royal bottom.

Another round of curses, and she kicked her flailing feet at him. "You did that on purpose."

He dusted the boot mark off his pants and tossed her mud-soaked boots at her. "Not everything is about you, Your Supreme Gloriousness."

She huffed and tugged her boots back on, ignoring the squelching noise they made. "Stop calling me that."

"If you say so... Your Elevated Highness." He chuckled at himself.

"Stop it." She gathered the borrowed cloak, stormed up to him—nearly slipping onto the forest floor—and jabbed her finger into his chest. The black of her irises took over. "I command you."

It was strange. The more cross she became, the more he wanted to push her over the edge. Back at the camp, he did everything in his power to stay clear of her wrath, but out here, he welcomed that fury.

It made things entertaining in a bleak situation. And he wanted to see how angry she'd get before she snapped.

"Whatever you say, Your—"

But the words died on his tongue as an awful sound roared from behind a group of barely budding bushes. Exactly the reason why he didn't want to go down this path in the first place.

The princess scuttled to the side and positioned herself so he was in front. He sighed.

Both watched the bush with bated breaths. Waiting... and waiting.

Another rustle and the bush jolted. Before he could grab Dark End, a shadow shot out and the princess screamed.

Six

The Princess

The fire crackled and hissed, blazing with a fury that no longer reflected the burnt-out ember of her heart. Isla was lost, deflated, and felt like a complete fool. This was a disaster. She was a disaster. Her leg was covered in disgusting half-dried mud that she hadn't been able to scrape off, a thick thorn was stuck somewhere in her right boot, her favorite vest was covered in stains, and she was certain a spider was living in the nest she now called her hair.

The wind picked up and her vision was obscured by smoke. It burned her eyes and though she was certain she would stink like fire for days, she sat as close as possible, willing some heat to return to her frozen hands.

The speared boar hovered to the side of the fire with a thick pole—carved from a branch—now sticking out of its mouth. Half of it had already turned a lovely dark color, its skin perfectly crisp despite the roaring flames licking its underbelly. Her stomach screamed at the mere thought of a meal, but she refused to ask when it would be ready. Instead, she glared at the meal that had tried to gut her mere hours ago.

After storming off on her own—foolishly, as she now knew but would not admit out loud, not to him—she'd barely made it a hundred feet into the field of trees before having to be rescued.

It wasn't her fault she was never taught how to spot a sinking pit until she was directly on top of it. If she had, then clearly, she would have avoided it at all costs rather than getting stuck in the stupid mud like she had.

Then that pesky boar came roaring out of nowhere, nearly skewering her in its first attempt before *he* thrust his blade into its chest. If that soldier hadn't returned for her, she'd probably be lying dead in the middle of this one-eyed goddess-forsakened forest, being slowly eaten by these damned bugs that wouldn't leave her alone, despite the layers of smoke she was engulfed in.

He sat across from her, poking at the flames with a long staff he had found and sighing loudly as if he was the one inconvenienced. Of course, this was all after he'd killed the boar, led them to a creek to wash the blood off their hands, and then found a suitable place to stay for the night.

Suitable was a stretch for this patch of dirt with a few fallen logs to sit on, and a grassy patch which she was told would be the most comfortable to sleep in.

To sleep in. *Outside.* In the middle of a forest.

How did her life come to this?

They were supposed to be just outside of Bluemoon Bay by now. Where she'd have one of her multiple aids already setting up her tent and fur bed, which she swore to never complain about again. One of her ladies would ensure that she'd have a large glass of wine in her hand and someone would have already cooked a delicious meal from the variety of treats she made sure they'd packed for her.

Instead, she was in the middle of a half-decayed forest controlled by people who wanted her dead, with nothing but the spiders, snapping beetles, cawing birds, and dead trees for company. That pesky soldier who'd been assigned to her this whole journey seemed to blame her for their current predicament, when it was all his interference that caused this.

If—no—when they got back, she'd see to it that all his titles and commissions were removed and that he was caned for his insubordination. Maybe even lashes.

The stupid soldier's uniform had been worn and in disrepair before being dragged halfway across the lands. He clearly was given a duty far above his capabilities. She'd have to speak to the commander about his choice of guardian in the future. No more Pedites if she could swing it. They were far too unpredictable.

The firelight lit up his chiseled, unshaven face, casting shadows across his annoyingly devoid-of-all-color eyes. Gray eyes that danced with too much merriment when he had to save her from losing her boot in a second sinking pit after already saving her from touching a poisonous but delicious-looking green mushroom. Every part about him infuriated her, especially when he seemed to be right at every thorn-filled turn.

A breeze tickled the back of her neck with its icy touch. She pulled the furs of her once white vest tighter and clutched the stupidly warm-looking cloak that remained in her lap. She refused to put on a dead man's cloak no matter how cold it was and had never let such a cheap material touch her skin in all her life.

So, she had sat here, brewing in an unusual mix of self-pity, uselessness, and anger, all while this soldier—this captain—set up a fire and makeshift beds for the nights. Her brother recounted stories of having to camp in the wilderness during the military training their father made him do. She thought it was all a good laugh at the time but never realized how tough it could have possibly been. Now, she was rethinking everything.

They had been days away from her ultimate destination, and now this had to happen. Her father would be furious at her for messing this up. Nobody would be safe from his wrath when she didn't show up to the meeting point on time.

What would he say when he found out? Surely, he'd find a way to blame this all on her, as usual. A shudder ran from the tips of her fingers to her spine.

It wouldn't do to get into her head too much, she didn't like it there. It was better not to focus on dark thoughts or else they'd fester and grow and become too much to stop.

For now, she was stuck with her brooding partner. Both equally cross with their predicament. Though Isla thought she got the worst part of this.

The soldier grabbed a thick log and began carving slices out of it with a dark blade. What was he doing—imagining her face on the other end?

When the silence became too much, she pointed at the fire and the neatly stacked pile of wood beside it. "How do you know how to do all of this?"

His hands froze. "From around."

She clenched her fists together. Was it that hard to give her a real response? If she wasn't already exhausted beyond measure, she'd command him to answer. But the words never left her mouth.

A beetle scuttled through nearby leaves and she jumped back; the circlet on her brow tilted dangerously. She pulled it off, ignoring the strands of hair it tugged with it. It was one of her favorites, picked out by her mother before she was born. While plain by all standards with its fine gold filigree and delicate leaf carvings, it held a hint of old flecked stone that you could only see when it caught the light just right.

It bore no ornate jewels or carvings of thorns and flames as was usual for their family. Plain and simple for a princess, yet she loved it above all the others she had.

It was one of the first things she remembered caring about and it was one that she always wore when she needed strength, just as she had needed it for their journey to Bluemoon Bay. She couldn't stomach the thought of parting with it once she left, even though her new home and new husband would surely want to outfit her in their maroons and sun symbols.

A month ago, the journey to the Koliats seemed like an impossible feat, as did her marriage to the prince. Now, sitting in the middle of a rotten forest and covered in dried mud, they both paled in comparison.

The soldier turned the boar again, sending a stream of juices into the flames below and earning a fresh set of sparks.

It occurred to her that she didn't even know his name.

This soldier had been guarding her for quite a while now, and she'd never once asked. It hadn't mattered before. Now, it seemed like important information she should know or it would become awkward shouting at a stranger in the middle of a dark forest.

"The others back at the camp," she started, twisting the circlet in her hand as she stared into the crackling flames. His head snapped in her direction. Dark gray eyes—judging eyes—bored into hers before following the movement of the circlet. "They called you Captain Cordrai."

A shiver rolled over him, and he threw the log to the ground. Isla could make out the beginnings of a feline face carved into it. He rubbed his shoulder and replied tersely, "That's what they call me."

"Is that your name then? That's not a very pleasant name and it doesn't roll off the tongue. How about I call you Cord?"

A small laugh escaped his lips, though his eyes remained dark. "You can call me that if you wish, Your Majestic Highness."

That name sent a wave of fury over here. "Fine," she said with a sense of bravado that she didn't feel inside. "Cord it is."

"We should find you a different name for when we make it to civilization. I'm not sure how deep in this forest we are but it's best to figure it out now." He hesitated before the next part as if he was uncertain how she'd react. "Isla isn't exactly a commoner's name around here and anyone with a lick of sense will recognize it in a heartbeat. They'll be looking for you."

A pit formed in the middle of her stomach, threatening to spread. She gripped the circlet until her hands shook.

"You better keep that out of sight too." He nodded at her mother's circlet.

She scowled, clenching her hands tighter.

A thick eyebrow shot up. "Any preference on name or do you want me to pick?"

The way the firelight danced in his eyes told her that was the last thing she should agree to.

She shook her head. Choice was something she was rarely allowed, let alone when it came to picking a new name for herself. Even if it was a decoy name to be used for a short time, she wanted it to be the right fit. The wrong name on an upstanding individual could destroy any confidence in that person and change the outcome of their future.

The dancing flames pointed her in the right direction. "My mother—her second name was Elena. It wasn't well known and I don't think anyone would recognize it. I want to use that."

He nodded. "Elena." His whisper barely reached her above the now-roaring fire. "That'll work for now. You should get some sleep, *princess*. We have a grueling journey tomorrow."

She scowled. "What do you mean grueling?"

An annoying smile filled his face, it grated on every nerve that wasn't already on fire from their day's hike. "Judging by how well you fared in the hour it took us to get here, I'm going to hazard a guess that tomorrow's all-day journey is going to be tough on your delicate feet."

Seven

Mira

Another day. Another bundle of useless rocks, another endless battle against the unmoving mountain that no one could hope to win. Bit by bit she chipped away, hoping that one day it would be enough to pay her price to get out of here. She wasn't even fully certain what that exact amount was and had yet to see someone pay off their debts or right whatever wrongs they committed against the Muratian kingdom since coming here.

A fact that she'd heard many of the workers bitterly grumbling about.

Beretta knew the guards well enough to know that her term end was merely months away. She made certain to stay away from anything that would add extra time to her *service*, as did Mira.

So, Mira worked as hard as she could without killing herself. It was useless to overdo it one day or you'd be exhausted and get lashes the next, and those were the worst, even the small ones. She clenched her scarred knuckles as she swung her pickaxe with venom.

The rock swelled and bulged as she chipped away––breathing in and out with each swing she took but refusing to give way. After an hour she rested her forehead against the rock, feeling beads of sweat tumble down her face to her neck and her back. She'd wipe them away but they'd just be replaced the moment she did.

Some days it was almost as if she could feel the heartbeat of the mountain calling through the lifeline of the stones beneath her fingers. It pulsed and swayed under her touch, and a few times she swore it led her to find firestone. Beretta always told her to keep those thoughts to herself before they sent her away with an illness, and that was not a good thing as those people never came back.

At least Beretta was by her side working tirelessly. Her fiery hair never seemed to dull, even with lengths between the surface and their tunnels, and neither did her spirit. She cracked a few jokes when she was able to catch her breath or noted which passing guards seemed like they would be best in bed, but mostly they worked in silence to conserve their breaths.

Gummy pummeled away next to them—she gave him that nickname thanks to the toothless grin he always wore—working as slowly as possible and spraying them with dust and dirt every few minutes no matter how much they complained. The giant, bald one that Beretta called Crag—they didn't know his real name—annoyed them with his constant whistling while he collected the useless sacks and carried them away.

Lucky Crag. It had been weeks since she got to do removal duty. It was so easy, it was unfair. Crag was friendly with the soldiers—even more than B—and it wasn't hard to understand why he was selected for the third time this week.

The fifth in their group was a straggly man, much too old for the work they were assigned, but he was here, nevertheless. His wiry eyebrows constantly had chunks of dirt in them, and he always looked on the verge of total misery. That one she called the Wasp thanks to his similarities to the annoying bug that lashed out if you got too close. It was best to keep your distance from him.

For some reason, he seemed to hate Mira and Beretta most of all. It was probably because during one of her first days here, Mira accidentally knocked over a stack of tools he was cleaning. In retaliation, he tried to drop a barrel full of heavy rocks on her and if it wasn't for Beretta stepping in before he crushed Mira, she may not even be here today.

Beretta had gone straight to the guards and he got twenty lashes and half rations for a week, while Mira and Beretta were sent off with only a warning.

From that day, Beretta and Mira were inseparable, and the Wasp's hatred for them couldn't be stopped. He made it his mission to hurt or mock Mira as much as he could, and it got to the point where the guards just stopped putting them in the same section.

So, it was surprising that they were assigned to the same group that day. Probably an oversight from one of the schedulers. At least Beretta was here to watch over her, so there'd be no squished limbs today. Hopefully.

A shower of rocks sprayed Mira, sending her into a coughing fit and scratching her eyes. Beretta was at her side in an instant, grabbing a large gray rock and pumping her arm back as if to throw it right at the Wasp's head.

"Don't—cough—don't bother," Mira choked out, waving her hand. "It's not worth it."

Beretta and the Wasp glowered at each other. He with his axe raised, the burn scars on his wrists shining in the dim light, and her with the rock in hand plus an unfiltered fury that would have withered any normal man and sent him running. The Wasp's hatred for them was clearly beyond reason.

This was bad. They were already on double duty and if they got caught fighting, then they'd be sent to solitary punishment. Mira couldn't do that ever again. She'd lose herself before the first day was done.

After ten seconds that seemed to drag for an eternity, voices echoed down from the tunnel. The dim light from the oil lamp flickered.

Guards.

Both Beretta and the Wasp nodded and lowered their arms slowly. The Wasp sent one final scathing glare at Mira that felt like he could see past her dirty clothes and skin and right into her soul—and he hated what he saw—before turning back to his work.

Beretta wiggled her eyebrows at Mira before dropping the rock in between them. "Some days I wish for a cave-in to fall right on his big, dumb head," she said, loudly.

The only sign that the Wasp heard was the way in which he doubled the strength of his hits against the rock, as if envisioning it were not rock beneath his dull tool but rather human flesh.

The voices down the tunnel grew and, before the next set of blue-clad guards could spot them, Mira and Beretta had already returned to work as if nothing had happened.

After the guards passed, Beretta turned her head to Mira, all while still continuing her strikes against the rock. They'd nearly freed a large chunk that had taken hours to carve out. Just a few more hits in the right place and it should pop right out.

"Maybe if I screwed that tall guard, then we could get an extra break?" Beretta mused between hits.

Mira groaned. "Don't tell me that's how you got those rations?"

Beretta scoffed and had the decency to look insulted. "Please. I have much higher standards than any of this rabble," she whispered the last part in case anyone was listening and wiped a bead of sweat off her brow. "May as well hook up with someone from the Hattien swamplands at that point. Although if we're down here any longer, I may have to start bringing those standards down a smidge before I combust from frustration."

Mira laughed, stifling it quickly behind her hand when the Wasp sent a deathly glare her way.

"Let's hope it doesn't come to that."

It was all Mira could do down here. Hope and pray to the goddess that she wouldn't die in these dark tunnels. That one day she'd be back above ground, and not just for a measly few hours of a long-needed break. *Really* above ground. Forever.

She didn't even know what she would do when she got up there. There were so many possibilities that thinking about it made her head spin. Even her dreams couldn't conjure up the surface that existed beyond this mountain; they only knew the rock, tunnels, and a dark comet that overtook everything. That was all she could dream of, even in her nightmares.

Ever since she arrived down here with a terrible head injury, she couldn't remember anything about her time before the mines. Trying to think of more gave her splitting headaches and made her so lightheaded that she nearly passed out. Even now her muscles grew tired, and her body craved a reprieve at the mere thought.

With a quick look to ensure no guards lingered, Mira leaned her pickaxe against the rock and dragged her hand along the side of the red wall, getting lost in her thoughts. She closed her eyes as a familiar warmth flickered at the edge of her fingertips, spurred on by the heat of the rock beneath her. The same pull that B always told her to ignore. But this time she focused on it. On the tendrils that spread beneath the rock. On the movement that she swore she could feel radiating from there.

"Argh." Beretta clipped the edge of a sharp rock and a piece of stone ricocheted off her. She fell to her knees and clutched her shoulder. Blood spilled from underneath her fingers—she had been nicked good.

"Get up," Mira hissed, kicking her pickaxe to the side. She grabbed Beretta's arm and tried pulling her up before one of the soldiers noticed. They didn't like when work stopped for any reason.

Crag's whistling came to an abrupt halt. He leaned against a cracked support beam with his arms crossed, watching them with narrowed eyes—not that she was surprised. The Wasp and Gummy continued strumming against the rock, but she noticed the terrible smile that curved around the Wasp's lips.

Her friend was in too much pain to get up, she was holding back quiet sobs. Panic flooded every vein in her limbs when a harsh voice called out. It was one of the blue-clad soldiers, a captain who loved taking flesh payment whenever he could. Beretta liked to call him Captain No-Neck, and the name was fitting.

"I said--" The broad-shouldered captain stomped up to them, twisting the leather strap in his hands. Mira's hand flexed. "Why are you two slacking off?"

Beretta's eyes flashed as she bit back a retaliation that must be begging to be released. An obvious sign that her friend was about to lose that thin grip on her tumultuous temper and this was not the man to lose it on.

"Well? I'm waiting."

The Wasp's smile widened as he chipped away at the mountain.

Everyone else paused to watch with hungry eyes. All waiting for the inevitable blowback they'd receive. The inevitable thrashing.

There must be something that could be done to save them from the whip. Anything.

"We found a firestone," Mira blurted. The words formed a life of their own and came out before she could stop them.

Beretta looked at her like she'd finally lost it, and Crag leaned further down the beam, resting his elbow on his knee, with a curious smirk on his face. The hunger in his eyes told her that he planned on fully enjoying what came next.

"Oh?" Captain No-Neck's eyes traveled over her face as he twisted the leather strap, then moved down the rest of her body in a way that made her want to recoil and hide, but she refused to move an inch. "I don't see it. Did you misplace it somehow?"

Crag laughed. A brazen move in front of a soldier, but he was on friendly terms with this one.

"I haven't dug it out fully yet." Mira swung her arm behind her while Beretta watched with wide eyes. They'd practically learned to communicate without words by now and she knew her friend would say: *Don't make this any worse than it has to be.*

The soldier studied the wall next to her with an awful smile tugging at the corners of his mouth. "I don't see it."

"It's in there," she assured. "I saw it. It's just—stuck."

No-Neck's eyes danced. "You have five minutes to put it in my hand or both of you will get the strap and no rations for three days."

A small whimper came from Beretta. The last time they went without rations, Beretta passed out mid-shift and was taken away. She came back twenty-four hours later and barely spoke for days.

The thought of the hollow look in her friend's eyes sent a shiver from her spine to her fingertips.

"Got an issue with that?" No-Neck sneered, his eyes traveling the length of her. "Better get started."

"Got it." Without a second look, Mira took up her pickaxe and wailed against the wall she was just surveying. No-Neck hovered nearby, watching with those same hungry eyes that would make the hair on her arms stand up if they weren't drenched in sweat.

Beretta took the distraction to wrap up her bleeding shoulder. She'd be ordered back to work no matter the outcome. At least Mira managed to buy her some time. She wouldn't get that same reprieve when she came up empty-handed.

She prayed to the one-eyed Halia that it was less than ten lashes.

What a dumb plan. What was she thinking?

Again and again, Mira hit against the wall, letting out the day's frustrations and anger. She allowed that rage to flow down her arms and into the unmoving mountain.

Please let there be something. She sent another foolish prayer to all fifteen goddesses, including the trickster Slin and Rallion, the goddess of the gates—for surely this was some new form of hell she was imprisoned in, she was certain of that now.

No-Neck and Crag stood shoulder to shoulder making crude comments as she worked. She tuned them out and focused on the sound of her blood rushing against her ear and the clatter of metal against rock.

Stupid Crag. Stupid Captain No-Neck. And stupid godsdamned rock.

That anger pooled within her and felt like it was going to burst. Her fingers became hot and would surely be shaking if she weren't gripping her axe so tightly.

At the next hit, she felt movement. She paused to catch a deep breath then pooled all her strength and rage into the next strike.

It couldn't be...

Something gave out and pieces of rock crumbled away like a stream of water falling down a mountainside. Once the river of rocks trickled to nothing, a larger one toppled out and fell onto the small pile with an echoing thump. It was red and similar to the rest of the wall around it to blend it. But this one was littered with black flecks that signified the firestone properties in it.

She picked up the rock triumphantly and it pulsed beneath her hand. Beretta said she'd never experienced that when she touched the firestone, but her hands had far more calluses than Mira's, and she wasn't as observant about these things.

Before she could open her mouth, the firestone was snatched out of her hand, leaving a cold breeze behind.

"Hey!"

"I'll be taking that in," the captain said in an icy voice. He tossed the rock in the air, catching it deftly in his other hand. "If anyone asks, I found it."

"That's not fair," Mira said. Burning anger flashed before her eyes and blocked out all reason.

"Mira," Beretta whined, still clutching her surely throbbing shoulder. "Just let it go."

"I found it!" Mira continued. She worked hard for that firestone and had every intention of being the one to get rewarded for it.

Thick leather lashed out at her and dug into her cheek. She stumbled back in a fit of pain and humiliation and anger. Before the whip could find its mark for a second time, her hand moved of its own accord and she grabbed the leather.

As soon as she realized what she'd done, she dropped the whip. "I'm so sorry. I don't know what came over me."

The Wasp snickered.

Stars exploded in her face and she was in a heap on the ground.

The soldier towered over her and his face told her that she made a very grave mistake. "You're about to have a whole mountain of pain tumble down on you." He raised his arm to strike again, but before it could make contact a second voice called out—one that she'd heard only a few times before.

Her heart skipped several beats.

"What are you doing, soldier?"

No-Neck froze mid-strike and the ends of the leather wilted. His eyes widened as the private came into view.

Mira scrambled to her feet and wiped her bloody cheek, hanging her head low while Crag and the Wasp's snickers continued to fill the air. They were certainly hungry for a show today—and likely to get one sooner than expected.

Beretta remained frozen in place, though her eyes were silently warning Mira.

"Pr-private Devlin." Captain No-Neck pointed at Mira. "This one was trying to steal the firestone, I saw her."

Mira's mouth dropped.

"That's not true," Beretta's shaky voice argued. She clenched her fists at her side as she looked at the captain with fiery disdain. "We just finished digging it up, and this—this—soldier took it right out of her hands."

The private whipped his head towards Beretta. He studied her reddening face before his mouth split into a dangerous smile that Mira wasn't certain if she should recoil from or feel relief at the sight.

Was she about to get into even more trouble? Was it to be the lashes or the pits? Either option was just as terrible, and now B would be dragged down with her.

Private Devlin had a winning smile that could make anyone forget their own name. He had an impeccably chiseled jawline with a scar running along the side of it. His blue uniform had not a single wrinkle in it, the dagger at his side was perfectly polished, and his rusty brown hair was always perfectly coiffed, even in the deepest of the mines. Even Beretta had occasionally admitted how dreamy the private was. Coming from her, that meant something.

It wasn't just that he was a god to look at and a dream to talk to, it was the way the other guards seemed to look up to him. He commanded respect and authority, even though he was one of the lowest ranking soldiers here. Beretta always thought he must be the son of a well-known general, and yet he remained the most level-headed of the soldiers she'd encountered.

It also helped that he was known to give the diggers extra rations when he was feeling generous.

Private Devlin's dark blue eyes moved between Mira and Beretta—still clutching her injured shoulder—and back to Captain No-Neck. "Are you lying to me?"

The captain withered under his glare, even though he held seniority over the private. "I found it myself," he said in a shaky voice.

Beretta laughed bitterly. No-Neck didn't have a fleck of dirt or hint of a blister on his hands. This man had never touched a pickaxe or a shovel in his life.

Devlin raised a thick eyebrow as his unwavering gaze remained on the man. "And you just happened to be digging in the middle of your shift, for fun, instead of watching your charges?"

"They were slowing down so I thought I'd help," the captain said stupidly.

Private Devlin leaned in close to No-Neck and whispered in a smooth voice that sent chills down Mira's spine, "Then where's your axe?"

The captain looked around desperately for help. There was not a tool nearby, and Crag had snuck out when the questioning turned around. He was always a smart man when it came to self-preservation.

When it became clear no help would come, the captain hung his head and stared at his shoes.

"I thought so. I'll take that." Devlin yanked the firestone out of the man's hand. "You," he barked, his long finger pointed right at Mira. She looked behind her as if expecting someone else but was met with only hard stone. "You're coming with me."

Eight

The Captain

It had been two days.

In the past two days, he fully understood every detail—every lock, every intricate inch of delicate carving, every seam, every inlet, every sway—that surrounded each veil that led to the gates of the twelve hells; for surely, he had passed through them all at least three times by now. He was so well-versed in them that the gatekeeper, Rallion, would recognize his face out of any crowd.

It had been two days of non-stop complaints, unreasonable demands, and countless threats to his title, family, and life. Two days wandering these cursed forests with no end in sight.

"How much further?" the princess—or Elena, as he needed to call her when they crossed paths with Muratians—whined, and it was not the first time she'd asked it that morning. It wasn't even the tenth time.

Pure annoyance stopped him in his tracks. He pinched the bridge of his nose and turned on his heel. Again, that inexplicable rage boiled up in his blood. He really should have left her the first night when she woke him with a blood-curdling scream as she thought a wolf-spider was crawling on her. It was nothing more than an innocent hunting spider, completely harmless, as he had tried to show her before she threw a rock at his head.

A lovely bruise was sprouting on his temple. He reached out to touch it and winced. This princess had good aim and a surprisingly strong arm. His reflexes must be waning thanks to his prior removal from regular duties.

And now she had more complaints.

The memory of her aim incised him, so he turned over the flap of his satchel and dug inside his pockets. "I don't know, let me check my handy little map that I... oh, that's right." He pulled his hand out, empty, and waved it around. "We don't have one. I can't tell you how much longer as I don't know where we are and where we're going."

The way her face shifted from twisted shock to scandalized indignation was worth the scolding he'd eventually get for that—if they made it back. It brought him a small solace in this gloomy forest.

He turned his head before she could see his smile and lose it even further.

If she could see herself, she'd probably freak out. Her furs were bloodied and mud-crusted; she had several layers of grime on her indignant face; her hair had fallen out of the fancy bun it once was in and hung in tangles down her back; and for some unknown reason, she was still wearing that damn circlet on her head that now had a spider's web on it, no matter how many times he told her to remove it.

After freezing throughout the second night, she finally gave up and put on the wielder's cloak. He didn't like wearing a dead soldier's uniform either, but surely Rallion would forgive this transgression given the circumstances.

At least her complaints about the cold had dried up after that.

Now, the moans about starving picked up again. He tried to give her some leftover meat from their first night, but she said she'd die if she had to eat another bite of that terrible boar. There wasn't much else that he spotted in this part of the half-dead woods, so for now, the princess had gone without.

And did she ever make it known how unhappy she was with that.

If he had half a mind, he'd have left her behind on that stump when she demanded her fourth break of the morning. Thank the goddess something had spooked her, or else he'd never had gotten her up from that rest.

They couldn't afford to break that much. Not when who knows what was on the hunt for them—well, her, to be specific. There had been rumors of the Muratian queen's obsession with amassing a powerful army, including a battalion she was full of their strongest wielders. It was said she was obsessed with strengthening the magic lines in Murat and a part of that plan meant stopping Velotia from creating allies of their own.

Isla's father, the Velotian king, was known for his aversion to wielders and merely kept the Agicae branch as there'd be an uproar if he broke from tradition. Dissolving an entire military branch was impossible without losing thousands of wielders. And no matter how much the king detested them, they came in handy. As evidenced by their entire predicament in these woods.

So, he refused to give the princess breaks as often as she wanted and forced her to wake up earlier than she'd *ever had to rise in her entire life*, all in the name of keeping them alive.

They'd tirelessly walked for hours today. Through a damp marsh, past a prickly field, and through branches and branches of thorny tendrils that scraped at his skin. Eventually, they found a cobble-stone path wide enough for a carriage, an excellent sign of potential civilization—or a bad sign, depending on how you looked at it.

Left with little choice, they followed it. They had to determine exactly where they were in order to find the best way home. They had to know how deep into Murat they were before coming up with any real semblance of a plan.

It had been hours now, and her complaining picked up with each passing branch that snagged her jacket or hair. She wasn't the only one tired and starving here, she was just the loudest about it.

A strange stone echoed against his boots as they entered a clearing of sorts. He doubled back and kicked away the shield of dirt that clung to it.

"What is it *now*?" she whined, dragging her feet as she doubled back.

It was no ordinary rock, but had sharp edges cut with fine black marble. He brushed off more tangled branches and several hundred years of dust to reveal a faded etching of a wilted blood-lily roughly the size of his torso.

The princess scoffed. "It's a stone. Nothing special. If I don't get breaks, then you most certainly don't either."

It pained him to admit that she was right. But he was curious.

The symbol was of the goddess of the gates, Rallion. Sister Death. The year of Rallion wasn't on the usual calendar rotation, neither was the star goddess, Hierel. Rallion's year was heralded by a black comet only spotted every hundred years or so. Her followers were devout, some would even say *radical* given the way they burned their own skin in an attempt to get closer to the goddess. As it has been several decades since the last black comet was spotted, they had clearly let this place fall into disrepair.

A quick scan of the clearing revealed more blocks of marble. Most were hidden away by time, nothing more than faint echoes of a grand temple reclaimed by the woods after being abandoned.

A passing breeze caressed the hair on his arm, but when he looked around, no branches swayed and there was no rustling of deadened leaves.

This place didn't feel abandoned. It was as if the goddess herself peered at them from beyond the twelve gates, her whispers passing from the trees to their branches and through the roots as she turned her eye toward the wayward pair.

No good would come of lingering here, under the eye of a goddess who never heralded good omens. Even the princess started to bristle and shift uncomfortably, adjusting the circlet on her head too many times.

Did she sense it too?

A flash of violet smoke in the distance. Another wisp.

He was done with ill-omens and ordered them to continue on, much to the chagrin of the princess who lamented about how she should be the one doing the ordering around here.

For the most part, he tuned out her ramblings, as he had become quite skilled at doing so by now.

In the middle of her tirade where she shifted between ranting about how she would kill for a hot bath and happily declaring she was going to have him removed from the military the moment they got back, a branch cracked.

The blood in his veins chilled, freezing his muscles in place, except for his head, which snapped to the side.

Even the princess sensed that something was wrong. She doubled back. That was the quickest he'd seen her move all day.

"Cord?"

He winced and ignored her, focusing on the thickly packed trees where the sound came from.

"What was that?" she whispered. She was now directly behind him and attempting to peer over his shoulder, which she barely reached.

"Somebody is here," he said quietly, running his finger over the chip on his pommel.

She drew a sharp breath.

His mind was buzzing with so many scenarios. Would it help to call out so the travelers knew they were friendly—sort of? Perhaps they could slip out and turn back before they were spotted.

But the princess called out in that shrill, but somehow still commanding voice, "Who's there?"

Laughter came from multiple directions, along with that damned rustling. The princess gasped and clutched his shoulder with her surprisingly warm hand. It took all his willpower not to abandon her in this clearing to deal with the problem she started. He was probably faster than her and could likely outpace whoever else was there. He and his brother used to race home all the time and he always won, even though his brother had years on him.

A knot formed in his stomach at the thought of his brother and their parting words. No. He was not a coward. He refused to be one ever again.

"Stay behind me," he said, even though the princess was practically attached to his shoulder.

Two men emerged from the thick trees in front of them, while another pair popped up behind, appearing out of two bulky bushes. They were all dressed in a similar mix of gray and blue-tattered clothing. The large one in front had a long scar on his temple and brandished a pair of daggers, while a stocky one leered greedily at the wayward pair.

Bandits.

That seemed to be the way their luck had been going. It could be worse. At least none of them looked like wielders. There wasn't a lot he could do against someone like that in these woods.

"We're just passing through," he said with a false bravado. He drew himself up to his full height, the grip on his shoulder nearing painful. "We don't want any trouble."

"That's a shame." The scarred one flipped a dagger in the air, the tip of it catching the light that filtered in through the forest canopy, before deftly catching it in his hand. "Because we do."

Something whizzed by their heads, just above his right ear. It didn't hit, so he didn't flinch. That warning miss was on purpose. The princess squealed and nearly crushed his shoulder.

The stocky bandits' eyes locked on her—or at least, what portion he could view from behind her human shield. "What's that?" He jerked his chin at her.

A crow cawed overhead.

Taking a look over his shoulder, Princess Isla's hood had fallen back, exposing that godsdamned circlet he'd told her to remove.

"Why's a dirty little troll like you got something so nice?" the scarred one asked, wiping his nose on the back of his hand.

"No." The short one from the bushes took a step forward. "You can tell she's not a troll under those layers, Benit. She may even be pretty, but we'd have to thoroughly check to be certain."

The words sent his blood boiling, tightening the skin around his bones. He flexed his still bruised fists.

"Don't you dare speak to me like that," the princess blurted from behind him, voice full of haughty indignation.

"Oh." The scarred one—Benit—stepped to the side, crossing one foot in front of the next. Circling like a vulture who had spotted a wounded prey. "This one thinks she can command us."

His throat dried.

This was what he was afraid of and exactly why he told her to keep quiet and—he carefully pried her hand off his shoulder—*out of the way.*

Perhaps he could find a way out of this without bloodshed. There must be a way. They'd have to tread carefully to make it out without pulling steel.

"But you are right, Tern." The scarred bandit dipped his head to get a better view of Princess Isla's face as she'd thrown the cloak back over her head. "I think this one may be pretty... but not pretty enough to order me around. I don't like taking orders." He hacked a glob of dark spit into the ground beside her.

The princess's face turned pallid green.

'Not yet,' he reminded himself as Dark End almost sang to him. They hadn't proven to be dangerous yet.

The bandit reached around him to grab her face. Reason abandoned him as a rush of blood pounded into his brain. He pushed the bandit, growling a threat as he did.

The remaining three's hands jumped to their weapons. Metal ground against sheath as swords were brandished. One of them even had a dull axe that painfully reminded him of Freya's Bone Breaker.

By the way the stocky one handled the hilt, it was newly acquired. The fourth one, who he'd only just had a chance to look at, was young and held his sword loosely. It was enough to convince him that these brigands were not as experienced as they put on. Perhaps they could be reasoned with.

After all, these were not Muratian soldiers out to kill them but rather marauders trying to make a life in this forest. They may even have families.

It was he and the princess who didn't belong. They were the ones on the run.

"Look." He eyed the closest one, Benit, keeping a hand splayed out so he couldn't get any closer to the princess. "I don't think you want to do this."

The bandit's eyes took in his defensive yet casual stance, and the borrowed blue and gold military uniform. For a brief moment, hesitation flashed in the bandit's dark eyes.

Briefly.

The princess ducked around him with a crazed burst of confidence. "Leave us alone you low-life band of pillagers."

Quicker than his reflexes could stop it, and partly because he was too stunned at her outburst, the bandit struck her across the face. She crumbled to the ground in a heap. Before Benit could raise his arm again, a dagger was lodged in his neck.

It all happened so fast he didn't even realize the blade had made it to his hand before it was gliding through hot flesh. Benit sputtered as he pulled it out, hot crimson spewing down his neck in ripples.

What had he done?

The other three bandits sprang into action and a sea of clouds fogged his vision. Dark End was already in his spare hand. Thanks to years of training in the army, plus all his father's games, his muscles remembered what to do even when his brain struggled to catch up.

The bandits were untrained and not expecting any resistance. They barely had time to register before he lunged at them, while the princess still babbled in the background from where she lay.

It was as if that cloud of darkness had overcome him, and his body and actions were not his own, even though he knew exactly where to dig each blade of steel. The larger one charged first, and he feinted left, easily ducking under his chipped ax. The end of a sword was lodged in the man's unprotected belly before he could turn back around.

The other two were right behind, sloppy and charging without a plan.

They never stood a chance and fell more easily than the first two.

As his hand let go of the last dagger, he had to watch the bandit's young eyes widen in surprise before dimming and closing. His body sagged to the ground along with the others.

A bird chattered from one of the tree-tops, oblivious to the carnage that took place beneath its timber home.

After tearing his gaze away from the petrified look still frozen on the young man's face, he turned to check that the princess was fine.

Princess Isla scrambled to her feet, holding a reddening cheek and whimpering as if she had been stabbed in the gut instead of slapped. Her eyes bulged when they settled on the lifeless bodies of their attackers. For once, she seemed speechless. *A small victory,* he thought grimly.

When she settled on her blood-spattered boots, she gasped, failing to hide a wet sob.

For some reason, that snapped something in him. "You're fine," he growled, trying to keep his hands from shaking. It wouldn't do if the hired protection lost it at the first sight of blood—well, second sight of blood. He should be used to getting it on his hands by now.

Another sob.

He added gently, "Let me see your face." He grabbed her chin and brushed away a matted strand of hair to check where she was hit.

She recoiled at the touch.

In a poor attempt to hide her disgust, she began adjusting that damned circlet on the top of her head and pulled a crisp, red leaf from her tangled mess of hair.

Boiling fury overtook him. Anger at the bandits for not leaving when they should have. At himself for not being able to control his emotions. And most of all, uncontrollable rage at her for pushing everything past a burning point.

He knew she wasn't fully to blame, but he didn't know where else to direct his temper. He lifted an accusatory finger to point at the top of her head. "I told you to get rid of that thing days ago."

The princess's face screwed into an angry spiral. "And I told you that's not an option."

"Look what happened!" His simmering rage grew to a blazing fire. "Look at what I had to do—because of you."

"Don't you dare blame this on me." She clenched and unclenched her hands into little balls as if she was the one who needed to reign in her emotions.

The sight did nothing to quell the storm inside him. "I am fully and completely blaming you for this. They were innocent."

She scoffed, nostrils flaring. "I doubt it. Did you get a good look at them?"

"Just because they weren't wearing fine silks behind the walls of a palace, doesn't mean they deserved to die." His stomach roiled over again and again. "We could have walked away if it weren't for your dumb tiara and loud mouth."

She scrunched her face, then said in a voice woven with derision. "Aren't you going to check them for supplies? Maybe they have more silver for you to steal too." The words struck harder than any physical blow he'd had this past week. "It's not my fault that you're a completely inadequate screw-up of a soldier who can't even handle a simple assignment."

"A simple assignment? *A simple assignment?*" If his voice could have gotten any more shrill, it would have set off all the animals in this damned forest. "I didn't ask to be marooned with a spoiled brat that doesn't possess a drop of wit or hint of self-preservation instincts, but here I am, with *you*. I pray for the day we drop you off to get those scars burned on your wrist next to your darling betrothed."

The same bird squawked indignantly.

The princess stepped closer to him, anger flashing in the depths of her deep brown eyes. She ignored his jibe about the upcoming wedding ceremony tradition. "I'm not the problem here. I've heard the others talk about you back at the camp. It's just my luck that I am stuck with the worst soldier across all our battalions who your own commander was talking about expelling as soon as we left the bay. I'd rather be marooned with a half-barrel of sleeping stink beetles than remain stuck with such a sorry excuse of a rotten soldier."

He recoiled as if stung by a viper snake. "That is not how it—where did you—how did you—" He clenched his hand at his side and took a deep breath. "Fine. I'll keep that in mind with our future interactions, *princess*."

With that he turned on his heel, stomping off down the darkest path, leaving behind a fuming princess and four warm bodies who should have known better. As he passed a second seal ordained with the same wilted blood-lily, he knew that the death goddess Rallion thirsted for repayment. Slin save him, for it truly was the year of the trickster goddess.

Nine

Prince Edmund of Velotia

The Crown Prince of Velotia was not a patient man, he was not forgiving, and he most certainly did not take kindly to any laziness, especially today.

It had been days since his sister was taken by Muratian forces, doing who knows what to her and undoubtedly putting her through insurmountable turmoil—if she wasn't already dead.

No.

He couldn't think like that. If she was dead, then the wielders would have known.

She was somewhere in there, going through even worse torment, and he was stuck with this poor excuse of an incompetent battalion until reinforcements could catch up.

He rubbed his shoulder, still sore from where that icewielder got him. Their healers did what they could to seal it up, but they didn't have time to linger and rest—not that he would let that slow him down. They were already so far behind and didn't know exactly where to look.

The attack on his camp happened at the same time his sister was taken, and he'd foolishly left his Siica contingent behind at the capital at his father's request. So, he placed his crown for safekeeping and changed into a simple black and silver military outfit on the advice of his guards. Forgoing his lavish clothes would help him blend in better––or so the general had said––and if he insisted on coming with them, then he had no choice.

They thought he'd get in the way and stall the rescue effort. He was determined to prove them wrong.

They were betrayed and too foolish to see it happening under their noses.

Annoyance bristled throughout every vein in his body. From the beginning, he told his father that he should have taken Isla in a smaller, discreet party instead of a pompous full military setup that would be an easy target. He refused to listen and laughed off the threats, saying that he and the commander were old friends, and he'd see to it that she was safely delivered.

No one expected the Muratians would pull as stupid and poorly-executed of a stunt as this—*twice*. They'd underestimated the Muratian queen's desire to stop this alliance at any cost, especially since declaring open war on Velotia, even if they had their reasons for doing so.

Things had been escalating since the Muratian king passed and his wife allowed their sons to terrorize their lands. They were more ruthless and vile than the old man himself, if that was even possible. Rumors were that the queen was a force to be reckoned with, especially since the death of her oldest two years ago. It was said that she'd lost it completely after his slaughter.

Many said the first prince's death was a twisted gift from Slin, given that the Muratian king was a second son himself. She despised when things were in proper order and injected chaos wherever she could.

Something like this was inevitable, and he was stupid enough to allow it to happen right under his nose. He felt that weight of responsibility like a sheet of rock on his shoulders.

It didn't help that he and Isla parted on terrible terms. Horrendous terms.

Admittedly, he lost his temper and was stressed thanks to their father's constant demands. He hadn't wanted to fight the way they did but he lost it and said things that he knew cut deep.

It wasn't something he was proud of.

That was why he took command of this joke of a battalion––on top of the half-battalion he'd arrived with. His father's orders to return home could be damned to the goddess. He didn't care that this new Pedite general was determined to bring her back safely and gave him his word—what a joke that was. Edmund should have sent him to his father's dungeons or given him a sound lashing for his part in this. The man had proven to be brash and emotional at best... and yet he was all that was left after the ambush.

There was no one Edmund trusted to lead this delicate retraction but himself. The others thought he didn't belong here, but they weren't the crown prince.

Edmund pushed back his tent flap, the rough material scraping his fingers. He chose a simple officer's pavilion, not bothering with the usual pageantry he would have on a trip such as this. This wasn't a jaunt with the royal army that included a full escort of Siicas. They had a purpose and needed to move fast, and—as he was constantly reminded—*he* needed to blend in with the rest of the army.

A group of Pedite soldiers sat around a roaring fire. The chatter died the moment Edmund stepped out of his tent. He was used to it. They were wary of letting anything slip around a royal family member, more so at this camp than any he'd been a part of before.

Isla must have done a number on them during their time together.

The thought brought a smile to his face that quickly disappeared when he spotted the Pedite general. They locked eyes. The general averted his gaze and rubbed his arm before scuttling away in the opposite direction, likely wishing to avoid another confrontation. He knew Edmund blamed him for the situation they were in, no matter how much the general stated he would bring his sister back and make the Muratians pay dearly.

Against his better judgment, he'd already allowed the general to take a small scouting party into Murat and they came back empty-handed. It wasn't like Edmund could just march several battalions of soldiers into enemy lands without massive repercussions. Their king—his father—sent explicit orders that they were not to enter Muratian land no matter what, but it was getting to the point that he wanted to throw caution to Slin and do exactly that.

Now this—this *general*—if he could even be called that—was pushing to be sent out again, this time into the Red Mountains. The others believed his hunch and recent scouts placed a lot of Muratian movement near the mountains, but Edmund wasn't sure. It was hard to know who to trust around here after everything. It was hard to make a move into enemy lands against direct orders without knowing where they were headed. And they *still* couldn't get an accurate read on Isla's location.

The Muratians that took her found a way to conceal her. Their wielders hadn't been able to get a good tracking on her besides a brief reading the first day before it disappeared altogether. Why that happened was anyone's guess, but at least they knew she was somewhere in the southern part of Murat.

Now they waited for another sliver of hope, which the general seemed optimistic about. His mood swings were hard to keep up with, but Edmund was less certain of their wielder's capabilities. His father's distrust of wielders had bled into him more than he cared to admit.

But they all had to work together, no matter how much Edmund disliked and distrusted this general and most of the soldiers here—all for Isla's sake.

"Is there anything we can help you with, Prince Edmund?" a Pedite with braided blond hair asked.

Freya. She'd saved his life during the attack and usually had a long axe strapped to her side, which he'd seen first-hand how proficient she was at wielding it. She tended to tail the general closely, always followed by another Pedite who tied his hair back with a silver band.

"I'm quite alright," he said, hanging his head. There was nothing that she, or any of them, could help with today. Same as the last.

The soldier nodded and returned to her conversation within the circle. They wouldn't deny him if he sat down to join in. They couldn't refuse their prince, but he had no desire to exchange pleasantries tonight.

A walk around the encampment would be perfect to quell his nerves. That way the men would be bolstered by his presence and he'd have something to keep his mind off of the terrible things they could be doing to his sister right now. Keep his mind from imagining what torment she must be going through.

Perhaps when he rescued her, they'd finally get a chance to squash this *thing* between them.

They never got along when they were young. There was no denying it. He was ten years her senior and their father never paid either of them any attention, never encouraged a bond between the siblings. He rarely encouraged *any* emotion among his children.

At least Edmund had his mother for those beginning years to show him what love really was. She showed him compassion and caring and kindness, and when she was taken from him, it was hard to remember any of her lessons while crushed under the weight of grief.

When Isla was born, their father immediately handed her over to the wet nurses and maids. He never took a moment to bond with his second-born, and neither did Edmund.

Edmund was so weary of the small babe that had killed his mother. For a long time, he believed his father's story and treated her as if she carried an ailment or a curse. The first time the maid brought him to see her, he stayed behind the door in fear of a creature that could fell a human like that, no matter how small and weak the baby seemed. After being coaxed in with the promise of sweets, he watched Isla for hours that first day, trying to figure out where her power came from. He waited in vain to catch a glimpse of any darkness beneath her frail skin.

It must be hidden deep within, he had thought to himself at the time.

As a boy of only ten years, it didn't matter that he spotted no sharp teeth or talons, and that she was a normal baby that meant no harm. All he knew was that this creature took away his favorite person in the world and was not to be trusted.

His father never discouraged that viewpoint.

When Isla was a toddler learning to walk, Edmund would push her to the ground when she came to him. Any time she stretched her tiny arms for a hug, he merely kicked her away. Once, she came to his room frightened of a storm, and he refused to let her in. Her maid took her away, screaming.

They fought and poked at each other for years until he was finally old enough to see that she wasn't some terrible monster that killed the loving mother who used to tuck him into bed every night with stories of blazing fire queens, knights fighting gallantly against beasts in a field of gold, and stones that held the power to change the world.

It wasn't her fault. There was nothing she did wrong. She was only a baby. She'd lost her mother just as he had.

Isla was his family. The only real one she had left, if you didn't count their ice-filled emotional void of a father. She was his sister, even if it had taken him a while to realize it. Too long, perhaps. And he'd never been able to put it into proper words.

Somehow, he always made things worse when she was around.

Their relationship blossomed into something worse over time thanks to him, and with the way everything turned out before her abduction, he didn't blame her if she never spoke to him again.

There were few things he regretted in his life, but the words he spoke during their last conversation was one of them. He didn't wish for that to be their final parting words. They couldn't be.

He had to find her and make things right. He would stop at nothing.

That was one thing he had in common with this *general*, at least. If anything, he had even more reason for this mission to succeed.

For this wasn't just the Princess of Velotia they took. It was his sister. They may have had their differences over the years—and many, many fights that it seemed like they would never recover from. None of that mattered anymore. She was his sister, and he was going to bring her back.

Ten

The Princess

The cold bite in the air had nothing to do with the blowing wind or the hint of frost she spotted on a dried leaf that morning. In fact, the small fire Cord erected had kept her quite warm. It was the attitude of her traveling partner that was arctic at best.

He stormed off after those bandits ambushed them. Isla had to run after him and nearly got lost in the woods, again, and he refused to speak to or acknowledge her for the rest of the day. The few times he actually addressed her were curt and snippy. It was worse than dealing with her father when he was in one of his moods.

The circlet remained clutched in her hands, still covered in the blood of that scarred one—what was his name again? She was never good with names and really needed to pay more attention.

A glowing ember landed on her boot. Her eyes remained transfixed on the flashing red and orange hues before brushing it off. The smell of the burning wood and pine was comforting in a way. It distracted her from her thoughts as she sat there, hugging her knees to her chest and wistfully dreaming of her warm bed at the royal palaces which usually overflowed with thick furs and fluffy pillows.

That room was nothing more than a distant dream now. All the comfort she would be afforded was a mossy trunk and this stupid cloak that smelled like a mixture of mud, smoke, and *death*. A shudder ran down her spine and she clenched her fists into tight balls as she remembered why that was.

Four more were dead. Because of her. Well, because of the Muratians, but they had been sent after *her* in the first place.

Their desperation to stop this alliance was odd. Did they know?

Cord poked the fire, sending another wave of sparks and ash into the air. She followed him closely all day in fear of being left alone in these woods. He didn't check behind to ensure she was still trailing and never asked if she was ready to leave after a break, he just got up and marched away, leaving her to scramble to lace up her boots while half-hopping after him.

He was mad. He made his point.

Could they get back to him condescendingly asking how much longer her royal feet needed to rest or begrudgingly helping untangle her from a branch while spewing complaints the entire way? Anything was better than this.

The words that she spoke earlier slipped through her tongue before she could properly think. She was in distress and couldn't control herself. This man, this soldier, was all that she had standing in the way between her and a slimy death in this damp forest. The trickster goddess was surely out to get her this year.

What would she do if he abandoned her? There had been a moment when he left to gather wood for a fire and the minutes stretched for so long that she was certain he wasn't coming back.

The shaky sigh she released when he came stomping back to throw a bundle of dried ashwood branches at her feet was almost embarrassing. If he'd heard it, he ignored it...just as he had ignored her all evening. It was insufferable.

Something had to be done––before morning came and he'd undoubtedly try to leave her behind for good.

It pained her to be the one to bend first. But her stomach was about to cave in on itself and he hadn't offered her anything to eat all day.

It had to end. Her stomach gurgled in agreement.

"I'm sorry," she said quietly, keeping her eyes on the flames. The words pulled against every instinct she had and pushed on every nerve. It had been a long time since she'd had to utter those words. She couldn't even remember the last time she had to apologize to anyone who wasn't her father or brother.

"What was that?" His head snapped up and even across the blazing fire, she could still feel the burn of those gray eyes piercing through her.

Judging her. Taunting her.

Stupid soldier.

"You didn't have to intervene," she bit out. So much for apologizing nicely. "I had it handled."

He snorted and grabbed a thick branch, the end of his blade shaving off the dark skin before attacking it vehemently.

They both knew she had absolutely *nothing* handled from the moment they landed in this forest.

"You're welcome," he replied, matching her tone. He turned the branch over and started carving something on its end. "You're welcome for not handing you over and taking whatever bountiful reward the Muratians must have for you."

She clamped whatever retort she had shut, understanding the threat behind his words. One deep breath to collect herself, to calm herself before trying this again. "I know this was unexpected and it hasn't been the easiest these past days, but I appreciate the help you've been."

"It's my job," he said irritably, hollowing out two small eyes and a beak. "Even if we're stuck in the middle of gods-know-where, it's still my job."

The level of bitter resentment in his voice surprised her. It was beyond anger at having to get his hands bloody, or wrestling with boars, or dealing with bandits. No, it was something beyond being marooned in the middle of Muratian lands.

She'd never had a guard assigned this long while traveling with a battalion, most didn't last. She had the usual Siica guards in the palace but they didn't travel away with her unless she was with her father or brother. And this one was forced into it by his commander. He was not watching her through his own choice. None of this was his choice as a Pedite.

It was enough to pique her interest. "Why'd you get assigned to me anyway? Who'd you piss off so much?"

Cord snorted and moved on to a small wing. "It doesn't matter," he said, though his eyes darkened.

Isla twisted the gold circlet in her hands. It seemed to have lost all its prior shine beneath the layers of dirt and blood. Any comfort it once provided her had faded. Now she stared at the cold metal and the etchings so delicate they seemed to mock her current situation.

"You were right before," she said.

"What's that, Your Splendiferous Regency?" She opened her mouth to repeat the statement but he cut her off. "Actually, you know what." He crossed his arms, allowing the half-formed wood hawk to dangle precariously in his grip. "I'd rather not know. We don't *have* to talk. At all. We can do this whole thing without pretending to even like each other. We both want the same thing and that's to get out of here in one piece. We don't need anything else, so let's just leave it at that."

The rest of her apologies died on her tongue. She ground her teeth together and clamped her mouth shut.

"You're right," she said. "Why bother lowering myself in such a manner? Let's focus on getting through this in one piece. If you think you can handle that?"

He scoffed. "I'm not the one who's been the problem here. If we spotted those bandits then that must mean there's a village close by. My guess is we should hit it tomorrow or the next day. Remember the plan?"

The biting edge of his tone sent her stomach into knots. Did he really think she was that useless?

"Yes. I'm Elena of Murat, and you're my brother. We got lost on our way to visit our uncle in Blackstone, which is hopefully close enough that our story will pass."

"And?"

"And..." She sighed. "I don't talk to anyone, and I don't look at anyone."

"*And?*" he hissed.

"I listen to everything you say without question and will keep my dumb opinions to myself."

A smile cracked at the corner of his lips but it only irritated her further. "Then maybe we can make it out of here after all," he added. "And we'll never have to see or talk to each other again."

"Fine by me." If she had her way, he'd be sent far away from her the moment they were back on Velotian soil and in the safe hands of the military. She'd had enough of this soldier to last two lifetimes, and he'd seen too much of her already.

Without another word, Cord threw the incomplete hawk onto the embers, took off his borrowed jacket, and wrapped it around himself like a blanket before throwing himself to the ground in a huff. He shot her a dirty look before turning on his side.

But Isla did not fall asleep, not for a long while.

It was hard to sleep amidst the overwhelming feeling of uselessness that threatened to overwhelm her. Deep down, the truth blazed.

This was all her fault. Everything. Just as it always was.

She twisted the circlet in her hands.

When they were young, her brother would terrorize her with haunting stories filled with boil-covered witches and beasts with fangs as big as her head. As a child, she couldn't distinguish between truth and fable, and would stay up worrying she would turn into a horrid creature while the sun slept. Eventually, she'd succumb to exhaustion, just for the nightmares to take over, and wake up drenched in sweat with shaking hands, and no one to comfort her.

Her grip on the circlet was dangerously tight. She could feel the leaf points digging into her skin.

Edmund always reminded her that she was the reason their mother wasn't around, why their father turned so cold and bitter, and that she was the cause of everything going wrong in their lives since the day she was born. Over the years it became apparent how true that was.

As much as she hated to admit it, it was clear why her father arranged this treaty with the Koliats. It was so he didn't have to deal with her any longer, and she could become somebody else's problem.

Now she'd created an even bigger mess. She was truly a curse on their family.

She threw the circlet into the fire and sat unmoving, entranced by the way the flames licked at the leaves and devoured the same gold bands that her mother once wore. It sank to the bottom, surrounded by hot coals that did nothing against the unwavering metal forged long ago. Eventually, it would be buried in the ash and dirt, like the rest of her reminders of home.

The next morning, she was rudely awoken by a sharp jab in her shoulder, followed by a few harsh words telling her to gather her things. The soldier didn't speak another word, and his cold eyes followed every slow movement while she scrambled to tie her cloak securely.

At least he didn't leave her in the middle of the night as she'd feared.

A hint of gold in the black pit caught the sun's first rays, nearly blinding Isla. Cord stared at the metal with hooded eyes then back to Isla's empty nest of hair. She jerked her chin and held his gaze, daring him to say something.

Anything.

Without a word he stuffed his blue jacket on and finished packing the rest of her belongings. He made a great show of smashing the logs and throwing dirt onto the remains of the warm coals, not caring that he sprayed dust on Isla. Finally, he patted the satchel he took from those Muratian soldiers and nodded that they were ready to leave.

Fine. If this was how he wanted to do things, then so be it. She refused to beg for a simple acknowledgment or grovel for any undesired companionship, so she followed him mutely.

The silence was overwhelming on the first day and made her want to scream or beat the nearest trunk, but she persevered. On the second day it was less dreadful. Still annoying. By the third day of it, she started to cherish the sounds of the forest, which slowly turned greener the more they walked. Surely that was a good sign.

They must have been deposited deep within the depths of the Black Forests if they still hadn't seen a village or any civilization yet, not counting the bandits.

He was still angry about that and showed no signs of reconciliation. Isla refused to bend. She'd already apologized, more than adequately given their circumstances. What more could he want? So, they walked in angry silence for three whole days and basked in uncomfortableness every night.

She didn't say anything when they had to double back after passing the same felled redwood twice. If he wanted her opinion he would have asked, and she didn't want to risk another outburst. She prayed to the one-eyed forest goddess that they'd eventually find their way.

On the fourth day, she woke with the rising sun without needing any help or prodding. She was shocked to see that she was the first one up. Not knowing what to do with herself, she spent several moments tracing the divots in the nearest cracked stump and counting how many rings lined its old bark.

On the bright side, at least her joints didn't hurt anymore and her muscles weren't screaming in pain. She'd never walked so much in her entire life, and it seemed like her limbs had finally forgiven her for the turmoil she'd put them through.

It felt like she hailed from the Wene kingdom, with their scores of traveling nomads that moved from place to place due to the harshly changing seasons. They'd certainly traveled enough through this forest to put those tribes to shame.

Boredom settled in her limbs, so she stretched and took in the woodland grove they had slept in. A bed of moss lined the ground and made for a decent mattress, keeping most of the spiders out of her way that night—at least, she assumed so. Several heavy branches hung low, creating a small canopy of half dead leaves that allowed rays of sunlight to peek through.

After peeling off her cloak-blanket, she caught sight of her dirty nails and frowned. She prayed to the goddess that she wasn't as big of a mess as she thought, though she had a feeling that wasn't the case.

All she craved was a simple moment to herself, so she took one last look at Cord's sleeping lump and padded to the nearby stream, miraculously remembering the way.

Bubbles of air broke through the surface as ribbons of glistening water washed past. The riverbank was soft and mushy, giving way when she set foot on it. Thankfully, she caught herself before falling in. After patting around she found a ledge stable enough to sit on.

Isla removed her borrowed cloak and peeled off the outer layer of her crusted furs, now a dark gray instead of the lively white it had once been. She tossed the ruined vest to the side. It could remain behind to rot in the forest, like her mother's circlet. She was determined to escape a similar fate.

After the fur was taken care of, she slid her jacket off and folded it neatly to the side. She'd need it still and now that the silver stitching was stained black, it was indiscernible as a garment once belonging to a Velotian royal.

She must smell like a mixture of a half-dead mule and a moldy trunk. Her only solace was that Cord smelled worse.

A songbird chirped overhead, hopping from one branch to the next.

She peeled back the sleeves of her once fine silk tunic and dipped her hands in, ignoring the sting of the frigid water. She rubbed the patches of blood and dirt on her arms, wishing, in vain, to wash all remnants of this cursed forest away.

Soiled water glided down her arm in battling lines. She watched crystal drops run off her fingertips before gathering a pool of water in her palms and splashing it on her face. It was nice to feel something other than grime on her skin.

When she dipped to grab another handful of water, she froze.

The reflection that stared at her was barely recognizable. It felt like gazing into the eyes of a stranger.

The frown on her face was set deep, just like the dark circles under her eyes. The bruise from where that bandit hit had turned dark yellow, and she had cuts on her cheeks from where she fought with branches. Her lips were dry and cracked, and her hair was a jumbled mess. She ran a hand through the gritty tresses and winced when it ensnared on a thick knot.

Something would have to be done about it or they'd have to chop it all off when she got home. There was only so much that re-pinning would help.

What would help her hair survive its trudge through the forest?

One of her favorite portraits in the palace showed her parents when they were young and they actually looked happy. Her mother wore the prettiest flowing white dress and fashioned her hair in a simple braid with lilies woven in. It was manageable and common; she'd seen workers around the palaces often spotting a similar style.

It would do perfectly.

After attempting, in vain, to get out the largest tangles—she'd have to figure out another way to attack the rest later—she wove her hair into a rough braid that hung over her right shoulder. It wasn't as nice as the one in the portrait, as Isla wasn't used to doing her own hair, but it would do.

The rest of her wasn't as easily fixed as her hair. She frowned at the series of scratches along her arms and the appalling condition of her tunic. What she wouldn't give for a bath or a fresh set of clothes right now.

She placed her hand in the cold water and lavished the way the liquid rippled past her hand, moving around it as if it always belonged. It reminded her of the waves that crashed the shores of Larial, where she and Edmund were sent away during summers to keep out of their father's way.

The frown that her reflection wore grew more defined. She splashed the water so she didn't have to look at it anymore.

Did her family know she was missing by now?

Surely, they must. The commander wasn't stupid and would have sent a missive immediately. Unless they were attacked too. No. The party that ambushed them didn't seem prepared to take on an entire battalion. The rest of the soldiers were likely fine, except for dealing with her father's wrath.

Was he worried about her or merely how this would affect their alliance with the Koliats? The answer wasn't one she wanted to know.

If she knew her father, he would have sent a full battalion after her by now, if not more. He didn't like it when his property was stolen.

The bird's song halted. A shadow loomed over her, cutting off the link to the barely risen sun and nearly sending her heart through her chest.

Before she could even turn around, that annoying voice spoke, "I thought you ran away. You can't just sneak off like that."

"I didn't know you cared." She twisted her head. It looked like in his rush to find her, her companion didn't even bother putting on his coat. His wrinkled, white tunic clung dangerously tight to the muscles in his arm.

Cord scowled; his dark hair jolted in every direction. "I don't care," he said gruffly. "It's—"

"Your *job*," she finished with a smirk that only seemed to irritate him more. Good. "I know."

A red blotch formed on his neck and he barely managed to sputter out, "Don't ever leave without telling me. Again. Something could have happened."

Isla grinned, glad she managed to get a rise out of him. She caught his eye and held his glare. "Nothing happened. So, you rushed over in vain."

He screwed up his face, seeming to struggle with himself for a moment. After some inner turmoil, something softened in his face and he gestured at the river. "What are you even doing here—deciding the best way to drown yourself again?"

This time it was her turn to scowl. She grabbed her leather jacket and stuffed her arms in the sleeves. "Get your stuff," she grumbled, taking care to bump his shoulder as she brushed past. "We need to get a start on the day before you manage to get us lost again."

Though she couldn't see his face, she imagined it was twisted in the most satisfying glower.

Eleven

Mira

"You're coming with me."

The command echoed off the cracked walls and dusty beams before ringing through her skull. Private Devlin stared at her expectantly, still holding the firestone tightly.

Mira's mouth hung open and she was about to utter a protest before catching the hint of a head shake from Beretta. *Right.* She clamped it shut.

There was no way she could deny him without facing even worse consequences. There was nothing she could do.

Beretta's eyes widened and pivoted around the room as if searching for something or someone to help. Blotches formed on No-Neck's face and a bead of sweat dripped down his temple. The other dredgers had made themself scarce.

There was no escape.

Mira nodded to herself. May as well get this over with.

Beretta's hand brushed against her sleeve as she passed. That was all the encouragement her friend could afford to openly send. It was more than enough to bolster Mira's confidence.

No words found their way through her lips, so she silently followed Devlin out of the tunnel, focusing on his dark boots and the small puffs of dirt each new step kicked up. A few of the other dredgers eyed them curiously and the soldiers called out to Devlin as they passed. They must all be wondering, like her, what sort of punishment she was in for.

After a few turns down a pair of familiar tunnels, Mira realized that he was leading her away from the bowels of the mountain. Could it be—could they be going above ground? To where the air was fresh and didn't taste like stale rock and mildew.

Another turn and she spotted a warm ray of light flickering ahead.

Too bright to be from a lantern.

Her heart stuttered and it took everything in her not to run toward that glorious exit. She had to remind herself that it could still be a special punishment planned above ground. It didn't mean anything.

Not yet.

Anticipation and curiosity vibrated through her with each new step bringing her closer to the wooden doorway. She tapped her fingers against the side of her dirty brown uniform to keep from shaking. Every inch of skin tingled at the prospect of fresh air, even the side of her face which still throbbed from where that soldier had hit her. It had been so long since she felt wind on her face that wasn't laced with dirt from the tunnels that she was half-certain her skin would combust.

Devlin passed through the doorway, large enough to fit a full cart, and disappeared into a curtain of brightness.

Mira took a breath and stepped through the doorway. An onslaught of fresh air attacked her lungs and burning light stung her eyes.

She stumbled and grabbed onto the wooden frame, holding up a hand to block the harsh light. A couple of deep breaths filled her lungs with clean air that smelled of woodlands and mountain water. She had nearly forgotten what this felt like.

The warmth of the sun caressed her face. She'd missed it dearly, especially the morning light and the way it lit every inch of her skin alive with a mix of fire and tenderness. It was like a piece of a long-forgotten memory brushing against every fiber of her body.

"What are you doing?"

Devlin had doubled back and was staring at her with those unyielding eyes. He was tall—at least a head above her—and had powerful, broad shoulders that she could trace by memory. She studied his face, including the glistening scar on his jawline.

"Sorry," she mumbled. "Was just taking a minute. The sun." Stupidly, she pointed at the sky.

"Well..." He blinked. "Stop it. Let's go."

Right. She squinted to rid the spots from her eyes but they refused to budge. He gave her one final look over his shoulder and she knew better than to linger. She ran to catch up and followed him to the sparring fields, which were not much further into the encampment.

Would she be used as sport in one of their training exercises?

No. She breathed a sigh of relief when they didn't stop at the training fields.

They walked past the quartermaster's offices, the bathhouse, and the soldier cafeteria, and barracks—lucky jerks. They got to sleep above ground whereas the workers were stuck below to sleep and eat. The dredger sleeping quarters were nothing more than a slab of cold rock with a dusty blanket and only the creaking of the mountain to lull them to sleep. Beretta and Mira always doubled up on the cold nights so they didn't freeze to death.

Every time she walked this path it was thrilling—in a morbid sense, as she never knew if she was in for a terrible punishment or some sort of pathetic reward. The more they passed the usual discipline spots, the more that spark of hope in her chest grew.

Finally, when they passed the last row of dusty offices, he led her into one of the barrack rooms.

"This way." He pushed open a creaky door and backed away for her to pass through first. Devlin was always well-mannered and kind to her, even in the darkest pits of the worst mines.

She wrung her hands together, thumbing over the lash scars on her knuckles as she waited for the goddess Laian's judgment.

The room was surprisingly plain, but must be one of the ones that Beretta told her the higher-ups used for meetings. In the middle lay a thick iron table, several high-backed chairs, and most of the far wall was taken up with an obnoxiously large portrait of a wrinkled man with fine furs and a sharp gold crown upon his head. She didn't bother asking who the man was; She'd been caned for less.

Devlin threw himself into a patchy leathered chair at the end. He leaned back and crossed his feet on top of the table. The firestone clattered onto the iron top and his dark eyes bored into hers as he waited.

If it could, her heart would have beat its way through her ribcage by now. She clasped her fingers together to stop them from shaking. "Am I in trouble—sir?" she added the last part quickly, always unsure how to properly address their guardians.

"Do you know why this is so important?" He tapped the firestone with the heel of his boot.

She shook her head and bounced on the balls of her feet, not knowing what else to do with her body. What did this have to do with her punishment for speaking against a soldier, even if she had been right?

He furrowed his brows and pointed at the spot next to him. "Sit."

The chair scraped across the floor as she pulled it out, sitting awkwardly at the edge of the leather chair. She waited for any clue as to what he wanted her to do next.

A knock at the door nearly made her fall off her seat.

A young aide brought a tray that had a steaming bowl of soup, a lumpy half-loaf of bread, and hot tea. Was that actual, real meat she spotted? The smell made her mouth water and her stomach rumbled embarrassingly loud. It had been so long since she had anything but mush to eat. Her body wasn't built for that kind of food even though it was all she remembered.

The boy placed the tray carefully in front of her, took one look between her and Private Devlin, squeaked, and backed out.

When the door shut, Devlin nodded at the food, lacing his fingers together and surveying her with those intense blue eyes. "It's okay," he said as an infectious smile filled his face. "Go ahead and eat. You did great work today."

Relief spread through her body and her muscles sagged, releasing that tension they had been carrying the journey from the bowels of the mountain.

Slowly, as if worried that this was all a fever dream, she pulled the tray toward her. She picked up the fine metal spoon with shaky hands, almost forgetting how to hold something that wasn't clunky or broken, and brought a heaping spoonful up to her mouth—all while Devlin scratched the scar on his jaw and watched her with a curious expression on his face.

Without bothering to ask again, she shoved delicious potatoes, roots, and some sort of spiced meat that her taste buds had long forgotten into her mouth, nearly burning her tongue. She didn't care.

It was delicious.

It was warm.

It was amazing.

Another mouthful was on its way in before she had time to swallow the first bite. By her fifth mouthful, she paused, remembering she had an audience.

Devlin waved his hand and chuckled. A lovely sound. "Keep going. It's fine." Another heaping spoonful met her with glee. "You don't need to worry about that soldier retaliating... I understand that he has it out for you."

As her mouth was too busy, Mira nodded. A dribble of stew made its way down her chin, which she hastily wiped, praying to Slin that he didn't see.

"He's a dick," Devlin said.

No-Neck hated everyone under his watch. That wasn't new. But he particularly relished in tormenting her and Beretta when there was no one else around to witness; she could only hope her friend was holding her own against him while she was away.

Now, Devlin, this soldier was a fascinating specimen and harder to read. He wasn't on any of their regular guard rotation so he must be stationed up here, especially judging by the shine on his boots. The rest of his uniform was in equally pristine condition from his crisp collar to the sparkle of his gold buttons.

He definitely didn't belong.

Devlin's eyes flickered towards the firestone laying in the middle of the table. "You've found a few of these before?"

Mira nodded vehemently.

"As much as the others may disagree, I always think that we should reward our hard workers instead of doling out punishments like they are a delightful pastry at a solstice banquet. Wouldn't you agree?"

She nodded again.

"I've watched you before, and you don't seem to slack off as much as the others. Am I correct?"

"Yes, sir."

He chuckled and she liked the way it lit up his eyes. "Please don't call me that. My father made me call him sir all the time and I hated it."

"Yes, s—private?" she corrected. Uncertainty laced her veins and her throat, nearly sticking her tongue to the roof of her mouth.

"That'll do for now."

For now. Those words and that dangerous half smile held the promise of something she couldn't name. Her stomach didn't know what to do with itself.

"Thank you for the food," she said quietly.

Private Devlin removed his feet from the table and sat up. He pushed the tray to the side. "That's actually not what I brought you here for. Like I said—I've been watching you closely these past weeks."

The last piece of meat clawed its way down her throat like a spiky pinecone. She gulped a helping of water to clear it, intensely aware of the portrait of the wrinkled Muratian royal watching her closely. Judging her.

Pretending not to notice, Devlin pulled a cloth from his inner pocket and spread it in front of her. It was a faded image of what looked like a dark blob with an unreadable ancient writing carved into the edges.

Not knowing what to do, she bit a chunk out of the loaf still in her hand.

He motioned her closer with his finger and lowered his voice. "I'd like to share something... but you must promise not to whisper a word of it to anyone else."

She swallowed, feeling the half-chewed lump of bread trudging its way down her throat. "Of course," she gasped. She discarded her spoon and studied the blade again. "What is it?"

"There are old stories from when the ten kingdoms were one, under the rule of the powerful High King who had magics untold of. Do you remember that from your studies?"

Mira shook her head. *Not since coming here.*

It was hard to remember anything besides the tunnels and rocks that encompassed her entire life. If he wanted to know which shaft had the most moisture and was best avoided, she could help with that. Everything else was lost to her.

"That's okay," he said gently. "I always thought it was a boring lesson anyways. Easily forgetful to young minds. There's a lot of backstory in there but the old High King's line was powerful. Very influential. He made most of our kingdom's strongholds and paved the great roads as they are today. They say he lived far too long for a normal human and ruled over Rocia for centuries. There are even more insane theories that the old High King's line comes directly from the sister goddesses: Hierel and Rallion."

Rallion.

Sister Death.

The gatekeeper of the twelve hells who guarded over the portal to the next veil. Mira didn't remember much from her time above-ground, thanks to her injury, but she vaguely remembered that from her studies.

"It was said the High King ruled alone for years, until he finally had two living heirs. Twins."

Her throbbing brain didn't remember that piece either.

"In some ancient texts, it was said that the reason the High King lived so long was because he managed to imprison death herself. He seduced her and trapped her, casting her in heavenly chains under the mountain during the year of Hierel when she was at her weakest."

The year of Hierel.

While the kingdoms of the Rocians honored the thirteen cycling years of the goddesses, Hierel and Rallion did not get their dedicated years on the heavenly calendar.

Their years were special, nonetheless, forewarned by Rallion's black comet.

The dark comet came first to signal the upcoming shift to the sister goddesses. Two chaotic years of ever-changing fortune followed.

It all started with the star goddess Hierel's year. Then came the goddess of death's immediately after.

A year of fortune and fortuity followed by a year of chaos and—well, death. The twelve gates were said to work overtime during those years.

Mira focused on the cloth in between them. That blob was a comet, she now stupidly realized. And the strange words along the edge were intertwined with a wilted blood-lily. Rallion's symbol.

The comet hadn't been seen for over a hundred years, until it showed its face several months—or was it weeks—ago.

Dreams of a black ball burning in the skies plagued her for as long as she could remember.

Devlin sprang from his chair and paced the length of the small room. He took one full turn before stopping in front of Mira. He tilted her head to the side, examining the flowering bruise on her cheek, before nodding to himself and leaning back against the table.

"Rumor is that the High King's grandchildren fought each other for the throne and he could never pick a favorite to take over before he passed. The magic that he wielded died out through the male line, as it is known to do, and the old man spent his remaining years worrying about his legacy. He died during Rallion's year. The first time the comet was ever spotted."

Devlin pushed the etching closer to her. "This one."

She ran her hand over the rough fabric.

"The legends say Rallion escaped and hunted him down to kill him herself, but I doubt a goddess would deign to lower herself to that level. It was said that he survived the first year thanks to the grace of Hierel, hence why it's her year first. But Rallion found him during the second. The ten grandchildren from his firstborn son fought each other for the throne. They devastated the lands, setting nearly everything aflame, as fighting monarchs tend to do," he said with a nod.

"In the end, they killed half the population and finally the lands split into the ten kingdoms, which we now have today. But the power the High King held was never heard of again from his male line."

Mira nearly scoffed. All this talk of goddesses and ancient weapons was utter nonsense.

But the fire in Devlin's eyes showed that he believed it to be true.

Devlin jerked his head at the cloth now clutched in her hand. "While the story about the goddess is absurd at best, there have been reports in our history of the old king's power—Rallion's power—rising again here and there. Rallion's followers are particularly vehement in pursuing every lead. It was said that the more rabid ones would burn marks into their own skin in an attempt to gain the goddess's blessing. Eventually, the old historians understood that the chains that bound Rallion may not have been chains at all, but rather stone. Stone that affects wielders' magic."

"The firestone," Mira breathed.

"Yes." He wiggled his eyebrows. "Likely the stories of Rallion and the old High King were stories made up to hide the true properties of firestone and its effects on wielders. This is one of the most firestone-rich mines we've found and I'm hoping we can find enough for what is needed."

"So, why the search for the firestone? What's the endgame?"

He snorted. "Obviously not to blaze villages to the ground." Again, he lowered his voice and stared at a point on the table. "My brother... he was once tasked to do the same as myself and was sent to other mines to collect the firestone, but he was killed by rebels two years ago. I want to finish what he started before anyone with ill-intentions can get to those reserves, as it can decimate our armies. The enemy has—either knowingly or unknowingly—stumbled upon a weapon of great magnitude that can topple our kingdom. I want to ensure we have something comparable."

"And you think that I can help?" she asked quietly. Her blood pounded through her veins and ricocheted off her skull as her brain tried to understand what he was asking.

"Absolutely." He pointed at the firestone, his dark blue eyes ablaze with unfiltered passion. She couldn't help but stare into them. "You seem to have a natural ability to find firestone, whether or not you realize it—I've noticed." Her heart skipped a beat. "You were probably born with these gifts. I'm not allowed down there for too long to search for myself. But maybe you can use that same pull to help me find more firestone and then maybe, together we can prevent a terrible war."

A weird sensation danced in her midsection.

No! She ignored any flutters that wanted to enter her stomach and killed any lofty thoughts of getting lost in those deep blue eyes. Those would do her no good.

"And what do I get if I help you?" she asked.

"Do you know how you got placed here?"

She shook her head.

"I'll help you find that out—find your life outside of here. And, if you help me find what I want..." he lowered his voice barely above a whisper and motioned for her to lean in close even though they were the only two in the room. Her heart stopped when he uttered those words she ached to hear. "I can help you escape this place for good."

Twelve
The Captain

It pained him to admit that when he woke up half-dead, barely registering his surroundings except to realize that Princess Isla wasn't there, he was nearly sent into a panic. He had scrambled out of bed and called out, only to receive deafening silence in response.

The silence was overwhelming and made his head dizzy as visions of overwhelming flames consumed him. Something terrible had happened.

The worst possible scenarios flooded his mind, each one more terrible than the previous. Had she wandered off to be eaten by a wolf or fallen off a cliff, as he continuously had to keep her away from several times a day. She seemed to have a knack for finding things that wanted to kill her in this forest, including the snapping vines, which she'd been caught in twice already. This entire gig was like attempting to keep a toddler alive who was determined to storm head first into peril every time he turned his back.

So when he woke up to find her spot empty, he knew something terrible had finally happened, considering he'd had to forcibly wake her each morning and listen to a string of complaints about exhaustion and her needing more *beauty sleep*. Something must have happened. He'd failed, *again*.

He searched the surrounding woods for her, calling her name like an idiot—as if he actually expected her to respond back. This was it for him if she died. He'd never be able to return home to make things right. His siblings would be conscripted now.

It was over. He was over.

There was no returning now that he'd lost his charge. He'd be hanged—if he ever made it back.

He trampled through the forest like a wild boar—or like the princess trampled around on that first day.

Just as his mind started to run through scenarios of the commander flaying every surface of his body and tossing him into a boiling tar pit, he heard splashing near the riverbank.

The *river*. He swore to the trickster goddess Slin, if she fell into the river, he was going to—

His boots froze to the damp ground.

She hadn't fallen and drowned in the river, nor had she been speared by another boar. There was no sinking pit in sight either.

In fact, she was perfectly fine. Though for some reason that irritated him even more.

The princess knelt at the edge of the stream, half-soaked, and seemingly lost in thought. *Not* lying dead at the bottom of a ravine as he'd imagined.

What in Hierel's name had possessed her to wander off without a word? He didn't think she was capable of rising without someone shouting in her ear, let alone managing to find her way to the stream without entangling herself in a batch of vines.

Before any semblance of relief could wash over him, he was inexplicably filled with rage. Angry that she had wandered off and worried him for no good reason. All because she wanted to scrub the dirt off herself.

Stupid conceited princess.

After exchanging a series of heated words, he packed up their dwindling supplies in a huff, refusing to speak to her the entire time. His anger seemed to bolster her, and she looked the most pleased he had seen her since they were deposited here.

And accusing *him* of getting them lost when all she'd contributed to their journey was trying to get them killed multiple times? It was laughable, at best.

At least she left behind that atrocious once-white set of furs. Now she donned her black travel leathers and the *borrowed* wielder's cloak. An odd combination but better than nothing. She had finally taken out whatever hairstyle she had with those fancy combs that were an easy giveaway to her royal lineage––even if she could barely form a proper braid with her untrained hands.

At least she looked less like a matted squirrel and more like a traveling commoner. A Muratian. Hopefully, she would blend in better… that was if she was able to keep quiet when they spotted any people, which was akin to asking for a miracle from the star goddess herself.

The angrier he got, the more pleased with herself she became. He even caught her humming a song after he got tripped up on a patch of hidden roots.

Besides that, they stayed silent, as they had been since the run-in with the bandits. She wasn't fully to blame for what happened, but he had lost his temper and saw red after realizing what he'd had to do, again.

There was so much blood on his hands that he never seemed to be able to scrub them clean, even though not a drop could be seen anymore. He knew it was there… and he loathed himself for it. The princess wasn't to blame for what he'd done in this forest. This wasn't the first bloodshed he'd caused.

That blame solely lay with one person.

While in the middle of climbing over a fallen trunk at least twice his height, he turned around to help her up, but she was twenty paces back in the shade of another oak, standing with her head cocked to the side and a curious look on her face,

"What is it now?" he huffed, trailing back to where she stood.

"Don't you hear that?" she asked. An annoying smile bloomed on her lips as she flipped her braid over her shoulder. "It's noise."

"Thanks for the clarification," he said dryly. But he started to hear it too and crouched down. "Get over here."

This spot was too open. He dragged her towards a thick chunk of trees. They were way past the point of asking permission to touch her now.

Unless he was mistaken, that was the distinct hum of voices and the clattering of hooves against hard ground. He pulled Isla behind a thick foxwood before they were spotted, keeping a tight grip on her arm so she wouldn't get any more bright ideas.

He held his breath as the noise grew louder––as whoever it was got closer.

That must have been a road of sorts they were on. And they finally found a trace of humans in the ghastly woods.

He rubbed a sweaty palm against his pant leg, still keeping a tight grip on Isla's arm. His skin was alive with a mix of excitement and nerves. Finding people was a good sign. A great sign potentially. As long as it was the *right* type of Muratians.

Whoever it was spoke with such a thick accent that he could barely make out a muffled word through the trees. After straining his ears, the few words he picked out were harvest, grain, and floods. Nothing about armies, missing princesses, wielders, or soldiers. It was enough to confirm they were farmers and likely posed no threat to a pair of lost wanderers, but still, it wasn't worth the risk to out themselves yet.

Isla shifted under his grip.

With a flush of embarrassment, he realized he practically had her pinned against his side. He dropped her arm and shifted away from her, keeping his eyes focused on the rough bark in front of him.

After what felt like an eternity in which he could hear every heartbeat and shaky breath she took, the voices faded into the forest.

As soon as she realized the same, Isla jumped away from him and smoothed her hand along the crease of her cloak. A crooked smirk was plastered to her face.

"It's a good thing *one* of us was paying attention or they'd have spotted us," she said in an annoyingly high voice. "Seems like I'll be handling your job in next to no time and you'll make yourself entirely useless, *soldier*."

His nostrils flared as his lungs released a torrent of air. He would rather impale himself at the end of a boar's tusk than admit she was right, so instead he said, "That would make this the first useful thing you've done in a while, I guess. From what I hear that must be a personal best for you."

It was her turn to turn a lovely shade of red. Not from embarrassment, but from anger. Something must have struck the proper target as her eyes looked ready to boil over. She clutched her hands together in a giant ball as her chest heaved up and down.

Once she calmed herself, she took a final, smoother breath, and brushed past him. "You are insufferable, do you know that?" she bit out.

He did. It was something the commander and his friends constantly reminded him of.

"Likewise, Your Supreme Gracefulness," he said, trailing after her. "We should keep to the thick part of the forest so that nobody can surprise us."

She kicked a felled branch and muttered words unbecoming of a princess, which is exactly what he told her. She then accused him of being a useless bodyguard again, which didn't help cool either of their raging tempers. They traveled into the thicker part of the forest, following the direction the voices had gone in the hopes it would lead someplace promising.

The trees grew close enough for their branches to intertwine together, creating an intricate canopy above which hushed any songbirds or outside noise. All he had was his own heavy breathing and the muted crunch of deadened leaves beneath their boots to fill the void.

The silence was uncomfortable, and if they found Muratians they needed to be on the same page. Fighting now wouldn't do either of them any good. He ran a hand through his increasingly greasy hair. "I'm glad you fixed your hair."

The scraping of boots against dirt faltered for a moment, and her hand jumped to the end of her braid.

"*Fixed it?*" she hissed. "Was it so terrible before?"

"You had a spider living in it, so—yeah, it was."

She scoffed. "I needed something to stop the tangles, or they'll have to cut my hair off when they find us."

"Well." He kicked a pile of dead leaves. "It's a good choice. Especially if you're trying to pass for a lowly peasant like the rest of us."

Her voice quieted, barely carrying above the soft rustle of leaves, "My mother used to wear her hair like this. I remembered it from old portraits around the palace... and I couldn't think of anything better."

If he could have found the way to remove his own leg to kick himself, he would have. It was common knowledge that the queen was killed birthing the very princess that had vexed him so the past week. Naturally, it would be a touchy subject for Isla.

"I'm sorry," he whispered. He knew the pain of losing a parent.

She shoved a spiky branch aside, allowing it to bounce back and whip him. "I doubt it." She scoffed. "Who do you think those men were? Anything we should be concerned about?"

He dodged another perfectly aimed branch that almost hit his head. "Sounded like farmers... common folk. Nothing to be concerned about."

"Good." She nodded, almost to herself, more than anything. "Don't want you having another fit for absolutely no reason."

Rage bubbled back up, as did his retort, which died on his tongue as soon as she snapped around, wearing a giant grin. It was then that he realized she was teasing him. *Teasing him*. And he could not give her the satisfaction of knowing her ruse almost worked.

Instead, he forced a grim smile on his face and closed the gap between them. She stood half a head shorter than him, barely coming up to his nose. But if she was intimidated, she hid it well. "There will be no need for any fits thrown this afternoon if people can just remember their place in all of this and *stick to the plan*."

The last part came out in a higher pitch than he would have preferred and the way the smirk on the princess's face grew, told him that she knew just how rattled he had been that morning... and that only infuriated him further.

Before he could open up his mouth to utter a jibe that would surely remove the smile from her face, she whipped around and cocked her head to the side. She held up a finger that still held the traces of a perfect cut and shaping beneath several washed out layers of forest and mud. Even a quick scrub in the river couldn't get rid of all the layers of filth.

With his mouth hanging open like a decaying fish, he paused.

The sounds of a distant brook floated through the trees. It was accompanied by the faint sound of metal against stone—hooves—followed by fainter voices that were almost lost amongst the trees.

They must be close. A wave of nausea threatened to come up when he went through all the scenarios in his head.

They'd wanted to find a trace of Muratians, but things hadn't gone over well the last time they ran into people in these woods.

The princess's finger curled and she gestured towards the edge of a small clearing. Before she could get near the opening, he grabbed her shoulder and pushed her behind him. He wanted that first look, and it was definitely not to ensure there were no snares or hollows she could get stuck in.

He crept behind a bush with curly blue-green leaves and pushed it aside to get a view. Finally, he could see the end of the forest.

In the valley below, was a small Muratian village, curled around a shallow river that looked to be nearly drained of all water.

From this distance, he could make out the drab colored buildings that must have been ignored for at least a decade. They looked like they were once painted a bright yellow, judging by the few sides that still held the color. A road—if you could call that line of muddy pebbles one—made its way through the center of the town, passing by wood buildings that had missing shingles, half-hanging windows, and fences only containing every other post.

They managed to stumble their way to the outskirts of some long-forgotten and clearly hard-done-by village. The question still remained as to which village it was and how far from home they were.

Something rubbed against his shoulder and made him jump. His hand was on the hilt of his sword, gripping it tightly.

"Finally," the princess breathed. She pushed a tangle of blue leaves out of her hair and clicked her tongue. "Some sense of civilization."

She moved as if to continue forward and stride right into the village itself. His hand shot out.

"Excuse me?" Her eyebrows flew into her hairline when he pulled her back.

"What do you think you're doing?" he shot back.

"Going into the village, as we planned."

"Don't be stupid," he said. "We don't know who or what is down there—and you want to just skip into town unannounced?"

Her nose wrinkled. "I thought that was why we followed the stupid river and those farmers' voices. Are you suggesting we spend another night in these cursed woods?"

"Calm yourself, Your Great Regalness. I'm not saying anything like that. We just have to be careful."

"Careful about what?" she whined, dragging on the last syllable for far too long. "I'm done being careful. I want to go home."

He grabbed her wrist, where the sleeve of her jacket was pushed past, and her skin was hot to the touch. "Don't forget that we are nowhere near home yet. And as downtrodden and harmless as that place looks, don't for a second let yourself think that it is safe for us."

Her eyes returned to the village, seeming to roll over every small detail as if to pick out potential danger spots from this distance.

"We sneak in. Take what we need and—"

"You mean to *steal*?" she hissed, her eyes flashing dangerously.

That was a part he had yet to inform her of. If he had it his way, they'd be in and out before anyone could notice a grain out of place. He didn't feel good about it, but it was the safest way.

"We're just going to borrow. Borrow without the intention of returning."

Isla straightened up, hands on her hips and eyes blazing with fury. "If you think for one second that I'm going to allow you—"

"Allow me? *Allow me?*"

"I have listened to your half-formed ideas for long enough." She poked her finger at his chest. "We're going to do things my way this time and that means—"

A branch crunched and they whipped around in unison. His grip was around the hilt of Dark End before his eyes could make out what caused the noise.

A voice called out, "What are you two doing sneaking about over there?"

Thirteen

The Princess

Isla's throat turned drier than the dead stump that tripped her up only minutes before. She opened her mouth but nothing came out. Beside her, Cord's hand clutched his longsword, running his finger along the hilt. Tension leaked off him in droves, unnecessary as it was, once she took in the pair who managed to sneak up while they argued.

A withered couple with matching gray hair—who looked to be bordering on Rallion's first gate—stood before them. They wore cross-patterned shirts with thickly stitched pants made from a stiff material she'd never seen, but it looked scratchy. Judging by the state of their attire and the deep tan marks on their skin, they must be farmers.

Neither looked harmful. She unstuck her tongue and gently pushed Cord's hands away from his hilt––a movement which hopefully went unnoticed by the intruders.

"Are you two lost?" the old lady crooned. Half of her hair was tied back with a piece of wool, while small curls escaped and stuck out at odd angles. Deep wrinkles lined her face and accentuated her kind eyes which took in their disheveled appearance, lingering on Isla's still dirty hands.

Feeling self-conscious for the first time, she pulled at the frayed end of her braid, as if that would straighten it out. They must be a sight to see for the poor farmers.

When it became apparent that Cord had no clue how to treat with these wayward travelers besides lobbing their heads off, Isla stepped forward. Those stupid, gray eyes bore into the back of her head as she remembered to keep her shoulders drooped and an unassuming smile painted on her face.

"We're hoping you can help us—my brother and I." She jerked her head at her escort, who continued to watch the couple through narrowed eyes while standing in an awkward defensive stance that she hoped wouldn't set them off. The lady passed a basket full of wild mushrooms from one arm to the next and adjusted the cloth around her brittle hair. "We were on our way to visit our uncle and got lost. We've been wandering the forest for days."

If there was one thing her instructors instilled upon her from an early age, it was how to be a gracious and welcoming host to win over the most taciturn of aristocrats. She may not know how to spot a sinking pit until it was too late, or which type of wood burned best for roasting wild boar, but she knew how to handle people. Her father—or her father's people—made certain of that.

The old man shifted from foot to foot, his scraggly eyebrows furrowed. They were married, judging by the matching burn marks on their wrists that was common practice across the ten kingdoms.

When completing nuptials, a pair tied their hands together with a simple rope and set it aflame. The scars were a permanent reminder of the forever vows a couple took under the goddesses' eyes. A reminder of the old ways of bonding souls together through a permanent scar on their flesh.

A shudder ran down Isla's spine at the thought.

"For *days* my dear?" The lady's free hand jumped to her chest. "These forests can be full of dangers. You're lucky nothing's happened to either of you."

"Lucky," she breathed. Her chest tightened. If that's what she wanted to call what they had gone through the past week then she wouldn't be the one to correct her.

"Horace," the lady said, head snapping toward the man. "Help these poor souls before the wrath of Laian comes down and smites you."

Horace was nearly skin and bones and sported a long curly beard that reached past his shoulders. The sleeves of his frayed tunic were pulled up past his elbows as he surveyed the pair skeptically—rightfully so. "What if they're bandits...or *worse*?"

Isla had to hold in her scoff. If anyone should be wary, it should be her and Cord, not these poor Muratian farmers.

The woman admonished her husband, "Do they look like bandits to you? They're half dead." She beckoned Isla closer with a calloused hand. "Why don't we help you into town and see if Saniam has a spot for you."

"Saniam?" Cord muttered; his face wrinkled in concentration. Isla dug her elbow into his side.

"He runs the local inn here, the Regal Heron," Horace said as if this was information they should already know. "He can get you set up with a hot meal and a place to sleep if you have the coin."

The man's eyes trailed over their disheveled outfits, including Isla's wielder cloak, which she clutched closer to her. They had no other belongings. A cold, hollow loss filled her as she remembered her mother's circlet that was left behind, buried in ash.

It pained her to admit that Cord was right about leaving it. It would have brought unwanted attention.

"We have some coin." Isla tucked a wayward strand that fell from her braid behind her ear and jerked her head at her *brother*. "Not much. Only what we managed to scrape up before starting our journey."

Even though she had chastised him at the time, she thanked the goddess that Cord took that dead wielder's coin bag... not that she'd ever admit it to him.

The man's eyes narrowed as he and Cord sized each other up. After a moment, he decided something and nodded.

"Perfect." The old lady, Edith, as she next introduced herself, clapped her hands together and demanded that they escort Cord and Isla into their village, Ackerslie. It had been so long since they had visitors pass this way and she was eager to hear any news from outside—which Isla doubted they could provide.

Hopefully, Cord was adept at making up stories. Something believable as she knew nothing about this area of Murat—or about the affairs of their greatest adversary, really. If the pair hadn't ventured away from their village in years, then surely any exaggerated news Cord could muster up would be welcomed.

"Have you been this way before, dearies?" Edith asked.

"No," Cord answered gruffly from his spot at the front of the path with Horace.

That one needed to lighten up.

They'd found a village.

A place with food, probably a hot bath, and even a place to sleep. An inn—even though she'd never set foot in one before—had to be better than the forest floor. Surely, there'd be no spiders there? And there'd be no Muratian soldiers, especially if it sounded like they hadn't had visitors in ages.

At least Edith bought their carefully crafted story. She spent the majority of their walk asking about their family back home and the ailing uncle they'd journeyed so far to assist.

It was so euphoric to have a new person to talk with that wasn't switching between yelling at her for some silly reason or ignoring her for another equally ridiculous one. Edith shared similar feelings as she hadn't spoken with anyone outside of their village in months.

Horace wasn't as welcoming as his wife and seemed more skeptical of their new arrivals. He asked, and not for the first time since coming across them, "You're at least a few days from Blackstone over here. Where did you say you came from, again?"

"Old Riverrot," Cord said, just as they'd discussed every night since landing here. By now, Isla could recite it without help as the soldier had drilled the details into her before allowing her to get her much needed sleep. There was no way even she could screw this up.

Cord, on the other hand, seemed to have lost some of his prior confidence under the sharp questioning of Horace. Thankfully, the soldier managed to find his voice and did not make a complete mockery of their story while following the pair along a hidden dirt road they were assured would lead straight into the village.

At least they had a sense of where they were now—or at least Cord must know where they were as Isla had never heard of this area. If only they had been transported someplace closer to the border and not a gods-forsakened village in the middle of who-knew-where. When Edith told him where they were, Cord's eyes darkened and he nodded solemnly.

Judging by Horace and Cord's discussion about news from across the river, it seemed like they were further than he had guessed. She'd have to wait until they had a moment alone to determine how far that was. Then she could allow panic to fully settle in.

"Are you cold, my dear?" Edith asked. She and Isla had grown tired of the men's somber talk of the war and fell behind on purpose.

"No." Isla rubbed her hands together to stop the shaking. "It must have been a breeze I caught."

"I'm surprised you didn't catch ill out there," Edith said. "These woods are unforgiving. You're lucky you only got out with a few scratches."

"Thank the goddess my brother is decent at tracking."

"I would hardly call his tracking skills *decent* if he got the two of you so lost. At least you are safe now and can follow the road toward Blackstone once you've had a chance to rest up."

Isla wasn't able to hold in the sigh that escaped her lips. The thought of a warm bed—any bed would do at this point—was enough to keep her going on without complaints of how the gravel road pained her already blistered feet. After a good night's rest, they could find the main road, head in the opposite direction Edith gave them, and be on their way home to forget this nightmare of a detour ever happened.

Except she wouldn't be on her way home.

Not ever again, she reminded herself, shaking her fists out.

At least she would be comfortable at Koliat. Comfortable. That was the best she could hope for with a man she'd never met. Anything was better than this. It had to be.

If it wasn't then she should have really just thrown herself into that river the day at the camp. A breeze kicked up a patch of loose leaves and sent them attacking her face.

"Your brother seems quite protective," Edith added when Cord glanced back for what must have been the twentieth time by now. "Older?"

Isla nodded.

Probably. He had to be around mid-twenty—not that she bothered to ask him. There was a lot she didn't know and it occurred to her that she should know her brother's age in case someone asked. They didn't go over any personal details in his nightly drills.

"It's nice to have someone who cares about you," Edith continued on. "Not everyone has that."

The contents of her stomach churned.

That *would* be nice. Her father viewed her as nothing more than a bargaining tool to strengthen his alliances. He couldn't wait to get rid of her. The relationship with her actual brother was just as sour, even though some days he pretended to care. Not that she blamed either of them.

Isla had been on her own for a long time before this. Marrying the Koliat prince would change nothing. She'd learned to take care of herself since she was old enough to understand the truth of why her father could never fully love her. She would always have to look out for herself first.

Her hands started shaking again.

"How long have you and Horace been together?" Isla asked, blinking hard.

The old man had been non-stop in his questioning of Cord their entire journey back. She should probably try to save him but he deserved it after everything he'd put her through.

"Sixty years last harvest," Edith said happily. "And I hope to have more if the war with the cursed Velotians stays far away from us. We've been lucky enough the past two years, but who knows what the death goddess Rallion has in store for us."

All Isla could do was grunt awkwardly. It suddenly felt much too hot here, even though it was starting into the cold season and she hadn't been properly warm in over a week.

"A terrible thing, really," Edith continued, taking Isla's noises as affirmation. "They've already sent the conscripts twice and our village has given all we have. But it's necessary to stop those monsters."

"Uh-huh." Where was Cord to bail her out and when did he wander so far ahead? Wasn't he worried that something could befall her?

At least Edith feigned ignorance to her discomfort. "Have you seen any of the impacts near Riverrot?"

"Nothing yet," Isla said. It was all she could do to hold the lie in the face of the poor woman. "I expect it's only a matter of time before war reaches us."

"I only hope that we can stop those savages before more death falls upon our lands."

"Me too," Isla said between rough breaths.

"Do you need to rest, Elena?"

Elena.

That felt strange against her ears even though she had practiced saying it out loud for days. When she told the Muratians her new name it tasted like ash against her tongue. It didn't feel right and she was worried they'd catch her lie.

Pretending to be some commoner felt as unusual as a bucking mule in a palace. She was out of place and certain everyone knew it.

"No," Isla said. "I just needed to catch my breath."

The callouses on her feet would never fade after all this, but her pride refused to take a break while the others were barely breaking a sweat.

The dirt path slowly turned into a rough cobblestone road thrown together with mismatched rocks that must have been castoffs from a main road. Behind them lay those blasted Muratian forests that she hoped to never see again, wrapping tight around the landscape in almost every direction. There must be a quick way home that didn't involve setting foot near them.

The only part that wasn't forest was the small, tree-lined lake to the west and the towering range of red mountains that spanned past the eastern horizon. She'd never seen peaks that color before.

In front of them was the village Edith had called Ackerslie.

It was smaller up close, with the buildings in more disrepair than she first noticed. It likely housed farmers and tradesmen, if she had to guess. She'd never have been allowed near a place like this before. Her father always deemed it beneath a royal princess.

But she wasn't a royal princess right now... that was what she had to remind herself.

As they drew closer, some of the villagers stopped and stared as if they hadn't seen an outsider here in years. She'd never been this close to this many Muratians in her life and Cord felt unnaturally far ahead.

If only these villagers knew who had just entered their small, peaceful village. What would they do if they found out the dangers her mere presence had placed them in?

Her pulse quickened. Every muscle in her body yearned to flee, but she took that feeling of uncomfortableness and buried it far down.

A few of the villagers called out in greeting to Edith and Horace as they passed, but none dared approach. One particularly scraggly man turned back into his shop at the sight of them, slamming the door shut. She didn't blame him for being cautious in the presence of strangers.

Up ahead, Cord looked the most stressed she had ever seen him, even worse than when he had to pull her out of a tangled vine pit. He kept looking back as if expecting her to vanish altogether and she spotted beads of sweat on the back of his neck.

"What made you two decide to venture so far from home just to visit your uncle, my dear?" Edith waved to a man in blacksmith's gear, who murmured to another outfitted in leathers with a bow on his back. Both watched the new arrivals with narrowed eyes. "These are troubling times to go off like that."

The smell of horses and dirt filled her nostrils, followed swiftly by the most delicious smell. It must have been that bakery they passed. Her stomach churned in protest at the thought of a hot meal.

Isla toyed with the end of her long braid. "Our uncle has fallen ill and has no one to care for him, so our father sent us to lend aid. Not that we've managed to make much use of ourselves since getting lost in the woods. I fear that our uncle will worry when we don't show up as planned."

"At least you made it someplace safe," Edith said. "If you'd gone any further south then who knows what would have happened."

"Why?" Isla blurted before she could stop herself.

Idiot. Surely a Muratian would know why going south was not a good idea.

Edith clicked her tongue. "The forests get even more terrible down there, with the dangers they hold. And if you manage to make it past that, then you'd be in..." She looked around, and lowered her voice dramatically. "Velotian territory."

Isla's heart frantically skipped a beat and she was worried the lady could hear it. What an absolute traitor of an organ.

"Don't worry dear," Edith said soothingly. She seemed to have picked up on Isla's uncomfortableness. "That's more than two weeks' journey on horseback and nobody ever comes out of that part of the woods. The next closest junction between our territories is southeast from here and is even further away. You don't have to worry about those Velotians coming anywhere near here."

Isla forced out a grin. All she felt on the inside was cold and darkness.

Weeks. *Weeks.*

Just perfect.

Isla cleared her throat. "I'm glad we found you and Horace. Now we can continue our journey before we get in anyone's way."

"Just be happy you didn't run into any bandits or thieves in the forest," Edith said idly. "They'd have skinned you alive."

The memory of the dead bandits flashed before her eyes. She was under strict orders not to mention that part of their journey no matter what. They had to stay clear of any stories that would rouse suspicion.

A small boy and his mother crossed in front of them, kicking up brown dust. The moment she spotted Cord and Isla, the mother grabbed her son's hand and ushered him across the road into the nearest shop.

"We don't get a lot of outsiders here," Edith said in way of explanation. Any of the unease that had filled her evaporated like the morning dew at the sight of the old lady's genuine smile.

"And here we are." Horace stopped underneath a busted sign of a heron and an axe that looked like it was one good wind gust away from falling. The rest of the walls were in equal disarray with peeling yellow paint and dirtied windows that gave no hint at what waited inside.

This must be the local inn they had been talking about. The Regal Heron. *Charming.*

Two weeks ago, the thought of spending a night in this run down place would have made her skin crawl and her breakfast turn up. Today, Isla would have traded half her royal jewels at the prospect of even a quick nap and a bucket of cold water to clean herself with.

Cord made sure she was behind him before allowing himself to be ushered in first. His hand flexed, as if it craved for the cool touch of steel, but he was too smart to grab for his blade. They exchanged a brief look together, both understanding that they'd continue their charade for as long as it took.

They weren't enemies of these people and should have nothing to fear. Not today.

They were Cord and Elena of Murat and these were their people. They had to believe it.

Fourteen

Mira

"What's got you in such a good mood?" Beretta asked for the third time that day, holding her gaze with a shrewd blue eye that reminded her of an ocean she'd never seen. She dug the blade of her shovel into a pile of discarded rocks and rested her chin on the handle.

A stream of sweat dribbled down Mira's back. Today was a hot one.

They'd been assigned down to the new tunnels to bust away with a dozen others, including two newcomers who looked as if they wouldn't last a week. The rock down here was tough, the guards were more irritable than usual, and the temperatures nearly boiling.

The poor newcomers kept tripping over themselves and constantly begged for a break. The guards merely laughed them off and kicked over a bucket of water.

A small part hidden deep in the cavern of her heart wanted to feel sympathy for them, but she quieted it. From the first day, Beretta taught her to turn her heart to stone in cases like this. It didn't do well to make friends as they'd either turn on you, try to shove you down a shaft, or eventually disappear altogether.

The only one she'd allowed herself to grow close to was Beretta and that was all she needed. They always talked about how they would one day make it out of these gods-forsaken tunnels together one day, and how the first thing they would do when they tasted sweet freedom was roll in a field of fresh grass.

The gruel in her stomach swirled into a storm at the mere thought of her deal with Devlin. She trusted him, or so she thought. But she'd never kept a secret from Beretta before and it didn't sit right. It felt unnatural keeping this from her.

But she refused to break her oath to the private the moment he left her sight. If she made an enemy out of him then her life would turn into an even worse hell—worse than the chaotic turmoil at the thought of lying to her friend. She was stuck. Stuck and she didn't know what to do.

What Devlin proposed was risky, and if his plan somehow failed, she didn't want to take Beretta down with her too. There had to be a way to help Devlin *and* not lie to Beretta.

Until she could figure it out, she had to remain silent and sit with the turmoil raging inside.

She wasn't only lying to Beretta. She was now plotting with one of the guards behind her friend's back. A plan that, if successful, could lead to her release from this prison... without her friend.

So much happened during her and Devlin's talk that she didn't think to include Beretta as a part of their deal. Could she convince him to add her in somehow?

She chewed her bottom lip. The private was kind to her and had always been friendly in the past, but how accepting would he be of an attempt to alter things? He could be turned off of the agreement and turn her in on some bogus allegation.

There was so much at stake here, and not only for her.

Beretta dipped her head closer when the silence stretched on. "You can tell me anything. We have no secrets down here."

"It's nothing," Mira said quietly. She adjusted the double braids that Beretta helped weave into her hair this morning and leaned against the red wall, ignoring the pain in her stomach. "I was dreaming of dinner."

Those blue eyes narrowed and she clicked her tongue. "It's going to be the same disgusting slop we've had for weeks and you know it. Maybe you were dreaming of that lovely meal you had the other day." Her eyes took on a devilish glint. "Along with the even more delicious company."

"Beretta!" She slapped her friend's arm. "It wasn't like that and *keep your voice down.*"

Crag and the Wasp stopped digging and leaned on their shovels. The Wasp rubbed the faint scars on his wrist as he watched hungrily.

Beretta scowled at them and lowered her voice. "You've been in a mood since coming back and I know it was because of that private you're always gushing over."

"Beretta, stop," she whined. "And I do not gush."

"You do." She elbowed her side. "And it's totally valid. Especially compared to some of the repulsive specimens we get down here." She jerked her head at the nearest guard, who was easily half a foot shorter than her and sported a chipped tooth and receding hairline.

Mira hesitated, then asked. "How many men have you been with?"

Beretta froze and scrunched her face. "A dozen. Maybe more."

"Any memorable ones?"

"Nothing since coming down here," Beretta said, a strange hollowness to her voice. "Though there were a few almosts that I never did manage to conquer before my sentence here."

"A pity." Mira had never been with a man before—not that she remembered. Though some days her vivid dreams of tangled bodies under a sandy canopy painted another picture. A pity that she'd never see those dreams come to fruition, not for a long time.

All that she had now was rock and dirt and sweat.

Beretta twisted her head and cocked an eyebrow. Her friend could always tell when she had something on her mind.

"Just thinking about home," Mira said vaguely. Home and the few shattered fragments she barely remembered.

"What about it?" Beretta said testily. "Do you remember something new?" Mira shook her head. "Forget about it. It's up there, and we're down here."

Her friend had long ago advised her to close up her heart and block out any memories from before the mines as it'd do them no good down here. An easy feat given how little Mira could actually remember of her time before this.

"I was just dreaming of the stars," Mira said with just enough wistfulness to convince her friend.

Beretta hit a slab of wall with particular venom. "I remember laying on my back and tracing the lioness constellation with my mind. If I close my eyes and try hard enough, some nights I can still see every dot that was up there."

"Same. If we get out, I want to draw a map of the stars and the sun and the moon, and anything else that I can see up there."

"When we get out," her friend corrected.

When. Mira's stomach churned, and it didn't have to do with the angry hunger she felt.

A whistle saved her from having to respond further, signaling the start of their break. Not a moment too soon as Mira was beyond exhausted. Both mentally and physically.

It probably had to do with the new nightmares that started last night. A black cloud that overtook every living person and creature, sucking the life out of everything it touched. She'd had other nightmares before, and all were broken by the solace of a glorious sun rising beyond the horizon, reaching out with its warm tendrils to take her away from this place.

Not this time. Apparently, she was whimpering in her sleep, so Beretta woke her and they stayed up side by side, reminiscing about what few details they could remember from above ground until a whistle called them to work.

Thanks to that, her body felt more ragged than usual and now a headache was starting to form.

After dropping their shovels, Mira padded to the food line in a daze and followed Beretta's heels closely to make sure she wasn't wandering. The day was barely half done and that was if the head guard didn't decide that they *deserved* to pull a double shift again to catch up.

The line took forever to move, so she rested her head against Beretta's back, hoping her sudden headache would disappear before it was time to head back.

Beretta stiffened and nudged Mira just in time to see Captain No-Neck limp by. He dragged his heel with each step and when he passed, drops of blood had started soaking through the back of his shirt.

Lashes.

So, the captain's thievery and lies had finally caught up to him. The yellowing bruise on her cheek throbbed at the sight.

No-Neck spat onto the ground, nearly hitting Beretta's boot. Her friend wound her arm back as if to hit him, but Mira grabbed her elbow just in time.

Mira whispered into the back of her ear. "What in Halia's name are you doing?"

"I'm sorry," Beretta whined. "It's just so unfair some days. I can't help it."

"I know, B." Mira grabbed a pair of dirty bowls and handed one to her scowling friend, nodding at the guard's retreating back. At least he didn't linger to cause a scene. "Life is a series of terribly unfair events, one after the other, piling on top until you think you can't handle it, but you can. We can—together. At least this time that captain got a smidge of his deserved justice."

And hopefully, one day soon, they will get a taste of their own justice. Once she figured out how to pull this off.

Mira sat and allowed her thoughts to wander towards the land above this dreary mountain including a bright blue sky with a shining orb lighting her skin on fire. That visit above only made her crave it more.

Her daydream was cut short when the Wasp passed, kicking a cloud of dirt into her bowl. Beretta hissed but didn't try anything this time, not with the guards so close.

Mira sighed.

This wasn't the first time. She'd had worse and continued eating as if nothing had happened and ignored the grit between her teeth.

She needed the energy to test Devlin's theory to see if there was a way to sense the firestone or if her finding it was all a lucky coincidence. But Mira had never been lucky once in her life, at least, as much as she could remember. If the goddess of fortune smiled down on her, then she wouldn't be here—would she?

And when they were sent back to work, she knew she had to try. She wanted to see, not only for Devlin but to test it out herself without any pressure.

Maybe her worries of abandoning Beretta were for nothing, and it *was* all coincidence.

There was only one way to know.

But it was hard to find a second alone as Beretta was always by her side and one of the guards usually watched them with a leery eye. It took hours until they were given a water break, and it was then that Mira hovered back by the wall, trying to be as inconspicuous as possible. Hard to do when everyone in this room kept shooting her dirty looks, especially Crag and the Wasp.

Was it her imagination or did the tall guard glare at her even more today? Perhaps word of No-Necks punishment got around and they blamed her for it. It wouldn't surprise her. Nothing did anymore. She got off with an above ground reward while No-Neck got the lashes. They surely wanted retribution for their comrade.

She'd have to convince Beretta to move from their usual sleeping spot tonight. She didn't trust the others not to pull something, and the guards would use any excuse to send her to the pits.

Casually—as casually as she could—she leaned against the wall and laid her palm against the russet stone. It was smooth and cool beneath her skin.

Crag and the Wasp laughed in the distance with the tall guard, but they didn't pay her any attention. The two newbies were whimpering in the corner and Beretta was busy trying to sweet-talk a second scoop of water from the stocky guard, whose stout expression looked like he wasn't going to budge.

Mira closed her eyes. Maybe that would help. She tried to concentrate on what the mountain felt like. Tried to reach past the hard stone to find warmth. To find anything.

Nothing jumped out at her. Nothing echoed back except for cold rock.

Every attempt that followed was a total failure. Perhaps she was wrong to get her hopes up of escape when clearly the soldier had misjudged what he thought was the budding of a potential wielder power.

What a shame.

When she opened her eyes, Beretta was still flirting with her guard, but a new one appeared at the entrance. Beretta jumped back, her blue eyes met Mira's and widened.

Private Devlin, in his impeccably clean blue uniform strode over to the head guard and spoke a few hushed words. The guard's head whipped toward her and he pointed, eyes full of glee. "You. You're in for a world of trouble."

Fifteen
The Captain

The inside of the inn—and he used that term loosely—was one of the saddest places he'd ever seen, and he'd seen his share of terrible excuses of buildings over the years. That said, anything was better than another night fighting with the insects for space on the ground.

Surely, it was worth the risk of staying here.

They had little choice.

If they exited too quickly, then they'd rouse suspicion. So, the only logical option was to stay the night. Then they could leave well-rested and ready for the treacherous journey ahead.

Thick wooden tables with mismatched chairs were littered throughout the desolate inn. A series of poorly folded and dust-ridden blankets lined a basket next to a raging fire with an iron pot filled with brown goo simmering among the flames. A bubble swelled and burst onto the worn floorboards.

A round man with half a head of hair and a thick, uneven mustache jumped up from what looked to have been a deep nap at the nearest table and greeted them the moment they stepped through the creaky door.

Another look behind reaffirmed that the princess still followed. Her face scrunched at the sight of the dark room and she seemed to shrink into herself so she wouldn't have to touch any grimy surface.

"Saniam!" Edith squeezed past Isla and greeted the innkeeper as if they were old friends. "We found a couple of lost travelers during our forage today and they are in desperate need of a room... and probably a good bath," she added, wrinkling her nose.

Isla looked aghast at the implication and sniffed the collar of her cloak.

"Do you have space for us?" he asked, casting an eye around the deserted common area.

Saniam scoffed and gestured widely with his arm. "As you can see, the entire place is yours."

He tried to get a good read of the innkeeper—this Saniam. When he used to bet back at camp, he quickly learned that it wasn't about playing the cards as much as knowing what your opponent planned on doing next. So far, he wasn't getting any of that shrewd cunning from the innkeeper, and he hoped it stayed that way.

Isla stepped forward, clutching her hand to her chest. She was nearly hunch-backed with an overdramatic slouch to her shoulders. He'd have to talk to her about not overdoing it next time, but he had to admit that she played the part of commoner better than expected. "We really appreciate this," she said. "As you can see, it's been a while since we had someplace safe to rest."

Saniam's green eyes narrowed. "Where did you say you two came from?"

Before Isla could respond, he stepped in front, hoping his face was calm and level, unlike how he felt on the inside. "Old Riverrot," he said, ignoring her exasperated sigh. "But we got lost on the way."

"Horace and I will leave you in Saniam's hands," Edith said, passing her basket to her husband. "Perhaps I can check in on you before your departure, if that's alright? I'd love to hear more about your journey. It's been so long since we had visitors."

Absolutely not.

"Of course," Isla said quickly. She flashed a winning smile that he hadn't thought she was capable of producing. At least she was convincing when she had to be.

Edith grabbed Isla's arm—it was hard to tell if the gesture offended the princess or if she was unaccustomed to someone touching her like that—but Isla recoiled instantly.

The lady snatched her hand back as if burned. "I'm sorry, my dear. I meant no—"

"It was nothing," Isla said quickly, rubbing the part of her arm Edith touched. "I'm just a little jumpy—after all we've been through."

It took everything in him not to groan. Perhaps staying the night *would* rouse suspicion if the princess kept acting as if she'd never come this close to rural commoners before.

"Naturally." Horace grabbed his wife by the shoulders. "And my wife seems to forget herself some days. Come along, dear. I'm certain these two need their rest and don't wish to answer any more intrusive questions for the night. We'll check on you tomorrow. Thanks, Saniam." He nodded at the inn-keep while steering his wife towards the door.

"But-but—" Edith stuttered as she allowed Horace to usher her out.

Poor Edith wasn't to blame. How could she have known that this traveler wasn't any regular Muratian, but a Velotian princess unaccustomed to a commoner acting so familiar with her? Nobody would have dared touch her like that while she was wearing that crown.

At least Isla had the decency to look guilty about the whole exchange and refused to meet his gaze.

The idea of a warm bed for the night was tempting. Too tempting for his exhausted bones to put up a fight. And the princess would throw a fit if he dragged her out now.

He took a deep breath and turned towards the stalwart innkeeper, who looked at them expectantly. "About that room?"

"Right." Saniam shook his head. "Two beds or one?"

"Two," Isla said quickly. He pretended not to notice the rising color on her cheeks. What would her father think of her sharing a room with another man right before her wedding?

They may have his head for this. They may have his head for a lot of things, starting with his failures that placed him in this mess in the first place two years ago.

All that mattered for tonight was keeping up the pretenses so that nobody thought any wiser. The sooner they could leave this town behind them, the better for everyone.

Saniam's thick eyebrows furrowed. "You two not a couple?"

"No!" he and Isla said at the same time. Both perhaps a little too heatedly as those bushy eyebrows shot up to Saniam's hairline.

"Elena is my sister." He placed his hands protectively on her shoulders to emphasize the point. At least she didn't recoil as she did with Edith, though she stiffened under his touch. "We'll take the two beds."

After placing ten silvers into the man's outstretched hand, Saniam nodded pleasantly. "Ya got any bags?"

Isla shook her head. After chatting with Edith the entire walk here, *now* was the time she decided to lose her voice.

Saniam looked his way and he adjusted the rucksack at his side as if making sure it was still there. "I got it."

The innkeeper studied the pair, likely riddled with layers of filth, leaves, and, hopefully, no visible blood. His nostrils flared. "If you want hot water for the baths, that'll cost extra."

Isla's head snapped to him and her brown eyes widened.

He sighed, digging back into the coin purse. "Fine." He dropped a silver with the Muratian king's head into Saniam's hand, then added a second one. "And can we get a hot meal sent up, too?"

After scarfing down several helpings of a questionable meat pie Saniam prepared and soaking in a lukewarm bath after Isla had stolen nearly all of the hot jugs for herself, it was finally time to settle down for bed. It felt amazing to be clean and the cold bath water didn't bother him as he was used to it in the Pedite camps. Even at home their family rarely had the resources for a hot bath. They didn't have the money for a lot of things back home.

Saniam opened a vacant room with a roaring fire and two slim beds that resembled something out of a dream after sleeping on the forest floor for over a week. Having arrived before the princess, he settled into the bed closest to the door and tucked two daggers under the stiff pillow. Just in case.

Thus far, he hadn't picked up on anything strange but for some reason, his nerves were still on edge. He checked the room twice, under each pillowcase and every layer of blanket. He lifted the faded green rug, and tapped on every inch of wall to ensure there was nothing lurking beyond.

The room was perfectly normal to his trained eye. The beds were probably too stiff for Isla's preferences, and too close to escape her father's wrath.

Maybe they should have asked for two separate rooms, but that would have been a strange request coming from supposed family. Plus, as safe as this place seemed, how was he supposed to guard her from potential threats, including herself, while sequestered in another room?

That girl needed constant supervision.

There was nothing left to check so he flopped onto the bed, ignoring the metal lump under his pillow.

It took all his strength not to fall asleep the moment his body hit the bed, which felt like a bed of fluffy moss at the moment. The rough blankets felt as light as clouds underneath his calloused hands.

The minutes stretched on.

How long could one princess take? The better part of an hour had gone by. In that same time, he'd managed to bathe, dress in the clothes Saniam left for him, and fully secure their room. Surely, the water was freezing by now and she'd managed to scrub every hint of forest off her like she'd complained about for days.

Right as he started to worry that something had befallen her, the door creaked open. Isla slithered in with dripping hair that hung loose down her back, wearing a matching set of night clothes to the one he had, except Isla was swimming in hers. She had the checkered beige sleeves pushed past her elbow, while the hem of the shirt hung to her knees.

She'd forgone the bottoms and he got a hint of pale thighs when she reached up to untangle her hair.

"What?" She paused with her hands in the middle of her tresses.

He snorted, ignoring his pulsing heart. What was that even? "You look ridiculous," he stammered out, nearly believing his own lie.

Flashes of her in the white tunic by the river threatened to pop up but he shoved that memory far down. Very far down. Yes, she would be attractive by any conventional standards, but this was the same princess that had constantly badgered and pestered him for days on end. He focused on all the insults she liked to throw his way, including the slights against his family home and upbringing.

That helped. For now.

They should have asked for separate rooms.

The princess's face screwed up while her hands resumed fumbling through a poor attempt at a braid "I'm clean. I'm dry. I'm full for the first time in days. And I'm finally out of those blood-stained clothes. Can you let me have this one moment of peace?"

Before he could answer with a quick retort, she kicked his bed-post.

"Apologies, m'lady." He dipped his head solemnly and gestured to the spare mattress before clasping his hands behind his head.

The princess threw herself face-first into the bed, letting out a long sigh that echoed into his own, tired bones. "I never thought I'd be this happy to be in a lumpy straw bed," she said loftily, kicking her bare legs in the air. He averted his eyes. "But here we are and I wouldn't trade it... although I do long for my old silk sheets."

"So many complaints, princess." He leaned on his elbow so she could get a full view of his eye roll. "It's comfier than the cots they had for us back at the camp."

"No way." She pushed up on both elbows. "The beds they set up were nothing special, but I always got a good night's sleep." That was quite different from what she used to loudly complain about in the camp. "They were decent mattresses for travel."

Flicking a piece of lint off his bed, he said, "Not mine. I don't think they afforded us Pedites the same luxuries as a traveling royal princess. Maybe the other branches, but definitely not the conscripts."

"Right," she said quietly. Her expression dropped and she flopped back onto her bed, tucking herself under the rough blankets. The bed post creaked as she shifted, but no complaints escaped her mouth.

They'd never deemed his branch worthy of any expenditures. Even the best rations went to the Agicae and Divites first, with the Pedites getting whatever was left. It was unfair, but he had known about his fate for years. His father ensured he and his brother always knew their role in life was conscription to pay down the family debts.

"What's the plan for tomorrow?" she asked.

"Find a horse before those two come back and head south as fast as we can before anyone realizes we've left." On their way in, he spotted a few mares that seemed like they could make the journey and noted a southern road out of town.

She turned her head and confusion flooded her eyes. "I thought we didn't have the money for a horse?"

An eyebrow raised, betraying his plan.

"You cannot be serious?" she whispered in harsh tones. "You want to steal from these people after everything they've done for us?"

"*These people?*" he repeated incredulously, getting up from his comfortable position to face her. The floorboards were cold against his bare feet. "These people are Muratians. They are your enemies and they would kill you in an instant if they knew who you were, *Elena.*"

She scowled. "They have been nothing but helpful to us. These people are not our enemies, and I won't stand for stealing from them."

"We're not going to steal from those two, I promise." There was no way those farmers could afford a horse worthy of taking anyway.

"It doesn't matter if it's from Edith and Horace or anyone else. It's not right."

Now was when she decided to find a conscience.

"Not to burst your special little princess fairytale, Your Colossal Excellency, but not everything in life is right or fair. A concept that may be hard for you to grasp, I know."

"Stop talking to me like I'm stupid, *Cord.*"

He scowled. "It's hard to do when everything that leaves your mouth *is* stupid."

This time, her voice raised. "Don't call me stupid. You're the one being stupid right now."

"Nice one," he said dryly. "It doesn't matter what your feelings are on this. We need a horse. Preferably two of them."

"Two now?" her voice neared that pitch that made him want to carve his brain out with a spoon.

"Oh?" He bent over and rested his elbows on his knees, not in the mood to prolong an argument that could rouse Saniam to check on the source. "Prefer to share a horse then? If you're that desperate to get close to me then you only have to say the word. I'm at your service."

He enjoyed the way her face turned from bright red to nearly purple. "Never in a thousand years, you unmannered ruffian. We are not taking *any* of their horses. If you try, I'll cause a scene."

A cold laugh escaped his lips. "That's an even stupider idea. Do you want to get caught? I know you seem to have a death wish but if you plan on doing something that'll get us killed, at least give me a warning so I can leave you behind before it happens."

"You can't leave me behind. You've been ordered to protect me."

He grinned. "Well, I don't see my commander anywhere around here. Who's going to tell him if you never make it back?"

A flicker of panic spread across her face. A part of him felt ashamed of the threat, but she had to know it was a brazen lie by now. The time to abandon her was days ago, in the middle of that cursed forest.

If she didn't make it home, then he could never make his amends. He could never pay off the toll he'd amassed.

"Please," she begged, voice barely above a whisper. "These people have done nothing to us and it wouldn't be right. How are we supposed to sneak out of here if we steal their horses? That'll tip them off and they'll send someone after us. Did you think about that part when coming up with your brilliant plan, soldier?"

He paused and thought through her point.

Stealing from impoverished townsfolk didn't thrill him, but he'd done worse to survive in the past. However, *if* missing horses caused them to raise an alarm, that could end up badly—for both of them.

Anger flashed through his veins. She was right.

"Fine." He threw himself back against the pillow, angry for no real reason. "You know that means we're walking then," he spit out.

Another creak told him that she'd also thumped back into her bed. "Fine."

"And I don't want to hear one squeak of a complaint out of you," he added, that heat threatening to bubble over. "Especially when we get near the rough mountain pass."

"I won't whine," she said darkly.

He threw himself to the side to face her. "You have done so every single night. How's this going to be any different?"

The princess turned on her side and glared at him with those deep brown eyes. "It's going to be different because I say so."

"Oh, my apologies then, princess. If you *say so*."

"Just go to sleep," she bit out.

"Don't tell me what to do," he snapped. "Remember that you're not the one calling the shots around here, *Your Majesty*."

Her face screwed up in pure rage that shook her entire body before she made a strangled cry and turned over in her bed.

Fleeting satisfaction was soon replaced with hollow guilt.

Whatever. Stupid princess.

He found a comfortable position and allowed the scent of honey and sweet lilies to lull him into darkness. Within moments he succumbed to a deep sleep.

When he woke, it wasn't to the sounds of birds chirping or annoying sunlight attacking his face, it was to a booming roar that shook the entire forest floor.

Except he wasn't laying on a layer of moss and dirt anymore. It was a bed of straw and hay that shook with his entire body.

"What?" He tumbled to the floor in a mess of blankets and limbs, struggling to break from his restraints. The satchel fell to the ground and clattered loudly.

The sound of laughter greeted him as he finally untangled himself and tossed the blanket to the side.

Another boom crackled across the roof.

Thunder.

Isla sat along the thick ledge of the dirty window, leaning her head against the pane and watching the streams pour down the glass on the other side. She was still wearing that oversized bed tunic, exposing most of the length of her leg and part of her thigh. She'd redone her braid at some point and it hung down her back.

She didn't bother turning to him when she said in a bored voice, "You snore even worse when you're comfortable."

"So do you," he bit back with a lie. He sank onto the edge of the bed, patting the satchel while his heart struggled to calm its frantic pace.

It was hard to tell the time when the sun was hidden behind a sky as dark as the nightly heavens. In the distance, the outline of the mountain range was barely more than a whisper against the skies.

"It's coming down awfully fierce out there," Isla said. "Saniam doesn't think we should head out today or we'll get swept away. He says he can put us up for another night free of charge, as long as you pay him for the food again. I think you overpaid last night."

That wouldn't do. Not at all.

The thought of staying here, in a Muratian village, any longer made his stomach churn. Someone could spot them and uncover the truth.

"What's with that face? You look grumpier than usual." She'd finally unstuck her gaze from the streams of water to study him. "You want to leave today—in this?"

As if on plan, a bright flash filled the window and a shattering roar shook the entire room. Isla pointed at the skies and stared blankly.

"We can't stay here any longer," he said stupidly.

The princess peeled away from the windowsill and stalked over in her bare feet. "I'm not going out in this. We'd never make it."

He towered over her, but she refused to shy away. Dropping his voice, he said, "The longer we stay, the more at risk we are. The more at risk *you are*."

"There's no risk here. Nobody has a clue who we are and as soon as this clears up, we can be on our way."

"When will that be?"

"Saniam thinks it should clear by tomorrow," she said. "Hopefully."

Her words finally registered into his brain. "When did you get a chance to talk about all of this? You didn't go downstairs *alone*."

A vicious headache was coming on, and the source of it had the audacity to look affronted.

After everything they'd discussed since arriving here, she'd wandered off again. This princess would be the end of him.

He paused in the middle of rubbing his temples. "Wait. Did you go down in *that*?" He pointed at the long shirt.

"I wasn't expecting anyone else to be up. Calm down, soldier," she said in an annoyingly commanding voice that she used on the soldiers back at the camp. "Between the thunder and your snoring, I could barely sleep. So, I went downstairs for some fresh tea and chatted with Saniam while you seemed content to snooze most of the morning away."

"You should have woken me." He twisted in search of his blades as his heart beat against his chest, squeezing the air out of his lungs. "I need you to think. Did you tell him anything that would tip him off as to why we are here?" Once he had the feeling of cool steel against his skin, calm spread over him.

Why did she have to make everything so complicated?

"Relax, soldier. That's an order." Her hand pressed against his and she loosened his grip on the slim dagger. "We just talked about the weather and the effect it'll have on the harvests. He seemed happy it was raining for some reason. Nothing anywhere close to mentioning how I'm Velotian royalty that was stranded here, and on the run, or about those men you killed in the woods."

"Lower your voice," he hissed, right as another boom sounded across the place.

"Please." She pulled the blade out of his hand and tossed it back onto the bed. "There's nobody around here. You need to stop worrying so much and enjoy the break that we've been given."

Break. She wanted to enjoy this *break*. In the middle of Muratian territory. She'd definitely lost it.

"Don't worry," she said. "Nobody's looking for us. So, let's not give them any reason to and take the time to regroup and refresh before it's back to the road and dirt beds for us. Judging by how long you slept, I know you need the rest too."

When he didn't answer she dipped her head to the side and added, "You won't be a decent bodyguard if you're exhausted and slow. We're going to stay for the day, soldier."

This time, there wasn't that usual condensation or teasing when she addressed him. Against his will, a smile tugged at the corners of his mouth. "Is that another order, princess?"

A smirk sprung to her lips. "Yes. Yes, it is."

Sixteen

The Princess

The fire roared with an all-encompassing brilliance today. Its flames flickered and bright sparks stretched towards her weary hands. The goddess knew how long it had been since she had a proper roof over her head, even if it was a half-caved-in, leaky one that had signs of mold sprouting in the far corner. If she closed her eyes and ignored the smells, she could imagine that she was back in the luxurious royal palaces, rather than the parlor of a run-down inn.

She'd barely had any time to take in the place when they arrived last night. As soon as was polite, Cord had ushered her upstairs before the innkeeper could start asking any questions. She understood. It didn't make sense to risk it.

Now that they were staying a while, there was no harm in relaxing. And she refused to stay cooped up in that stuffy room alone with him.

After a few threats on her part, Cord got dressed and followed her downstairs for breakfast, or lunch in her case. The place was empty except for them and Saniam, who mostly kept to himself cleaning glasses behind the bar.

They'd remained next to the large fire for the rest of the afternoon. Mostly in silence. Saniam passed by now and then, asking a curious question or two but nothing concerning.

Things between her and Cord had settled into a tense understanding upon reaching Ackerslie. They were surrounded by enemies who weren't really enemies and had to stick close. She understood that, as much as she liked to push on his nerves whenever possible.

Cord rested his head against the high-backed chair. His eyes flittered shut and it was hard to tell if he was sleeping or merely relaxing his eyes like he had told her he was. At least the snoring hadn't started up yet.

She had long ago moved from her chair to sit in front of the fire, attempting to absorb as much of the heat as she could. It was as if her limbs knew they'd be back on their cold, damp journey as soon as this downpour let up, and they craved the heat.

Maybe it was foolish, but she allowed her senses to relax and enjoy their moment of reprieve, while she could. There was something calming about being warm and comfortable while the heavens cried all around them. They were cut off from the outside world, including their pursuers and any Muratians who would cause her harm.

It allowed her to pretend this was all some bad dream she would wake up from and find herself back in her room at the palace. But once this nightmare was complete, a different one would take over.

She distracted herself with several dusty books Saniam brought over from a crooked shelf. There were a few farming almanacs, a text on mining techniques, and a battered book about the old gods and goddesses and their origins. There were a few new names she'd never heard of, so she spent the morning pouring through the book while Cord pretended not to watch. He was focused on carving a piece of wood Saniam found for him into a fish.

As a child, she'd never been allowed to read the old volumes her father deemed too radical for a princess, even though she loved devouring anything she could get her hands on.

This was a far cry from the royal libraries in Aurial, but given this past week, the small pile felt like a treasure trove.

She was engrossed in stories about the ancient god Luriel and his fifteen goddess wives who were responsible for the lands, the skies, and the heavens. It sounded like Luriel didn't do much and the goddesses were responsible for everything from the rains, to the soil, to the wind and rivers and trees. Basically, everything that was needed to live and breathe and survive.

Then again, everyone knew that the magic passed down from the female line was stronger than the male lines, thanks to the grace of the goddesses. It was a fact she was too familiar with.

Saniam slid two bowls onto the wooden side table and said it was hunter's stew. Isla's nose turned up at the dish stewing since they got in last night. Cord told her the perpetual pot was known to last for months or even years in places like these with the innkeeper adding new ingredients every so often to keep it *fresh*.

It was hard to tell if he was joking or not. Surely no one was that desperate for a meal around here. *Surely?*

She didn't want to seem rude, so she took her first hesitant bite, aware of Saniam and Cord watching her closely. An explosion of spice and flavor met her. She'd never tasted something like this before and began shoveling heaping spoons into her mouth in a manner not becoming of a Velotian princess, pausing only to tear into the charred biscuit Saniam handed her. Even that was silk on her tongue.

Saniam chuckled, his green eyes sparkling. "I thought your brother said you were picky."

Cord's face split into a terrible grin. He lifted his bowl and blew on it. "You have no idea."

Isla kicked his shin and she didn't care that Saniam saw. In fact, the man laughed even more and scuttled away muttering about siblings. As soon as he turned a corner to go into a storage room, she smacked Cord's arm, harder this time.

"Ouch." He rubbed his arm dramatically. "What was that for?"

She leaned in. "I thought we were being careful."

"I am. We are. It wasn't even a lie so what's the problem?"

All she could do was make a disparaging noise and continue with her meal.

As she finished the last bite, the outside door flung open. Cord jumped up, hands flying instinctively to his side but nothing was there as Isla had convinced him to leave his weapons upstairs.

A short, hooded figure shook off the water from her cloak. Edith had returned. She wore a radiant smile, despite being soaked and surely freezing, and had a bundle tucked under her arm.

"Looks like it might let up tonight," Edith said, removing her topcoat and handing it to Saniam who appeared out of nowhere.

Cord slowly sank back into his seat, extremely interested in adjusting his freshly cleaned Muratian jacket. He tugged at the gold stitched collar around his neck. Those prominent blue colors must have felt as foreign to him as they did to her.

Edith placed the bundle on the table next to their stew and settled in one of the high-backed chairs next. "Did Saniam set you up with a nice room?"

"Yes, he did," Cord said, eyeing the old woman wearily.

That was a slight over-exaggeration. Though Isla wouldn't dare complain, not to him, especially knowing where they'd likely be sleeping tonight.

Saniam wiped his hands on his pants. "Should I get another bowl ready for ya?"

Edith sent him a winning smile. "That would be lovely." She nodded at Isla. "Did you sleep well?"

"Yes." Isla cracked her neck to emphasize her point. "Some of us better than others. Far better accommodations than we've had lately."

"I can imagine—thanks," Edith said as Saniam dropped a bowl of bubbling stew in front of her before retreating behind the bar.

While Edith blew on her spoon, Isla's eyes flickered to the package she'd brought.

"I noticed that your cloak was in awful condition." Edith looked over to Cord who had finished his stew and resumed lounging with his eyes closed. She lowered her voice and dipped her head in close, "And I know what you are."

Isla's heart stopped.

Cord hadn't heard or else Edith would no longer be sitting across from her.

After unsticking her tongue from the roof of her mouth, Isla stumbled out, "Wh—what do you—what do you mean?"

Edith leaned back and clasped her hands together. "Your cloak," she said plainly. "It is a magic wielder's cloak. I recognized it as we had one in our village, years ago, before they were all conscripted away." Her eyes darkened. "We never saw her again."

"I don't—I never have—I'm not a wielder," Isla said, finishing with a flood of false conviction. Her heart resumed its racing, for a different reason now.

"If you're on the run from the armies, then you can't stay," Edith said. "We're small and lucky enough to be kept out of the queen's sight, but anything that could bring us trouble is not welcomed."

"We mean to leave as soon as we can," Isla said quickly. "And I don't want to do anything that would bring eyes to your village." Or to her and Cord.

Edith's smile returned, reaching her eyes. "I know that dear, and I meant no accusations. I'm not one to judge someone's life circumstances." She nodded at Cord pointedly. "Stay with your brother. He seems to have a good head on his shoulders and your best interest at heart. I'm sure he'll lead you down the right path."

That was the hope.

Edith's thin hands unwrapped the cloth and pulled out a deep blue and green travel cloak with gold trimmings. Muratian colors again. "I still want you to have this."

Isla took the cloak and ran her fingers over the rough material and traced the vines woven into the fabric.

"It's nothing fancy," Edith said quickly. "And don't you worry about money. It belonged to my daughter, who we lost a few years ago. It's been doing nothing but attracting moths—and you look like you're more in need of it."

The old lady's eyes darkened as they focused on the blue and green cloak, lost in some long-forgotten memory.

"I can't accept this." She ignored that stabbing feeling in her heart and turned to Cord for help, but his eyes were still closed.

Useless bodyguard.

Would Edith still want her to have it if she knew who Isla really was? It was hard to tell as the old lady seemed so welcoming, so understanding, but that was when she thought Isla and Cord were lost Muratian siblings, not a Velotian royal and her escort.

"You can, Elena, and you will. The goddess knows that you need something better for the rest of your journey than that tattered old thing, especially since it's so recognizable. Plus, it would warm my heart to know my daughter's cloak will help someone else's journey."

Isla forced out a smile despite the guilt that rushed through her. "Thank you," she breathed. "You have no idea how much this will help."

Edith patted her arm and her voice returned to its normal volume. "I'm just glad to help someone in need. I'm certain your uncle will be pleased for the aid and will be happy to see you arrived safely."

"Yes." She pushed her braid behind her shoulder and laid the cloak across her lap. "He most certainly will be."

At this mention, Cord cracked a gray eye open. Isla shook her head to indicate she had everything handled.

Edith clutched her hands together and didn't meet her eyes. "When you get to your uncle's village, if they happen to have a temple there, would you light a candle for my daughter? We don't have one here and I wish to make an offering to Rallion—however late it may be—I made a promise to the goddess when she was taken from me and payment must be made."

Isla swallowed a lump in her throat. "Of course. I'll light two candles for her, one from myself as well."

All Edith could do was nod.

After turning to talk of the spring harvest, Edith lingered for a bit. Horace joined after checking on their crops, and Saniam pulled up a rickety old chair and brought tankards of ale for everyone. Isla sniffed at her overflowing jug that smelled like bitter citrus.

Over the years she'd been allowed a glass of wine or two at supper, but ale was one thing that never flowed in the palace halls, not even in the encampment—at least, it wasn't when she was around.

She was going to enjoy this.

Before she could take her first sip, Cord snatched the jug out of her hand.

"My sister can't handle her liquor," he said to the others' questioning glances. "And our father wouldn't want her overindulging." He finished his tankard far too quickly, before starting on hers.

Isla scowled when Saniam brought her a cup of pulp-filled juice instead. Cord looked positively delighted. So, this was how it was going to be? He'd pay for that when they made it to Velotia. She'd ban him from ever touching a drop of ale again in his life.

Could she even do that? It didn't matter, she'd find a way before taking her place among the Koliats.

With nothing more than juice to parch her thirst, Isla brooded. At least she had better company than the moping guard she'd been marooned with for days. While Horace mostly kept to himself, Edith and Saniam more than made up for the surly farmer with stories of the village and its history.

There was an old mining outpost at the base of the red mountain less than a ten minute horse ride from here. It'd been shut for ages and when the mines closed, this village lost much of its income.

"It's a ghost town up at the encampment now," Edith said. "A hollow memory of what once was here. The post and the mines are all abandoned, and many left for good. A terrible thing really."

"What happened?" Isla asked.

Horace shot a look at Edith before she answered. "They used to mine for firestone until the cave in. The royal guard came and took the last of the reserves before shutting it all down."

"Firestone?" Isla repeated. The word sounded familiar on her tongue, like a lost memory that had been misplaced. Most likely from one of the drab lessons her father made her go through.

"Yes," Saniam explained. "The stones are meant to heighten or block a wielder's powers, depending on the wielder. It's quite unstable stuff but the king and queen found a lot of value in it, as did the old High King Edom, for he was the one who started the mines ages ago."

"Right," Isla said confidently. A Muratian would know that, so she pretended this was not news to her.

Edith patted her husband's leg. "There used to be legends that the old High King's lineage was blessed with gifts by the star goddess, Hierel, and the goddess of the gates, Rallion. That's how he first discovered the firestone, which can be used to bolster gifts from the goddess Hierel and inhibit gifts from the goddess Rallion. It was used in old war prisons quite effectively."

"So, the High King wanted to elevate his lineage into history?" Isla asked.

"As all kings want, my dear."

Isla had heard the stories of the old High King, but never this version. His grandsons fought after his death, splitting the lands into ten kingdoms. The oldest five brothers took the best lands: Murat, Velotia, Koliat, Rambey, and Lenoc island—who had closed their borders for decades now—while the others were given the less habitable lands, the poorest lands.

The High King's lineage was diluted through Isla's family, the same as it was the other kingdoms. The royal lines had become somewhat incestuous, but they always took great care not to mix too similar bloodlines.

It was strange to think that she was related to such a man, but as magic passed through the mother's side, then any of his powers would have died out along the son's line.

The door creaked open and a man with a brown leather jacket entered, waving at Saniam for a tankard. With the rain in full force, it seemed like most of the villagers' work had paused. Others came in throughout the day for a hot meal or to check out the newcomers for themselves. Isla didn't think anything of the villagers passing by, but Cord tensed up as if he expected the Muratian Queen escorted by an entire battalion to walk through those doors every time they squeaked open and let in a fresh spraying of cold water.

That soldier needed to learn to let loose or he'd wither away from stress before they managed to make it home, and she couldn't navigate to save her life.

The storm's wrath calmed by the time they prepared for bed, which in her opinion was far too early. Cord wanted to ensure they got a good night's rest as he didn't think they'd get another opportunity like this again, but she had a suspicion he was exhausted from entertaining Edith and Saniam all day. Isla would have stayed there all night if she could; she was more than prepared to entertain all kinds of people, thanks to her father's countless lessons. But when Cord sent one of his signature death glares, she knew it was best to follow before he lost it completely.

So here she was, in the middle of their room in a ridiculously oversized shirt that sent Cord into another fit of laughter, and she still didn't feel any hint of sleep yet.

Cord, ever the worrier, wanted to go through the plan for the next day.

"I'll be more optimistic once we've crossed the border." He tugged his shirt off, briefly exposing a chest with muscles toned by years of drills. She craned her head to get a better view, but he quickly covered up with his matching bed shirt. "Stop staring. It's not becoming of a princess."

"I still feel bad about leaving so early like that." Isla kneeled at the edge of her bed, ignoring the warmth that crept into her face. What would her brother think of her now? "Edith wanted to see us off in the morning. She's been a big help and it's rude to vanish like that."

That scowl returned to his face at the mention of the farmers. "That's not happening and you know it." He peeled back the top layer of blankets from his bed. "If you know what's good for us and those villagers, we'll sneak out before anyone notices. Trust me."

"Well," she said slyly. "You better wake up in time, as you know I'm terrible for sleeping in."

"That won't be a problem," he said, his entire demeanor oozing confidence that was likely fueled by the five tankards of ale he'd consumed.

"We'll see," she muttered. Even though she'd never been given ale before, she had seen firsthand the effects it had on some of the men.

Not that she was bitter, but she planned on sending an extra prayer to the trickster goddess tonight for him to wake with a raging headache.

Isla settled in her glorious bed and pulled her blankets up to her chin, relishing in the comfort of the fire and the lack of insects scuttling at her feet. Tomorrow's sleep would be an entirely different story.

"I can't wait to be back home," she said wistfully, tucking her hands behind her head.

"Not home though," he corrected with a finger in the air.

A cloud of darkness overcame her, blocking out the prior warmth she felt. She shook her head to clear those thoughts. "No. Not home. But it will be my new home."

"Hm."

"What?" She rolled to her side to face him. "What was that?"

He twisted his head. "You don't sound too excited about getting those scars burned on your wrists. I thought you couldn't wait to marry Prince Brenner."

That was brazen, even for a half-drunk soldier. It sent her blood boiling. "And why should I be thrilled about marriage to a complete stranger to seal an alliance with the Koliats? Would you be jumping at the prospect of leaving your home behind?"

This was the first time she'd said it out loud and it felt like a boulder was removed from her chest when the words were released. She wasn't sure why she finally vocalized it, as she was taught to keep feelings like that to herself. Perhaps it was exhaustion or maybe she realized that she didn't need to pretend here.

This was always her destiny for as long as she could remember. It was only a matter of time before her father finally found a sovereign willing to pay his price. Now her time was up.

Cord's eyes widened and she hated the way his voice softened when he said, "That's something I'll never have to worry about, princess."

At least it wasn't an apology. She couldn't take any more of those.

"Lucky for you." She threw herself against the stiff pillow, imagining it was one of the dozen silky ones in her bed back home. "But we do what we have to do to help our family."

"Yes, we certainly do," he said darkly.

His tones sparked a flame of familiarity as she used similar ones when talking about her family. She rested her hands atop her stomach, playing with the rough fabric. "So, what's your issue with your family then?"

"I don't think we have time to get into that. We'd need days."

Fair enough. It would take weeks to get into her family's tangled history as well. "I don't even know if my brother or father would have bothered to get off their marbled seats to search for me themselves."

"I'm sure they are worried about you."

"And what impact this will have on their alliance, you mean?"

Silence answered her.

"I know the truth, and I'm not mad about it. At least I'll have a lovely banquet waiting for me. I can drink all the sweet wine—without people snatching it away—and eat dozens of honey cakes until I'm ready to burst. Maybe I'll even get them to make some sugared jango-berry tartlets."

The thought of a giant feast with all her favorite foods made her mouth water and sent her stomach into a loud protest.

"I've never tried them," he said wistfully.

"Really?" She cocked her head.

"We didn't all grow up in palaces. There weren't many pastries or exotic berries in the village I grew up in, and we definitely didn't have giant, overly decorated banquets to attend for Pedite conscripts in the army."

"They are not all they're made out to be," she said darkly. "But the food is worth it. You'll love it, and you can try all the varieties when we get back."

"When we get back?" He laughed. It was hollow and mirthless.

"Yes. I'm sure they'll hold a giant feast when I'm back. If not, I'm going to make them. You'll be rewarded of course."

But there would be not a drop of ale allotted for him, she'd make certain of it. Fair stakes for a fair game.

"I don't think you understand how this works," he said plainly. "There's no fancy party or feast waiting for me. My reward—if I'm lucky—will be to keep my head and pray I'm not banished completely. The best I can hope for is that they won't take this out on my family."

"But—"

"I'm on my last chance here. And that included guarding you and making sure nothing happened before we got to Bluemoon Bay... yet, here we are, stuck in the middle of our enemy's territory after nearly getting killed, twice. Do you call this a success?" He waved towards the fireplace and at the bucket collecting rainwater spilling in from the ceiling beams. "They probably think I had a hand in all of this. After everything I've done, I'll be lucky not to be killed the moment we set foot in Velotia."

"That would never happen," she said stupidly.

"I wish we all got to grow up in the same dream world as you. Going to balls, fancy banquets, and having someone to wait on your every need."

"It wasn't like that all the time..."

Again, he laughed. "That wasn't how the rest of us had to grow up, knowing what fate eventually awaited us in the conscripts. I didn't have a choice when I left my family. None of us did. Maybe when we get back, you'll see the difference more clearly than ever. We'll have very different welcoming parties."

The commander would understand when they got back. All of this could be easily explained.

Except a small part in her brain told her that Cord's words rang true. She knew the commander, but she knew her father even more... and even if she was returned safe, someone would have to pay.

Isla recalled her father's temper and how he treated staff that didn't execute his orders perfectly on plan or how easily he dismissed their last High Commander after losing a small territory that really didn't affect their standing in the war. It never ended well when her father was disappointed.

Eventually, Isla said, "Sounds like it's more trouble than it's worth to take me home. I don't know why you don't just kill me yourself and slip off while you can. Or better yet, turn me in and take whatever bounty there is and build yourself a new life. A better life."

He stared at her, dumbfounded for a moment. Then his face split into a wide smile. "Some days, you really make me want to consider that option, *princess*."

"I'll keep that in mind, *captain*." With a scoff, she threw herself on her side so that she no longer had to stare at his stupid face.

Seventeen

Mira

The trickster Slin was surely playing with her. This had to be a dream.

The spread of food on the table was beyond anything she'd been able to dream up on her best nights, and she had an overly active imagination, as Beretta constantly reminded her.

This was no dream. The iron table had an assortment of sliced game meats, glistening vegetables, steaming sweet rolls, and at least five different colors of cheese that she had only heard about from B's stories.

The Muratian king leered at her from his portrait, casting his usual judgment against her.

Leaning against the hard table and looking exceptionally pleased with himself, was Private Devlin. He wore that same half smile and his dangerously blue eyes watched her closely while he spun a chipped porcelain plate on its edge.

Her head hurt. So, she wasn't getting punished?

When she didn't speak, he asked, "Do you like it?"

"Yes of course," she said, hoping there was no visible drool sliding down the side of her mouth. It was hard to tell if this was a trick or real.

She knocked her knees together and twisted to face the arrangement. Crisp air blew in from the cracks under the door and windowsill.

It was perfect. Everything she could have imagined. The smells—the smells—she couldn't pick out what came from what dish, all that she knew was it all smelled incredible. The only thing missing from the feasts of her dreams was an overflowing platter—or two—of deserts to pick from. Yet, she didn't reach for a single thing.

"I'm confused." She tore her eyes from a plate of steaming greens. She hadn't seen this much color in her food in—forever.

"Why?" His eyebrows knitted together. "Oh, is it because of what I told the guard? Sorry about that. It's just that they don't like giving up dredgers for just any old reason, and I had to make something up. They love when you get in trouble, so that seemed like the best excuse. Plus, I didn't want them to suspect anything."

Mira frowned. It was strange to hear someone speak so callously about the pains she had to endure daily. How nice it must be to be so far removed from the daily agony of the workers below.

When she didn't answer, he added, "Maybe just limp a little when you get back to help sell it a bit?"

Limp a little. He meant for her to lie again. Pretend like she had received a punishment instead of—whatever this was. Where would it stop?

He scratched the scar on his jaw and stared around the room. "That was callous. I'm sorry. I know it wasn't the brightest idea, but it was all I had. I didn't know how else to get you out of there."

Mira grabbed the silver fork in front of her. The smooth texture still a stranger to her calloused hands.

"I'll think of something better next time."

"Please do."

That meant there would be a next time.

Devlin took a seat across from her and whipped out his blue napkin with a flourish before placing it delicately on his lap. He waved at the table. "I had to pull a lot of strings to arrange this. But I won't lie and say it was all for you."

She froze in the midst of stabbing a thick slice of ham, worried she had misinterpreted his words.

His eyes sparkled. "Go on. I meant that this food was brought in as we have the commanders coming tomorrow. It's for you—and me—but it's also a little bit *borrowed* for now."

"Borrowed," she repeated quietly.

If anyone found out she had taken the commanders' food, there'd be lashes for days... or the pit. A shudder ran down her spine.

"We better not let it go to waste then." He pulled the closest plate toward himself and dished out a spoonful of spiced root vegetables before moving on to the platter of meats. "They won't notice it missing. Trust me."

Trust was hard lately.

Through narrowed slits, she watched as he continued to pile meat after meat onto the plate, all while her stomach screamed at her to do something.

The protests from her gut combined with the amazing smells that made her mouth water were too much. She attacked her plate with restrained gusto, remembering with horror how unladylike she had been that first day he brought her here.

If there were lashes to be paid, the first bite of juicy ham mixed with creamy potatoes was certainly worth it.

"How has the digging been going?" Devlin asked. He rested his cheek in his palm and twirled the dull knife between his fingers.

"It's been—difficult these past days," she admitted, staring at the meat on her plate. "I've not been well, and we are in a new sector. I haven't found anything."

"Not well?"

"It's nothing," she said quickly. "Headaches and such. But tomorrow I will try again."

A clatter of metal on metal as the knife dropped onto the iron table. Then he was in front of her tilting her chin up to face him.

"I know it's not easy, but I have to reinforce how much time is of the essence in this matter. The queen wants results and I'm afraid if we don't give her something soon, then a debt must be paid."

His eyes darkened and he leaned against the table, barely missing the plate of potatoes.

"Queen Grimha is obsessed with the ancient wielder blood-lines––just as Rallion's followers are. Some may say too obsessed, especially since the passing of the king and their eldest son." His eye twitched. "But the firestone, along with a special weapon, can win us this war before other, crueler beasts are needed to be called upon."

Mira knitted her brows. The others spoke about wielders and the magics they possessed such as firewielders, mindweavers, trans-porters, and so many more. They were both equally blessed and dangerous beings.

It was no surprise that the queen was so interested in using them and other beasts to win this war.

"You're not the only one risking everything here." Devlin leaned in, studying her face closely. "How do you find the firestone like you do?"

"I don't—I don't know."

"I think you do. Whether or not you want to say it out loud."

His blue eyes studied her face. She was painfully aware of the way her heavy breaths traveled through her chest in giant heaves and of the dryness that spread down her throat.

What he was suggesting was impossible.

It was insane. It was deranged.

Yet, something small nudged her, reaching from her fingertips all the way to her chest. It was the same spark that helped her find the firestone that day.

He nodded as if her silence was confirmation enough. "It's per-fectly normal to be afraid of those powers within you. I've had close friends taken away to go to the army camps. Many were taken away from their homes when they were young to start culling their wielder powers. Not everyone understands."

Mira cast her eyes down.

"Remember what next year brings?" he asked. "The sister goddess years. Hierel's year."

The years forewarned by the black comet. Rallion's comet. Mira could never forget the same comet that had haunted her dreams even though she hadn't remembered seeing it with her own eyes.

"The year of Hierel is foretold to be a year of power and prosperity," she said.

"Immediately followed by the chaotic year of Rallion, not that you hear many people talking of it. They think if they ignore it, then it'll go away, just like this war. But Rallion's year is one of the most powerful.

The goddess of the gates.

It was known that the year of Rallion was filled with death and destruction, if you believed such superstitions. Her followers certainly did and they were a passionate lot, burning themselves in some cases.

It was known that the year of the fire goddess Insmia accentuated wielders who mastered the element of fire the same way the trickster goddess Slin's year accented mindweavers and Poron's year was for the healers.

Mira wasn't certain what the sister goddess years meant for wielder powers, only that the next two years could either mean great things to come or complete chaos.

Devlin rested his long fingers on the edge of the table. "The sighting of the comet heralds new things to come. New beginnings. We have two months until the solstice and the changing of years."

If that's the way he wanted to interpret the tumultuous years of the sister goddesses, then she wasn't going to correct him.

"The coming of the sister years means we have to work even harder to ready our weapons and wielders for the coming war, no matter the cost."

She noticed the way his eyes darkened at those words. Who had he already lost?

Devlin got up and circled the table. "I'm not as familiar with these things but what I do know—from studies I've read—is that it all starts with you and your control. It may be strange at first. It may be draining, and it may be uncomfortable, but I think you know, deep down, how to help me. If you are strong enough. I can help you learn to channel that power. Are you willing to help me?"

The way he looked at her with those pleading eyes, she wanted to give him everything. Her head started nodding before her mind could catch up.

That lethal smile stretched across his face, crinkling the ends of his eyes. "Then let's try a couple of simple exercises."

"Here." Mira edged up next to Beretta, shoving a cup of lukewarm water into her hands that Devlin had given her on the way down. She angled her body so the nearest guard couldn't see the exchange.

"What is—"

"Hush, B." Mira grabbed the spare shovel next to her friend's dirty boots, keeping an eye on the two guards who harassed her upon returning. "Or they'll take it."

With wide eyes, she nodded and quickly downed the liquid. "You know, I didn't know if I'd ever see you again when you left. And the Wasp was gloating the entire time. I thought something bad happened to you, and yet you look perfectly fine." Beretta grabbed her arm and squeezed. "We're going to talk about this later."

Mira nodded—she expected nothing less—and dug in the loose ground in front of them, taking advantage of the groove Beretta had already made in this section. She'd tell her as much as she could, while leaving out important details.

At least they were on light shoveling duty today by some miracle of the one-eyed goddess.

By the time she finished shoveling a decent pile of rocks into the rusted cart, Mira was absolutely exhausted. The session above ground was draining in a different way. After finishing two plates of food, Devlin had her try a few concentration exercises he found in an old journal with a wilted blood-lily on it. She wasn't able to get much done and the poor soldier was visibly irritated by her lack of any progress.

She still worried he would search for someone better to help him. Her chest tightened.

It felt good to be needed in some way that wasn't just digging or shoveling—even if she was terrible at it. It made her feel alive again. Plus, the food was amazing, unlike anything she'd remembered tasting before.

No. She'd have to try harder. For the treats, or so she told herself.

And she couldn't do that while shoveling light rocks like this, as much as it was a glorious break against the usual grueling excavation work. They were only removing already dug-up rocks, not freeing it from its unyielding prison. She'd never find anything with this shoveling.

Even though she told Devlin she'd wait until tomorrow to try again, she couldn't afford a delay. Not while he may be reconsidering their arrangement altogether.

Her shovel slipped from her hand and dropped to the dusty floor with an echoing clatter.

Everyone's head turned to her, including Crag, the Wasp, and that Captain No-Neck who tried to steal from her. Beretta's eyes widened in warning, and she knelt to pick it up for her.

The Wasp inched closer with that hungry look in his eyes. She wondered what he was like before all of this. Surely, he wasn't this miserable of a wretch all his life, if the marriage scars on his wrists were any indicator.

No-Neck stormed up to them, as much as he could while wincing and limping every time he jostled his back, and kicked the shovel out of Beretta's hand. "What's going on, scum?"

"I have blisters," Mira said in as stupid of a voice she could muster. Beretta was looking at her like she'd lost that faint grip on sanity.

"Pick it up," he said in a deadly voice.

"I can't." She raised a calloused and scarred hand to his face. "The shovel hurts my hands."

No-Neck's face split into a terrible grin—gods his breath smelled terrible. "Then it's back to the digging pits for you, *dredger*. The new pits."

Mira's face contorted into a worried frown and she suppressed a shudder at the thought of going back into those dark tunnels.

Another clatter as a second shovel joined the first.

"My hands also hurt," a confident voice said from behind her. "I guess I'll have to go dig too."

No. No. No.

Mira closed her eyes and held back a scream. *Beretta*. Not with her half-healed shoulder.

No-Neck's smile turned positively gleeful as he pushed both of them to get moving.

"What in Halia's name was that about?" Mira nudged Beretta as they were led past the scowling workers, and towards the pit to dig for their newly assigned double shift.

"Ouch." Beretta grabbed her shoulder dramatically. "Not that side, remember."

No-Neck didn't bother looking back as he led them down and down and down. He was too busy whistling gleefully to himself.

"You shouldn't have done that," Mira said.

Beretta scoffed as she rubbed the dirty bandage. "I wasn't about to leave you to suffer down here all alone. What kind of friend would I be?"

"You didn't have to." As much as Mira protested, deep down, she was glad for the company.

A day in the digging pits was strenuous and exhausting to no end, plus there were dark tunnels that led to nowhere where the wind made the worst sounds. It was either freezing cold or boiling hot, and the temperature constantly fluctuated between the two options several times per hour.

"I couldn't stand being left alone with the Wasp, and besides," Beretta said, ducking her head under the low beam that marked the entrance to the digging pits. "You're up to something, and how am I supposed to find out what it is when there's half a mountain separating us?"

"Are you sure it's worth it?" Mira asked as the gleeful captain handed them over to the pit guard for assignment.

The straight-jawed guard handed them a pair of chipped pickaxes and sent them down a secondary tunnel with no lights and they had to crouch to fit in.

"Absolutely," Beretta said, bumping her elbow against the rock wall. "I want to know what you've been up to."

"Fine," Mira said quietly. "But if a word of this reaches anyone, I'm dead... and so are you."

Her friend stopped in a small opening where they could stretch their arms and raised a hand as if to swear a godly oath. "You don't need to tell me twice."

The howling wind blew past them and a chill filled the air.

"How about here?" Beretta whispered, looking over her shoulder at the dark tunnel that could barely fit a large child. "I don't want to go any further."

"This spot is fine." Mira sent her a wry smile and raised her axe in the air, before slamming it down against the unmoving rock sheet.

"And I hope you think it's worth a double shift down here, because it's nothing all that exciting."

Beretta nodded fervently, bringing her own pick above her head. The hard rock groaned around them in protest, as if a part of the mountain were alive. Alive and watching.

Mira always hated coming down here, but today she was determined.

Within an hour Beretta decided that no secret Mira could unload on her was worth spending the afternoon in this cold, dark tunnel.

"I want to go back up," Beretta whined. She wiped dirty sweat off her forehead and leaned against the wall, massaging her shoulder. The pit guard hadn't been around in a while so the pair took advantage of the solitude to take an unsanctioned break. "Not just back to the regular tunnels, which I already miss, but above ground. I can't believe you got to go up. *Twice*. Take me with you next time."

"Well, it's only going to keep up if I can actually manage to find more firestone," Mira said. She'd only told Beretta vague details about her deal to find the firestone for Devlin, nothing more.

It was common knowledge that they were searching for firestone, so a guard bribing a particular dredger to help him find it so he could receive more credit wasn't unusual.

A pang of guilt spread through Mira at the lie, but she wanted to keep some secrets between her and Devlin only. The thought sent her heart into patters.

"I can help," Beretta said, her eyes lighting up enthusiastically. "Do you think he'd want—"

"I don't want to push anything," Mira cut across. "Give it some time and let's ease him into it somehow."

"Good idea." She winced and grabbed her shoulder. Crimson blood was starting to seep through.

"See," Mira scolded, ripping off the bottom of her brown tunic and replacing the dirty bandage with a slightly cleaner strip. *Slightly.*

"This is exactly why you should have stayed up there. You've opened the wound again."

"Don't worry about me," Beretta said darkly. "It's you who has to watch yourself. If that soldier starts favoring you in front of the others, it'll only make things worse."

Things were already worse. Mira could handle anything that came her way as long as the prospect of leaving this place still loomed ahead.

"And that's why we are not going to tell anyone," Mira said pointedly.

"I *know*," she dragged out the last syllable. "Keep my big mouth shut. Got it."

Mira threw her pick to the ground. "The guard still hasn't come back. Keep resting and I'm going to search for it."

"How do you—?"

She held up a hand. "Hush, B. I need to concentrate."

Her battered friend sat crossed legged on the floor, pressing her shoulder and staring at Mira with wide eyes. Not at *all* distracting in the least.

How did she manage to do this before? Mira ran her hands along the smooth, blue-gray surface of this area. They were deep here. The reddish hue that reached to the surface was long forgotten about in these parts. They were near the section that once collapsed on a group of miners, causing them to close down for years.

They reopened this particular section for their group to expand into and Mira couldn't help but question the safety of this place. She doubted the guards cared if the mines collapsed all around them, except for the fact that they'd have to find new dredgers to take their place.

Best to try to find the firestone as quick as possible then get back to their regular duties—if they were allowed after their double shift was over. In her haste, she didn't stop to think what would happen if they kept her down here longer. And now Beretta had followed her.

No pressure to find the firestone now.

Perhaps Devlin could help get them back to regular duties. That fluttering in her stomach returned. That was only if she managed to find more firestone and prove she wasn't a complete screw up. Prove that he chose right.

"Are you doing it now?"

Mira winced. "Quiet B."

The prospect of a reward and returning above ground warmed her. She imagined a table covered with dozens of assorted pastries filled with savory creams and topped with glistening sugar. Countless desserts that would make her sick when she devoured them all, but she wouldn't care at the time.

It would be worth it.

She could practically feel the warmth of the sun caressing her face. Its welcoming rays reached out to embrace her, kissing every inch of her skin. The memory made her feel safe. Made her feel wanted. Loved.

A tingle flickered at the tips of her fingers and spread further up her hands. She closed her eyes and allowed the warmth to thrum throughout her body as if it were that powerful sun beaming down on her. She continued to run her hands along the stone as she held onto that small memory. That distant memory was less than a faint echo at this time, but still managed to reverberate across her bones.

Wind howled from the end of a slim tunnel, sending a wave of shivers down her spine.

No! She had to ignore that.

As she dragged her hand along the wall, a piece of stone pulsed beneath her fingers. It felt hot to touch and nearly burned her. She yanked her arm back. Even in the dim light she could make out a faint handprint on the stone that pulsed once, as if to call to her, before fading. She shook her head and couldn't find it again.

"What was that?" Beretta asked from her spot on the floor. She had moved to her knees and bounced on her heels like an impatient child.

Mira rubbed her hands together. "Nothing. Let's try here." She pressed her hand against the same warm spot. "Exactly here."

With a renewed energy that even managed to summon Beretta from her respite, the two of them chipped away at that spot in the stone—the spot that felt as hot and welcoming as the sun. They struck the rock with all their strength, ignoring any sore muscles or injured shoulders.

It was only the two of them in this cramped tunnel, too small for the other dredgers. That didn't matter. All that mattered was their target. Beretta believed in her without question, so Mira struck against that unbending stone.

Again and again and again.

Until the outer layer finally gave away, sliding off in a perfect gray sheet. Behind it, a perfect red stone spotted with shining black flecks revealed itself.

A shadow flickered past. Beretta gasped and covered her mouth.

Rough hands grabbed Mira and threw her back. She landed against the wall, feeling something crack. Stars formed in front of her vision, blinding her momentarily.

"What's that?" The pit guard plucked the stone out of its rock encasing. He turned it over in his hand, examining it with a blood-shot eye. "This is a big one. He'll be pleased."

Beretta's biting voice rang out, "*Actually*, we were the ones that found that."

The guard paused and studied both their faces as his eyes whirred in contemplation. His spare hand flexed on the holster of the wooden rod attached to his belt. Even though he had to crouch to fit in here, he could move faster than them if he wanted to.

Mira's back protested at the sight. Not again.

Feeling bolstered by her discovery and the fact that she managed to find that firestone using her senses, Mira said, "Remember what happened to your friend?"

The guard stepped back and something new flashed in his eyes. Fear.

Beretta had never looked prouder.

"I'll let them know you found it," he said quickly.

"We both did," Mira corrected, pointing at Beretta.

The guard nodded and backed out, looking over his shoulder at the pair as he left.

Once he was out of sight, the two friends exchanged delighted giggles. Beretta skipped to her axe and pretended to chip away at the mountain, taking great care to make as much noise as possible.

Minutes passed.

Hours.

Nobody came to celebrate their discovery.

To Beretta's grave disappointment, they weren't called up for any grand feast or reward—not that it happened every time firestone was found—but she still wanted *something* in exchange for their hard work, and the goddess knew that she deserved it.

As much as she hated admitting it, Mira echoed the same feelings. It was foolish to expect that feast of a reward for every small pebble of firestone she found, no matter how she craved the fresh air and that rewarding smile telling her she did a good job.

She couldn't go up every time or the others would get suspicious—that's what he told her. They'd notice the special treatment and realize something was happening. The last thing she wanted was for Devlin to get in trouble because of her.

So, she resigned herself to the expectation that nothing was coming. Beretta complained about it to no end.

The next day they were sent back to shovel duty without a fuss, which was the perfect break for their tired bones. No-Neck wasn't there, so the one-eyed goddess had finally decided to smile upon them.

And when Mira went to bed that next night, she peeled back her dirty bedroll and discovered a small bundle hidden underneath. Beretta had gone to relieve herself and the others were off singing an old farming song about yellow skies turning black.

Without anyone seeing, Mira went to a dark corner and unfolded the cloth to find four sweet rolls and a thick slice of orange cheese.

Before a guard could ask what she was doing lurking in dark corners, she tucked the reward into her shirt, ignoring the stabbing guilt when Beretta returned, not caring to remove the secret smile that forced its way onto her face.

Eighteen

The Captain

Rallion herself must have trudged up through each of the twelve hells to wake him this morning. There was no other explanation for the pounding against his skull and the high-pitched trill of that annoyingly loud voice.

"Don't be grumpy just because *you* didn't wake up with the sun like some of us," Isla sang, tucking her braid into a loop on the top of her head. She looked far too happy when she shook him awake with the sun hanging halfway up the morning sky.

Allowing himself to imbue even one drink was a mistake. A big one. Continuing to have several after the first tankard was verging on insanity.

And now he'd be hearing about it from that girl for days.

So, he did what came natural to him and placed the blame on Isla, while angrily shoving his arms through his shirt. "If you've been up with enough time to pack, get dressed, *and* sneak downstairs to eat breakfast, then you should have roused me much sooner."

His chastising did nothing to dispel her uplifted mood. It only seemed to bolster the grin on her face. "You seemed to be enjoying the slumber—if the snores were any indication—and I didn't want to disturb you." She put on a dramatic frown. "I was hoping you'd be less miserable with the extra sleep. I guess not even a full night's rest can cure that."

He pinched the bridge of his nose and inhaled deeply, sending a prayer to every goddess he could name. "I don't want to argue today. Let's just head out before anything can happen."

"Always the worrier." She tossed his cloak at his head and jerked her chin. "What's the hold up, soldier?"

He scowled and upon realizing his shirt was inside out, had to tear it off in a flurry with the sound of giggles accompanying him. This princess really was the worst.

After settling their final tab with Saniam—with their blood-bought coins—they were ready to resume their journey with a fresh pack of supplies he bartered from the taciturn innkeep. The princess was loath to head out from the comforts of the inn and had dragged her feet all morning. But he was keen to get moving before people could ask too many questions.

The sun was up and the villagers would be out and halfway through their day.

The danger wasn't apparent to her as she'd been sheltered most of her life, but he noticed how the townsfolk watched them yesterday. He paid attention to the intrusive questions they asked and the way a few followed his every move. Horace, especially, dug in deep when he wasn't satisfied by their responses, and there was no way Edith was actually that sweet.

They were out of those gods-forsakened woods but by no means did that mean they were away from danger. It was best to head out before more questions could be raised.

So, here they were, finally dressed in their clean clothes that he could still somehow feel the blood stains on. At least they were dry, fed, and—more importantly—about to be on their way.

The original plan was to get up before dawn and make a quiet getaway *without* a horse. But someone decided to be an absolute terror about the entire plan and made things even worse.

Now not only was Saniam here to see them off, but Edith and Horace had managed to show up as well. Both stood just outside the inn's entrance, dressed in similar wares to how they'd been that first day, looking expectantly at the pair.

So much for slipping away quietly.

A hand smacked his arm.

"Don't look so inhospitable," Isla said when he sighed for the fifteenth time. "They are merely here to see us off on our journey."

Edith had another bundle held in her arms, which she handed to Isla, who passed it back to him. "I know it's not much, but I wanted to make sure that you had some freshly baked biscuits for your journey. You lot looked five steps away from Rallion's first gate when you showed up here and I won't have that happen again. Are you certain I can't convince you to stay an extra day or two?"

Isla's eyes widened and she turned to him with a drawn pout that would mean nothing but trouble for him later.

"Absolutely not," he said between gritted teeth. He held up a hand to block out the blazing sun that beat down on him, serving as a callous reminder of how late the hour was.

Edith gasped at the abrasiveness while Horace looked every which way but at them. At least someone else seemed as impatient as he was to see them on their way. He'd been checked out of the conversation and had barely uttered any response besides a shrug or grunt every now and then.

An elbow dug into his ribs. "What *my brother* means to say is that we've been off the path far too long and don't want to keep our uncle waiting any longer. We'd love to, but we can't stay."

Edith looked confused for a moment then nodded. Some sort of understanding passed between her and Isla that he didn't like. What exactly did he miss yesterday?

A horse whinnied from its spot tied to the outpost of a small butchery. He frowned. They really should have tried to take one before anyone was up. Their journey would have been so much faster but this godsdamned princess was stubborn and really was going to get them both killed before the end of this.

"Well." Edith clasped Isla's hand in her wrinkled one. This time the princess seemed prepared and didn't cower or jump from the contact. "I shall pray to the goddesses that your journey is swift and shall pray equally as hard for your uncle's health."

The smile on Isla's face faltered for a sliver of a moment, but she recovered quickly. No doubt the lie weighed on her.

Horace approached with his hands tucked in his pockets. "The skies to the north are clear." He stared at the blue canopy as if he could deduct the coming weather from a mere glance and a flick of the finger to test the winds.

"Perfect for a quick journey," he said with as much pleasantness as he could muster.

Unease still flooded his veins and knocked at the corners of his mind, even though he couldn't place why. It was more of a strange feeling in the air that floated down from the red mountain. He'd feel better when this place was behind them.

The princess would start complaining the moment they stepped out of earshot from this run-down village.

Isla had already made snide comments under her breath since he told her that they had to go north first, in the direction of Blackstone so that nobody caught on to the fact that their journey would lead to the southern border with Velotia. She thought nobody would notice if they headed in the proper direction or not. He knew it wasn't worth the risk.

They'd have to make their way back close to the red mountains so they weren't spotted. That was the only way.

Edith gestured at the dark blue and green cloak Isla wore, clipped together with a brass leaf on her shoulder. "It suits you."

Isla had thrown the dead wielder's cloak in the fire the moment they retired to their room last night. Now he knew why.

Before he could usher Isla out of there, a stumpy man wearing tanned leathers approached. Horace grabbed his wife's shoulder and steered her away before she could utter a word—at least he looked sheepish as he did so.

A lump clung to his throat at the sight.

This was the same man who watched them closely upon their arrival two days ago and came into the inn last night for a pint of fresh ale and steaming bite to eat, or so he had said. The ale at Saniam's tasted as though it had never been fresh and the food was tepid at best.

A hint of a faded blue uniform peaked out from under the worn leathers. That combined with the bow strapped to his back and a broadsword glistening at his side gave away the man's true identity.

A Muratian ranger.

Of course. He was an idiot.

Before the ranger could get close, he stepped in front of Isla, who had already shuffled back. He flexed his fingers that were craving to jump straight to Dark End, but it was too soon for that. "Is there something we can help you with, ranger?" he asked in level tones.

Perhaps there was no need to panic and the man was here to see them off like Edith and Horace. Maybe the ranger was eager for news around the rest of the kingdom, even though those questions could have been asked the other night.

The ranger adjusted his bow and wiped a bead of sweat off his temple. "I was merely in the neighborhood and wanted to see our visitors off myself."

Isla snapped her head to survey the ranger with one of her signature condescending glares that could wither any normal man. The ranger kept his composure and did not back down, though the way his eyes kept darting around told a different story.

Acting as if he was adjusting his belt, he positioned himself to easily grab his broadsword at a moment's notice. "Is that all?"

"Where'd you get the uniform from?" The ranger pointed at the gold embellishments on his borrowed Muratian uniform. "It's not as maintained as it should be." He jerked his head at Isla. "Same with the wielder cloak you wore when you came in... deserters?"

"You have this all wrong, Wesley." Edith had broken out of her husband's grasp and pushed past a small child and his mother who had inched closer to watch the interaction.

They'd drawn a crowd. They should have taken their chance in the storm, Slin, and her hatred of proper order, be damned.

It took everything to keep his hands at his side. There was a chance they could still talk their way out of this and nothing would have to turn physical—there *had* to be a way out. "We're not deserters," he said smoothly, trying to act annoyed they'd even suggest that. "We're on leave."

Their exchange was like a game of liar's dice, in that moment right before the final die tipped to show the winning number—or the number that would destroy everything. It was all waiting on that final reveal to see if their side came up.

"Where's your leave papers, then?" The ranger's eyes flicked from Isla and back to him. "You know about the wielder conscriptions the queen has on. Nobody's exempt."

"We got lost in the forest," Isla said from behind him. He closed his eyes and prayed to Luriel. "Our stuff got destroyed and it wasn't exactly a priority."

"Likely story," the ranger said. "But I'm going to need some form of papers before you can leave. Your *brother* can go on ahead, but not you."

"That's not going to happen," he said, thumbing the chip on Dark End's hilt. A small movement—one noticed by the ranger who tensed and jerked his arm backward.

"We received reports of a group of dead bandits not too far from here. Which way did you say you came from again?"

Isla gasped.

"Wesley, please," Edith said. "As if these two could be capable of something like—"

"I sent word ahead to the next village," the ranger said confidently, as if he thought that would help deter them. "In case you're thinking of slipping out before we're done chatting."

The blood in his veins turned to ice. He couldn't move. Couldn't think. "What did you say?" he asked, his voice echoing oddly in his ears.

A shaky hand grabbed his arm followed by a steady, commanding voice. "It doesn't matter, Cord. Let's leave."

"I'm afraid I can't let you leave," the ranger—Wesley, she called him—said, his eyes darting around. "*We* can't let you leave until we sort this out."

Three other cloaked men appeared behind them and metal unsheathed from its casing as they all drew their swords.

A squeak from Isla. It looked like there was no talking their way out of this one. *Again.*

In the distance, a flock of birds took off from behind the red mountains.

"Wait," Edith said, struggling to push forward now that her husband held a firm grip on her frail wrist. "These two mean us no ill-will. I believe you are mistaken, Wesley. You should hear them out."

The four rangers shifted uneasily, but the grips on their swords remained strong. They were village rangers in the middle of nowhere. That didn't mean they were inexperienced. Definitely more experienced than those bandits in the woods judging by their cool stances.

"*Cord,*" Isla's voice warned from behind him. He winced at the poorly concealed layers of terror he heard in it. She rarely let her shields drop like this and he knew why. She was finally starting to realize there were consequences to their presence in this cursed land.

There was no other way.

"We don't have to report them," Edith said, grabbing the arm of the one she'd called Wesley but he pushed her down. Horace went to grab her but the shorter ranger held him back.

"Edith," Horace said in his cantankerous voice. "You have been misled. I believe these two to be—"

A shovel fell over and the sound spooked one of the cloaked men. The man charged with his sword brandished, but he didn't seem to be going for him. He was charging toward the easier target of the princess.

Without thinking, he pushed Isla further back. Back and safely out of the way. Her screams mixed with the thundering of his heart overtook out all else.

Every sense was heightened. Every muscle alert and ready for what came next.

The man's blow was blocked with a swing of his broadsword. His spare hand already had a dagger in it and he plunged it into the man's side before he could register something was wrong.

"Stop!" the princess screamed.

Horace struggled against his restrainer, trying desperately to get to his wife who seemed frozen to her spot on the ground.

The ranger, Wesley, was fast—unnaturally fast—and he was so distracted by the first charging man he didn't notice Wesley sneak up on him until something hit him from behind. A sharp blow from the back of a bow sent Dark End clattering to the side.

Edith scrambled to her feet to get closer to them, ignoring her husband's calls.

A second hit to his head sent bells ringing and stars erupting behind his watering eyes. His lungs spasmed, making it hard to see. It was hard to think when all he could hear was the ringing and the screaming.

The last ranger had grabbed Isla by her hair and tossed her to the ground. She called to him for help, her voice trembling.

Before he could retrieve Dark End, the ranger brandished a shining long sword. He was trained well. Not out of shape and out of practice like the others. The long sword was in the air and slicing toward him.

Time slowed down and warped. His brain stopped working, as did every limb in his body despite the blood that furiously pumped through every vein as if attempting to escape its confines. All the warmth cast from the sun was sucked out of the air.

Before the ranger's blade ever made contact, Isla threw her hands up, as if to hide behind them, and screamed.

The scream vibrated off the blade, the ground, and the dilapidated buildings. It probably made it far past the red mountains and shook the air as if it wanted to cleave the skies in two.

It rang in his inner drums and against his skull. His hands jumped to his ears, as if they could block out the terrible ringing, and a dark cloud rushed over everything.

The ranger clutched his head as if in pain, as did several others. Edith fell to the ground, shouting for everything to stop.

That dark cloud encompassed everything, yet the sun still shone as bright as any day. That dreadful rush of darkness spread from Isla and shot out as quick as it came, touching everything it could reach within twenty feet.

It brushed against him briefly and a dreadful cold filled his body. The satchel at his side pulsed and the darkness moved on, not before sending him retching to his knees in pain. After the pain and nausea subsided—only seconds had passed though it felt like an eternity—he lifted his head.

Isla's fingertips were as black as the night sky. A terrible power rolled off her hands.

Wielder powers.

He'd never seen a wielder with an ability like that. He'd only read about them in books and lessons—or in old fables.

When her scream finished, the power that burst out so suddenly, darted back into her, draining everything it had touched. The dirt ground, once brown in color, lost what little moisture it had and dried up, crumbling beneath them, the wood posts caved in on themselves, collapsing into a pile of cinders, and skin peeled back into ash, melting and withering into nothing.

Those people that the darkness touched were reduced to ash.

When it was over, Isla collapsed to her knees. Her eyes were wide—either in shock or fear—before turning nearly white and then closing. Her entire body shook and when he looked at her hands—her hands—they were still blackened.

Deafening silence clung to the air before someone screamed. Horace knelt in the ashes, holding the shriveled, blackened, lifeless body of his wife as what was remaining crumbled into ash in his hands.

Isla's hands jumped to her mouth. "I didn't—I don't know—I didn't mean for this—"

"Monster." Horace pointed at her with an ash-covered finger. "Deathpuller," he whispered. His eyes burned with a hatred akin to an erupting mountain.

Those still standing backed away at the mention of that word. Some cowered and covered their faces while sobs wracked their bodies at the loss of their friends and family.

"I didn't mean for this," Isla choked out in between shaky breaths. Half of her face was covered in ash from the ranger that hit her.

"Deathpuller," another villager whispered.

The small boy they saw on their first day wailed for his mom, who got caught in the outburst and was nothing more than black dust.

Somehow that scream broke him out of whatever stupor had kept him frozen. Somehow his limbs managed to move, even if his brain could barely function. They had to get out of there.

Isla stared at her blackened hands and he now understood the look frozen on her face—it was probably the same one etched into his own.

Absolute horror.

Eventually, something snapped in place in his head. An understanding of why the Muratians—why the queen—wanted the princess so badly.

Nobody ever told him that she was a wielder.

He kept looking between the princess and the pile of dust that was the villagers.

As he watched a hunch-backed villager dither away, he knew they couldn't stay. Not now. They had to get back home. They had to get away before Muratian soldiers came—or worse.

One look down at the princess and her shaking hands—still painted stark black—was enough to know he had to get her out of here, for everyone's sake. He grabbed what was left of a blanket and threw it over her hands.

As the rest of the villagers were either frozen in fear or already running away, nobody bothered to stop when he grabbed the last horse that had not turned to ash and untied it from the post. He secured the rucksack safely on the side and with great delicacy—and against every rational inkling of self-preservation he possessed—he grabbed the stunned princess and heaved her onto the lanky horse's back before vaulting in place behind her. Propriety be damned to all the goddesses.

No one attempted to stop them on their way out of Ackerslie.

Nineteen
Prince Edmund of Velotia

The goddesses were determined to test his resolve.

No matter how many assurances he sent his way or the number of missives with detailed outlines of their plans that were overindulged with false confidence, Prince Brenner of Koliat still decided to hand every ounce of caution over to Slin and had joined up with their scouting party—to everyone's utter dismay. The trickster goddess loved when things played out of order so he shouldn't have been surprised. Not when the stars still favored her.

The Koliat prince arrived with an entourage of fifty maroon-clad aides, soldiers, wielders, and high-born party-members that were, apparently, *absolutely necessary.* What a pompous ass.

Their assistance wasn't needed. In fact, it was more of a hindrance than anything.

Thank the goddess that the Pedite general finally put an end to his idiocy and demanded Brenner leave half of his party behind before they ventured closer to the border. He didn't seem afraid of the Koliat prince or the Muratians, but he'd had the most upfront experience of them all. He didn't seem afraid of much since Edmund had met him. He was focused on their goal.

Too focused. And the reminder of his past failures incensed Edmund.

Still, the general had proven useful so he had no choice but to keep him around. Brenner, on the other hand, was utterly incompetent and his soldiers left an imprint everywhere they touched.

The Koliats had already gone through the Pedite camp and taken any supplies they needed, stating that *this type of soldiers* had no need of extra blankets and could survive on fewer rations. Edmund let the first raid slide but now they were starting to set their eyes on the Divite cots and had even looked towards the Agicae's special fur-lined cloaks. The general asked if he could knock the prince flat on his ass and Edmund had half a mind to allow it.

There was a lot to be said for how Brenner's men skirted around the Koliat prince, a habit his Velotian soldiers had started to take on as well—especially the female ones—though none would explain further when asked.

Edmund had a terrible suspicion as to why.

It was hard to believe *this* was the man their father wanted Isla to marry. Well, maybe not that hard to believe. Their father was only concerned with strengthening their alliance with the Koliats and nothing else.

The thought of his sister sent pangs of guilt twisting into his stomach again. Would that feeling ever go away?

No. Not until they found Isla safe. If they had to go over to the isolated kingdom of Lenoc for aid, he'd sail to the remote island himself. He had to explain himself to Isla and beg forgiveness for words said out of anger. Words that had cut more deeply than she let on. He thought he had time to apologize, to make amends. That time was cut short by the Muratians.

Getting to her was hard to do with Brenner and the Koliats impeding their efforts. Their ostentatious reputation was well-warranted, even by Edmund's high standards.

The axe-wielding Freya, along with the other one, Malin, had taken it upon themselves to unofficially escort the new prince around.

As they were Pedites, the prince refused to acknowledge them even to tell them off, so he allowed their presence.

Smart.

The last thing they needed was the Koliat prince getting hurt—or hurting others. They didn't need another kingdom going to war against their father.

Everything balanced on the edge of a spinning, fine-tipped sword—ready to topple over at the first hint of complication.

Edmund approached Freya under the pretense of adjusting his boot. He leaned against a large pine and kept his focus on the encampment ahead. He ran a hand through his hair, an action that his father always said was unbecoming of the crown prince. "What has he done now?"

Freya sighed heavily and adjusted one of her braided loops. "He grabbed one of the princess's ladies, Alynna, and demanded attentions in his tent." She twisted the hilt of her axe tightly and jerked her shoulder at the shaggy-haired Pedite soldier who hadn't left her side since this all started. "Malin and I stopped him before anything could happen, and we sent Princess Isla's ladies to wait at the secondary camp. There's no need for them until we find her, and it's best to keep any further temptation out of sight."

Edmund pinched the bridge of his nose. This prince was going to get himself killed before they could find his betrothed. "Did you tell your general?"

Freya scoffed, and the other soldier adjusted the silver band in his hair. "I'm not an idiot," she said. "He wouldn't be here if I did."

"I don't get it," Edmund said. "Why doesn't he wait back with the rest of his men? He's doing more harm than good being here."

Freya raised an eyebrow.

"Right. I know. I know." They all whispered the same about him. "Just—just keep an eye on him. *Please.*"

"We have been," she huffed. Sunlight glared off the axe blade threateningly.

179

"Keep doing it, I meant." He turned and paused. "Keep him out of trouble. Keep him alive. And let me know what else you hear about him, please."

The soldier nodded solemnly before returning to sharpen her axe. Malin hadn't even looked his way once during the exchange. He—like his general—thought Edmund was a useless asset they were forced to bring along. Edmund had every intent on proving them wrong.

As his mind swirled back to the Prince Brenner issue, he only found himself growing angrier and angrier. The more Edmund learned about him, the less he liked. A pit in his stomach formed at the thought of his sister marrying this man. A small part of him—a naive part—thought he could convince his father otherwise, now that he knew his true character. Everything in him knew that pursuit was futile. Pointless.

There was nothing he could do about it at this point, his father would say. The deal was done and it was already too late. Edmund never paused to think that he would never see his sister after all of this was over. Not really.

There was no doubt in his mind that after his sister was married off to Brenner that she'd rarely be allowed to return home to visit her family, if ever. So, any peace he wanted to settle with her had to be done before then.

The Koliat prince wasn't concerned with what the Muratians may be doing to his sister, his only concern was that she was retrieved intact and the marriage went on as planned. Just the same as Edmund's father.

Their father had certainly been picky about who he selected for Isla. He'd denied requests over the years, even ones from the Muratian king himself—long before he passed. Thank the goddess that his father never accepted that agreement, given how relations had broken down over the years since. It didn't help that King Gorvo was a second son thrust onto the throne nearly thirty years ago when

the eldest son vanished, never to have been seen again––or died hor-
rifically depending on the storyteller––and Edmund's father always
thought this one was never bred to rule. Too *weak*, as he'd called him,
to be bonded with through marriage.

Apparently, he thought the Koliats were a better option.

It didn't help matters that—to his utmost horror—the Koliat
prince had somehow found out about Isla's *gifts*. A fact that his
father went through great lengths to conceal throughout her whole
life, so why divulge that secret to her betrothed? And why not tell
Edmund that others knew?

By the grace of Hierel, the prince wasn't off put by Isla's gifts.
In fact, Brenner was impressed and curious to know more, though
Edmund didn't know if that was worse. Edmund pushed the fact
that few people knew about Isla and that things should remain that
way until they found her safe. Until the wedding ceremony was
sealed in scars.

In a strange twist of fates, Prince Brenner actually agreed with
him. The less people that knew about Isla, the better––for now. His
father would be displeased if word spread. He'd always despised the
wielders and refused to acknowledge the fact that his daughter was
one of them.

A twig snapped and a twitchy messenger approached, standing
awkwardly to the side until Edmund waved him in.

"What is it?" he asked briskly, eyeing up the parchment as if the
paper itself had wronged him.

The messenger turned red-faced and squeaked out, "Another
message from the palace, Prince Edmund."

"Put it with the others." There was no urgency to open it, and
he debated if it was worth reading at all. He already knew what the
letter contained.

Another demand from his father to return home and resume his
duties as royal heir, abandoning the rescue for the others to complete. It could join the eight similar missives he had already received.

Each becoming more and more demanding as Edmund left them all unanswered.

A laugh bubbled up from his throat at the thought of his father furiously writing each letter, only to have every single one ignored. Edmund couldn't remember the last time he'd told his father *no*, but it felt freeing.

There would be a price to pay when he returned. That was for later. For now, he had to continue on with the efforts as planned and pray to the goddess that good news awaited them.

Twenty

The Captain

This was not what he signed up for.

Well, none of it was, but this most definitely was not what he expected to be dealing with when the commander shoved him into this gods-forsaken post. If only the commander had truly known how spectacular of a punishment he'd managed to sign him up for this time.

What in Rallion's name happened back there?

His brain had yet to catch up with the rest of his body. It was left behind in the shadow of that mountain, right in the ashes of that poor village. A part of him hoped the villagers could call for aid quickly, but the rational part knew that meant their location would be revealed sooner.

The Muratians would know how to find them now and likely drew close. The thought of what would happen when they did turned his stomach into stone.

A wielder.

A wielder.

A fucking wielder!

Why didn't he know about this? How did he miss the signs?

The pit in his stomach felt like a knife scraping his innards. It's not like he had been entirely truthful to her about why he was assigned to her in the first place. They'd both kept the truth veiled from one another.

But again, how didn't he spot this sooner?

The princess hadn't spoken all day and refused any of the rations he had prepared, even after practically shoving them under her nose. She must be starving. Though he barely ate for days after—after his incident.

The glaze in her eyes told him that she still swam in that sea of thoughts. Too far gone to complain about sharing a horse or the fierce winds that had picked up when they passed near the mountain range. She didn't squeak out one word of complaint when he helped her dismount—careful not to get close to her hands—to lead their *borrowed* horse across a frigid river, soaking their boots in the process.

It was like traveling with a wraith.

A silent, death-summoning wraith that could explode at any minute—killing him, their horse, and everything within eyesight.

But he wasn't dead, he reminded himself. He was as close as any of the villagers, so why was he spared?

It seemed like Isla had no control of—whatever that was—but yet he remained unharmed.

Why?

He felt her powers reaching out before something stopped it. The cold darkness touched him briefly then backed away as if spooked. He shot a guilty look at the rucksack he'd taken great care to carry with him since that day in the forest.

Starting a fire was out of the question, no matter how cold he was. Even with their wet boots hanging off a branch to dry, Isla hadn't complained about the turn in weather. Instead, she clutched her new cloak tight around herself as if she wished to disappear into the worn cloth that the kind farmer gave her.

She didn't acknowledge him when he asked about it. She didn't acknowledge him when he tried asking about anything really. He understood, though the silence ate at him. The snarky comments and constant complaints was almost preferable to—*this.*

It felt like he would burst from all the questions pooling within.

The way that black power snaked out of her, he'd never seen anything like it. Never felt a power like that and he'd worked closely with the military wielders before—whenever they needed something from the Pedites, that was.

After the shock wore off and he could move, the sight of the ashes where people once stood sent shivers down every inch of his body—it frightened him to his core. It took everything in him to get her out of there and head straight south, towards the border. It didn't matter anymore if the villagers saw where they were headed. They knew they had been deceived.

Their lie had been laid bare in the worst way possible and those villagers paid the price.

They never should have stayed the night.

Since then, half of the time Isla had tears running down her face, and the other half she stared into the void, surely plagued by dark thoughts.

Looked like he was right about needing a horse after all. He really wished he hadn't been.

After their initial escape he let Isla ride the steed all day as she needed it more, even though his bruised—and hopefully not broken—ribs were screaming in complaint and the side of his head was pounding from where that ranger got him good. Overall, he was in sore shape.

Still, she needed it more.

The horse they had acquired was a lovely chestnut color, and despite his lankiness, a missing ear likely caused by frostbite, and tangled mane, he had been a sturdy beast so far.

They traveled long, and he made sure their tracks were covered, hence the journey through the icy river to throw the scent off for the ones that would eventually follow.

Isla hadn't uttered one peep the entire day. She didn't ask for a break or food or water or to take a nap to rest her feet. She allowed herself to be led like the dead walking through a ghost swamp on a full moon.

When a family with a full cart passed them halfway through the day, on what he thought was an abandoned road, Isla didn't even bat an eye. The jolly father asked about the condition of the roads ahead, all while the two small children ran around the horse, trying to catch his tail and pointing at his missing ear.

Isla didn't move when the small girl asked where she got her pretty cloak, so he made up a story that his sister was mute.

It was only after the family had left them that he finally relaxed the hand tucked into his jacket and released the death grip on his dagger. He didn't let them stop for hours after that.

It was late into the night by the time they stopped. The horse couldn't go much further, and he didn't think his legs could either. They huddled under a makeshift covering tied between two trees. His hands were freezing and he was still wearing that gods-forsakened Muratian military jacket that he took off that dead body nearly two weeks ago.

Why didn't she tell him she was a wielder? Wielder powers manifested at a young age, usually when the child learned to walk. This couldn't have been a recent development.

The villagers had called her a deathpuller—a nickname for ashfeeders. The magic was old and unheard of for centuries. It was said the first ashfeeder was cursed by an ancient demon—or a goddess, depending on who told the story.

Ashfeeders were harbingers of death and destruction. And the entire time the Velotian Princess he was protecting yielded those very powers without him knowing. No wonder the king was eager to marry her off. It was known that he had a strong disdain for wielders. How did he react when his daughter turned out to be one of the deadliest kinds?

A sickening pit formed in his stomach as he remembered the smell of rapidly decaying flesh. At the sight of skin and bone withering away as if it were nothing. He shivered. An action lost on Isla who was too stuck in her own mind to have noticed.

Ancient magics like that were usually passed through the mother's line. Not a lot was known about Queen Isabella before she married King Augustus. Would the king have still married her if he knew what she carried dormant in her blood and that it would eventually pass to his heirs?

Was the king frightened of his own daughter? The speed in which he arranged this marriage to Koliat was a good indicator.

The thought made his heart sink into a cavern.

He needed a distraction, so he grabbed a loose log and started carving. What should he do today?

The horse whinnied.

Perfect idea. He pulled out his dagger and allowed his hands to take over. They knew what to do by this point.

"If we ride hard tomorrow, I think that we can make a good headway," he said to himself, just as he had been doing all day. They'd spent days without talking before, especially after the bandits. This time the silence weighed heavily and he longed to be rid of it.

Isla stared at the felled log in front of her. Her hands had returned to normal, but she clutched them so tight that they turned pale, matching her blood-drained face.

"That old horse made it longer than I thought he would," he continued, carving out the beginnings of a long face with two holes each for the nostrils and ears—wait—one ear for this one. "I thought there was a good chance the chestnut would pass out before noon or his heart would give away crossing the river." He winced as soon as the words left his mouth, but Isla made no indication that she heard him.

He scratched his chin, running the hilt of his blade along the stubble that had started to grow. "We should probably give him a name. Any suggestions?"

Her head moved ever so slightly to the right.

Was that a *no*?

"We never had any horses growing up, obviously, but my brother and I used to pretend with one of the old, downed trees that had branches that stuck out like a horse's legs. I mean... looking back it probably was nowhere close but at least we had an active imagination, like our mother always used to berate us for. Nothing like the purebred steeds I'm certain were at the palace or those fancy riding toys I've only ever heard about—I'm sure you had one?"

He raised an eyebrow questioningly, working on the thin lines of the horse's mane.

Not even a finger moved this time, but her eyes connected with his. They were devoid of all emotion. Haunted.

"Figured you would have," he said, a hint of a smile teasing at the corners of his lips. She probably had the pick of any fine breed she wanted while growing up. "But that horse that we pretended to have, we used to call it Rigel." He frowned and attacked the rest of the body including the legs—which were always difficult to master. "Or was it River? I think it was River. Let's call this one River. How does that sound?"

A toad croaked in the distance. The first sign of wildlife since setting up camp.

One of her shoulders shifted in a motion that he pretended was a shrug.

"River it is," he said happily, carving the same muscles along the horse's back and moving on to the shape of his hooves. All while Isla did nothing but sit and stare.

Done.

He held out the wooden horse and examined it under the pale starlight. It wasn't his best work but the light here was terrible and he didn't dare risk a fire.

The horse—River—flicked its tail as if he approved, both of the name and the carving.

"We should probably get some sleep so we can get started early tomorrow." He clapped his knees and stood, placing the wooden River at the base of a birchwood. "We didn't see anybody along the paths today but that doesn't mean there won't be. We'll have to be extra vigilant to get you home in time for that fancy wedding and those sugar tartlets that I know you've been dreaming of."

Isla didn't move an inch, but her eyes darkened to focus on whatever demons battled in her mind. He'd killed before, hells, he'd even killed *for her*, so it was nothing new to him. Something told him she never had to deal with this magnitude of destruction before. Not by her own hands.

Living with the guilt was something that never got any easier. He *knew*.

Perhaps her father had sent her off in the hopes that she'd never have to face that terrible guilt. To see their faces in a dream as clear as if they were standing next to him right now and hear their voices louder than his own.

Now she would know. She would always know.

When a fresh set of tears streamed down her face, he pretended not to notice. Instead, he flattened a spare pack into a suitable pillow, which he left beside an unmoving Isla in case she decided to get some rest. He doubted it, but still, just in case.

Sleep, no matter how terrible or little of it achieved, tended to wash away the prior day's worries. It could turn the worst events into mere memories rather than a fresh horror painted in your mind. Every day made the guilt fade a little more.

As for him, he leaned against a hard trunk and pulled the rough blanket Saniam had given him over his lap. He wouldn't get much sleep either as he planned to keep watch for the first part of the night.

Now that the Muratians knew where they were, she was not safe.

Twenty-One
Mira

It had been days since she last saw the private. *Days.*

But the stash of snacks under her blanket and the extra ladleful of stew she was given on occasion told her that he was lurking around somewhere. There'd also been no other incidents with No-Neck since he was punished for stealing the firestone from her. Nobody suspected about their meetings—not even B, who was over-observant to a fault. So why was he avoiding her?

It was probably because of the new commander that showed up.

After retrieving the piece in the pit, she had been called up for only one more practice. That time there was no fancy meal beside a small plate with stale bread and a day-old baked fowl. Devlin winced when he gave it to her and said that they had to be more careful, especially now that some Commander Maylot had arrived on site and kept close tabs on everything—and everyone—that went in and out of the mines.

Mira was disappointed but tried her best to force the food down. Then he put her through three hours of intense training in an attempt to call that heat—that flame forward.

"You need to think of yourself as more than a conduit," he said, reading from that tattered journal with wilted blood-lilies. The gold buttons of his blue uniform were undone, exposing a crisp white shirt that clung to his muscles as he paced the room. "You are the instrument through which the ancient magics are wielded."

Whatever that meant.

"If you can't find a way to control your powers, they will consume you. You'll become a dangerous weapon that could explode at any moment and we don't want that. We want you to become a targeted, precise weapon."

Right. Right.

It pained Mira to admit that, once again, she found it hard to focus on their session, especially with Devlin circling her like a feline and rambling confusing instructions every other minute.

It was an utter disaster.

And now she was back in the pits with Beretta by her side, trying to get it to work again, without success. For some reason, she couldn't find that spark—that magic—which should flow easily.

Beretta grumbled constant complaints about the humidity down here. Why did she ask to be assigned with her *again* if she still wasn't feeling well? Anything would have been better than the digging pits, and Mira already told her not to follow this time.

Naturally, her friend refused to listen to reason.

The heat was worse and the rocks were tougher today. They'd both sweated through their brown tunics and were a mess. A hot bath would be to die for right now and Beretta agreed.

"Next time you find some of that stone, let's share it again," B suggested while happily chipping away at a tough protrusion. "Maybe we can sit in the sun together, only for a bit."

"That would be lovely." Mira closed her eyes and envisioned lying against a stump with the sun shining on her face and her friend right beside her.

The dream disappeared quickly.

Devlin would want to continue their practices in private—no matter how little progression she had achieved. Even her most trusted friend wouldn't be allowed up. It was the same reason why she didn't tell B about the meals or extra food he was sneaking her. She was afraid it would all stop if Beretta found out.

The more people that knew, the higher chance word would get out.

"I feel like I've forgotten what the wind feels like," Beretta said dreamily. "The closest I get is when Gummy burps in my face after surprise meat pie day."

Mira covered the giggles with the back of her hand and pretended to adjust her shoe when the other dredgers paused to glare at the commotion. At least the Wasp wasn't here today. The way the skin at the back of her neck prickled when he stared and the constant degrading comments were too much to handle some days. She'd never be able to concentrate on finding firestone with those vicious eyes tearing through her.

Beretta huffed out a deep laugh, then she froze. The other workers snatched up their tools and quickly went back to work. An unreadable expression filled her friend's face—it was so brief that she thought she'd imagined it.

A shadow moved behind Mira. She whipped around with her pickaxe poised to strike. "What is—oh." The pick dropped to the ground, and she stared sheepishly at her feet.

"Were you going to hit me?" Devlin asked. He scratched the back of his neck.

"Sorry," she mumbled, refusing to meet his eye.

He tilted his head so he could see her. When she looked up a smile filled his sharp face. "It'll take a lot more than that axe to hurt me." He winked.

"I would never—I didn't mean to—I wasn't—"

Beretta coughed.

At the reminder of their audience, Devlin changed instantaneously. He straightened and dusted off the sleeve of his jacket. When he spoke, his voice had lost all of its prior mirth. "You're wanted for work in another section."

Beretta's pick clattered to the ground. "What about me?" she asked indignantly.

"Finish up here," Devlin said, not even bothering to look at her directly.

"But I—"

"That's an order." The coldness in his voice sent shivers up Mira's arm; he was fantastic at putting on a front. He nodded at her. "Come along, you."

With an apologetic look at Beretta, Mira followed his lithe footsteps past the other scowling dredgers and down several winding tunnels that she hadn't been through before. None of the guards looked twice as they passed but the Wasp stopped to watch them with his custom glower aimed directly at Mira. She held her chin high and ignored him.

Devlin's light voice returned the moment they were away from the others. He turned and bounced on his heel. "I decided that I had enough of the air and the sun and wanted to see you in action for myself."

Mira didn't bother telling him that she'd stalled in every way. Then he'd send her back and find another, and that was the last thing she wanted. She wished to draw this out as long as she could.

Captured by the light in his eyes, all she could do was swallow and nod. Then they were off again, ducking under a molded plank that was clearly meant to keep the miners out. When she thought they were headed toward an unopened pit, he turned left, grabbing a torch off a sconce as he passed.

The wind howled and yelled down here, protesting their intrusion.

The paths became narrower and narrower until it was so small that only one person could squeeze in at a time.

It was hard to see and she kept bumping against the sharp rock. She cracked her head against a jutting stone, he reached behind and grabbed her hand. His grip was firm and confident.

The contact made her want to explode out of her skin and she was painfully aware how sweaty and dirty she must be. She should have stopped to change her shirt—not that she had a spare—or grabbed some water to clean her dusty face. Why did he have to come today of all days?

When they emerged from the tunnel, the lantern light spilled out to fill every crack of a large cavern that looked to be carved by hand.

"What is this place?" she asked, twirling around to get a better view. The rock down here was nearly black and looked like it was damp, but a quick touch revealed it was completely dry. It reeked of mold and mildew.

Devlin ran a hand along the dark wall. "This is one of the many caverns the ancients carved. An underground river runs nearby—that's why it smells terrible here."

"Oh."

Oh?

That was all she could come up with? She'd been anxiously awaiting her next chance to see him and all her meager brain could manage was *oh*.

If Beretta were here, she'd be slapping her forehead.

"It reminds me of the caves near my home that I would explore with my brothers," he said. "Though this place smells much worse."

Again, Mira was silent. There wasn't much that she could remember from her time above, let alone anything about her family—surely, she had one, once.

He stuffed his hands in his pockets, looking sheepish. "Sorry for the show back there, but I wanted to get you alone and couldn't come up with anything better."

The wind barked in protest against the hard rock.

"Don't be," she said, ignoring the pathetic sputtering of her heart. "Anything's better than digging."

She ran her hand along the length of the opposite dark wall, pausing to examine the layer of dirt that had accumulated beneath her nails.

Then he was next to her, grabbing her dirty hand for the second time. "Want to try again?" he murmured, placing her hand back against the hard stone. "See if you do better with an audience?"

Heat burst from where he pressed her hand into the stone and she was certain her face resembled the same color as the red firestone they worked so hard to uncover.

Then the heat was gone. She looked around in confusion and he was now leaning against the far wall, watching her intently. He swallowed, then gave another encouraging nod.

"I don't want to distract you from your mission," he said quietly. "My brother was a gifted swordsman before he—and he hated when I watched him practice with his sword master. He said it was too distracting and would throw rocks at me until I left. Eventually, I learned to watch from the safety of a dark corner where nobody could spot me." That menacing smile returned, though a darkness lingered in his eyes. "I don't want you resorting to that, so say the word and I can hide around the corner."

If only he knew how his mere presence sent her brain whirring. She needed several layers of mountain between them to lull the distracting thoughts in her mind.

Mira shook her head.

The heat in her cheeks refused to go away, so she turned back to the stone and focused on bringing that heat currently pooling below her stomach toward her hands. She pretended she was in a deserted corridor with only Beretta murmuring quiet encouragements and loud distractions.

There was no pressure to find the firestone then. She was only testing her abilities—which she still had yet to fully understand.

What had worked before?

Remembering the warmth and what it was like above ground. All she had to do was imagine happy memories of bathing in the morning sun's caress. In its encompassing warmth and the comfort it brought.

In the distance, drops of water dripped onto stone, echoing like a waterfall in the dark cavern as she paced the room, pressing her hand into the stone while Devlin continued to watch. The heat of his gaze threatened to burn her neck, no matter how she tried to pretend he wasn't there.

After her fifth pass of the entire room, the rock beneath her hand grew warm, lighting up her skin. Triumphantly, she turned to Devlin, ready to tell him about her accomplishment and the breath whooshed out of her lungs.

In her complete focus, she didn't notice that he had inched close. She tried to jump away but there was only cold stone behind her.

"I—I found it," she said, releasing a shaky breath. At this range, she could trace every line of his perfect face, including the shining scar on his jaw.

"Perfect. Excuse me." He grabbed her shoulder and gently moved her to the side before placing his hand over the exact spot hers had just been on. "Hmm," he muttered. "It doesn't feel any different to me."

He turned and leaned against the rock she was just inspecting. Their shoulders were almost touching. They were close. So close that when she turned her head, she could see the flecks of black in his blue irises and trace the perfect waves of rusty-gold highlights in his hair.

Those blue eyes narrowed. "How do you do it?"

Mira tore her eyes away from his and leaned her head against the hard rock behind her. "I don't know. I can just—feel it—if that makes any sense at all?"

"No." He chuckled. "But hey, at least you can control it better now. These exercises, finding the firestone, help you get a grasp of your power, but I know you can do so much more than this." He turned back to inspect the rock wall with his hands on his hips. "Still, the firestone is useful to imbue in blades and chains so we should probably take it. I guess we didn't think to bring any tools to dig it out, huh?"

"I—uh—no, we did not." What a dummy she was. A poor excuse of a dredger.

"That's alright." He twisted back to face her. "It's not as much about the firestone as it is you understanding your power, and how to find it and harness it."

That was hardly harnessing anything. Mira was skeptical that she had any real powers besides a better-attuned sense of touch and she said as much.

"Don't discount yourself," he said, grabbing her chin so she was forced to look at him. "Wielders are rare, and learning to control magic is not for the faint at heart. There are so many different kinds of wielder powers and each varies in degrees of difficulty to master. Those that don't learn to respect their powers can become a menace to themselves, those around them, and this kingdom."

There was an intensity in his eyes as he spoke.

"The right power in the wrong hands can spell doom for the entire kingdom. Do you understand?"

Mira nodded.

"Your power is one of the rarest and will be hard to gain a semblance of control over, especially once you leave the confines of these mines. But it can be done. That's why I want to help you, so it doesn't destroy you from the inside."

All she could too was blink stupidly.

"Next time I see you, I'll show you some passages from an old journal that details Rallion's comet and the wonders that happened the last time the sister goddesses years happened a century ago. It mostly focuses on Hierel's year. Rallion's is more vague on details, as usual."

"Why is that?"

He wrinkled his nose. "People are superstitious and fear the unknown. The year of Rallion is thought to bring about death and destruction, when really, it heralds change. It's not always a bad thing, but it does mean a lot will happen for wielders when we enter Hierel's year."

If only that gods-forsakened comet hadn't bothered to show its face this year, then she wouldn't have to be here reading up on it when she'd rather try practicing again. Why did the comet have to show up now?

"And that's why it's so important for me to figure out if I have powers now," she said slowly. "Before the year of Hierel turns?"

"Yes," he said softly, still holding her cheek. His lips curved up, crinkling the skin at the corners of his eyes, which traveled down her face, stopping at her lips. "You're more important than you realize."

The breath that loosened from her lungs was ragged and heavy. It took considerable strength to remember how to haul a second helping of air back in.

The baying cry of the wind picked up.

Louder this time.

Closer.

Except this time, it wasn't the wind growling and crying. It was something else.

There was only one entrance to this cavern, and whatever was making that noise was coming from it.

Mira gasped. Devlin dropped his hold on her and jumped to the side. Steel slithered out of its case and into his hand. If her heart hadn't plummeted to her feet, it may have stuttered at the sight of him standing there, broad-backed, with his eyes fixed on the dark entrance.

Long moonlight-colored claws came into view first as—whatever it was—slithered along the side of the rock, moving as if it were one with the mountain. It had four limbs and was humanoid in appearance, but its face—it was hard to see past that terrible face. Where there should have been eyes and a nose, was nothing but a gaping mouth with rows of thin teeth.

It took a ragged breath and that terrible sound—that *howling*—came out of its mouth.

Devlin elbowed her, nudging her behind him as the thing jumped from one wall to the next. "What the fuck is that?"

Before Mira could do anything more than scream and throw her hands up, the creature launched at them. Its mouth stretched so it was twice the size of its head and all she saw was row upon row of jagged teeth down its throat.

Devlin charged and in a flash of steel, the creature was split along its neck and its torso. It fell to the ground in a gurgling heap, pools of nearly black blood gathering around it.

Mira stood there with her chest heaving—frozen and utterly useless—while Devlin bent over the creature. He took his long sword and before she could look away, plunged it into the creature's chest.

That terrible gurgling stopped and silence washed over the cavern.

Her limbs were finally free from the spell that held them in place, and Mira gasped.

Devlin whipped around, eyes flashing in the dim light until he realized it was only her behind him. He dropped his sword and ran over, grabbing her arms. "Are you alright?"

"Yes," Mira sobbed, turning away so he wouldn't see the flush in her cheeks or the tears forming at the corner of her eyes.

Once again, his hands found their way to her face and forced her to look at him. "There were rumors of cave dwellers in this mountain range but never thought I'd see one. They travel alone so there should be nothing to fear. You're safe now."

Safe.

You're safe now.

The words echoed across the cavern of her mind. She wanted to feel it. To trust his words, but she wasn't safe down here. Nobody ever was.

His blue eyes captured hers and he swore. "I should have checked before bringing you down here. This was all my fault."

"You couldn't have known," she rambled. "And it's dead now."

Why did it come out now? Was it attracted to her powers?

Devlin's blue eyes narrowed. "What are you thinking?"

She let out a shaky breath. "I'm thinking—I'm thinking that I should get back before the others notice."

He laughed, dropping the hold on her face. "Get back to what—breaking your hands by digging in the dirt with those other dredgers? Take your time. There's no rush. There are worse things held back by the gates to the godlands, that thankfully haven't been released."

Dredgers.

The way in which he said that word sent her blood boiling and clogged her throat in ice. "Those dredgers are not to be laughed at," she scolded, biting the inside of her cheek from lashing out further. "And the one you found me with is my friend."

The color drained from his face and his eyes widened. "I'm sorry. That was callous."

It was the truth. Was that what he thought truly about them? About *her.*

"I'm sorry," he repeated.

She didn't care that his apology sounded genuine. She didn't care that his eyes pleaded for her understanding. She didn't want to look at him anymore. "You should probably take me back. Us dredgers have a quota to keep and someone will notice my absence. I don't want to get more lashes."

Was that disappointment she saw in his face? Shame?

Good.

Mira was too incensed to care. All she wanted was to get back before the hot tears pooling in her eyes spilled over. What an idiot she was to think he ever thought any different of her. She stepped over the body of the dweller and refused to look back.

Twenty-Two
The Princess

The sun didn't jolt her awake that morning, and its usually tantalizing rays refused to warm the frost she felt inside. She'd been awake for hours, though she'd barely moved from the spot her body had trapped her at. Cord had also been up most of the night, jumping at every sound and pacing with his hand on the hilt of his sword as if he expected a Muratian soldier to pop out from every flowing branch. Eventually, he slept. Maybe for an hour or two before the sun rose.

Sleep wasn't an option for her. As soon as she let herself drift, the nightmares would start and she wasn't certain if they'd ever end. The darkness would come in and would consume her until she was nothing but a cold, black mass.

So, she stayed up and allowed the intrusive thoughts to consume her as easily as a rushing tide overcoming all in its path. When she couldn't bear the way Cord kept peeking at her, worried she'd combust and take him with her, she decided to close her eyes. The darkness threatened to come back.

Every rustle of leaves, every movement of branches spread a whisper where she went. The trees seemed to bend away, afraid of the one who pulled death to her.

Deathpuller.

If she slept then the nightmares would consume until there was nothing left. So, she forced her mind awake while her body screamed for sweet sleep.

Only when he started packing the horse, River, did she finally find the strength to crack open a dry eye, finally listening to whatever was inside of her that nudged to keep going. Perhaps it was encouraged by that nagging voice, which had been grating on her ears for nearly two weeks now, as he spoke to River in a soft murmur too low for her to understand.

She lifted her head as he stroked the chestnut's neck, brushing his fingers through its tangled brown hair in a show of affection he'd yet to show on their journey. The horse's good ear flicked in response. If she could care, she'd be offended he thought a horse was more deserving of an agreeable behavior than a crown princess.

Something slipped off her shoulder and fell to the dirt below. She frowned, not remembering falling asleep with anything on.

It was a blue jacket with faded gold linings. A Muratian jacket.

When did he have a chance to do that? She swore she didn't do more than close her eyes at the time.

Cord finally noticed her movement and leaped away from River, recoiling into himself as if he was caught slacking off in the camp instead of merely getting their horse ready. His eyes traveled to the jacket her hand picked at and widened. Before she could register anything, he snatched the jacket away.

"I was hot last night so don't expect it again," he mumbled. That usual angry gusto was missing, and he looked at her with nothing but pity.

It was better than the fear painted on his face after seeing what she had done to the villagers. Anything was better than that.

Isla couldn't muster a response or even a pitiful shrug. It was all she could do from breaking down again... or worse.

She stretched, feeling life finally start to come back into her fingertips. After her *outburst,* a deep trill passed through her, from her fingers into her veins, her muscles, and into every aspect of herself that she couldn't shake. It finally dissipated at some point overnight while she counted the number of stars overhead.

It had never been this bad before. She'd never lost control like she had yesterday. Everything happened so fast, and there was nothing she could do to stop it.

She lost control when that ranger grabbed her. And then they were going to kill Cord and she needed him. But they were all too close, and she couldn't stop. Couldn't hold it.

The way they looked at her after and called her a monster. They were right. They were all right.

An overwhelming cloud of doom threatened to collapse her lungs in on themselves. Every breath was excruciating and every movement of her chest felt as if a rock had caved in on it. The tremble in her hand started up again. It terrified her.

When she was young and alone, she taught herself to embrace the darkness and let it fill her, before letting it leave her. It usually worked... *usually*. So, she tried again that morning, sitting there unmoving until the shakiness left and that last tinge of darkness disappeared like the morning dew.

With a shake of her hands, she rolled to her feet. It was a struggle at first as her left foot spasmed, still half asleep. Warmth emanated from the cloak Edith gave her, and she could almost hear the words the lady spoke to her before things turned ugly.

Cord watched as she gathered her few blood-bought belongings, with his eyes flicking back towards the path every few seconds. Perhaps he was worried she'd have another outburst and kill him too. He was probably eyeing the quickest escape route.

If her mouth wasn't so dry, she'd tell him there was nothing to worry about. That she was drained and wouldn't be able to duplicate it, even if she wanted to... and she didn't want to ever touch that power again. If she could give it up, she would.

It was something Isla had sought out for years under the direction of her father, and it was something that she bitterly knew was impossible. No wonder he wanted to get rid of her so unceremoniously—her brother too. They couldn't wait until she was someone else's problem.

She was hoisted onto River's back and being led down a small trail.

It was a good thing River recognized these paths, as he didn't falter once on the rocky ledges and knew when to jump over a hidden branch. He only stopped every so often to nip at an overgrown strand of grass.

Time passed strangely, as it had the day before. Before she knew it, they were stopped for breakfast—or was it lunch—and Cord passed her one of the biscuits Edith had baked for them. There was no strength in her hand or her heart for it, so she kept her arm limp and allowed it to fall to the ground.

Normally, she would have shrieked when Cord dusted off the biscuit and placed it back with their other rations, but no noise came out. Her throat was on fire, and she allowed him to help her with a drink of water, as her limbs were too weak to hold the bag herself.

They were back on the road again. Everything passed in one giant blur of hooves and dirt and rocks. Her companion spoke at length throughout the day. This was the most she'd heard his voice. Sometimes he spoke to her, mostly it was to compliment River. She only registered a few words about his training days and something about his brother.

Eventually, the sun's final rays were pulled behind the mountains, casting a dark shadow across everything. Cord led her and River off the path to find a suitable place to sleep, apologizing that they'd have to sleep on the ground again—as if he somehow thought she wished to curse another village with her presence instead of sleeping with her grief in the dirt where she belonged.

She didn't know those villagers, not really, and she'd only met Edith two days prior, but the guilt still lay strong as if she'd known them for years. They didn't do anything wrong except welcome her into their village.

The stars were out in force tonight, casting enough light to see most of the path, so they continued further into the woods. Cord was weary of who may be behind them for they'd surely have learned about the destruction by now. It was only a matter of time before they caught up. A part of Isla begged to be caught so the Muratians could end her pain and make her pay for what she had done.

Horace was right. She was a monster.

By the time Cord set up a small camp, her mind was in shambles and her hands wouldn't stop shaking, no matter how ferociously she wrung them out. She shoved them under the layers of her cloak so that he wouldn't see. He couldn't know how close she was to completely losing it.

Cord stood with his hands on his hips and surveyed the small grove with fierce interest. River swung his head and nudged at Isla for scratches, but she couldn't move from her spot beside him.

"I don't think we can make a fire tonight either," Cord said. "Probably won't be able to until we cross the border... I—I hope that's alright?"

She nodded. A warm fire didn't seem as inviting as before. She was afraid of what she would see in those ashes. That anxiety welled up again at the prospect of another night lying with the vision of the light being snuffed out from the villagers' eyes before they could even run.

There was nothing they could have done. It all happened so fast. So quickly. It was all her fault.

At one point she felt a warm hand cupping her face, turning her to look into a pair of gray eyes. She blinked slowly, then there was coldness, and he was across the grove fixing something in his pack.

It was easier to distract her mind when they were moving. There she could focus on the movement of River's muscles beneath her or counting the steps from her companion as he walked alongside them, never once asking to switch, and instead walking on what must be exhausted feet, no matter how much training his ramblings claimed to have had for scenarios like this.

Now they were at a standstill, she had nothing to stop that black cloud from returning like a gale against a weak flower. She was alone against the full chaos of the goddesses that raged within.

Cord had already laid out two makeshift beds as he did last night, so with trembling hands, she attempted to make herself useful and remove River's bridle. She needed to move them before something worse happened. She needed to quell the storm inside.

Even though she'd had numerous steeds at her disposal back in Aurial, she'd never had to tack or untack her own horse and wasn't sure how it was done. The shaking hands didn't help matters either.

When she got caught on a knot, she swore and tugged again. That only made things worse. Everything she did made things worse.

River whinnied and nudged her, as if he could sense her distress. His good ear laid back flat and she wondered how he lost the other. What merciless creature would have done something like that?

The black of River's eyes was the same color as the ash at Acker-slie. The way the horse whined consolingly and rubbed against her reminded her of Edith's kind touch. The same kindness that was trying to help them when Isla—when she...

That well of blackness swirled and expanded and grew out of control. She gasped when her fingertips started to blacken.

No. No. No.

This was like a never-ending nightmare.

Not again.

Twenty-Three
The Captain

After they'd left that poor village behind, he'd closely watched the princess for signs of her powers re-emerging—even if he wasn't an expert at spotting wielders and the signs were different depending on each kind. Still, he kept a sharp eye out for anything out of the ordinary.

After crossing that river the first day, he worried the freezing temperatures would set her off. It didn't. When she refused to eat or drink, he started to get worried that it would make her unstable. Again, nothing happened. Even lack of sleep wasn't a catalyst for an outburst.

When no signs appeared on the second day, he naively thought they were in the clear. That she was fully drained or something.

He was wrong. As he'd been many times since setting foot in these lands.

The first indication that something was off—well, more off than usual—was River's peculiar whine. The surely exhausted creature stomped its feet and shook its head, his ear nearly flattened. He'd never had a horse of his own, but he knew enough about them to know that River was spooked.

He scrambled to his feet with Dark End in hand as if it were an extension of him, ready for whoever found them. A quick scan showed him that the small clearing was empty. No one had come for them.

River was backing up—away from the princess—kicking at the dirt with his hind legs.

It was Isla. Something was wrong with Isla. She stood frozen and stared blankly at her hands.

River's tail swished angrily, bouncing off nearby branches.

The air shifted like the charge felt before a coming storm. This was exactly what he felt back in the village, right before—

The air crackled as an unseen power threatened to pull everything in. Pull him in.

"Stop!"

The scream broke her out of whatever trance she was stuck in. River shook his head and stomped his hooves in protest, shuffling further away from the princess.

Fear infused her eyes as another tremor ran through her hands and up her arm. "I—I can't stop it," she said in a wavering voice he had yet to hear from her—a frightened voice.

Not again. Not today.

Despite all of his better instincts, he closed the distance between them. "What can I do to help?"

Now he could see what had set River off. The tips of her fingers were darkened, just as they were at the village. Curiosity overcame sense and he reached out to touch them but she snatched them away.

He flinched and she recoiled at the sight. So, he tried reaching out again.

"Don't touch me," her voice cracked on the last word and the darkness spread.

He threw his hands up as his heart thundered against the cavern of his chest. "Just calm down."

"Don't tell me to calm down right now," she snapped, her chest heaving in and out. "Don't try to pretend like everything is alright, and that I didn't just murder all those innocent people back there."

"I hardly think they were all innocent," he said in a lame attempt to break the tension. A bead of sweat trickled down his forehead while River nickered.

"Stop it." The blackness spread halfway up her fingers now, making the muscles in his abdomen tighten. His instincts, screaming at him to run were in a heated battle with another part of his mind.

If he had half a semblance of sanity, he would already be running as far away as he could. His last shred of common sense was lost around the time he helped Isla out of her third sinking pit in the forest. There was no running now.

Not if he wanted to get her back safely and fix everything.

"Just get away," she screeched, throwing her hands to her side. The grass around her feet curled. River backed up, swinging his head nervously.

A reckless thought entered his mind, remembering how he was spared in Ackerslie.

Taking care to fight down the oncoming flinch, he stepped closer and grabbed Isla's hands. They felt cold and hot at the same time, like a flaming piece of icestone. Once more, she tried to pull her hands away but he kept his grip tight.

"I don't want to hurt you, too," she said.

"Then don't." He forced calm into his mind even though the quickness of his pulse told a different story. "I don't know much about this stuff but I assume sending yourself into hysterics doesn't help any bit."

Anger flashed in her eyes and she tried to wriggle away. "Don't you dare patronize me right now. I am not a child."

The skin beneath his heated up. Deciding to drop her hands before his own melted off, he nodded at the duo of blankets he had already set out. "I know. I know. Let's sit down and wait for it to pass."

"Sit down? Right now?" she asked in a shaky voice. "Are you insane?"

He scoffed. "What else do you want to do? Do nothing and wait for you to blow half this forest away?"

When he saw the hurt in her face, he winced as if his own words had ricocheted and stung him instead. Right. Bad choice of phrasing. The way his dumb mouth was behaving, he'd be the one solely responsible for his own withering death in these cursed woods.

"I didn't mean that," he said, even though they both knew it was a hastily covered lie. He was there and had seen what she had done to that village. "Just—come sit."

She looked skeptical, but after River snorted, she followed him and sat cross-legged on the ground, muttering under her breath and wringing her hands together as if she thought that would stop the spread.

If only he had paid more attention to the Agicae soldiers and how they controlled their powers. He'd kept his distance from wielders in the past, so this was completely foreign to him.

Talking wasn't helping. Anytime he opened his mouth, it only made things worse, so he clamped it shut. If he was calm and composed, then perhaps she would pick up on that and follow suit.

A bird crowed in the distance, then a second one.

Above them the lights continued their bright sparkle, echoed by streams of blue paint against black skies. He'd never seen the sky colored like that before. It was something that the ancients said happened only on nights when the sky goddess Hierel danced for joy, leaving smears of color in her wake.

Even the heavens mocked him.

After losing himself in the celestial lights for a bit, his eyes found their way back to Isla, who stared with glazed eyes at a point above his shoulder. Her hands had stopped most of their shaking and, unless he was mistaken, the black had retreated to only her fingertips now.

The blue swirls above reflected off her face, highlighting it as easily as the morning sun. Several chunks of hair had fallen out of her long braid, which she hadn't bothered to fix since they left Ackerslie.

Normally, she would have cared about finding the comfiest spot to sit but she made no attempt to move from the rough patch of dirt she had settled in. It was almost as if she craved the discomfort.

There was a lot of familiarity he felt for what she was going through. He wished he could take away her pain. That was something there was no spell for and no cure but time. He'd killed before, but always intentional and usually in defense.

This was something new. If it were him that had caused that much destruction, he'd be a crumpled heap of misery. He had to do something to help.

He'd seen Isla's worst in Ackerslie, perhaps it would help her to know she wasn't the only one responsible for needless death.

Perhaps... perhaps he should tell her.

"Do you know why they call me Captain Cordrai?" He stretched his cramping legs and pulled out a hardened biscuit to chew on. "Back at the camp that is."

A line formed across her forehead and she shifted. "Because that's your name," she said quietly.

His shoulders shook in silent laughter. He almost forgot. "No, it's not."

Isla's eyes widened.

"It's a common nickname they use in the military branches. It's not my name."

Silence as she blankly stared at him. At least she wasn't focused on her hands anymore.

"It's an old saying from the ancient languages. It means coward."

"What?" she squeaked out.

"Why do you think I was assigned to you as punishment? The same punishment I've been trying to claw my way back from for two years now. Commander Skallen said if I was able to finish this last thing without a hitch, then he'd reinstate my badges." He nodded at her. "Obviously, I think we can both agree that's not going to happen now."

It seemed like the goddesses had it out for him. They had to after giving him so many devastating blows in life.

She opened her mouth, as if struggling to formulate a question.

"My father was a captain in the military too. A Pedite conscript thanks to his debts. He used to train us every day, starting with play swords. He always had dreams of grandeur, always wanting something more which he could never achieve. He piled up gambling debts and knew we'd be conscripted to pay off his taxes, so I think all that training was his way of preparing us—or apologizing."

To this day he wasn't certain which one it was, though he could still clearly remember the allure of those betting pits when his father brought him. The temptation was so strong then, even as a child, he couldn't imagine what it was like for his father who always had higher dreams he could never achieve.

"He died when I was ten, but that didn't stop him gambling away everything, including the house. My mother and my younger siblings are on the verge of starvation to this day. I send back everything I can to them."

He eyed the satchel he had discarded by his bedroll and wrapped his arms around his knees. He'd do anything to help his family, to finally clear those debts. His stomach churned.

"I was on assignment with an entire battalion under my command. It was my first big one as a senior captain and if everything pulled off as it was supposed to, I was on track for a promotion to Pedite general. It was an easy job—protecting an important town called Liopen, near the shipping ports and right on the border with Murat. We were there for weeks with nothing exciting happening. Rumors popped up every now and then of a contingent of Muratian soldiers moving through the kingdom. We didn't pay it any attention."

Everything, from the simplest details like how many birds were in the skies, to how many soldiers were under his command—every small, unimportant detail was burned into the recesses of his brain.

"We were supposed to stay in the village as a precaution. They hadn't spotted Muratians in the area for months... and my men were growing bored. So—so was I."

He paused and released a long breath.

"There was a wealthy farmer nearby that needed help clearing his land of some beasts that had settled in and were destroying his crops. They'd already had a harsh double winter, and he couldn't afford to lose the field. He promised good pay and we—*I* needed the money. I figured we could make the trip, less than a day's ride out, and be back before anyone noticed. We—*I* didn't know—at the time—that those rumors of Muratians were more than rumors. There was a group of scouts nearby."

Despite how big her eyes grew, he couldn't bring himself to meet them.

"When we got back the entire town was up in flames. There were no survivors."

He ignored the sharp intake of breath from his companion. At least she tried to hide it behind her hand.

The flames were so high and so hot that it felt as if Insmia herself had set the town ablaze. They couldn't put it out and had to wait until it had burned to complete ash.

"I'm sorry," she said quietly.

"For what?" he asked. "It was my fault."

"You didn't mean to—you didn't kill those villagers. The Muratians did."

He shrugged, hoping the gesture would hide the conflict swirling inside. "But I handed them the town. I may as well have swung the sword myself—and all for what? The promise of some coin." He swallowed. "We—we followed the Muratians responsible past the border. We found them and we slaughtered them."

A pause. Then she said quietly, "They deserved it."

"Nobody deserves a death like that," he said darkly. The Muratians tried to reason with them, tried to plead for their lives, but they were so blinded by rage that they didn't listen to anything they said. He deserved an equal or worse reckoning. Surely Rallion had his name listed somewhere. "There were—dire consequences because of what we did."

Isla nodded, as if she could possibly understand.

He wanted to tell more—explain everything. She deserved to know what he did and what he caused because of that day. So much death that he still hadn't atoned for. And now—*this*. They were stuck in all of this mess because of him. And she deserved to know why.

There was no way they could have known who traveled with that group of Muratians.

A part of him begged to tell her while another pleaded with him not to. The cowardly side won and he said, "War and battle are never kind on innocents. Not all of those Muratians were innocent but some were. Now that we are in the beginning of what may be the largest war since the old High King, you can bet the forest floor will be stained red by the time peace finds us again."

Anything they could do to stave off the future battles—anything—must be done. And that included brokering an alliance with the Koliats and getting Isla back safely, even after all of this. He couldn't stand to see any more innocent blood spilled because of him.

Some dark memory filled her eyes. What he wouldn't give to know what she was thinking right now.

"Don't you worry about me though," he said, ignoring the pang of guilt in his chest. "This is my burden to bear and trust me, I bear it."

Barely.

"How?" she asked with a voice that just carried above the rustling of leaves.

He tilted his head. "What was that?"

"How do you bear it?"

He scratched his chin. Good question. "You just do, somehow. It gets better every day, bit by bit. You never forget though and you do better next time. The way I look at it is that you have two choices: allow the guilt to consume you and become a walking shell of a human, or you can live with it every day, promising to never make the same mistakes again and never abandon your duties, no matter how many times it complains about spiders in her hair."

She let out a small chuckle.

"I know that's probably not the healthiest advice," he said. "But that's all I have. Wallowing in your guilt isn't going to help us out here. So, if you do want to make it home then you need to find a way forward or tell me now if you can't."

He could see the conflict in her mind. It was easier saying the words then following them through, and he knew from experience.

"If you want to make amends then we need to get you home so you can go through with that fancy wedding to the Koliats and help stop this war from growing into something terrible. What happened to Edith and those villagers doesn't have to happen anywhere else. You can stop that. You can make things better."

Her eyes darkened again. After a moment, she nodded.

"It will get easier," he said. "One day, you'll wake up to find the pain is slightly less, and it'll become easier. At least you won't have any visible scars to bear."

He hesitated, then turned around. Before she could protest or he could think it through, he peeled off the blue and gold jacket, and pulled up the back of his shirt. He hadn't shown anyone yet. Hadn't even been with another woman since it happened so as to avoid answering unwanted questions and watching their eyes fill with shame.

The scars he bore were engraved in his flesh as a constant reminder of his failure and shame. He'd never counted them himself, but there were fifty-six lashes. One for each Velotian life lost in that village.

Fifty-six constant reminders of his failures, of what he caused—not that the voices in his head weren't enough to remind him. He was even too weak to take them all in one sitting that it had to be done over several weeks.

The commander told him he was lucky they didn't count the other lives lost because of his actions. There wasn't enough skin on his body for that.

Warm hands touched his back, leaving a prickling sensation across his skin before they were quickly pulled away.

"Sorry," she mumbled when he turned around. Her face dropped as she focused on a jagged rock between them.

He shrugged and pulled his jacket back on. "It's my shame that I have to live with. Everyone knows. It's not a secret... that's why they call me Captain Cordrai around camp."

She stared at him with a gaping mouth. After opening and closing it several times, an array of emotions crossed her face. She finally settled on a cross between indignation and anger. "You mean to say that this entire time I've been calling you by a name that's not even yours like an idiot, and you didn't say anything?"

"Yeah." He chuckled. Anger was good. Anger was easier to control than despair. "You were a terror, and I thought it was hilarious at first. Besides, you didn't even ask, you just assumed. It's a known slang among us commoners, and I guess you haven't spent enough time with us lowly folk to have heard it before."

Her face screwed up, wrinkling her nose in a cute way as she let out a long puff of air. "No. I had not."

"I was going to correct you... eventually. I needed something to humor myself with during those long days in the woods. Then it just became funnier the longer it went on."

"Hilarious," she said dryly, pushing her hair out of her face.

"I hated when they called me that, but when you called me it that first night, thinking it was an actual name and never even bothering to ask, well, you took some of the power out of it. I didn't mind as much."

"I guess you're welcome," she bit out, digging her heel into a patch of dirt.

"Hey, look." He pointed at her hands. "It's all gone now. No need to worry about you accidentally turning me into ashes."

The look on her face told him that she was slightly disappointed about that. It only made him laugh so hard that he spooked River out of his slumber.

The horse grunted his annoyance.

Her face dropped and she held up a hand. "Wait. Wait. Wait. Wait. I don't even know your name then. What is it? Is it something stupid like Girolde or Abernathie or Jim?"

"*Please.*" He sent her a scathing look of disgust. A part of him contemplated not telling her. It would drive her absolutely insane but she had gone through enough the past few days and he was determined to start anew. "It's Rian."

"Rian," she repeated. It felt strange hearing his name coming from her after she'd been calling him that gods-awful nickname. "It's still stupid."

"So is Isla."

She made a face and stuck out her tongue. Very mature for a princess.

He tilted his head as a new burst of blue and green swirled above them. "No more secrets," he said without looking at her. "If we want to get through this together, then we need to work as a team and trust each other."

"A team," Isla repeated. "And we get out of here and do what we can to fix this war."

"Together." He grinned then added quickly, "Except for when things get heated. Then I'm in charge."

She scoffed. "I'm still the higher ranking one here."

"With no years of actual military experience," he tacked on. "Or any basic survival skills besides an uncanny ability to find every hidden root in this forest."

If his words made any impact, she kept it well hidden. She stretched her arms out, flexing each finger and staring as if it were the first time she'd seen them.

"Get some sleep," he said. "I know you were up most of the night and you'll need it tomorrow."

"Speak for yourself," she said, adding a layer of haughtiness into her voice that wavered slightly. It was a good effort, he had to admit. "I wasn't lulled to sleep by the dulcet sounds of your snores as usual, so I know you were up pacing half the night."

"I didn't know you saw me."

"It was hard to ignore that clunky stomping. I thought a pack of wild boars had returned to finish us off... and you *lied* to me about your dumb name. *Rian.* So bland. So—so common."

Any of the prior sympathy he had for her evaporated. He turned his back to her and settled on his side. "Go to bed, Isla."

"You too, *Rian*," she said in a way he knew meant to be insulting but the uncertainty in her voice only made him laugh. A river of blue light continued its dance above as he willed himself to sleep, ignoring that strange unease that settled in his stomach and the terrible guilt that filled him as he remembered the pleas from those Muratians two years ago.

Twenty-Four
The Princess

Isla.

That was the first time he hadn't called her a depraved version of princess or your excellency or that damned alias, Elena. Nobody called her by just her first name unless it was her family and even then, it was rare.

It sounded *strange* coming from him.

Rian.

The embarrassment came back in full force. It was a relief to feel something besides the crippling grief she was drowning in before. She'd been cycling between anger, total despair, irritation, and embarrassment. A modest improvement but it was something.

Now, she was back to being annoyed. How was she supposed to know that wasn't an actual name? That it wasn't *his* name. It would have been obvious to anyone else. Apparently, not to her.

At least he thought it was funny. A great joke at her expense. That's what she got for assuming things.

At least she wasn't the only one keeping things from their little group, even if she understood why he kept his past hidden. She'd done the same. River had proven to be the most trustworthy of them so far, unless he was hiding a pixie or a shrew under his mane. At this point, nothing would surprise her.

At least Rian had a chance of escaping his mistakes. She was cursed with this burden forever. Every time she lost control, others would be at risk. And now, she could never erase the look of the fear on their faces before everything turned to ash.

All because she lost control. Never again. She clenched her fist so tight that her nails nearly broke skin. She had to do better, like he said.

Everything with that soldier made more sense now. Like why he was so bitter about being assigned to her and why he was even more concerned about what would happen if—no, *when* they returned home, as she had to keep correcting herself.

What else wasn't she aware of? She had the impression he'd been holding back on his story, not that she blamed him. Her family started the conscripts hundreds of years ago for those behind on their taxes. A father could sign his babe up the moment he was born, and his debts to the crown would be settled. Debts to her family—her father. The Pedite army was bursting with soldiers conscripted from a young age. It was no wonder why they all hated her, why *he* hated her.

No doubt that washed-up commander would try to place the blame on Rian. Well, she would make certain that didn't happen. If anything, this entire mess was the commander's fault for not setting up enough patrols that day. There was no way this could be turned on him, even given his past.

If it wasn't for Rian, she would have been dead or captured long ago. The only reason she made it this far was because of him and they would know it when she got back. If she had been stranded on her own, the outcome may have been totally different, especially considering the stickiness of that first pit or the ferociousness of that boar on the first night.

All her life she was brought up with a purpose. She thought she was better than others thanks to her father's bloodline, but strip her of her title and swarm of aids, and what was left?

Nothing.

A hand shook her out of her daze. Had she managed to doze off? She cracked an eye and darkness still enveloped everything except for the outline of Rian crouching beside her.

Even in this light, she could envision the frown on his face and the crease lines under his eyes. "I spotted smoke not far from here," he murmured, keeping his voice oddly level. "We need to move before they can catch up."

She bolted upright, all thoughts of drifting back to sleep long evaporated. "What?"

"I think it's a hunting party behind us. I don't know how far back, but I'd rather not wait and find out."

"Do you think they're tracking us?" Her eyes darted around their makeshift camp, checking for signs of a possible intruder hiding.

There were only the two of them and River.

"Yes. Whoever they're with was dumb enough to start a fire, probably some high-up general that can't go without a hot meal." He blew a wayward strand of dark hair out of his eyes. "Idiotic of them. Great for us."

Perhaps they deserved to be caught and payment made to Rallion for what she did. It would set so many things right.

As the dark thoughts swirled in her mind, Rian caught her wrist in a tight grip. He didn't cower from the touch and held tighter when she tried to pull away.

"None of that," he said sharply, holding her gaze. "Not today. We need to make haste."

The look he gave her told her it wasn't worth the argument. She flung off the cloak that she'd been using as a blanket, ignoring that pain in her heart every time she looked at it, and gathered up the small bedroll.

River was already tacked and kicking at the dirt and leaves, still energetic for an old beast. Rian must have been up for a while before he roused her.

It took less than a minute to finish packing up the rest of their *camp*, by the end of which, Rian was hoisting her onto River's saddle and vaulted in place behind her. She was completely useless—more than before—and it should bother her but she didn't have any room in her hardened heart to feel anything else.

They would have to move swiftly and needed to double up for as long as River could handle it. It felt strange having another body pressed up against her. Certainly, her father would never approve, but it was the only option besides capture.

She vaguely remembered riding together while leaving Ackerslie but those hours after everything passed like a haze.

Her escort hesitated, then placed a hand on her hip to reach around to grab the reins.

"You ready?" he asked in a rough voice, as if he had just woken even though she knew he'd been up for hours.

All that she could do was gulp and nod, hoping that was enough.

With an encouraging word to River and a tug of his reins, they were off. The sound of hooves against dirt and rocks echoed into the night—hopefully not too loud.

Isla barely allowed herself to breathe as they were whisked away. Spiky trees blurred by, followed by brightly flowered bushes that shone in the starlight, then tall grass that tickled her legs, and a cobbled road River happily trotted through.

At one point, he directed River towards a running stream barely two hands deep. It curled along the path, and Rian said it would help cover their tracks. He apologized every time a splash of water hit them, but Isla didn't mind. The cold water jolted her back whenever her thoughts strayed too far.

River kept up a brief canter, dipping in and out of the water every few minutes. It wasn't until the sun's rays reached from beyond the horizon that the horse finally slowed to barely a trot.

A hand tapped her side and she jumped. "I think we're in the clear for now, and River needs a break when we can find a covered spot." He leaned back and cracked his neck, sending shivers down her spine. "I need a break too."

"Is he okay?" she asked, worry flooding her when the horse slipped on a loose rock.

"He's perfect." Rian thumped River's side. "He's doing great so far, considering——"

"Considering we stole him," she said darkly. "From those villagers after I—I—"

Those thoughts threatened to consume her once again. To drown her whole self out completely and wholly and take over everything that she was and had ever been.

"Hey!"

A pair of strong hands shook her, shaking her away from the turmoil.

"Not today, remember?" he said in even tones. "Let's not destroy anything until we run into some Muratians, okay?"

Isla's hands shook when she pulled them away from the pummel, afraid to touch anything. "O–okay," she murmured, clutching her hands to her chest as if that could ground her somehow—save her.

"You got this," he said. His voice held more conviction than she'd felt in years.

For as long as she could remember, she was always taught to hide this power, to restrict any outbursts. The last thing her father wanted was word getting out that she was a wielder. A dangerous one at that.

A powerful one, no matter how he tried to force it out of her.

If anyone other than their family had found out, she shuddered to think of what her father would do to them... and yet Rian was one of the first to see the full destruction of her curse and not shy away. He hadn't abandoned her at the first opportunity, like she expected that first night. He somehow seemed even more determined to finish out their journey together.

The determination to right his name must be powerful, given his own terrible truth. If something happened to her, then Isla was certain her father would make his family pay, if he hadn't already. Her father was not a forgiving man and did not take well to threats against himself or his legacy. Isla was a part of that legacy, whether or not either of them wanted to admit it.

The shaking stopped and the cold left her hands. Rian, thankfully, didn't comment on it.

She grabbed the saddle's pommel gingerly and clung to it as if it could stop anything bad from happening, focusing on the crow's morning song and the way the tendrils of light stretched ahead of them. Warm streams of gold and pink filled the sky as the sun burst over the horizon.

It warmed her.

It soothed her.

She always loved the feel of the sun against her skin and would sneak out hours before her maids woke just to wait on the castle ledge for a chance to catch those glowing beams that came with the first morning's rising.

She closed her eyes and tilted her head back as far as it would go. The rays sunk into her skin and began soothing her soul in a rare moment of peace. There was nothing that calmed her better.

Rian cleared his throat.

It took her a minute to realize that she had rested her head against something warm and solid.

It was something warm and solid that wiggled beneath her.

Right. She jumped and shifted forward so that she barely touched him. She was not alone on River today. With her thoughts being so scattered, it had slipped her mind.

"Sorry," she mumbled.

If she had a mirror, she was certain her face would resemble a burning coal. It was a good thing she was facing away from him too.

Rian grunted a response and shifted behind her, increasing the distance they were separated. Was he that uncomfortable being close to her after what he'd seen in Ackerslie? She didn't blame him. Just like she wouldn't blame him if he eventually ditched her in the middle of these gods-forsakened lands.

River dipped back into the water, which kissed her ankles and grew much faster. Soon they met a juncture and their small stream poured into a larger river. There was still no sign of their pursuers.

They came upon a bridge large enough for wagons to pass when Rian pulled the reins to stop River.

"What?" she asked.

"Let's take that break and get him some water," he said, thumping the horse's side. He released the grip around her waist and leaned back, head craning from side to side.

Did he expect some troll to be lurking under the bridge? Those creatures died out decades ago after being hunted to extinction. It was only those trailing behind they had to worry about.

Rian edged River up on the ledge of the stream, then jumped onto the grassy bank before Isla could blink. He wrapped River's reins around the pommel and held out a hand to help her dismount.

Remembering what happened with the sunrise brought that blasted blush back to her face, so she turned and fumbled her way down the other side, using the horse as a barrier. She patted River's chestnut side and murmured a few words of appreciation, staying hidden until she was certain her face had returned to a normal color.

Summoning all the years of training her father made her go through, she lifted her chin, put on the most indifferent expression she could muster——hoping that it was enough to even convince herself that she had it all together——and stepped around River's narrow head.

When Rian's eyes met hers, a strange expression filled his face. Feeling unnecessarily uncomfortable, Isla brushed past him back to the water's edge and scooped a handful of fresh water. She was shocked at how cold it was against her hot skin, despite being consistently sprayed by it on the journey. She allowed the icy drops to slip through the gaps in her fingers.

"This water is fed from one of the glaciers over there." Rian pointed towards the snow-capped mountain line in the distance. "It's freezing, but fresh."

She turned to stare at him, then quickly remembered herself and dipped her hand back in, relishing the cold against her skin.

After letting the water fall through her fingers again and again, she brought a clear scoop to her mouth, imagining it was a crystal chalice and she was back home. Rian was right. The water tasted better than anything she'd drank before. She pushed back the sleeves of her cloak and rinsed as much of her arms she could reach before dabbing at her neck.

She froze when she realized that Rian was still watching her, one eye half-shut to block out the sun. "What is it?" she asked sharply.

He rubbed the back of his neck. "We can't stay too long."

"I know that." She splashed ice water on her face once more, while River lapped up a drink beside her. It was soothing for her frazzled nerves, and she had no desire to leave anytime soon.

Rian's head snapped to the side, like a predator catching scent of an injured hare.

"What do you—"

Before she could finish, she was pulled into the water, sputtering as she was half-dragged through the waist-deep flow. River followed behind obediently. She grumbled when her toe hid a sharp rock and realized he was ushering them under the shadows of the bridge. They stopped in the darkness of its shadow, completely drenched and kneeling in the glacial water.

Rian's hand snaked around her waist and the other rested on the bridge of River's nose, keeping the beast calm, though the horse looked to be enjoying his impromptu dip in the water. Isla was less thrilled.

"Quiet," he whispered, though the warning was hardly needed. The grip on her side was almost painful, but he didn't let go.

There was no room for embarrassment as the thunder of hooves against stone was now clear to her untrained ears. As it grew louder it sounded like at least a dozen horses, with even more footsteps accompanying. Boots met wood and echoed against the trill of the water.

Rian's hand twitched against her skin. She linked her fingers through his to keep them both calm.

Her heart beat frantically against its cage with each new footstep echoing overhead. She barely allowed the breath to escape her lips, fearful they would hear it. One glance up showed that Rian had similar worries. His dark brows were knotted together and he had his head cocked to the side, listening closely.

How did they catch up so soon?

Stupid question. They were Muratians. They knew these lands and must have found easier terrain to pass through. How they got here didn't matter. All that mattered was they had run out of places to hide.

River shifted in the water but kept silent. Rian pressed his forehead against his.

A voice icier than the water they were standing in shouted, "Keep moving, or I'll have your heads."

Isla recognized it as the Muratian wielder who ambushed her back at the camp. It nearly made the blood in her veins freeze.

"Are you certain they went this way?" a male voice drawled. It sent the wet hair on her arms on edge and even River snorted in protest before Rian quieted him.

"Yes," the wielder said happily. "Those villagers were quite talkative by the time I was through with them."

A shudder ran over her body.

No. A tremor. Not now.

The hand linked in hers tightened. She focused on that pressure. On the small tendrils of warmth that seemingly came from his presence.

Losing control would turn disastrous.

"I'm surprised they weren't more willing given what she did," the male said, authority lining his tones. "Quite destructive. Very powerful."

The thought of those poor villagers made her weak. She would have lost her balance and slipped further into the stream if it weren't for the grip now fully supporting her weight.

"We'll find her," the woman said, before shouting another threat at a group to hurry. Minutes passed while voices overhead continued to shout and the sound of carts scraped by.

They waited long after the last boot dragged against stone and the last hoof met gravel. By then Isla was shaking, both from nerves and the cutting temperature. So was Rian.

"Are you good?" he whispered. His arm slid down her waist, finally releasing his grip. He didn't mean the cold.

A finger trailed along the side of her cheek, bringing warmth back into it.

She nodded, lifting a hand to show him the shaking was from the water only. She managed to keep the darkness at bay.

They were both silent as he handed her River's reins and pulled himself onto the riverbank. He paused. Nothing happened so he held out a hand and helped her and River out of the water.

Once they were firmly on the moist ledge, he wrung out his Muratian cloak and exchanged a dark look with Isla. They were both thinking the same.

The path ahead was no longer viable. They'd once again have to continue their journey through the Black Forests of Murat—the same part that Edith once warned her against, as the southern section was known to carry dangerous perils they had yet to see.

There was no choice. They had run out of options.

Twenty-Five

Mira

The walk back from the cavern was the most uncomfortable she'd felt since coming down here. Devlin made no effort to grab her hand as she kept it tucked in close. He made multiple attempts at small talk, but Mira refused to budge, no matter how her stupid heart ached for it.

Yes, he had saved her worthless life, but then turned around seconds later to insult her and the other miners. What was she supposed to think of him after that?

When he brought her back to the pit stating that she had served her punishment, she didn't look over at him twice and picked up her shovel, attacking the mountain with venom until she was dismissed to catch up with the others. B must have gotten out early. Hopefully, her shoulder wasn't acting up again.

She dodged Crag and the Wasp and lined up for a pitiful dinner ration they scraped the bottom of the pot for, which she scarfed down before heading to the sleeping quarters. Beretta was already sitting along their two bedrolls in their usual spot tucked away in the corner, far away from the others. It was the only way they could get a peaceful sleep.

A heavy breath released from her chest. Finally, a face that she was happy to see. A part of her was worried when she didn't see B in the food lines, but maybe she'd had enough of the other miners.

"You will not believe the day I've had," Mira said, kicking aside a dirty rag that must have been a worker's shirt at some point. She undid the knotted braid Beretta had helped weave into her hair that morning and ran her hands through the greasy tresses.

Beretta stared at something in her lap.

"I hate everybody and everything," Mira added. She threw herself onto the floor in front of her friend and sat cross-legged. "Remind me to stay clear of the guards from now on. *All* of them."

A mirthless laugh bubbled up from Beretta's chest.

Mira tilted her head so she could see her friend's face. "What's wrong, B?"

Beretta dragged her eyes to meet hers "You were gone so long that I thought I'd get your bed ready since you'd probably be exhausted when you got back."

"Thanks, I—"

"I even saved some of my rations since I wasn't sure if there'd be any left for you. I was worried you weren't eating enough lately."

Beretta leaned over and folded back the blanket to reveal an assortment of buns, dried meats, and even a crusty piece of smoked cheese that had a chunk out of it. Mira had planned on finishing it tonight when everyone was asleep.

The blood in her veins turned to ice, freezing her in place. "I can explain—"

"Can you?" Mira winced at the heat in her friend's voice. "*Can* you?"

"I was planning on—"

Beretta threw the cheese against the side of the wall where it broke into pieces. "So, it's not the first time then. Here I've been, scrimping and saving to make sure you're taken care of. I share my leftovers with you. I've picked up the slack when you were too slow so you wouldn't get in trouble. I've given you my entire meal when you were sick all so that you could get through the next shift in one piece and you've been hiding *this* from me."

"You know that's not true. I didn't mean—"

"I've had your back since you got here and made sure nobody touched you. I did everything for you because I thought we were friends. Clearly, it's all one-sided. How long has he been sneaking you extra food?"

Mira clamped her mouth shut.

There was no answer she could give that could explain her selfishness. She didn't know why she hid it from B. She'd shared so much with her friend, but this—a selfish part of her had wanted to keep what happened between her and Devlin between the two of them. If B knew about the food he snuck her, that would have led to more questions.

Questions that Mira didn't want to answer at the time.

After what he'd said in that cavern, she could care less about Private Devlin and keeping his stupid secrets. She'd tell the entire guard at this point.

"You know he's probably doing all this just to get into your pants," her friend bit out. Strands of fiery red hair cascaded around her face as she vaulted to her feet.

"Please, B."

"Or has he already fucked you?" Her eyes trailed the length of Mira, as if trying to see where he'd laid hands on her. "I didn't know you were that desperate for a nice meal."

"Like you?" The words left her mouth before she could stop herself. Beretta had always been open about using the guards to get extra benefits—benefits she usually shared with Mira. "I didn't mean it," she added quickly. "Not like that."

Beretta's eyes flashed dangerously. "Everything I have done has been for you—*for us*." She threw a hardened biscuit at Mira. It bounced off her shoulder and fell dully to the ground. "I can't believe I thought we were friends."

"We are," Mira said, stepping closer and trying to grab her friend's hands but B tucked them behind her back. "I was being stupid. I wasn't thinking. But it doesn't matter now as it's—"

"You aren't the first, you know," Beretta said, her voice ice cold now. Almost unrecognizable. "The guards are always looking to get one of us off into a dark corner with the promises of a few paltry pieces of bread. Did he take you down one of the old shafts to a dark cave where it was just the two of you? Is that where he took you? Did he tell you that you were *special*?"

"It's not—he hasn't—I've been trying to help him. You know that."

Beretta snorted. "That's rich. *You don't even know him.*" She grabbed a stale roll and lifted her arm to throw it. She paused, then shoved it at Mira. "Here, you obviously need it more than me. I guess it's worth more to you."

"Wait, B." She grabbed Beretta's shoulder when she passed. If only she had the chance to explain.

Beretta winced and pulled her arm away.

Right. Her injury.

Her cold eyes traveled from Mira's toes all the way to her face as if seeing her friend for the first time. She shook her head. "I'm going to find someplace else to sleep tonight. I can't stand the sight of you."

Mira's heart plummeted.

Before she could mumble another inexcusable apology, Beretta had already turned on her heel.

This couldn't be happening.

If Beretta knew the full truth of why she hid those snacks, then maybe she'd understand... understand that she was trying to protect her. To keep her out of it, in case things turned bad.

A nagging part of her brain reminded her that she could have found a way to share her treats with Beretta without revealing the entire truth. If she really wanted to, she'd have found a way around her promise to Devlin.

She risked it all, and for what? A pretty smile from him or a stale biscuit as a feeble attempt at buying her silence. So stupid. How unbelievably stupid she had been acting. How terrible of a friend she had been.

A dark wave slowly filled her. The guilt made her queasy. It made her angry.

Godsdamnit.

Mira kicked a large rock, then screamed when it caught her toe.

"Rocks got you?" a raspy voice called out, making her jump.

She thought she was alone. Nobody ever came to their little corner and the last person she expected or wanted to see was the Wasp. Yet there he was leaning against the entrance with his arms crossed.

He watched her hungrily. "You're difficult to find on your own. Where's your little friend?"

She swallowed hard and straightened her shoulders, putting on a falsely confident front. Today really was shaping out to be the worst day yet. "Beretta went to get us some water. I expect she'll be back soon."

"Will she?" He scanned her through half-lidded eyes. Eyes that were glazed with a fiery hatred that burned solely for her. Nothing she did ever made that loathing fade.

"Yes," Mira replied in a hollow voice. She tried to edge around the room. There was a small space left in the opening that she could get through if she was quick enough.

He stepped towards her, nostrils flaring.

Mira hurled herself at the entrance but the Wasp was too fast. He grabbed her around the waist and threw her into the wall. The back of her head made contact and bright spots formed all over her vision.

She was yanked to her feet and he kept a tight grip on her arm.

"That's not what it sounded like to me." His nails dug painfully into her skin. "I think you're lying. I think she left you all alone. Abandoned you. And that's not a very good *friend*, would you say?"

Mira struggled against his grip. "Let me go or the guards will see. We'll both get a lashing."

"I don't care about the lashes, you stupid girl." Venom laced his voice but it was nothing compared to the pure loathing in his eyes. It was beyond reasoning.

She tugged her arm again but it could not escape his cold grip. "Well, I do, so you'll have to excuse me."

"I don't take orders from you," he spat. "Don't you ever try to order me around, you little—aargh."

Mira flung her free arm crazily and her nails took a chunk of skin out of his cheek.

He tossed her to the ground, kicking up dust and scattering the morsels of food that she'd hidden from Beretta.

A painful kick landed against her side, nearly tearing her in two. It was followed by another, then another.

The last thing she remembered was him shouting at her while the pointy end of a rusty pickaxe hurtled toward her head. She threw her hands up and screamed.

Darkness burst and consumed everything.

Twenty-Six
The Captain

When this was over, he vowed to never set foot in a forest again.

The twisted woods laid ahead, stretching halfway into the heavens and just as far to either side. The thick canopy blocked all remnants of sun. Darkness loomed heavy within, urging them to attempt another way.

There was no other way.

This was the safest—and quickest option—as he had to constantly remind himself. Unless they wanted to walk headfirst into a full battalion of Muratian soldiers. The same ones, according to Isla, who ambushed her outside the encampment in the first place. There was no mistaking why they were here and who they were after.

The death of the Muratian prince was not easily forgivable, and the Muratians wanted a taste of justice. That must be why they pursued Isla and him so relentlessly. Why they set up that ambush in the first place.

So, the forest it was.

The thought of spending days traipsing through these dreadful woods made his stomach queasy and his lungs heavy. Catching up with the Muratians wasn't something he wanted to entertain.

They'd already removed River's saddle and tack. Isla was hopeful that the horse would continue with them, but he refused to go near the woods and started bucking as soon as they got close to the forest edge. Smart beast. He was smarter than them.

It was a shame, Isla had said, as she'd grown fond of his comforting presence which she'd joked was better than Rian's morose attitude.

Rian allowed the jibe as it was the first attempt she'd made at humor since Ackerslie. Plus, it was a fair point. River was the only one he spoke with that first day when she refused to acknowledge him. At least River had listened to the stories that wouldn't stop flowing from his lips in an attempt at filling the awkward silence.

So, they both said a quick goodbye to their one-eared companion. Isla gave him an extra long hug around the neck before setting him off, wiping her eyes from a dusting of dirt—or so she claimed. Hopefully, the horse wouldn't cross a sharp-clawed beast while on its own. Rian didn't dare voice his worries to Isla though. They had enough to worry about as they took their first steps into the heart of the Black Forest.

A light fog had settled upon the ground, fully covering the forest floor from sight. Knowing Isla's penchant for finding wayward roots, the fresh misting would make this a difficult journey.

As thick clouds drifted past, he instinctively reached for her hand—only to keep her from wandering off. Days ago, she would have shuddered at the contact, as would he. This time she didn't pull away and allowed him to lead her effortlessly. Perhaps the connection brought her the same spark of comfort.

Their first steps taken were timid. He tested the ground with a toe before putting his full weight on it. Once they realized the mossy ground was nothing more than that, and the spindly trees were harmless, they both relaxed and walked with purpose.

A weight lifted off his chest when the fog lightened after fifty feet and the sounds of distant croaking toads returned to the air.

Perhaps those villagers were wrong about this part of the forest and their warnings based on superstition rather than fact. He doubted any of them had been to this part in ages.

Once more, he didn't voice his thoughts to Isla, as that would only bring up the painful memories she was struggling to push down. At least the tremors fully disappeared after he threw her in the river. Perhaps the cold or the threat of capture shocked them out of her. It certainly quieted any complaints from his companion.

After a few minutes he realized he still had her hand in a tight grip. He dropped it as if it were a burning log and stuffed his hands in his pockets. Isla scoffed but he didn't dare turn to see her face.

As they lost sight of the forest edge and the light dimmed, a chill settled in his bones. It was as if the sun rested even though he knew it to be floating high beyond the thick canopy above them. It didn't help that they were both still soaked from their jaunt in the river. Nightfall would be rough without the option to start a fire again.

All they could do was continue on and pray those soldiers didn't turn around too quickly once they realized their prey was not on the road ahead. Would they know to look to the forests, or would they try another route? Rian tried his best to cover their tracks but there were other ways to find a person if the Muratians had the right kind of wielder with them. He prayed to the goddess that they didn't.

At least this part of the forest was thick and dark. It would be easy for her to hide if it came to it. He'd had years of training in the military, but that wouldn't help him against dozens of Murat's best soldiers.

A small part of his brain nudged him, reminding him of the important fact he didn't dare speak out loud. Isla could handle them all with one thought if she wanted to... if she even knew how to do that again. He wouldn't ask her. He saw the way it tore her up, and how easily she lost control. They may not get as lucky next time—*he* may not get as lucky.

They hadn't talked about it since Ackerslie, not directly. There were so many questions dancing around his head but he didn't know how to ask without upsetting her.

Did the king know?

Stupid question. Obviously, her own father would have known. Right?

Could she only turn things into deadly ash or what else could she do? *How* did she do it?

Ashfeeder.

That's what they used to call those who wielded that kind of power. What did it mean?

There were so many other things he wanted to know—when it was time. If it ever got to that. He nearly had to remind himself that once they made it out of these forests, they would be safe in Velotian lands and she'd be returned to the care of Commander Skallen.

He prayed to the goddess that he'd somehow be rewarded for returning the princess safely and could send some of that money back to his family. If not, he had other options. He clutched the satchel at his side closely. Surely, they'd see what trouble he went through to make things right. They had to.

They trudged through the forest, both similarly lost deep in their own minds. The silence wasn't as maddening as it was before. It was calming. Settling even.

He and Horace had spoken at length about the mosses that grew on the trees in the Muratian forests. Black grew on the western side, red on the east. That was how he knew which direction to head, even without the sun to help them.

At least that man gave him one true piece of information, even if he did betray them. In the initial heat of his betrayal, Rian wished he had killed Horace. But the Muratian was doing what he thought was right and protecting those he loved. And what good did that get him?

He'd now have to live with that guilt for years. Maybe less—if what was said about the Muratians was true, then those villagers would pay for allowing the princess to slip through.

Something snapped, echoing through the dark forest.

He grabbed Isla around the shoulders and pulled her against him. The pattering of her heart pounded against his breast pocket.

Neither spoke for a moment, and the sound didn't happen again. Perhaps it was merely a bird or some other critter?

He released his grip and nodded to continue. While it may have been merely the movements of the forest, Rian couldn't shake the idea that something watched them. It was as if the forest itself was alive and knew they walked paths they didn't belong in.

Both he and Isla had a mutual, unspoken agreement not to stop for a break until absolutely necessary. So, they walked on and on, keeping a calm, steady pace.

It must have been about half past midday when Isla first broke the comfortable silence. They'd been traveling for hours without any creeping noises or a single person tripping.

That must be a new record.

"What are your plans once this whole thing is complete?" she asked, stepping over a vermin mound without so much as a complaint. "After we get to Bluemoon Bay, and your wretched assignment is finally over?"

"Once our assignment is finished..." He pulled on his bottom lip. "When it's over, we were supposed to get leave to visit our families. That is, if I'm still in the corps. If not, then permanent leave or the stocks."

"You will be fine," she said confidently.

"And for you?" he asked, not sure what was bordering on intrusive questioning or not. He held a hand to help her over a downed oak that must have easily towered thirty feet high at one point. "Time for that fancy feast and the marriage scars you've been dreaming of?"

He could only imagine the elaborate party the Koliats, already known for their ostentatiousness, would put on. It'd be enough to clear his family debts in one swipe—the whole village's debts at that point.

"Hmm," she said slowly, hopping over the trunk with his aid and landing confidently on the moss below. "I guess it would be time for that. I haven't allowed myself to think that far ahead, even before we got marooned here."

The way she spoke about her future nuptials was not the way one would expect a cheerful bride to. It didn't surprise him given the way these royals bartered their offspring as if they were bargaining chips at the betting pits.

The toe of his boot caught on a root and Isla smirked. The closest she'd come to a smile in days. They both froze when the wind picked up, carrying hints of a creature's howl.

"It's likely far away," Rian whispered, praying to the goddess it was true.

Isla rubbed her hands together. "Probably," she murmured.

He kicked away the fossilized shell of a dead crustacean that must have climbed its way here years ago. "Looks like neither of us are exactly thrilled to find out what is waiting for us."

"It would seem not," she said moodily. "But duty calls, as it always does."

"Always," he repeated, catching her eye for the briefest of moments before they both looked away.

And with that they continued the rest of their journey in that familiar silence.

By the time night swept through, it was impossible to see the terrain beneath their feet or what lay ahead. When Isla tripped over a hidden vine that she swore had moved and scraped the palm of her hand, Rian decided they would call it a night before one of them walked off an unseen cliff.

"Are you certain we've gone far enough?" she asked as he wrapped her bloody hand in a torn piece of cloth. Even in the dark, the worry in her brown eyes was obvious. It made the lining of his stomach turn over.

He sat across from her on what remained of a downed redwood tree, which was somehow annoyingly damp like the rest of him. "It's too dangerous, and I don't want to risk any serious injuries.

Besides..." A smile filled his face. "I know how much you need your beauty rest, Your Resplendent Highness." He released her wrapped hand. "There, all done."

"Ha. Ha." Her voice was laced with exhausted sarcasm. She settled next to him and took a dried piece of meat without complaint. "First things first. When we get back, I don't care who's there or what they want me to do, we're both going to have the biggest and most delicious feast they can muster with whatever supplies our retrieval party has on hand. And nobody is going to stop us."

"I like that plan." As if on cue, his stomach growled. "Pastries too?"

"Absolutely. I'm certain they can pull something together, even in the middle of a military camp."

"Hells," he said. "I'd even personally go find a baker from a nearby town for you."

"And then," she continued wistfully, eyes staring ahead as if she could see it in front of her. "We're going to sleep in the most comfortable beds, in a heated tent, for hours past what is socially acceptable."

"Meh." He shrugged his shoulders. "Soft beds are overrated. I'm doubtful the commander will afford me anything besides a plain tent. And I can guarantee I'll be up early preparing for travel with the other Pedites. *But* I'd still take my travel cot in the Pedite quarters over this soggy moss."

Isla chuckled, her laughter breaking through the dampness of the gloomy forest. "At this point, seeping in a travel cot sounds wonderful."

He shrugged. "You can still take the nice bed, I don't mind. You deserve it after everything."

"Very generous of you." A shudder ran through her body.

He froze and watched her closely, worried she was about to have another *attack*. "What is it?"

"Nothing," she said, refusing to meet his eyes. "Just a breeze."

But no branches had swayed and not a single leaf had so much as crinkled since they sat down. He crouched in front of her and grabbed her hands, which were still ice cold. That cloak of hers wasn't drying as quickly as his Muratian uniform.

He swore. The river. "You should have said something."

She rubbed her arms vigorously as if that could dry her damp clothes in seconds. "Nothing you could have done."

"Take that cloak off for starters," he scolded. He helped peel off her wet outer layer and hooked it on a nearby branch. It should dry by morning. The rest of her travel leathers that she had worn since the beginning were still damp, but not as bad as that blasted cloak. "We don't have any other clothes, but you can take both blankets tonight."

"Don't be ridiculous," she said as he unfurled the bundle of cloth they managed to accumulate. "Then you'll freeze."

"I'm not the precious cargo, remember? I'm tougher than I look."

They'd gone through colder nights during training exercises when he first joined the Pedites. They were sent out for two weeks with no supplies or jackets in the middle of the coldest season and were somehow expected to survive on their own. Freya and her sister were experts at making a fire out of nothing and Malin built them a sturdy shelter that managed to keep out the snow and rain that plagued them.

If he could survive that, a chilly night in the forest would be nothing.

Isla's brows knitted together. "Are you certain?"

"Absolutely." He tossed her the two blankets. "Get some rest. When it's light—lighter—we can set out again."

A hint of a smile lit her face and she nodded.

They quickly set up a spot in between two roots that would serve as the perfect pillow. He leaned against the root opposite her—close enough for their feet to meet in the middle—pulled his jacket in tight, and watched as she curled up under the blankets.

He tucked his hands under his armpits so they wouldn't lose their warmth. At least it wasn't snowing or anything—though he didn't want to press his luck with Slin by voicing those thoughts out loud. Normally, he would have kicked his boots off by this point to allow his feet to breathe, but he wanted to preserve as much heat as possible.

Isla had wrapped both blankets tight around herself, covering every inch up to her neck. After a minute the shivers came back, despite her poor attempts to hide them.

Rian sighed. Loudly.

"I can't help it," she whined as another series of shakes rolled over her body. "You know I'm not built for the cold like some people."

"I know." He weighed their options carefully, considering this wasn't a fellow soldier that he was camped with but a princess of Velotia, the second in line to the throne, and his current charge.

A frozen princess would get him nowhere.

Against his better judgment, he tapped the spot beside him. "Come here."

"*Excuse me?*" Her head shot up.

"You're going to either freeze to death, which will result in my head being removed from its spot, or you'll catch sick, which will turn you into an even more insufferable travel partner than you began as, and then I'm going to have to leave your whiney royal bottom behind, which will still result in loss of head for me."

"I am *not* sleeping with you," she grit out. Despite the cold, a faint flush filled her cheeks.

"Trust me. I'm just as disturbed about this arrangement, but seeing as I'd rather keep us all alive, *come here.*" He pointed beside him. "It's just to make it through the night."

She huffed. "Fine. Fine." She gathered up the blankets and shuffled over on her knees. "But don't you dare try anything funny, soldier, or I'll make sure the commander sends you om assignment to the wastelands for years."

He scoffed. "Like I'd be stupid enough. If anything, I'm the one putting myself at risk here, Your Superior Royal Highness."

When she scooted into place next to him, he lowered himself into a more comfortable position so she could fit.

Rian laid on his back and she curled into his side, resting her head tentatively on his chest. He tossed the blankets around them, making sure to fully cover her first. He already felt more than warm enough at this point.

From this close he could trace every freckle that covered her nose and could count every fluttering eyelash. He instinctively went to wrap his arms around her and froze.

"What?" She lifted her head up and her features were flooded with confusion.

"I swear to Rallion, Isla, if you tell anyone about this, *I'm* dead. Seriously."

"I know. I know." She rested her head back down and let out a sigh, squirming until she seemed to find a suitable spot. Her hands laid on his chest, before she snatched them away and tucked them into herself. "I won't breathe a word of it to anyone. It's just to get through the night."

He allowed his arms to wrap around her—in the name of warmth. Instant heat spread through his body and he focused on the dark canopy above them, trying to trace out the shapes of the tree branches in his mind while ignoring that slight flutter that started up in his heart every time a hot breath tickled his neck. He wanted to touch that brown hair, free from its braid and splayed across his chest, but kept his hands frozen in place.

In a voice barely above a whisper, he repeated, "To get through the night."

Twenty-Seven
Prince Edmund of Velotia

Edmund stormed out of the idiotic general's tent, nearly giving a poor aid a heart attack and sending several young captains scrambling away from their game of dice. He glared at the gamblers. Clearly, everyone in this camp had too much spare time and weren't focused solely on the rescue efforts like he was. He doubted that the general made any efforts to stop them. If anything, he probably encouraged them.

If Edmund wasn't fearful of his father's wrath after ignoring his summons, he had half a mind to write him and request a new battalion instead of this lot. He wasn't supposed to be out here, it's not like his father would willingly send him any supplies or reinforcements.

Alas, he was stuck with this deplorable group of soldiers, lest he risk alerting his father to his whereabouts.

Just as they were stuck with him. It was hard to tell which side was more annoyed by the fact.

Being this close to the border was risky. The general spoke of crossing over past the Black Forests if they could get another good reading on Isla's location like they had the other day. It was the first time they'd had any spark of hope.

The Agicae general was confused why they were having a hard time getting a reading on her, and the only conclusion he had was that something else must be interfering with the search.

Idiot. Edmund wanted to rip off his stupid sword and flame badge and banish him someplace frigid.

Obviously there was a major interference as the Muratians were likely working just as hard to hide her as Edmund and the others were at finding her. Perhaps that Pedite general was correct after all. He did have more experience than any of them in those forests.

Edmund wasn't ready to concede that perhaps *the general* was correct, and that he alone knew the best way to find her. He refused to listen to that soldier since the day they saw the comet.

A dramatic sigh came from behind him, which he ignored.

When an annoying hand clapped the back of his shoulder, Edmund closed his eyes and sent a prayer to the goddesses—any of them that could help in this moment. He was answered with silence.

"Tough batch," Prince Brenner said in that deep voice Edmund had grown to hate. "But I see their reasoning. We can send a small group into Murat, but two princes would create a new target altogether. It's best to stay back. Could you imagine what would happen if we were caught?"

Edmund rubbed his shoulder, the injury from that damned icewielder still refused to leave him. He focused on the tree line ahead. Everything this prince said grated on his nerves, especially when he was making sense.

"There are reports that one of the Muratian princes was near the borderlands past the mountain range, but nothing we can do about that. Let your general and his men handle it."

To an outsider, it may have seemed as if the Velotian prince was deep in concentration. Inside, Edmund was seething.

The mere suggestion that he should stay behind while a group of ingrates led the efforts to rescue his sister was more than laughable.

"We should meet up with the main camp we left behind. I have a cook who makes the best stewed fowl, and several ladies who can be at our disposal at the snap of a finger."

What a ridiculous proposal. He couldn't formulate a proper response. Brenner knew he had a wife. Edmund had the ceremony scars to prove it—albeit he hadn't seen his wife in months and they barely tolerated each other. The audacity of his suggestion still rang true.

With a chuckle, the prince clapped his shoulder again and returned to his tents. Edmund curled his fists into a ball, crushing the newest letter from Aurial that had several depictive threats from his father.

The Pedite general was right. They'd have to send a group into Murat—a small group. And Edmund had every intention of allowing Prince Brenner to return to terrorize the Koliat camp a day's ride away.

Edmund knew what he had to do.

Hours later as the small group that was hand-picked by himself and the general packed up to leave, Edmund had already donned his newly acquired silver and black cloak, taking great care to obscure his face as much as possible.

They had just enough horses for the small contingent, which was perfect as they'd need to travel light and fast—especially if a quick exit was required.

Before he could finish adding a roughly packed bag of supplies that he thought would be helpful, something grabbed his arm and threw him against the side of a spotted horse, who neighed in protest.

Edmund found himself being stared down by that cursed Pedite soldier, Freya, who the general insisted would accompany him on their journey.

"What do you think you're doing?" she hissed.

Edmund opened his mouth to remind her who she was speaking to but stopped himself before the words ever left. His mouth hung open as he struggled to come up with a good excuse for why he was dressed in an Agicae uniform and about to mount this warhorse.

"You cannot be serious," Freya said, staring as if he'd been possessed by the whim of the trickster goddess. Her eyes lingered on the sword and flame badge pinned to the shoulder of his cloak. "I'm taking you to the general."

"I am serious," Edmund said, refusing to wither under the glaring look she was giving him. "And if you think about alerting your general, I'll cancel everything."

"Don't be stupid. Remember the ice wielder? You'll get in the way, just like the attack on the camp."

"I won't," Edmund said confidently. "None of you are going without me. I'll stop this entire operation if you out me."

Freya released the painful grip on his arm and backed away, rubbing her temple and swearing under her breath. Her usual looped braids were pinned tightly against the top of her head.

"Nobody is to know you travel with us until our return." He nodded. "I swear upon Rallion's deathful gaze, *my prince*, if you get in the way of the rescue, I will remove a limb before we cross back into Velotia—an important one."

To enforce her point, she pulled out her sharp battle axe and twisted it menacingly.

Edmund brushed his sleeve and adjusted the hood of his cloak. "You have my word."

"Do not let *him* find out you're here or he may very well be the one to remove something important himself." A twisted smile filled her face. "Try not to get yourself killed, and do try your best to keep up."

Before he could respond, she disappeared into the shadows of the tents, cursing to herself.

Edmund huffed and returned to readying his steed. He cursed when his hands fumbled at the tricky knots, never having learned how to tack a horse for himself. At least he knew the basics and what it should look like. He somehow managed to tie his supplies, hopefully tight enough so the pack wouldn't fall during the rough journey, and was ready.

Ready to ride. Ready to enter Murat. And ready to find his sister.

As the general called for the small group of soldiers to head out, Edmund clumsily vaulted to the back of his horse. He spotted the blond hair of that soldier, who looked in his direction and—thanks to the grace of Hierel—merely nodded. Edmund felt a weight float off his chest, and his heart resumed near-normal pacing.

The Pedite general passed and his eyes barely traveled over Edmund for more than a second. Good. The general gave the signal to head out, and Edmund released a long breath.

It was decided.

Edmund would go undercover with the others into Murat—consequences be damned.

Twenty-Eight

Mira

Fuzzy images wafted in and out of her dreams. Darkness covering everything. Light bursting over the horizon. A dark ball of fire in the sky. Flames and ash and blinding sunlight all melded into one giant painting that she couldn't decipher as the images kept moving too fast.

Blinding pain. Pain that overtook everything and turned her into something new. The pain went away then came back even worse than it started.

It eventually stopped and turned into a dull throbbing against her skull.

She wasn't sure how long she was there in the darkness.

Lost. Alone. No sense of self.

It could have been hours or days or weeks or months.

When she cracked an eye open, she wasn't greeted by the hazy red light from the tunnels as she had been expecting, but a warm yellow light that hurt to look at. Sunlight.

That was sunlight peeking in through a nearby window.

She clamped her eyes against the onslaught of brightness and may have drifted off again. It was hard to tell. When she opened her eyes next, that bright light remained in the same spot and she tried to get up but every bone in her body protested.

The stabbing pain below her ribcage was a painful reminder why she was here.

The Wasp.

He'd attacked her. Tried to kill her, and very nearly succeeded judging by the way her body felt as if it were dragged up from the step of Rallion's first gate.

A cool hand was on her forehead and a familiar sigh greeted her. "Your fever broke. Good."

Mira's eyes struggled to focus on anything that wasn't a blurry yellow or red blob. She blinked hard, then found flaming red hair that cascaded down thin shoulders. Beretta.

"B." She tried to sit up but her muscles didn't remember how to function. A hand on her shoulder pushed her back down and the pounding against her skull came back with a vengeance. The room spun and darkness may have come back for her or it may not have.

Eventually, everything came back into focus and she found the face of her friend staring back at her with worry lines carved into her face.

"Are you feeling any better?"

"Better than what?" Mira croaked out, focusing on a batch of freckles on her friend's nose.

Beretta raised an eyebrow. "I don't know. Better than death?"

Mira dug under her scratchy shirt and felt soft bandages covering where the axe had broken skin.

Beretta, who had been sitting in a chair next to her *bed*—yes, it was an actual bed—leaned back and let out a low whistle. "I thought you were dead. When you weren't dead, then I knew the infection would surely take you." Her eyes flickered down to where Mira's hands rested over her wound. "I should never have left you."

"Don't feel bad," Mira said. "I deserved it."

"I'm a terrible friend."

"So was I. Maybe this was the trickster's wicked sense of repayment."

A wet chuckle from her friend. "You deserved a sound talking to, but definitely not on the level of getting stabbed. At least, I'm the only one that should be allowed to stab you. Not *the Wasp*." Her face screwed up in indignation. "When I heard screaming, I grabbed a guard and we barely got there in time. You were unconscious and the guards they—they took him away."

"I still owe you an apology," Mira said.

"And several days' rations," Beretta added with a smirk, her eyes still glossy. "But I will admit, this rickety old chair is far more comfortable than sleeping on the hard rock down below... and the *sunshine*." She lifted her head back and golden rays hit her face. "Gods, I missed it."

"Glad you benefitted from my near-death experience." If Beretta hadn't arrived when she did, who knows what gate Mira would be crawling through now. Her friend had saved her life, again, even though Mira was undeserving after her lies.

"That's what friends are for," Beretta's eyes narrowed and she studied her face again. "You are looking rather peaky, are you certain you feel fine?"

Mira's heart leaped into her chest upon hearing the word *friends*. After everything Mira did, after everything she kept hidden from her, she wouldn't blame Beretta for removing herself from their friendship altogether.

Mira's eyes were finally able to focus properly and she studied the room they were in. They looked to be in a private room in the guard barracks. Nothing fancy by any usual standards. Yet, compared to down below, this was a palace.

Beretta followed the path of her eyes. "They brought us here when you turned for the worse. Good thing or else that stagnant air would have made your wound fester even more."

She grabbed a slice of bread from the nearby table and stuffed it all into her mouth. Apparently, Mira had interrupted her meal, which she'd hungrily resumed attacking.

Mira caught sight of fresh red lines on her friend's hands, several marks up her arm, and a purpling bruise under her eye.

"It's nothing," Beretta said, her words muffled by the slice of bread. "I got in trouble at first—for what happened. They blamed it all on me."

"What?"

Beretta pushed back a strand of hair that nearly got caught in her hungry fervor. "Don't worry about me. I sorted it out."

Mira shook her head. Even that movement made everything spin again. The goddess of fortune, Imoten, must favor B based on the number of times that girl managed to talk her way out of trouble.

Beretta swallowed a thick slice of jackfruit, then a devilish smile lit her eyes. "You spoke in your sleep. You called out a particular name *several* times."

There was no mistaking the heat that rushed to her face. It was a good thing Mira was too tired to care about the blush that would not go away, and she didn't bother asking whose name she said.

The grin on B's face doubled in size while her eyes continued their fierce blaze. "It's a good thing you've been flirting with that guard or else we'd never have been brought up here."

Mira feigned ignorance and focused on the moldy ceiling beams.

"I swear he must be related to an important commander to have pulled something like this." Beretta crossed her legs and carved up a slice of fowl to wave in front of Mira's face. "A proper bed and a private room. I refused to be left down below and instead of getting more lashes, I was allowed to keep watch over you, as he said he had urgent business to take care of."

Mira didn't want to talk about Private Devlin. She didn't know how she felt about him anymore after hearing the way he spoke so poorly of them all.

If only the traitorous stuttering of her heart would catch up to her brain.

"Again, I can't thank you enough and I can't apologize enough."

Beretta waved the hand holding her knife, spraying Mira with a speck of meat. It smelled amazing and made her stomach roil over, though she knew better than to eat so soon. She didn't want Beretta's meal to end up in chunks on the floor because she couldn't keep it down.

"You can thank my quick thinking that got us these fancy digs... my quick thinking and that gorgeous guard who seems to be quite taken with you."

That pesky blush refused to go away and sent Beretta into a fit of laughter that made a patrol guard come check in on them.

At some point, Mira must have dozed off again, and she didn't know for how long.

The next few days went by in a similar hazy fashion. She drifted in and out of sleep. Every time she woke, Beretta was by her side, either holding her hand or brushing sweaty strands of hair out of her face.

The pain below her ribs became manageable and the headache drifted between being tolerable or feeling akin to a thunderstorm blasting through her skull.

At least she was in a comfy bed. At least she was warm and breathing fresh air and—alive.

When she next opened her eyes that lovely sunlight was missing. A dark hue had settled over the room but she could still see Beretta in the wicker chair beside her, staring at the stars and the moon as if she couldn't get enough.

Mira understood.

"Can't sleep?" Beretta asked without taking her eyes off the crescent glow.

"Something tells me I've had more than my share of sleep lately." Mira pulled herself up on her elbows. This time she refused to let Beretta help her or scold her that she was too weak.

At least the headache was gone.

"They brought me tea." Beretta pointed at the table as if it were the most glorious sight she'd seen in years. "I think they accidentally made an extra pot and had nothing else to do with it, but hey, I'll take their leftover scraps any day. Look!" She brandished a dark piece of rock the size of a nail in front of her. "They definitely forgot to remove this."

Mira scowled at the rock.

"It's chocolate," Beretta corrected, breaking it in half. "Have some. It's supposed to do wonders for illness, or so I've heard."

That sounded promising. Mira popped the dark substance in her mouth and was overwhelmed at the explosion of tastes. It was velvety and smooth and amazing. It started off bitter but turned into the most glorious thing she'd eaten in her mediocre life.

"Good, right?"

"Amazing," Mira corrected.

"Better enjoy this while we can. Now that you are better, they'll be sending us back soon." Beretta focused on her fluffy pillow. "It was a nice break, right?"

"I'm sorry," Mira said. Perhaps she could try faking a fever again? Anything to buy them more time. "I wish it could have been longer."

"Me too," she said wistfully.

It would be hard to return back to that terrible, dirty, smelly, underworld after living in the sunshine for days. But that was their lot in life. Both of them. Stuck together in this dreadful cycle of horrors from which there was no escape.

Twenty-Nine
The Princess

Falling asleep came easily while exhausted and wrapped in a cocoon of comfort and warmth and safety. It was the first dreamless sleep she'd had in a while.

When she jerked awake the next morning, everything was cold and hard and—lonely. Both blankets covered her and still carried a hint of horse mixed with another smell she couldn't place.

At least she didn't freeze to death throughout the night. That was a positive.

She peeled the blankets back an inch and wiggled her toes, massaging the sore muscles on the bottom of her feet. If only River wasn't so frightened of the forest, then he could have saved her heels from the fresh blisters that had begun to burst. She prayed the old horse would manage to find a wild herd or someplace to call home. Rian seemed less certain he would make it on his own, but Isla had faith the old beast would survive.

Rian sat across from her with his blue jacket unbuttoned and hanging loosely off his shoulders. His focus was set on a black twig he was flipping between his fingers. When his eyes snapped up, a small smile jumped to his face, immediately replaced by a deep frown.

The twig dropped to the dirt.

"You speak in your sleep," he said in a dry voice.

"I do not." She threw the blankets off indignantly. The sudden shift in his mood confused her. "How long have you been up?"

"A bit." He shrugged. "I thought I heard something and decided to keep watch. It turned out to only be a pair of tree mice."

That was more alarming than the thought of bandits or brigands. She jumped to her feet and was ashamed of the squeal that came out of her lips as she scrambled to the top of the nearest tree root.

"Why didn't you say something sooner?" she scolded.

The forest filled with the sound of his chuckles while he merely sat there and watched her frantics without moving an inch to help. "They're long gone by now so you can stop your royal panicking."

"Are you sure?" Her heart skipped a beat and her stomach was doing somersaults for some reason that had nothing to do with the mice. "How do I know there's not another one lurking somewhere?"

He clutched a hand to his chest, eyes crinkling at the corners. "I'm offended you'd think I would lie about something as serious as this."

She scowled and hopped to the ground. "We don't have time for this," she said briskly, brushing off a leaf that had stuck to her shoulder. "We should get moving before a battalion of Muratian soldiers show up. And you better save your energy for when they get here."

"What's saying I don't just hand you over and take whatever ransom they are promising?"

Isla refused to be goaded into an argument, especially since she woke up in a good mood for the first time in days. If he was going to take whatever payment Murat had, they both knew he would have done that long ago. It was too late for him at this point.

Instead, she shot him a fiery glare and rolled up the tattered blankets, perhaps a bit too aggressively, but it helped keep her mind from wandering back to how closely they'd slept that night.

As a Velotian princess, she'd had her share of aristocratic pursuers spouting flowery words and frothy promises, holding hands when no one was around and sharing stolen kisses with some of the promising ones. Never anything like that.

Never in a position so—*intimate*. Her body and her mind didn't know what to think of it, especially after the turbulent storm of emotions she'd gone through the past few days. Traitor of a body.

A shadow passed over as she swam in her thoughts. Rian tossed a wood carving at her—a mouse—before scuttling away, laughing to himself.

The audacity of that soldier.

They set off in minutes. It was the same routine they had done for days now, and she didn't have to be asked anymore. Follow his lead, don't ask stupid questions, and don't fall off a cliff or into a pit again. The last part was harder than expected with the fog that appeared and disappeared at some unforeseen whim.

They walked in silence for a bit, as seemed to be customary. Rian led the way, checking the terrain gingerly when he thought it was too soft and loudly pointing out a sinking pit in the distance with far too much glee in his voice.

At some point Isla tripped over another vine that came out of nowhere, nearly tumbling to the ground altogether if it wasn't for Rian's helping hand that caught her before she landed in a pile of thick underbrush. He may have held her arm for a second too long after she righted herself. Neither said anything as she took a moment to fix her hair and adjust her cloak before they continued onwards.

The forest grew darker and quieter.

Too quiet for her liking.

She'd never spent much time ducking between branches and waltzing around trunks, but she knew it shouldn't feel like this. Something in the air made her skin crawl and sent her heart into tatters, so she kept close to Rian, who seemed startled at first but made no comment when their arms brushed.

After they had their mid-day *meal*—she thought he used that term too loosely—they passed through a dense patch filled with billowy, red-veined trees and far-reaching branches that moved like waves in the sea. All the songbirds and croaking toads quieted, and there was no rustle from small critters slithering along the forest floor.

A cold chill shifted down her spine when she caught sight of a violet-colored wisp hanging from a branch. It was gone before she could take a second look at it.

After tripping over a thick vine, her foot squelched into a muddy spot, nearly getting herself stuck, again. It took two good tugs and she managed to release her foot all by herself. She turned with a gloating smile, wanting to make sure Rian saw that.

Something warm snaked its way around her foot and pulled.

"Wha—?"

Before the word could escape out of her mouth, she ended up flat on her back and staring at the dark canopy, too stunned to move.

"*Isla!*"

A pair of hands pulled her up as something dark shot out from the ground. It clubbed Rian in the stomach and sent him flying into a thorny, black bush.

A vine? *It was a vine.*

Before the creeper could get her a second time, she rolled out of the way, and scrambled to her hands and knees.

She tried crawling away. Crawling to Rian or their discarded supplies but a slimy vine gripped her wrist and squeezed, pulling her back to the ground. Panic exploded when her hands started to burn.

No.

Her fingertips turned numb and all she could do was stare while the creeping undergrowth tightened its grip, making its way to her chest and constricting. It tightened and tightened, doing nothing to help the panic that made its way to her shaking hands. Her darkening hands.

The little bit of air in her lungs was forced out and she gasped, trying to catch any small breath of air, but the force of the vine kept squeezing and squeezing and squeezing. Burning water filled her eyes and spilled over.

Darkness would consume everything.

Consume her.

Boots shook the ground and shining silver drove through the vine, cleaving it in half. Glorious air soared back into her lungs as the vine withered away into the underbrush.

Waves of relief washed through her, adding to the drops already spilling from her eyes.

"Are you alright?" Rian threw his sword to the ground and pulled off the piece still clinging around her waist. His calming presence soothed the initial fear that she thought would overwhelm her, and he held her shoulder while giving her a minute to calm down.

Now was not the time to lose control. Keep it together.

After several heaping gasps of crisp air, the shakiness stopped. Rian didn't seem to notice or care about the retreating blackness at her fingers and was more focused on pulling a red leaf out of her hair, glaring at it as if daring it to move.

"I'm not hurt," she choked out, examining her now-normal hands. "It shocked me more than anything. I guess this place is a bit livelier than we thought."

"I'm sorry, I should have kept an eye out—"

"For vicious greenery with a vendetta?" she said with a wry smile. "It was just a plant."

Rian turned to examine the grove they had unceremoniously paused in. In the distance, a creature warbled a terrible howl and crashed through the forest.

They both froze—Rian's grip remained tight on her shoulder—waiting an eternity for whatever it was to turn their way. Isla sent a prayer to the trickster goddess to spare them this one time, promising to light a casket of fruit wine on fire the moment they were out of this safely.

The crunching footsteps led away, and Rian was the first to break their vigil. "Let's get out of this place before anything worse finds us."

As Isla enjoyed the air in her lungs, she couldn't agree more.

They found a spot that looked safe enough and set up their dirtied bed rolls next to a gnarled tree while Isla watched the amusement afforded by Rian's poor attempts at removing dozens of burrs that had lodged into his jacket and pants when he fell into that bush. She rubbed her hands together absentmindedly, more out of a habit rather than trying to keep her power from spilling over and erupting into everything.

A scowl filled his face every time he pulled a yellow spike out of the jacket, a few pulling the skin beneath as he did. He made good work on those lodged in his arm, before reaching around and twisting himself up in an attempt to reach those in his back.

When his hands failed three times to pull out a nasty batch near his spine, a bubble of laughter burst through. She couldn't stand to watch the struggle anymore.

She kicked aside her blanket and knelt in front of him, ignoring his scowl. "You're absolutely terrible at that. Let me help." She twisted a finger. "Turn around."

"I was handling it just fine," he said moodily, still turning as instructed. "But thanks."

With no prior experience with these things, she decided to attack the biggest batch all at once. She tugged the yellow cluster as hard as she could and his skin moved with it. He hissed and twitched his shoulder before she could get it out.

"Sorry," she mumbled.

Perhaps all at once was not the best strategy. It hadn't occurred to her that the spurs had lodged themselves so deeply.

He waved his hand. "It's fine. Best to get it over with quickly."

"If you're certain?"

He nodded, so she plucked away with gusto. One at a time now. How did he manage to get so many stuck on him?

The answer was obvious.

Saving her stupid life again. That was always the answer.

A distraction was needed. For him. For her. Something to keep her mind away from the dark thoughts that crept along the recesses of her skull like a spider. Always lingering.

"So," she said slowly, while her hands continued their work. "They all call you Captain Cordrai back at the camp. That can't be fun?"

She pulled a thick spike which must have hurt by the way his shoulders jumped. "They don't *all* call me that. My friends don't, but most of the others do."

"Still, it's not very nice." She screwed up her face as the next one refused to go easily. After some tugging, she pulled out a thick spur with drops of blood on it. "For what it's worth, I don't think you're a coward."

A coward would have left her. A coward would have turned her in.

There were several spurs in his hair, which she began to carefully remove. The strands under her fingers were surprisingly soft given their rough environment.

At least her patient had stopped with his complaints. Her distraction worked.

"The girl with the axe?" she asked casually, resting a hand on his shoulder while the other wove into his black hair in search of missed spurs. "I've seen you talking with her—when you were watching me before, that is."

"I thought noticing things like that were beneath you. That's Freya. She and her sister were conscripted alongside me at fourteen and have been with me through a lot. I'd trust her with my life. Even if we're not on the best terms since—"

"Since Liopen," she finished for him. He nodded solemnly. "Must be nice to have friends."

"I'm sure you have plenty back at the palace."

"It's surprisingly difficult to find trustworthy people when you're in a position like mine."

"I'm sorry," he said.

"Don't be. It's better this way. All done," she said happily as she ran her hand through his hair one final time. "There's no one to use or hurt you if you don't let them get close enough."

He twisted around to face her. "I get it. There's a lot of bad people out there, no matter where you come from or where you call home."

"There is."

She noticed the way his eyes followed as she flexed her hands and shook out her fingers. As soon as he caught himself staring his face flushed.

"Sorry," he mumbled, focusing on a rock next to his knee.

"I know you want to ask," she said. "You can. I think I'm ready to talk about it."

Instant relief washed over his face. He must have been holding it in for days. "How long have you—you know?" He jerked his head at her hands.

"Since the moment I was born." She refused to meet his eyes. The cavern in her chest turned into an empty pit.

A sharp intake of breath showed that he understood her meaning. It was easy to put the two together, once one knew of both the truth of her powers and of the mother that died giving birth to her.

At least he didn't make her say it out loud.

"I don't know how it happens or why," she continued, shifting from resting on her knees to sitting in a similar cross-legged fashion. "They believe my mother's line was linked to powerful wielders. My father refuses to talk about her so I don't know if she knew about it or if she had any *gifts* either."

"Does your brother?"

"No," she said quickly, tucking a loose strand of hair behind her ear. "At least... I don't think so."

It was something that crossed her mind many times. That'd be pretty terrible of him if had hidden it all these years, but seeing how their father treated her because of it, she wouldn't blame him.

These powers killed her mother when she was merely a baby. All she'd ever been taught was to fear them.

"I was the only one who inherited this curse. That circlet was all I had left of my mother. The woman I—I—" She hung her head. "It was her favorite. That's why I didn't want to part with it at first."

His eyes darkened and something flashed across his face. Had she scared him off again?

He cleared his throat. "Is that why you were out there that day back at the camp? Because of—?" He nodded awkwardly at her hands.

"That and other reasons."

"I'm sorry," he said. "For all of it."

"I've learned to live with it."

"Have you, though?" His expression hardened. "Sounds like you don't know how to handle it at all. I don't mean it like—not like that—I merely meant that it seems like you never learned to use or control it. Just contain it."

"My father would rather be stabbed in the eye than admit we needed help. So, I was always told to keep it in check instead. I've..." she hesitated, "I've tried to find a way to remove it. To take it away. But there is nothing."

"I don't think something like that can just be turned off," he said kindly. "When we get back you could talk to the Agicae general at the camp—"

"No." Her tones were harsh but definitive. Panic flooded her at the prospect of what would happen if they found out. "Nobody can know. *Nobody*. Do you understand?"

"Of course." His eyes met hers and he held her stare. "You can trust me."

A toad croaked in the distance.

Tracing the faded patterns at the hem of her cloak, she said lightly, "I hope so. Or you'll have much bigger problems to worry about than everyone calling you a coward."

She allowed the threat to linger in the burnt-pine-soaked air. Her father had gone through great lengths to keep her powers a secret. There was no limit he wouldn't cross to ensure it stayed that way.

"Noted." His eyes traveled down to her lips, then shifted to the dark canopy above them. "I think this is as good a place as any to call it a day."

Agreed. She was in no mood to fight with this forest anymore. If it weren't for Rian, she would never have escaped those vines. If she were caught unawares, and without him, she'd likely be dead on the forest floor.

Isla sighed.

"What is it now?"

She paused. Her father would never approve, but he was far away from them. "Can you teach me how to defend myself?"

"From a tree?" He wiggled his eyebrows. "Cutting words aren't working anymore?"

"*Rian.*"

"If you could learn to control—" He gestured at her hands. "—*It*, then you would be unstoppable. But I don't know anything about that. There is a reason there are wielder masters. If it were easy, then anyone could do it."

"Not that," she said quickly. "Never that." She looked at his broadsword, which rested against the base of the tree. "How did you learn?"

"My father trained us from childhood, so I've had years of experience. But if you want to know the best way to hold a sword." He jumped up and went to grab the chipped hilt. He paused with his hand outstretched. "On second thought, I don't want you accidentally chopping off a limb."

"*Excuse me.*"

"How about we start with something small." In a flash, he was flipping a black dagger between his hands. "Something small and light—and, hopefully, less deadly to someone who can barely walk through a simple forest without tripping."

"*Ha. Ha.*" She joined him in a small clearing, far away from their possessions—what little they had. She grabbed the smooth hilt and ran her finger along the side, catching the hint of a faded bell etched on its side. When she noticed Rian watching her closely, she dropped her hand and prayed to Halia that the shade of the forest hid her blush. "What do I do?"

"For starters—keep your elbows locked and point the sharp end at your enemies." He moved behind her as if afraid she'd count him in that category. "Something small like this may not cut through armor or thick leather, but there are always weak spots."

Heat exploded at the back of her arm when he grabbed her elbow and adjusted it.

"Which are?" she asked, glad he couldn't see her face from his position.

"Plenty. For now, go for an easy target like the neck." He inched closer, nearly fully pressed up behind her. He slid his hand down to her wrist and the other grabbed her waist. "Like this." He moved her entire body in a swiping motion. Then he repeated it.

"Imagine your enemy," he said. "A stupid soldier who won't let you have a second helping of dessert."

"Or a simple tankard of beer?"

"Exactly." From the sound of his voice, she imagined a smile tugged at his lips. "Now you try on your own," he said.

That heat was gone. All that was left was a cold emptiness at her back. She shook her head in a feeble attempt to clear it of any distracting thoughts—like how she could feel every muscle of his tighten behind hers and how she could imagine—

"Give it a try."

Right. Isla shuffled her feet in a grand show of fixing her stance, then envisioned what she thought the face of that wielder woman looked like—thin and cold, with black eyes that lacked any life or emotion—and she put all her force into her body and swiped where she thought a neck would be.

"Nice. Try again. Don't focus on the target too much but rather your movements. Imagine your arm hitting the target and it will. I like to name my weapons so I can imagine it's them doing the killing and not me."

Isla dropped her eyes to stare at a cluster of leaves in the dirt. "What's your sword called?"

He paused briefly before saying, "Dark End. Fitting, isn't it? As that's all I seem to offer."

"I don't think so." She tightened the grip on the dagger, focusing on the pattern of a particularly spikey leaf. "I shall call this one Shadow Death, since that's what I bring."

Rian didn't reply.

Determination filled her, so she tried again. She swiped at the enemy in her mind, imagining whoever it was turning to dust under the blade. It felt good, so she slashed Shadow Death again.

Then again.

And again, and again.

Cutting into the air as if it were the one who had marooned her here, as if it were the thing hunting her down. She didn't know how long she stayed there fighting invisible enemies. Releasing all her rage and sorrow and frustration on the forest air, screaming at it like that would actually do something.

Eventually, that warmth was behind her again. Rian caught her elbow and placed his hand on her shoulder.

"I think that's enough for tonight," he said, his breath tickling the back of her neck as he plucked the dagger out of her hand. "If there's any ferocious bunnies out there, they should be frightened."

Isla said nothing. She stood there with her chest heaving, trying to catch her breath as she stared at the spot where the bodies of her invisible enemies would lay. She'd never lost it like that, but she liked it.

Rian tucked the dagger into his jacket and turned toward their small camp. "Let's get some rest so we can set out early—whenever that is."

Isla padded over to her bedroll, brushing off the stray spurs she had tossed onto it earlier. Rian settled into a spot ten feet away from her, keeping his eyes on the ground.

"Thanks," she whispered quietly. After a few moments where she stared at a clump of dirt, her breathing finally settled. So did her mind. For once, it was calm and devoid of any vicious storms. Isla liked it.

She lay on her side, tucking the cloak around her as a new draft started up and reached into her tired bones. Why did it have to be so cold here?

Something must have shifted in the air as she didn't remember being this freezing last night. She tossed and rolled in her spot, sighing loudly when she couldn't find a comfortable position. A root dug into her back and her knee kept slamming into a large rock every time she stirred.

Stupid dirt floor. Stupid forest.

Memories of a warm cocoon flitted back. A glorious sleep in which no breeze snuck past her blanket, no noisy bugs interrupted her, and, *most importantly*, no nightmares plagued her.

This would not do. She threw back her blankets, sat upright, and huffed louder than before.

Rian cracked an eyelid and peeked at her through a narrow slit. "What is it now, majesty?"

"I'm cold," she whined, dropping her shoulders.

Both gray eyes snapped open and stared at her in an accusatory manner. "Your cloak dried last night. You are fine."

She wrapped her arms around herself and aimed the best pout that always worked on her nurses and instructors. "It's still freezing, and you picked a terrible spot for us."

"This spot is no different from any other night. And it's not that much colder..." Even he didn't seem to believe the lie.

It was as if he fought a battle within himself. She could see the turmoil pooling behind his eyes and knew he fought with his stupid sense of duty.

But it was cold and last night was one of the best sleeps since arriving here. One that wasn't plagued with stupid nightmares or waking up stiff from the harsh ground.

"That's an—order," she added, not sure if it was a question or not.

"Is it?" An annoying smirk filled his face.

"Unless the thought of sleeping next to me repulses you so much that you'd rather us freeze to death." Her heart stuttered as she waited for a response.

"First off, no one is freezing to death tonight and it's not just the repulsiveness of it," he said exasperatedly. "It's also the threat of—"

"Losing your uniform when we get back," she finished for him. "I got it. And you weren't so repulsed that night in Ackerslie when I caught you staring at my bed dress."

A hint of red rose to the surface of his usually calm face. "That was because I'd never seen such a ridiculous sight in my life."

Isla snorted. It was rare that she won something over him, and she was definitely counting this as a win.

This wasn't as big of a deal as he was making it out to be. So what if she was betrothed and about to be married? Prince Brenner would never hear a whisper about this from her. And he certainly would never hear about how she had caught herself staring as Rian undressed that night in—

That terrible howling started up again. Further this time. Or was it closer? It was hard to tell in this place. Her hands turned clammy and she scratched the side of her neck. Even Rian looked unsettled.

Something in her expression must have convinced him, for Rian sighed and lifted the side of his blanket.

A pulsating heat filled her chest and she scrambled to collect her own tattered blanket. Within seconds she was wrapped in that spectacular cocoon of warmth again. It was easy to find that perfect spot that she fit in. That perfect comfort that soothed her. She had to hold her hands together to keep them from exploring as they so desperately craved too.

Without needing any prompting, he wrapped his arms around her in a tight grip that melted away her stress and worries. Within seconds she was lulled into a peaceful sleep.

Thirty
The Captain

They'd spent days in the deepest part of the forest without sign of their enemy pursuers. That wasn't to say it lacked activity. These forests were brimming with mischief, and he had to be on constant watch. The whole place seemed to be alive and clearly didn't want intruders. It was as if it knew they didn't belong.

The vines were the first part to fight back, then came the diving redbirds that loved to snatch a chunk of their hair, a rock that wasn't really a rock but rather a well camouflaged snapping beetle that tried to take off his arm, and a sharp cliff—that he swore came out of nowhere—leading to a pit filled with venomous snakes.

Whatever howling they heard that second night disappeared for days, only to pick back up again with a voraciousness. The creature those sounds belonged to didn't come any closer, as if it were lurking just outside of sight and smell.

Edith was right.

This part of the forest was worse than what they previously traveled through. Yet they continued on, as what was behind them was more terrible than whatever these dark woods could throw at them.

They had been wandering the woods for eight days now. Always headed south. Always following the moss to keep the direction true. Towards safety and home. And whatever else may come with that.

During the foggy parts they passed the hours in silence, worried about attracting attention from any unwanted creatures that lingered just beyond sight. When the fog lightened up, they spoke at length about a variety of topics, including lighthearted stories of her brother playing pranks on her as a child, which to him sounded dreadful, but Isla said she'd grown accustomed to it over the years.

It wasn't like his relationship with his elder brother, Oliver, was any better. They hadn't spoken since, well, since he messed up at that village and ruined everything, brought dishonor upon their family, was responsible for so many deaths, along with a bunch of other reasons.

At least Rian's younger siblings didn't care about whatever shame he had gone through. Word didn't pass through to a village as small as theirs, so perhaps they didn't understand the severity of what he'd done. Of what he caused. He'd surely never explained it to them and was happy to keep them in the dark. Though a part of that may have been because they needed his money to survive, it didn't matter how it got into their hands.

They kept away from any matters that were too sensitive, including Isla's upcoming nuptials or any talk about her father. He didn't blame her for avoiding the subject of her wedding. The more they traveled together, the more apparent it became that the only one who wanted those scars on her wrist was her father, and maybe her brother.

They focused on lighter topics like his conscription training or his friends, which she was interested in hearing great details about their early conscription days together. They'd built a good routine now. They'd walk as far as their feet could handle or until it got too dark to continue on. Rian always led the way in case there were dangers hidden from sight, and Isla kept close to him. Very close.

Even her complaints were down to a minimum... or he'd grown accustomed to them at this point. When she wasn't complaining, he grew worried, but she seemed fine enough—on the outside. Things hadn't changed much from when they were first dumped across these gods-forsaken lands.

Except every night, after he showed her a few defensive moves he was certain the novice could master, Isla decided that the forest floor was too uncomfortable for her royal bones and demanded that they combine the bedrolls to make for a loftier cushion to sleep on. It was unfitting for a royal soldier and a princess, but she insisted, and he wasn't one to disobey an order, not anymore.

It was cramped and uncomfortable. She murmured in her sleep and twitched constantly, keeping him up for hours on end with hair scratching at his face and neck. As she technically ranked above him, she stole most of the patchy blankets and he couldn't say a word. Half the time she used him as a pillow, all so that he was left to sleep on the rough, forest floor. It was absolutely terrible.

Or at least that's what he told her.

It was easier than putting the truth into words. He laid awake for a multitude of other reasons he would never speak out loud.

This night was turning into the same as the others, the dark gloom had seemingly lightened up by this point in their journey. Perhaps the overhead canopy of twisted branches and dark leaves was starting to thin out or they were nearing the end of the worst of it and things were starting to look up. If his calculations were correct, they should be closing in on the edge of the forest any day now.

Leaving the Black Forests meant stepping into Velotian land and, hopefully, some semblance of safety. There was still a lot that could happen, depending on where the forest would spit them out.

Rian had settled at the base of a towering redwood ten times the size of him. Isla sat next to him, close enough that their shoulders brushed every now and then, with her fingers working through the tangles in her hair, which she complained would never come out at this point.

"I guess you'll just have to cut it all off then," he said after she sighed for the fifth time. "Must be hard having to brush it out for yourself. Your poor, delicate, royal fingers." He nudged her leg with the heel of his boot.

"Pfft." She blew a strand out of her eyes and crossed one leg over the other, their legs now fully touching. "Don't be so dramatic."

He scoffed but didn't bother pointing out which one of the two of them had been responsible for most of the dramatics since arriving in Murat—and it definitely wasn't him. Why was his heart pounding so frantically?

Isla bumped her head against his shoulder. "At least nobody ran into a thorn bush today. I don't think that jacket can take more harm and neither can my fingers." She shoved them in his face so he could see the fresh set of scars.

"Apologies, my lady." The only reason he landed in that bush was because he had to double back because *someone* had dropped her bedroll after they scaled down a rocky cliffside and was too tired to go back and retrieve it. That was how he fell into the second, somehow stickier, thorn bush.

At least this one didn't attack back like the thrashing vines they'd come across several times. By now they had learned to step over anything that wasn't clearly dirt.

"Do you think they're still searching for us?" she asked, wrapping her cloak firmly around herself and pulling the blanket across their laps.

"For you," he corrected, playing with the hem of the blanket. "Yes."

"Do you ever wonder why they wanted me—the Muratians?"

"Well," he said slowly, flicking a dead leaf off his jacket sleeve. "I'm certain they didn't want this alliance with Koliat going through and were clearly desperate to stop it."

"Why wouldn't they just kill me that day in the forest? What was the plan?"

"Ransom? Torture?" he supplied honestly. There were other reasons he had thought about but didn't want to voice to her. No sense in worrying over it until they got back.

This alliance had to go through and the war had to be stopped. He was determined more than ever to do his part, no matter the cost.

"Hm." She slid into a more comfortable position. "Good thing they were terrible kidnappers, I guess."

"Says the one that fell face first while trying to run away from them."

"That root came out of nowhere and I was only doing as you said."

"The one time you did."

Isla sighed and turned on her side so she faced him with those deep brown eyes. She was so close that her forehead almost touched his arm. "It's been more than once," she said sleepily, her eyes fluttering shut. "You do have good ideas... every now and then."

"Coming from you, I'll take that as a compliment."

With still tightly shut eyes, she laughed before nuzzling her face into his side. He shifted uneasily when her finger trailed along his chest before poking him in the side. "Don't let it get to your head."

Every muscle tensed before he remembered to breathe out. He prayed to Hierel that she didn't notice how shaky his breath was. "I wouldn't dream of it, Isla."

A branch cracked. Loudly.

All of the former exhaustion was sucked out of his limbs. He was on his feet in an instant, his discarded sword in hand.

Isla didn't bother objecting at being so unceremoniously dumped on the ground. She stared at him with wide eyes, drowsiness a distant memory for them both. The forest turned quiet—except for the sound of something dragging against the ground.

What was that? she mouthed to him.

Rian shook his head, focusing on the slithering sound making its way across the forest floor. Where was it?

Every hair on his body stuck up on alert, and a terrible chill spread down his spine into his toes and fingers. Something was there—and it wasn't human.

He tapped Isla's shoulder to be prepared and fixed the sweaty grip on his sword.

A shadow crept along the nearby path, reaching out from the base of a curved tree. Everything in its path leaned away, even the branches groaned and stretched away from the creature.

The *smell*.

It smelled like a mix of mountain air and ice and dirt all at once. The creature was corporeal—not fully here—as if it were a walking spirit with half its body past Rallion's fourth gate. It was tall, at least seven feet and from the parts of its body that weren't covered in a dark cloth, had a pale blue skin stretched over thin bones. He couldn't see its face but knew it stared at him, looking into his soul and taking all the breath before turning to Isla.

An elemental. A forest-walker.

It turned its head to Isla, and she let out a small squeak, clutching the bottom of his jacket in a death grip.

Rian's body froze and his grip slackened, while he could do nothing but stare at the elemental like an idiot. Regular steel wouldn't work if it decided to attack. If it decided they were intruders in its forest that needed to be removed.

His heart thundered wildly, begging him to do something—anything. But he couldn't move.

The creature moved closer to them and what little air Rian managed to find, was drained from his lungs. The elemental passed over him and stood in front of Isla, who still remained seated on their bedrolls, staring at the creature.

It stretched a bony hand to her—Isla's body was now wracked with shakes—and ran a blue finger along her cheek.

Before Rian could even begin to think about how he could take down an elemental, it retracted its hand as if burned and stepped back.

It turned and something dropped from its wispy robe. The air returned to Rian's lungs when it started to slink back into the forest as if nothing had happened. As if it had merely taken a curious glance at the intruders in its forest.

Isla didn't move. Neither did Rian. Not for a while.

Only once fully certain it was gone and his chest resumed a normal pace, did Rian nudge the flower on the ground. It was a wilted blood-lily. He didn't think they grew in these parts.

Isla didn't take her eyes off the flower. If anything, she was more disturbed than when the elemental first showed up.

His heart sank. *Of course.* A wilted blood-lily. The symbol of Rallion.

Rian picked up the flower, which had turned a strange luminescent white, and tossed it into a bush, where it could wither and die for all he cared.

Was that flower meant as a warning or a blessing of their passage?

Either way, he didn't want to find out.

Isla now wrapped her arms around her knees, looking like nothing more than a lost child. Rian dropped next to her and pulled her into his lap, running a hand over the top of her hair like his mother would do to calm him down as a child. The other pressed tightly against her back, holding her against him, keeping her with him and comforted.

That was all he had to offer—comfort. He had been utterly useless at deterring the elemental, and if it had chosen to attack, there was nothing he could have done to protect her.

Useless.

"It was nothing," he said, not sure which one of them he was reassuring. He pulled the tie out of her hair and wove his hands through the strands.

Isla nodded, hiding her face in his chest and pressing her hands against him. She was still shaking, but not the bad kind that destroyed everything type of shaking. This was the human kind that came from very real fear.

"I don't think it'll come back." He eyed the path it disappeared down to ensure there was no new movement. The musical sounds of the forest had returned in force. The elemental must have returned to its home—wherever that was—but still Rian didn't release Isla.

They may have stayed like that for hours, eventually her shaking stopped and his heart stopped skipping beats. Morning would be here soon and they *needed* rest. He moved them back into a lying position, curling around her body with his own.

"You need to try to sleep," he said. He lightly pressed his lips to the top of her head and attempted to remove her from his lap but she shifted and wrapped her legs around his waist, shaking her head so he kept on holding her.

"I don't know if I can sleep after that." She said into his neck. "It was terrible. I can't stop seeing its face. Can you tell me something real—something about your life back home?"

He cupped the back of her head. "What do you want to know?"

"What was it like? Not just the time you were conscripted, but before."

"What was it like not growing up in a palace, you mean?" Her body shook, this time caused by a small bout of silent laughter, so he continued, "My father was obsessed with training my brother and I. He wanted us to go into the military to pay off his debts; he always dreamed of a luxurious life, and it cost him in the end. Any *games* we played were really training sessions in disguise. It took us far too long to figure that out, longer than I'd like to admit."

She pulled back. The thin line of her lips curved into a smile and he caught himself staring at it. "Something that hasn't changed over the years, I see."

"I'd like to say I've honed my powers of observation since then, but there's still room for improvement. Anyways, as I was saying." She chuckled and placed her cheek against his chest, still tightly wrapped around him. "We spent a lot of time outdoors and *prac-*

ticing, but never had the actual tools or real horses or exquisite feasts to come home to."

"No fancy horses or meals," she repeated, voice thick with exhaustion. "Got it."

He toyed with the ends of her hair. "My father was a good man but was broken from something in his past. Thankfully our mom was an amazing cook and could make the best meals out of the simplest ingredients. We didn't know how little we had for so long..."

He continued on at length about some of the trouble he and his brother would get up to around their small village, lavishing in the breaks they got while their father was away on assignment for weeks or even months at a time. It wasn't long before Isla's breathing turned heavy and she stopped responding, but he continued his story as it was the only thing keeping his thoughts from focusing on that blue face beneath the elemental's hood, or the frightening patter of his heart that wouldn't let up for other reasons.

A small breeze rustled the nearby leaves and made him jump. He wrapped his arms tighter around her, not wanting to wake her to move just yet. He stared at the intricate branch pattern in the canopy overhead as, once again, he knew sleep wouldn't come easily.

∾

The sounds of something shuffling through the leaves woke him out of a restless sleep. He bolted upright in a dead sweat and untangled himself from Isla.

"What in the goddess—?"

He clamped a hand over her mouth, awkwardly kneeling next to her in a position that made his knees scream. He may have been too closely pressed against her side, but that didn't matter. All that did was whatever caused that noise.

Was the elemental back to finish them off?

Slowly he removed his hand from her mouth, sliding it down her shoulder to grab her hand and help her to her feet. At the same time, his free hand jumped to the hilt of Dark End.

The heat of her hand pulsed dangerously against his and still he didn't release it. There was nothing to fear from her.

The rustling returned, followed by a deep growl. It was not human.

That was equal parts great news and horrifying at the same time. It must be large.

It must be whatever was making those gods-forsakened noises the past nights.

There was no time to quietly pack up their bedrolls or what little supplies they had left. He had fallen asleep with Isla with his satchel and sword still on, so that was all that would be coming with them.

Squeezing her hand so that she understood, he waited until the last possible moment. Until he was absolutely certain this beast would come crashing through. He kept a tight grip and told Isla to run.

Thirty-One

Mira

The day before they were to be taken back below was when he returned.

Devlin.

They had been topside for days at this point, to which Beretta had been quietly gleeful.

Once the soldiers up here realized that Beretta was neither injured nor incapacitated, they demanded she make herself useful or they'd send her back under the mountain. They took her out for hours at a time to clean the unused barracks while Mira was left alone to heal, sleep, or stare through her glorious window for hours on end. Each time Beretta returned, she painted a face of grave misery until the guards left her for the evening.

Once they were alone, Beretta's angsty scowl turned into a bright smile. They both loved being up here, and even though she spent her time scrubbing floors until her knees and knuckles hurt, Beretta said it was easier work than any day they had below.

Neither dared express how happy they were with this arrangement or the soldiers would put an immediate end to it. They refused to allow the dredgers a glimpse of happiness for too long over here.

"I wish we could stay up here forever," Beretta said wistfully. She had positioned herself to stare out the small window while her fingers worked vigorously patching up a sleeve from the pile of tarnished uniforms a guard dropped off earlier.

The soldiers up here had no idea how truly difficult life was below. That one had laughed when he kicked the pile of uniforms towards Beretta, looking far too gleeful to be barking an order at a lowly dredger. B's eyes darkened for less than a second before clearly remembering where they were.

At least her friend snapped out of it before doing something she'd regret.

They'd just been brought a mid-day meal consisting of stale bread and forest mushrooms, when Private Devlin burst through the door. He donned his finely pressed blue and gold uniform without a button out of place or speck of dust to be seen. His dark blue eyes found Mira, briefly, then focused on Beretta, who remained in the chair at her side, frozen in place by his sudden interruption.

"Can we help you, private?" Beretta asked in a cool voice. "I heard you were not due back for a few days."

If she were close enough, Mira would have kicked her before B got them both of them sent down below with her snark.

"Plans changed." His eyes trailed back to Mira. She was hyper-aware of the tangled mess of her hair, which she'd yet to have Beretta fix, and the dirtiness of her days-old tunic still caked in a mix of soot and her blood.

"We're heading back down soon," Beretta blurted out. Mira held back her groan. "That's what the guards say."

"I know. I heard," Devlin said.

Beretta's eyes clouded over and she grabbed Mira's shoulder. "We've been helpful up here with the cleaning efforts, private. The other guards even said so."

"Which one was it that attacked her?" Devlin said, his dark eyes pouring into Beretta's. The unwavering command in his voice made her shrink into herself.

"They call him the Wasp," she whispered, pressing her hand into Mira's shoulder so she couldn't move. "The guards have taken care of it. I saw them remove the body."

The body?

No.

The Wasp was a terrible old man but he didn't deserve this. The hand at her side quivered, and she pretended to adjust her bandage to hide it.

A smile flashed over Devlin's face. "That is good then."

Though from the sound of his voice, she thought she sensed a hint of disappointment. Had he wished to be the one to do it himself? He was certainly capable of it, if her experience in that cavern was any indicator.

"What about the other one—the one that helped him?" he asked. "They said that there was more they uncovered."

Beretta spoke, but her words became hazy. Everything around Mira started to become a blur as her headache came back in full force. She must have fallen back asleep because when she opened her eyes next, Devlin was gone and Beretta was helping herself to a hot kettle that was steaming on the small table.

When she saw Mira's eyes on her, she jumped up. "How are you feeling?" she asked with furrowed brows. "I think you passed out earlier. I tried to get them to call for a medic but they wouldn't send one."

Mira ran a finger across her forehead. She wasn't feverish anymore but clearly needed to take it easier. That would be hard to do when they were due back in the mines so soon. She prayed to the goddess that she was able to keep up when sent back below.

Beretta traced the lip of her chipped cup. "I was hoping they'd keep us up here after seeing how useful I've been these past days. It sounds like they still want us below."

"I'm sorry, B."

"Don't be." Beretta stared into the steaming liquid. "It was stupid to hope I could change their minds."

Mira grabbed the cup out of her hand, set it on the table and grasped her friend's hand in her own. "It's not stupid to hope. We've just been the unlucky ones who Rallion frowns upon instead of Hierel's graceful smile. Misfortune is our lot in life."

Beretta's eyelashes fluttered. "So, it looks to be."

"But not forever," Mira added with unfounded optimism. Something had to change. Something soon. She felt it pulsing through her blood and seeping into her bones. It took her nearly passing beyond the first gate to realize that this was not the place she was destined to die in.

Beretta didn't look convinced, but Mira had enough conviction for the both of them this time.

The next morning, they both dressed somberly, preparing for someone to take them back below. Beretta tore up strips from the hard mattress to reinforce Mira's bandages so nothing would interfere with their work back below.

They both sat in silence, drinking in the morning's light that filtered through the window as if they could get enough. As if they'd never see it again.

A knock at the door and both their head's pivoted.

Except it wasn't the guard who promised to return and deliver them below. It was the private again.

Both she and Beretta could do nothing more but stare at him.

First to find her voice was B. She stuttered a poorly formed greeting and half rose from her seat, but he paid her no attention.

"I wish to speak to Mira." Devlin's eyes burned into hers. "*Alone.*"

Beretta sent her a worried look. Her eyes searched hers, likely wondering if she wanted to be left alone with the private.

That was a question Mira wasn't certain she could even answer. Her heart and head battled with each other, fighting for dominance.

Not that it mattered what Mira wanted—what either of them wanted. They were nothing more than property to these guards who could command them at will. There was no real choice, only a thinly veiled illusion of agreement.

"It's alright, B," she said quietly.

Devlin's head swiveled toward her friend. He'd likely never bothered to learn her name before all of this and probably still wouldn't after they were sent back down.

Beretta nodded, perhaps a little too vigorously, and stormed out of the room muttering to herself. That girl was going to get them both flogged.

Silence stewed in her absence.

Devlin stood by the door, now a picture of nerves and awkwardness that she didn't think him capable of. His pristine uniform with crisp colors stood out in this room of drabness.

If she'd waited for him to speak first, she'd already be halfway down those mines.

"What do you want?" she asked. Surprise filtered through at her own abrasiveness.

Devlin, to his credit, didn't flinch or show any sign that he noticed her cold attitude. He rounded the room and kicked the chair out with his boot before taking a seat.

Mira pulled her feet onto her bed and tucked her messy tresses behind her ears.

"I'm sorry," Devlin said slowly. "I was out of line the other day."

Mira stared at him. He scratched his splotchy neck. The scar along his chin shined brightly.

"I'm sorry for not seeing you for who you were. The truth is that I used you, and I shouldn't have, but I'm glad it was you. Everything I said about wanting to help you was the truth. You *are* special."

Her damned heart had the nerve to flutter at his words. Stupid traitor.

"I know you probably still hate me, but I want to make this right. All of it. I want to show you something," he added in an odd voice. "Are you well enough to walk?"

She had to be, considering they were being sent back to work the mines today. B had even helped her take a few turns around the room as practice. She swallowed and nodded.

Devlin extended a hand to help her up, but she ignored it. She wasn't completely invalid. And a small part of her didn't want to show any weakness.

Not to him. Not today.

Was he only apologizing because she had been nearly killed, or did he truly regret his words that day in the cavern? Now she'd never know.

When she stepped outside an annoying group of clouds moved to block the sun's rays from reaching her. She grumbled internally. This may be the last time she was up here for a while, and she was looking forward to feeling that familiar warmth one last time. Direct sunlight and not just whatever filtered in through the poorly cleaned window.

"Come on," he said, placing her hand on his forearm to help her down the rickety steps and along the worn-out path. "I'm sorry I was away while you were recovering."

Mira frowned. This was a stark comparison to Devlin's usual radiating confidence. He almost sounded unsure about himself.

"I was away on assignment but returned earlier than I was supposed to. I wanted to see you before you were sent back down."

Back to the mines with the other dredgers, she thought bitterly.

"I expect I'll have to leave again soon, and I don't know when we'll get our next moment alone together."

Her stomach flipped at these words, and her fingers flexed upon his arm.

"Where are you sent to, when you leave?" she asked, a bolt of bravery filling her. Nothing mattered anymore and she'd be sent below soon.

His step faltered momentarily, but they continued on, passing the empty barracks that now donned sparkling clean windows. Where did Beretta get to?

"My higher-ups send me where I'm most needed to help this war. I have some choice, but not much in the matter when my orders are cascaded directly from the queen."

Directly from Queen Grimha. Beretta was correct, and there was definitely more to Devlin than he let on. At least he was as honest with her as he could afford. He didn't owe someone like her anything and she appreciated the gesture as it was meant to be—a peace offering of sorts.

Mira hated the way her silly heart fluttered at the thought. Even her brain was determined to betray her when she said, "Will you be sent back here when you are done?"

Will you come back to visit again? That was the question she really wanted to ask.

A smile curved from the corners of his lips. "Yes. And I hope we can resume our work together—if you'll have me again."

"Yes," she breathed. "I would like that very much." Perhaps there was some hope for getting out of here after all. She was equally as guilty for using him as he was her.

They walked in silence until they reached the end of the camp. This was as far as she'd ever been allowed before. The air smelled fresher here, especially when the wind picked up like an untamed gale bursting from a storm's edge.

Nobody else was out at this end of the camp, and the tree line was right there. A wave of freshly scented pine and grass hit her senses. A small part of her wondered what he would do if she took off. He had a long sword. Would he cut her down or turn his back and let her go?

The others would eventually find her and payment would be swift. They may even take it out on Beretta now they knew the two came as a pair. Perhaps that was a mistake on B's end, letting them see how close their friendship had grown. Anything that could be used against the dredgers to bring more pain was done gleefully and without remorse.

When she tore her eyes from the tree line, she saw that Devlin's face was fixated on a point just over her shoulder. She followed towards what he was staring at so intently and gasped.

A row of four wood poles, carved from the same pines that had now blurred in her view, stuck out from the muddy ground along the camp's edge.

Attached to each pike was a half-decaying figure clad in tattered brown garments now stained red. Their throats had deep slits and there were terrible gaps where their eyes should have been.

The sight brought her delicious breakfast tearing up with no warning.

Devlin hopped away so it didn't spill on his immaculate boots. A second wave of nausea came over her and she dry heaved, spitting up a mix of bile and soggy oats. It took a moment for the queasiness to stop and she wiped her mouth, gasping for air.

She had to turn away from the bodies before another onslaught could hit. Her hands trembled uncontrollably and every muscle in her body couldn't stop shaking.

Before she lost the contents of her stomach, she managed to get a look at who they were. There was no need for a second look.

The one on the far right was recognizable even without his eyes, Crag. The only solace was that he was long since dead. The other was that guard, Captain No-Neck, along with two other guards from the pits who she had never bothered to learn their names, but they'd made their disdain for her known.

A warm hand rubbed her back but she recoiled from the touch.

"Why would you bring me here?" she asked in a shaky voice, closing her eyes tightly but all she saw in the darkness was their bodies.

Devlin crouched in front of her and her eyes opened to see his intense face "They were the ones responsible for hurting you. That dredger up there." He jerked his head towards the pike Crag was skewered on. "He helped that one you call the Wasp, so did the captain. Those other guards were too lazy to notice what was happening."

Mira clamped her hand over her ears to stop a loud ringing. A hammer was surely pounding against the inside of her skull, begging for release.

This could not be happening.

"Why would you do that?" she asked as hot tears spilled onto her boots.

"I did it for you," he said, heat lacing his voice. "They were going to do it again. That one wasn't going to stop until you were dead."

"I didn't ask you to do that," she shouted back with equal anger.

"You didn't have to. I had to do it for you. They were going to tell the commander everything. You have no idea what I've done to protect you."

She didn't care. Didn't want to hear anything from him. It sounded like he did it to protect himself more than anything.

"I've done everything to protect you and help you, and this is the thanks I get. I thought you'd be pleased."

"With that?" She pointed at the bodies and tasted bile on her tongue. She forced it back down. "Are you insane?"

"Maybe," he said, and his blue eyes went wide. "I wanted to help you. Everyone told me against it—all my advisors, but I didn't listen. I saw something in you that I see in myself. I want to help you. I want you to trust me. I couldn't stay away."

The thudding of her heart nearly drowned out all else. Blood rushed through her veins along with something else—some other emotion. There was nowhere to look—she couldn't look at the bodies or his face—so she stared at his shiny black boots.

"I have to go back down below," she said.

"You don't have to," he said. "If you don't want to. They'll listen to me—they have to."

Mira shook her head and continued focusing on his boots until her eyes hurt.

"If you promise to stay here with me and dedicate yourself the same as I have, then you could stay up here."

Again, she didn't respond.

"They don't want you here. They think it's too dangerous and that's why they allowed the attack. But I can help you, only if you promise."

"Promise what?"

"To never leave. To stay by my side forever so we can weather what comes next *together*."

It was tempting. Every fiber of her body begged her to accept... almost every portion. There was a small cage hidden away, locked deep down that told her *no*.

But those bodies behind him told her that could never happen. Everything about this place was meant to trap them, to punish them.

It had to be another trick. It had to be.

And she had to escape before it was her body displayed on a pike.

There was nothing she could think of, her brain was empty of all. All that she knew was she had to get away from this place before it sucked her in and consumed her wholly.

So, she ran.

Perhaps Devlin was shocked at her doing something so stupid that he froze. Perhaps he let her go. Either way, she pushed past him and ran towards the tree line. Towards that dark forest that would surely be the death of her.

She was so desperate to get away that she didn't stop to notice that the Wasp's body was missing.

Thirty-Two
Prince Edmund of Velotia

"Don't make me send you back over the border," Freya hissed as she pulled his boot out of the thick mud. Brown goo sprayed everywhere, including his already dirtied face and his now-torn wielder cloak.

If Edmund's spirit hadn't already been broken by these lands, he had half a mind to think she'd done that on purpose.

The soldier's face seemed to be a strange mix between annoyed and amused. No—it was definitely annoyed.

At least she stopped to help, even if she cursed at him the entire time she did. Even if she likely sprayed him with mud in retaliation. Her uniform remained safe from the onslaught of murky sludge.

It wasn't like he had a choice but to accept her prickly aid.

Nobody else had bothered to stop to help one of their stuck party, everyone was too on edge from the terrible sounds and lingering darkness the forest emanated since their arrival. Every leaf seemed to watch them and each sway of thick branches cast shadows that made some of the more tenured soldiers jump.

Edmund didn't like the way the hairs on the back of his neck wriggled each time a passing breeze brushed against him or the way the brown birds stared at him as they shredded their songs across the forest canopy. The sun struggled to make its way through the thickness of the leaves and that ridiculous fog refused to dissipate.

All in all, this was a terrible place and nearly made him regret his decision to join with every passing hour.

The Pedite general wasn't afraid like the rest of the soldiers. He seemed more familiar with these lands, always knowing what to expect. In fact, he pointed out a series of snapping vines before one of the captains stepped on it. A shame Edmund didn't possess his tracking skills, then he'd be leading this mission instead of hiding in the shadows, and that general could have been left behind in the camp like the failure he was.

Edmund wiped the splash of mud off his face and glared at Freya. "I had it perfectly handled, thank you very much."

"Whatever you say," she drawled. "Remember what I said before. If anyone ever finds out you are with us, you'll be dead before you can utter a stupid breath of a word."

Before he could add a witty comeback, Freya had already stormed away. She stopped ten feet away, turned, and traced a finger across her neck. Then she shot him a disparaging look and trotted off after the general and his group.

A shoulder shoved into his back, setting off his icewielder injury, and nearly tipping the hood of his cloak back.

The *audacity*.

The Divite soldier brushed off his dual sword badge and sneered as he passed. "Move along Agicae. Stop holding us up."

It took the last few ounces of patience Edmund possessed to dump out a sludge of mud from his boot, ensure his hood was properly secured, and join the rest of the group, ignoring the pain from his jolted wound.

He'd have a word with the Divite commander when this was all over. He'd have several words with his father's highest leaders after this.

No doubt his father would have received word that he was missing by now. His wrath would surely flatten even the vilest of forests. The thought nearly brought a smile to Edmund's muddy face.

Nearly.

When he got back, perhaps he could tell his father that he stayed behind, as requested, and even attempted to return home, as *demanded*, but his party got lost outside of Bluemoon Bay.

He snorted, earning a look of disgust from the nearest Pedite.

As if his father was stupid enough to believe that.

Prince Brenner would have surely noticed his absence and blabbed at the first chance. When Edmund returned to Velotia, he would have a furious king to deal with—if his father ever bothered to drag himself down from Aurial to get him.

When Edmund tripped over his third root of the night, all he could think of was how this had better be worth it, or somebody was about to pay dearly. And he already knew who.

The Pedite general flung out his arm, stopping the party from the front. "Do you hear that?"

Edmund froze, straining his ears for any sign of noise besides the babble of the forest. There was nothing there.

As he opened his mouth to speak, a breeze picked up. It was different from the usual gale of the forest or sway of the leaves, as if something dark passed overhead and underground all at once. As if something in the forest watched them closely.

The idea of something in this forest watching them was enough to shrivel his heart.

Whatever it was passed by as quickly as it came. A few of the soldiers released a long breath while the soldier next to him shook out his shoulders.

"What was that?" Edmund whispered.

The soldier next to him gave him a withering glare and moved on, shoving his shoulder as he passed.

A blond head at the front turned around, checking that he was still with them.

Though he'd never admit it out loud, Edmund was seriously second guessing his choice to accompany them into these cursed lands—needlessly. There was nowhere he could go at this point, not without giving himself up.

The group walked in restless silence, echoed by the unnerving stillness of the forest. Edmund was no great tracker, but even he sensed something remained lurking just beyond their eyesight.

Thirty-Three
The Princess

The hand wrapped around hers was the only anchor that kept her from tumbling to certain doom. She'd barely had time to register what was happening before Rian grabbed her and dragged her along through the forest.

Whatever had been howling every night finally found them.

Thunderous footsteps barreled through the brush behind them. It was hard to tell exactly how close it was as she'd never been properly trained as a tracker. She relied on the way the skin on the back of her neck prickled and how the snarling sounds that continued to grow louder to tell her that it was close.

The noises were definitely behind them. Then beside them, as if trying to cut them off—or steer the direction of their escape.

So, she clung to the hand and tried to keep up as best she could, focusing on where her feet were going instead of figuring out the path ahead, as she had someone to lead her. One foot in front of the next, taking care to jump over a dead stump and never faltering when they barreled through a thorny bush that would be a pain to pick out later.

The terrible growls plagued their every step, urging her heartbeat into a dangerous pattern.

They ran and ran until every breath turned into jagged daggers tearing through her lungs. Her legs wanted to collapse but whatever chased them refused to let up, and she didn't want to find out what type of face—or claws—matched those sounds.

Another step. Then another.

The fog grew thicker as they ran. Until the ground beneath her foot was no longer there and hung in the air for a fraction of a second before she was sent tumbling head over foot to the ground. It may have taken seconds or minutes to reach the bottom—it was hard to tell with her head pounding, and the newfound dizziness from the fall.

Every inch of skin would surely bruise and she was surprised none of her bones were broken.

"Are you alright?" She was pulled to her feet by the same hand that remained clutched in Rian's the entire time they fell down the cliffside.

Blood trickled from a cut above his temple but he looked relatively unharmed—and considering the giant cliff they'd just tumbled down, that was a feat in its own.

When she tried to breathe it sent her into a coughing fit. "I think so," she stumbled out, trying to untangle herself from her cloak. She refused to let panic overtake her now.

He grabbed her chin and studied her face, lingering an extra second on her eyes as if he thought to spot an injury in there.

"Your satchel," she said stupidly, pointing at the cloth bag at his side. "It made it."

His eyes darkened and the hand on his bag flexed. "We left everything else behind. I don't know what we're going to—"

Another branch snapped and Rian spun around, his reflexes as quick as ever.

How had that beast managed to find another way down so fast?

But it wasn't a growl or a snarling creature that she heard next. It was a human voice. A taunting voice. The coldest voice she'd ever heard.

Isla felt the blood drain from her face when she recognized that vile female speaking. In their haste to escape whatever chased them, they ran straight into a clearing filled with the Muratian soldiers hunting them.

It really was the year of the trickster goddess.

Rian shifted to stand in front of her, but not fully blocking so she could still see around his shoulder.

The clearing they'd landed in was filled with ankle sized vermillion shrubs, still half-dead at their tips, and a few large oaks circling them. There was nowhere to hide, and running would be nearly impossible with a cliffside at their back.

Three dozen—maybe more—blue and gold soldiers now circled them, leaving no gaps for escape.

A cold pit formed in her chest at the realization, pulsing outward as fear gripped her muscles.

Rian drew his blade. The others didn't even flinch.

"Planning to fight us, fool?" the cloaked woman said in that taunting voice. "You're outnumbered. Unless..." She stepped around a blue-clad soldier. "Unless you plan on doing to us what you did to those poor, defenseless villagers."

Rian flicked his head to the side. She knew he was checking on her.

Isla's body tightened at those words. She felt that familiar pumping of blood start to creep out, that dark ember throbbing and begging to be let out. A part of her yearned to release it, but she remembered what happened last time and shoved her hands behind her back.

"I didn't think so. Not without killing your companion." The woman turned to someone behind her. Another two hooded wielders flanked someone hidden past a line of six burly bodies. This one must be their leader, judging by the pristine shine of his gold badges, far too many for one so young, and his uniform was in too good of shape for a lowly soldier. "It's just as you thought," she said to the leader. "She has absolutely no control."

Isla's face flushed and she dropped her chin.

"She doesn't have to fight you," Rian said with waves of confidence that she wished she could muster in the face of so many enemies. "And you didn't do so well last time we met."

If she could see the wielder's face, Isla was certain it would be drawn back in a sneer, especially based on the venom she spat out, "You merely got lucky, soldier."

As she stepped to the side, Rian's body shifted with hers, as if he determined her to be the most dangerous adversary. The leader's head was barely visible above his shield of soldiers but his eyes were trained on Isla, ignoring Rian's presence altogether.

Rian didn't have to speak, but one quick glance Isla's way was enough for her to understand his meaning.

Stay out of the way.

That was something she didn't need to be told twice. She'd learned her lesson the hard way and more than once. Stay out of the way and run when you get a chance. That was what he wanted; that was what he'd told her to do if something like this happened. There was no way he could take them on his own.

They'd gotten lucky that day back at the camp, she knew that now. They'd been expecting her to be alone when she found that creek. Had likely been watching her for a while at that point. They hadn't expected much from a Pedite soldier, as most think them untrained and lacking the same combat skills as the other regiments, but Pedites were the ones sent to the front lines of the worst lands and were the most resourceful, and Rian had been through the worst of them all in the past two years.

But this time the Muratians knew what they were up against and would not be caught off guard again.

The blue and gold soldiers shifted, waiting for direction. The wielder lingered back, staying close to their leader.

Good. She'd be more worried about his safety than harming Rian or getting to Isla.

Isla and Rian were backed up with an unforgiving wall behind them and Muratians everywhere to the front. There were a few spots that they may be able to escape through, if they got lucky and the soldiers moved the right way.

But the goddess of fortunes had rarely been on their side since their arrival.

Someone gave a silent signal to attack, Isla wasn't sure who or what it was, but a thick-bearded soldier lunged at them. He attacked alone as if testing their theory about Isla's powers.

These Muratians weren't idiots. Their first attempt to kill her outside of the camp had failed, and they'd clearly learned from their mistakes.

Rian raised his sword, ready to make that strike which she knew would land its mark. She had full faith in her guard—her companion—to take him down. She'd seen him fell lesser men.

Isla backed up so she was flush against the cliff they'd fallen down only minutes prior and prayed to the tricker goddess for a miracle. She owed them one.

Rian stepped forward, planting his heel in the dusty ground.

The first soldier didn't make it to them. Before he could close the gap, a roar shook the forest ground, sending leaves tumbling from the surrounding oaks.

All heads snapped to the side and a creature crashed through a crimson bush to their right. The attacker faltered, and Rian took his chance to cut him down while the man's eyes were focused on the beast.

Before absolute chaos erupted, all that Isla managed to get a glimpse of was a dark muscled body akin to a feline, with a long stretching neck and slits for eyes. It easily came up to her chest and must weigh as much as a mare. Its eyes were blood red and blazing with rage and violence and—hunger.

A seropa.

Isla had learned about such beasts in the tales her night maid used to read her before bed—the kind told to youngsters to make sure they listened to their elders or ate their entire meal. This creature was surely sent from Rallion herself to drag them to the first gate.

The beast burst forth as a harbinger of death and sent the Muratian soldiers scattering. It seemed to have no target for who became its next meal and charged for those closest to him—a trio of broad-shouldered soldiers.

Rian shoved her out of the way as a staff-wielding soldier took a swipe at them. She heard a sickening crunch as a connection was made with his shoulder, praying it didn't break bone. She landed in the dirt and leaves, clawing out of the way of swinging limbs and shining blades.

Screams and snarls filled her ears, and she couldn't catch her breath. She wanted to help but her stupid limbs wouldn't work, her brain was barely functioning. She was useless.

Utterly useless.

A hand tangled in her braid and wrenched her to her feet. It felt as if half of her scalp was ripped off as a terrible musky laugh rang in her ears.

Something connected with the side of her face, and she was thrown to her knees in a pile of dirt and rocks.

"Stay there," the soldier's voice said, kicking Isla in the side.

Pain radiated everywhere along her ribcage. She may have broken a bone with that blow.

The creature jumped and charged at a group of nearby soldiers with a vicious snarl that rattled her bones. The female wielder grabbed their leader and pulled him away when the seropa got too close to them. Then Isla's face was shoved back into the dirt and a knee was pressed against her back. She couldn't see anything. Couldn't see Rian.

She dug her hands into the dirt and tried to get a hold of any piece of her restrainer that she could, lashing out desperately and with no real plan. Her nails scratched the man's arm, and he screamed, earning her another kick in the side. The pressure against her skull was on the verge of unbearable, and her head would surely be ripped off at any moment.

The Muratian soldier laughed at her. *Laughed.*

She opened her mouth but instead of calling for Rian, she inhaled a cloud of dirt that was kicked into her face.

The man's knee dug painfully into her spine and his hand pressed at the back of her neck. "I said don't move."

A snarling sound raged nearby, and the voice that had just laughed at her now gurgled in pain. The pressure against her back and neck were gone and she rolled out of the way.

The soldier held his neck where a small dagger was now lodged. Rivers of crimson pooled out from the opening, running down his hands and arms.

Rian was about twenty feet away, his hand still outstretched from where he launched the dagger. A smile pulled on his lips when the man slumped to the ground.

Before Rian could utter a word, a thick-set Muratian soldier nicked the side of his arm, and he nearly dropped Dark End. His eyes met hers briefly before turning to focus on the new assailant.

Isla remained frozen—clutching her throbbing side—before that awful sound boiled up again. Footsteps shook the ground and thundered towards her.

The seropa sprinted with its sharp claws glistening in the little light that made it past the tree canopy. Its thin red eyes were focused on its newest prey, weakened on the forest floor. Focused on *her.*

Isla didn't even have time to sit up before the beast jumped over the dead Muratian and lunged for her with its jaw open, showing a dual row of sharp fangs stained red with blood from the Muratian soldiers. Its breath smelled of death and destruction and all Isla could do was scream as it closed the gap in less than a second—too fast for Rian to make his way to her.

This was it. She was useless on her own. Always had been and always would be, no matter how hard she tried.

As her body started to turn limp in acceptance of Rallion's swift fate, someone screamed her name. Nobody had ever cared if she lived or died beyond her usefulness in completing a treaty or how she could help them get ahead in life. Nobody had ever cared for *her* before.

She raised her hands as something vibrated through her entire body. Her entire being.

This was not the day she planned on dying. Not like this.

The seropa clamped down on her wrist and burning pain shot up her arm. It blinded her and blocked out everything.

With her free hand she scratched at its face, trying to get to its blood-red eyes or its nose, like Rian had taught her. Panic crashed through her like a tsunami—threatening to take over everything.

Consume everything.

Destroy everything and everyone. Including Rian.

That couldn't be allowed. She refused to be overshadowed by it anymore.

Isla reached into the pit of herself. The darkest part that she'd always kept hidden. Kept down. And she pulled on it. She pulled and pulled until cold heat sparked in her chest, and she focused it.

Wrangled it and focused it outwards.

The beast squealed and tried to pull away once it realized what was happening, but she clutched onto it with her good hand and forced that pressure into it. She forced that dark pit away from her and into the fanged beast trying to kill her—and only it.

The sound it made was a terrifying mix between a shriek and howl. Stuck in a trance, Isla watched as the black that had pooled at her fingertips burst outward and into the beast. For a terrifying moment—just like at that poor village—she could feel every pump of its frantic heart and every ounce of blood that pushed through its veins, before it was all yanked away.

The rush of energy flooding into her overwhelmed her and, once again, she collapsed under the weight of her powers. Her curse.

Darkness filled her vision and she couldn't move, despite the sound of steel clashing against steel that remained. Fresh dirt filled her nostrils and she realized that she was face-first in the ground again. Blood pounded against her ears and she struggled to lift her head, which felt a hundred times its normal weight.

A shiny black boot came into view next to her face and a light dust cloud was kicked up. This was it. The end.

She squeezed her eyes shut against the final strike, waiting an eternity for them to just get it over with.

Instead of a hearty kick or a deathly blow greeting her, a voice said, "Princess Isla. Are you alright, my lady?"

The shock was enough for her to regain some control over her limbs. She twisted her head up, expecting to see another blue-clad Muratian soldier coming to finish her or finally glimpse the taunting face of that wielder. Instead, she was met by the breath-stealing sight of a black and silver Velotian soldier.

Thirty-Four

Mira

Branches whipped by in a confusing blur of greens and blacks and browns––passing so quickly she wasn't sure if it was a branch that scratched her as she rounded a large bleeding oak or if it was the bite of a sharp blade. Both felt equally painful against her worn skin and thinly soled shoes.

The only sounds that met here were the crunches of leaves beneath her body and the thundering of her heart against its cage.

The thought of staying back there with those bodies was too much. The thought of staying with him was too much. The only option was to keep moving. Branches clung to her dirty clothes and tried to trap her, but she pushed past them and continued. A flicker of violet flashed by, so brief she may have imagined it.

A part of her was pulled toward him, in some twisted way. An even larger part urged her feet to keep moving and to get as far away from this place as possible. She'd allowed her mind to become muddled while down below and wasn't sure if her inner thoughts could be trusted anymore.

Not with both halves of her brain currently at war with each other.

Eventually, the battle distracted her so that she missed a giant tree root, which she swore sprang up out of nowhere and tripped her.

She landed in a messy sprawl of limbs and dirt. The injury at her side howled in pain as she likely broke the stitching. The screaming pain was echoed by a curse to all the goddesses which she yelled into the ground.

Something moved below her, snaking around to her wrist. "What in the—"

It pulled her arm, dragging her along the forest floor with its unrelenting grip. Through a thicket of bushes. Around giant oaks and through a mud pit.

She struggled and twisted but couldn't escape its grasp.

Shining silver came crashing down upon it and the green vine withered away into darkness. Everything felt like it was still spinning through.

A chuckle came from behind her and she groaned, turning on to her back. So much for a quick escape.

"Watch out for those roots. They seem to have a mind of their own out here."

That godsdamned private had followed her. "I had it perfectly handled on my own," she spat out with a sizable amount of condensation that she was unaccustomed to escaping her lips.

Devlin crouched next to her wearing that damned crooked grin. "Why'd you run?"

"So, I could have a nap in this lovely pile of dirt," she said, fishing the ground beneath her.

Instant regret washed over her. She shouldn't be so callous with her words. She ran away. She *ran* away from the camp. Devlin could have her lashed or worse. They could also punish Beretta now that it was known they were close.

"Excellent location to fall flat on your face," he said lightly. A hand was extended, but she smacked it away and struggled to her feet in front of him. "Any further and you may have met some really nasty snapping vines. You got off easy, trust me."

And that one wasn't nasty? Curiosity bit at the back of her tongue but she refused to rise to his bait. Instead, she focused on brushing off the red-tinted leaves that clung to her dirty shirt.

"If you wanted a stroll in the forest, you could have just asked."

Summoning all the icy thoughts she could, she sent him a withering glare. It did nothing to quell the pounding of her heart or stall the way her boiling blood raced through her veins. She hated the effect he had on her without seeming to try.

He dropped his gaze and his expression became somber. "I'm sorry about the bodies. That was callous."

"You think?"

"I wanted to show you that you are safe here. I thought you'd be happy."

A laugh bubbled up from her chest, but she shoved it down before it could escape. "How could you ever think that would be a joyful sight? Those men are dead. They had families, lives."

"They decided their fates when they allowed the attack on your life. You know we don't allow that kind of violence here... especially not to you."

Thump. Thump. "You should take the bodies down. Let the dead rest. Rallion would be displeased and you don't want to anger the goddess."

He screwed up his face in contemplation, then nodded. "You're not like what I thought you'd be," he whispered, reaching out for her hand. "I didn't expect this when we first started to work together."

She pulled away as a flurry of confusion clogged her brain.

Pain flashed in his blue eyes. "I thought I'd have you convinced by now."

"Convinced of what?"

"Trusting me."

"Why should I ever trust you?" Mira pulled away, clutching her side.

There were only two people she trusted in this camp, including herself. Devlin was definitely not on that list. Not after everything.

He grinned. Before an answer could escape his perfectly shaped lips, a terrible sound rang in her ears.

"Get behind me," he said, eyes narrowing as he stared into the dark forest.

Mira refused to move. "I'll take my chances with whatever beast that was, thank you very much."

"If you go any further, I can't guarantee you'll make it back safely."

Mira looked down the dark path behind her and looked back at Devlin. Certain death seemed like a good option at this time.

His eyes searched her defiant face, then trailed down. "You're hurt."

Mira looked down and swore. Crimson stains were starting to seep through her shirt. It looked like she'd torn a stitch or two after all.

Before she could utter another word, he raised his hand to her side. She jerked away on impulse, but he grabbed her hand and kept a tight grip on it. "Don't move," he said in a calming voice.

"Wha—?"

The words caught in her throat as he pushed his hand into her side. All she could do was stare at him stupidly and wonder which goddess had possessed him.

At first there was only stinging pain. Before she could shout, something cold and icy burst from her side. It was pain and bliss all mixed together, reaching down into her insides. A faint light burst out of the spot where his hand touched her side.

The aching pain of her wound was gone and all that remained was a dull throb.

When she pulled up the side of her tunic and pulled off the bandage, it revealed nothing there. The only hint that there was once a gaping hole in her side was the odd tingling in her skin, as if her mind still remembered the injury but her body didn't.

Devlin watched her closely. A bead of sweat formed on his temple as he waited for her reaction.

A thousand questions filled her mind. It was hard to pick out one that resembled a coherent thought. "You're—you're—"

"Like you," he finished. "Not exactly like you." He held up his hands. "I can't do the things you can."

"I don't know what I can do," Mira whispered.

Devlin shrugged. "Not yet."

"How long have you been this way?"

"A while." He smiled sadly. "My mother—she changed once she found out I was a wielder. She sent me off to the camps with the conscripts to train. There were years that I barely saw her except for family events, and my father was too busy to notice. It—it wasn't easy, but I do know what you are going through." He cocked his head and took a step towards her. You've barely begun to tap into your powers but from what I've seen of them, they're virtually limitless."

She took a step back. "But you've barely seen them."

"I've seen enough to know," he said plainly. "And since Rallion's comet was seen months ago, I'm sure we've only seen the edge of what you can do. My mother was a devout follower of Rallion's ways, and her people have been reading the signs for years before all this."

Mira's back hit a tree and she gulped down ragged gasps of pine-soaked air.

Devlin placed a hand on either side of her face and she was painfully aware of every pale freckle on his face and every swirling shade of blue in his eyes.

"We should go back," she said, her mind blanking of all else. She was a prey captured in a predator's clutches, yet her mind wouldn't work properly.

"Nobody saw us leave," he said calmly, allowing his eyes to bore into hers. "I meant everything that I said before about you feeling safe. I want you to know that."

"Why?" The question slipped from her lips before she could stop it.

"Because you're special," he said, not moving from where he had her trapped. "You're more special than you realize… and I want to help you reach your full potential—beyond the firestone."

A piece of rock that was floating in her stomach plummeted. "Only that?" she asked quietly.

His eyes traveled to her lips. He bore the same hungry look he had that day in the cavern and it made every sensible thought in her brain evaporate on the spot. "You know the other reason why."

The two parts of her spirit resumed their vicious battle. She should run. She could scream. She could fight back. But that other half of her was nervously waiting for what would happen next.

That second half won for now, as it tilted her head into a nod. It didn't have the power to make her speak the words out loud, not yet. She was afraid it would come out in a jumbled mess and scare him off.

Something darkened in his eyes and it was like a trance was broken in them both. He grabbed her face and tilted her head toward him before slamming his lips into hers.

The half of her that wanted this, that half leaned into his kiss with a fervor she didn't recognize. It was like someone else had taken control of her hand and her lips. She had no memory of being with another man before this—but then again, those past memories were always hazy—yet her hands worked their way expertly along his arms, across his chest, and into his hair.

She was fueled by a fiery passion that filled every drop of blood furiously pumping its way through her body. Heat and longing filled her. So did confusion and something else.

As his hands and lips worked their way to her neck, that confusion spread like wildfire. Surely the trees would have caught ablaze by now.

He took her confusion for timidness and muttered against her skin, "You're more perfect than I could have dreamed up. I'll never let anything happen to you again."

The words snapped something in her and visions of those decaying bodies came back to her no matter how hard she tried to bury them. She pushed him away. She couldn't do this. Not now.

Something dark filled his eyes and he looked hurt. She didn't blame him. Not when her own emotions were a tangled web not even she could decipher. He didn't deserve this. Didn't deserve whatever poor excuse of an explanation her half-wit brain could come up with, so she didn't bother with one.

A howl sounded again, but neither of them moved. He waited for her. Expecting something.

Mira had nothing more to give, she straightened her dirty tunic and said in a hollow voice, "Take me back. *Now*."

Beretta was right. She didn't know him. Not fully. And he definitely didn't know her.

All that talk of helping her escape was nothing but false promises to get her to trust him. And she'd fallen for it like a fool. She'd clung to that desperate sliver of hope, attached to a beautifully tempting body and entrancing eyes.

Foolish.

That is what she was. What she had been.

No more. No more falling for those pretty lies sung by a sweet voice that only masked some ulterior motive that she still couldn't place.

No more.

As she thought through a foolhardy plan, her mind settled. One way or another. Tomorrow would be her last day in these gods-forsaken mines.

Thirty-Five

The Captain

The sight of the rolling beige and black tents was as familiar to him as the hilt of his sword, but for some reason, he felt out of place today. Like an intruder.

It had been so long since he was in the presence of the Velotian military that he'd foolishly allowed himself to forget how much contempt most of them held for him. Here he was, being escorted through the makeshift camp by two burly Divite soldiers, wearing a torn Muratian uniform, covered in a mix of blood and dirt, all with a princess in even worse condition than he was.

It did not look great for him—especially as the one who was supposed to protect her.

To keep her safe.

Rian pulled the strap of his satchel further up his shoulder and kept his eyes on the black cloak of the wielder in front of him. A bead of sweat dripped down the back of his neck and into his shirt.

The Agicae wielders kept him away from Isla while tending to their wounds, as if worried he'd harm her. Isla was pale and shaking when they showed up—after the Muratians had scattered, and the beast was turned to ash.

At least they didn't see her use her powers—thank the goddesses for that. The Velotians were more concerned when Rian ran to check on Isla, and he nearly ended up gutted right then and there.

It took Isla stepping in to convince them he was a Velotian, despite the blue uniform.

They took great care in making sure the princess was fully patched up before haphazardly mending him, and only enough so he could make it on one of the steeds they'd brought for the journey. He understood. They wanted him weak in case he tried to pull anything before they made it back to camp for questioning. He'd have done the same.

They had been so close to the edge of the forest when they found them—and made it outside of Muratian lands in no time with the help of his comrades.

They were home.

They made it to Velotia, even if he was still being treated like an enemy raider.

There was no need to wait to find out what the rest of the camp thought of his and the princess's initial disappearance. The soldiers didn't hide their sneers when they saw him. Some whispered that word he hadn't heard in so long that he'd nearly forgotten the name they'd branded him with.

Coward.

They marched around the dust ridden, beige-tented Pedite camp, and went straight towards the rows of pristine black Divites tents. Each step dragged on forever and his body wanted to burst from his skin—anything to get away from these stiff tents in a camp he didn't belong.

Commander Skallen stood there with his shining black and silver-lined uniform and the multitude of badges on his left arm, waiting with several of his officers with shining dual sword badges. Rian's eyes went straight to the look of fury on the grizzled commander's face. The man struck a unique fear into the Pedite soldiers whenever he inspected their camp. They knew he didn't care for them like the rest of his precious military branches and would always favor his Divites over them.

Except when it came to the worst duties. Those he reserved for the Pedites he despised most. That was how Rian was assigned guard duty over Isla so long ago. The worst punishment Skallen could devise for him, and how right he had been—at the time.

They stopped directly in front of the grisly commander, and Rian flexed his fingers. The Divite kept a tight grip on his arm so he couldn't run. The blue uniform he was clad in, no matter how dirty and faded it was by now, stood out among a sea of black.

Even after Isla protested their treatment of him, the soldiers ignored her. And the look the commander gave him told him exactly how this conversation was about to go.

Rian's chest tightened. As if he should have expected anything less.

"Princess Isla," the commander drawled, returning his hungry gaze to her. No doubt the king had been placing immense pressure to return his daughter safely. Now, Commander Skallen could take all the credit for the rescue efforts—and the reward. "Words cannot express how relieved we are to have you safely returned."

The person Rian had grown to know in the forest had disappeared. Another one stood in her place as she drew herself up, her face fixed in a haughty frown that he remembered all too well—having been on the receiving end of it many times.

"Thank you for your men's assistance, commander," she said in even tones that were devoid of any emotion. Rian had been around her enough to recognize the fiery anger concealed beneath her cool surface. "There is a group of Muratians not far from where we were. They are the ones responsible for the attacks, and you should send your men after them immediately."

The commander dipped his head. "I'll send my best ones, Your Highness."

Your Highness.

In their last days together, Rian had almost allowed himself to forget who she was and where his place lay in all of this. The vice-like grip on his arm was a painful reminder.

The commander still didn't acknowledge him. He remained focused on the princess. "You may use my tent until we can fetch your things from the old camp. We had to leave most of your escort behind, given the need to move swiftly. We do have two of your ladies with us who can attend to you and help you, ah, freshen up, while I deal with this soldier."

Isla's head snapped to where Rian stood, several feet behind, still with their *escorts*. He gave a constricted wave, and fury flashed briefly across her eyes. It was so quick he was unsure if the others understood what it meant. He'd seen that look many times by now.

"What exactly do you mean by that, *commander*?" She stepped toward Skallen; her chin tilted upward so she could look down the bridge of her nose at him despite being half a head shorter.

The commander swallowed. "With the ambush in the woods and your disappearance—naturally with the captain's history, we have to do a full investigation to ensure—"

"*Investigation*? What kind of investigation?"

Rian could only see the back of her head but was certain the princess's eyebrows were halfway to her hairline by now.

"You see, my lady, we need to ensure—"

"No." She closed the remaining gap between her and the commander. For a short woman, covered in half the forest's leaves and with a large twig still tangled in her hair, she was quite the commanding presence. "Your captain not only saved my life several times, he risked his own to ensure my initial escape and safe arrival home. There's nothing to investigate."

A bead of sweat dripped down the commander's forehead. His face turned purple while he stuttered through his next sentence. "Well—it's protocol—have to ensure no ill intent—I'd prefer if we—it's protocol, my lady." he finished pathetically.

"And I said it's not necessary. That's an order, *soldier*."

While dressed in the tatters of once fine travel leathers, with a tangled mess of hair, and a face half-covered in dirt, it was almost easy to forget this was a Princess of Velotia.

Almost.

Perhaps the commander had also briefly forgotten who stood in front of him. Any doubts had been washed away with the condescending way she dressed down his rank—one of the few who could do so without a sound lashing. Commander Skallen was rendered speechless.

That was a first.

All the clueless commander could do was nod at the Divite next to Rian, who begrudgingly released him with a shove. The commander shot a fiery glare his way that Rian refused to meet.

Rubbing his arm, he tried in vain to grab the princess's attention. A duo of finely dressed ladies—*her* ladies—swarmed her. They pointed at the state of her attire in horror and whisked her off before another word could be said.

So that was it, then.

Rian was left alone to face the gale of Commander Skallen, along with the accusatory glances from the rest of them. All they could do was stare. They couldn't disobey a direct order from Velotian royalty.

Or could they?

There was one way to find out.

With a winning smile sent at the steaming commander, he took one step backward. Nothing happened.

Then he took another. And another quick one.

They did nothing to stop him.

Without a second glance, he picked up his pace and all but ran away from the commander before he could change his mind and lock him up. He didn't stop to catch his breath until he was long gone.

It was easy to find the Pedite camp with its tiny beige tents tightly squeezed together, the patches on several already visible from a distance. Nothing had changed there.

Nobody seemed to be expecting him, so he made his way quickly through the tents as he was not in the mood to be questioned today. It felt like he had been gone for ages. He didn't know what to expect when he returned but it felt different. It felt empty for some reason.

A thought came to him briefly of going to find Isla, but that wouldn't be proper. Not to mention, he doubted the commander would let him get within eyesight of the princess ever again.

Everything happened so quickly that they didn't get to say goodbye. Now she was back where she belonged, and so was Rian. Even if it felt strange to his bones. He was so used to looking out for her every next step that he didn't know what to do with himself. What use would he be now that he had finished his mission?

At least he had escaped punishment—for now.

Which was why it was best to find someone who could tell him what in Slin's name had been happening while they were away. How bad was this going to be and how happy would they be to see him?

The first familiar face he found, Malin, was sharpening his longsword. He was easy enough to recognize by the silver band in his shaggy blond hair that General Xavier never managed to make him cut. His black and silver private's uniform was badly wrinkled, as if he hadn't cleaned it the entire time they were missing, and half the buttons were undone. Good to see that he hadn't bothered to change that either.

Rian strode up to him, unsure what type of greeting was in store.

Malin paused mid-stroke. He blinked and stared as if he'd just seen Rallion herself trudge up from the ninth gate.

He stood.

"Rian," he said happily, clasping his arm. He stepped back and surveyed him from toe to top. "What in Luriel's name are you wearing? I'm surprised you didn't get stabbed before setting foot in this place."

"I know," Rian said wearily. It wasn't for lack of trying on the Divites' part.

"What happened to you?"

A few of the other Pedites had finally taken note of a blue-clad soldier in their midst and paused to stare.

"Not now," he said pointedly, flexing his empty hand. "I've had a long day."

"Let's get you set up with a tent." Malin wrinkled his nose and adjusted the band in his hair. "And a bath. You smell like you need it. And most importantly, let's get you a new uniform before somebody skewers you on the end of a sword—or me for talking to you."

Rian breathed a sigh of relief. At least he had one ally in this camp.

After finally scrubbing himself clean with half-used camp water, getting a tent and cot set up, dumping the few possessions he managed to keep, and putting on a familiar black and silver uniform that Malin managed to dig up, Rian finally settled down to rest his achy legs far away from the Divites and Agicaes. His side still throbbed from that half-healed injury. If he were anyone else, he'd try to find another wielder to get them to finish the job, but he knew better than that.

Malin brought a bowl of thick stew along with a slice of lumpy bread to eat, which tasted like a glorious feast at this point. Rian allowed the silence to spread as he ate his way through the best meal he'd had in days. *Days.*

"So," Malin drawled with a mouth full of food. "It was that bad, huh?"

Rian shook his head. He didn't know the half of it.

"*What happened?*" Malin asked.

Boots scraped against rock, announcing the presence of a Pedite soldier with blond hair braided into loops that were tied together at the ends with scraps of leather. She still had her favorite chipped axe at her side and wore a thick leather Pedite uniform that had seen many battles.

Freya.

They hadn't spoken in weeks, even before he became stranded in Murat. When he came back from Liopen, she had distanced herself from him, rightfully so given what he'd done. What he'd caused. They'd barely spoken any words that weren't about their assignments since then.

Rian rose to unsteady feet. Before he could speak, Freya held up a hand.

"Princess Isla has requested your presence," she said curtly, refusing to meet his eyes. "*Demands*—is more the word I'd use. I'd suggest you come along promptly."

The way that her eyes rolled at that last part tugged a small smile to his face.

"Good luck with that." Malin scoffed. He shoveled down a mouthful of stew, nearly choking and sending himself into a coughing fit.

After thumping him on the back, Rian passed his bowl to Malin to finish, and followed Freya's retreating figure. She hadn't even looked back to ensure he was following.

They walked in silence throughout the maze of tents with her keeping a brisk pace.

Now that word had spread of their return, others noticed as he passed. The first cluster of soldiers all stopped their training exercise to silently watch them walk past. The second group of Agicae warriors sneered at Rian, and one spat at his boots. He pointedly ignored them and so did Freya.

When they put the Agicae camp behind them, Freya turned around. A long braid whipped over her shoulder that nearly took out his eye.

"I was really worried about you, you know," she said, glaring at him as if everything were his fault.

"Thanks? I guess."

"They thought you had a part in it and, for a while, I'm ashamed to say that I believed it too." She stared at his boot. "Can you blame us? Then we received reports that you two were spotted by a village and that you saved her from some sort of eruption."

A bitter laugh escaped his lips. That was putting it lightly.

Thank the goddess, that was the only rumor that had spread through the camp.

"We were able to track you, or her at least, with one of the Agicae. We couldn't go directly into Murat without their magical sensors being tripped. Not until we knew for certain. The Agicae knew you were moving south so we got as close as we could."

That's how they found them so quickly in the forests. No doubt the Muratians had a similarly powered wielder who tracked them from their end.

"The Agicae tracked Muratian soldiers close to you—with one of their princes at that—so we knew we had to send some of our men in. The commander was worried they'd get caught and turn things worse, but General Xavier convinced him, and it all turned out."

The Muratian Prince. So that's who that one was. It made sense now.

Freya shuffled her feet. "I'm glad you're alive... and I'm sorry—for abandoning you after Liopen."

"It's fine," he said gruffly, shoving her shoulder. "I don't blame you. I would have done the same. At least I always bounce back, right?"

"That princess is a piece of work." She rolled her eyes. "And I thought she was taxing *before* the attack. But she wanted to talk to you and, *apparently*, it can't wait."

He drew his eyebrows together and rubbed his face. What had she done now?

"Exactly," Freya said, misinterpreting his sigh as one of annoyance. "I don't know how you managed to make it so long without cutting out her tongue. I would have left her to fend for herself, but you're a far better man than I am."

That and the fact that he had to make things right. He couldn't fail his kingdom another time.

They'd made it past the black Divite tents and came upon a bright red one, far more ostentatious than the rest. The commander's tent.

She gestured at the entrance. "Here we are." She thumped him on the back and said grimly, "Good luck. We'll catch up after."

He wanted to stop her, to tell her the truth and so much more, but the words couldn't form. So, he watched his friend saunter back toward the Pedite camp, leaving him outside of the commander's tent—no—it was Princess Isla's tent now—to fend for himself.

There were no less than ten guards placed around her tent. Two Agicae and eight Divites.

Naturally.

They all watched him approach with hands on the hilt of their swords. Rian hadn't bothered wearing his weapons since discarding the Muratian uniform. That'd only serve to incriminate him more in their eyes.

The same Divite that had so graciously escorted him into the camp, sent him a withering look and pulled back the flap of the tent. He muttered *Cordrai* as Rian passed, spitting on the ground in front of him.

Rian ignored him and entered, not sure of what to expect. The only time he'd been inside of a superior's tent was to be chastised or punished, so he didn't have a lot of great memories of these red tents.

The inside of this one was different.

He caught a fleeting glimpse of a massive bed covered in a plethora of dark furs at the back, and a thick oak desk filled with papers and candles to the side, but his attention was on the middle of the large tent where a long table was set up with the most amazing sight he'd seen in weeks, perhaps all his life.

Thirty-Six
The Captain

The star goddess herself couldn't have scrounged up a better assortment of options or planned a better feast.

Plates filled with at least a dozen different kinds of fresh vegetables, exotic fruit he'd never had the chance to try in his life, and at least four different kinds of roasted meat weighed down the thick table. Two crystalline cups filled to the rim with some sort of expensive red wine were placed in front of overly ornate sets of plates and cutlery. A tiered tray was set in the middle with over two dozen miniature bites of a layered dessert Rian had never seen before.

It was a meal that shamed the harvest feast that his mom would work all night to tirelessly pull together.

And it was all for him.

Isla—the princess—stood to the side, wearing a new, crisp set of black leathers with a lace collar peeking out, and a silver fur-lined cloak pinned to her shoulder by a flaming signet. Her hair was up in one of those impractical, ostentatious updos interwoven with strips of beaded silk probably meant to highlight her slim cheekbones, but most importantly, it showcased the radiant glint in her brown eyes.

He opened his mouth to say that she looked terribly overdone in her new outfit and that the color drowned her face, but the lie wouldn't form on his tongue, so he closed it like an idiot.

The princess's expression dropped and it made his heart twist.

Someone coughed, and it was only then that he noticed the two women in long white dresses standing to the side. The princess nodded at them and spoke in sharp tones, "Alynna. Susanna. You may leave."

They both sent a questioning look to their ward. However, it was not their place to remind her of the inappropriateness of being left alone in a soldier's company—especially one who arrived dressed in Muratian colors—so they cast him doubtful looks and sulked out. One threw a final warning look over her shoulder as the tent flap fluttered shut behind them.

As soon as they were gone, the princess's shoulders slumped. She splayed her hands out and gestured toward the overflowing table, biting on her lower lip. "This is all I could get brought in from a nearby village. They didn't have much."

A laugh escaped his lips at the absurdity and her eyebrows jumped in clear confusion. She didn't think this was enough?

"I'm sorry. I'm sorry," he said quickly, before her confusion could turn to rage. He pointed at the overflowing table. "That's supposed to be for just us two?"

She nodded, eyes wide.

"This is more than enough. You have nothing to worry about."

That radiant smile came back in full force, nearly blinding him like the sun. It lit all his limbs on fire, flickering briefly before he stifled that dangerous flame deep down.

"Then sit." She gestured at the two spots seated at opposite ends of the long table. Apparently, fancy meals required as much space as possible between the participants. He wouldn't know, since he'd never seen anything as elegant as this.

When he hesitated, she asked, "Why not?"

He rubbed his arm. "I shouldn't be here—with you. I don't want people talking."

She shrugged. "I don't care about that anymore. I believe that a return feast was promised, and I mean to keep my word."

The aroma of sweet ham hit him in full force, and his stomach protested every second the meat wasn't in it. He nodded. "Then a feast it is."

There were so many forks in front of him that he didn't know where to start, so he picked a middle one that looked most normal to him. The princess already started grabbing pieces, starting with an entire calf-bone by the looks of it.

"What?" she said innocently. "I haven't had a good meal in forever, and you've seen me at much worse. Go ahead, there's nobody here but us."

Without needing to be told twice, he attacked the plates nearest him. He didn't care which ones, just that he got his hands on as much food as possible. He piled on two slices of roast along with spiced sprouts and mushrooms, then poured some sort of cream sauce on top of it. If his stomach could handle it, he was determined to try a bit of everything.

Across the table, his companion filled her plate with similar gusto. All forms of decorum forgotten in the face of all this food. It was a good thing her ladies weren't here as witnesses or they'd turn faint.

"Your commander was not happy when I told him I wanted to host a grand meal. He was even more irritated when I told him he was not invited." She grabbed her glass and took a dainty sip of wine, paused, then decided on several large gulps.

"I bet he was ecstatic when he discovered who your esteemed guest was."

She snorted into her glass. "That man really does have it out for you."

That was something he hadn't expected to go away so easily.

Rian grabbed his glass and pointed at her shining, clean hair. "Did you demand all the hot water in the camp again, Isla—sorry, *princess*?"

She froze.

Rian set his glass down.

"You don't have to call me that," she said softly. "We're still friends, aren't we?" Her brown eyes widened with some emotion he couldn't place.

Was that what she thought they were? Friends.

He scratched the back of his neck. "I don't know... it's not proper, is it?"

She shrugged, and he pretended not to notice the way the light caught her eyes. "I don't care. We trudged through a freezing river together. We shared a room together and slept in the dirt together. The name feels *weird* coming from you."

"When you list it that way... Isla, it is then," he said.

She tapped the side of her glass. "It felt strange not having you around to criticize my every step. It was even stranger having my ladies attend to me while I bathed and dressed again."

"Well," he smirked. "As much as that does sound tempting to witness, I don't think your father would have approved my guardianship over you extending to the bathhouse... and *please* don't tell people we slept in the dirt together. Especially using that specific phrasing."

"Right, you want to keep your head in place," she drolled. "Then maybe you should stop talking about my bathing habits so much."

He scoffed. "*Please*. The last thing on my mind will be about what you do in that gods-forsakened bath for hours on end."

The thought of it didn't fill him with utter revulsion, as he had hoped it would. He squirmed under her close watch.

Isla chuckled and returned to attacking her plate. They ate in silence, besides the occasional groan of pleasure, and sharing quick glances every so often but both were equally focused on their meal. Too focused.

When she lapped up the last drop of sauce with a steaming bun, she pushed away from the table and stood, licking her lips. "Did you try the layered sponge cakes? They look amazing."

"Not yet," he said in between mouthfuls of ham.

"They're from the commander's private stock. Another reason he's unhappy with me, as I had my ladies raid it." She shrugged as if Skallen's unhappiness was only an annoyance rather than another potential item in a long list of things that could be used to expel one of them from the militia. It would end up his fault, just like everyone else was.

She plucked a cake from the top tier, grabbed his hand, and placed it delicately on top.

Rian could worry about the commander taking his frustrations on him later. Right now, he had to focus on steadying the frenzied pace of his heart. It couldn't decide if it wanted to freeze and crack in two or gallop away into the skies. He was certain the indecision turned his face bright red.

Instead of returning to her seat, Isla leaned against the table and watched expectantly. For some reason the proximity made his throat dry up—even though they'd been much closer during their nights in the woods. He grabbed his crystal glass and took a swig. Because Slin had it out for him, the liquid got stuck on the way down and sent him into a coughing fit.

A helping hand thumped his back and he sputtered his way to clear lungs. His face was definitely the same shade as his wine now.

In his debacle, he'd crushed the sweet in his palm. Isla scoffed and grabbed a napkin.

She wiped the crumbs and cream off his hand. "So uncivilized, soldier."

Another skip of his heart. "We didn't all grow up in fancy palaces, princess."

An eyebrow raised at the use of the title, but her smile didn't falter. He found himself studying the curve of her lips. "No. We didn't."

When her eyes met his, something changed. He was aware that her ladies could return at any moment, and that their closeness would be considered improper by all means, especially in a private tent surrounded by guards who would love any reason to hand him over to the commander, but he was intensely aware of the fact that she still held his hand.

He should pull it back and tell her to return to her seat. That they should finish their meal that she'd dreamt of for so long. Remind her that she had a betrothed to get to and that their time together was drawing to an end.

For some reason, the only word that came out of his mouth was, "Isla."

The hand that held his twitched but did not let go.

"Yes?" Her brown eyes did not waver from the gaze they held his in. She blinked. Waiting.

Somehow his brain managed to start working and allow his mouth to speak again. "We should probably finish the lovely meal you worked so hard to expropriate for us."

"Should we?" She squeezed his hand and pulled it to her chest. Her eyes darted to his lips, then back up to trap his gaze.

"I—ah." The food he ate was performing a convoluted dance in his stomach, and there was fluttering against his chest that he couldn't stop. It distracted him from everything that wasn't her. All he could focus on was the curve of her lips, the crinkle at the edge of her eyes—how they sparkled in this candlelight—and how she was still holding his godsdamned hand.

She laughed, shaking the hand that she still held close to her. A strand of hair loosened from the nest on her head.

With his free, but shaky, hand, he brushed it out of her face and tucked it behind her ear. She turned her head so that his hand cupped her cheek. The heat from her breath tickled along his wrist.

At this moment, it felt like it was the two of them alone in that forest again.

He ran his thumb along the edge of her jaw, memorizing every curve, every line of her smooth skin. She pressed her lips against his palm.

Heat exploded from his hand, spreading to every limb in his body. It blocked out all semblance of sanity, of rationality, of honor, and spurred him to vacate his seat and close the gap between them.

He paused an inch away, but the intensity in her eyes was permission enough.

When he pressed his lips against hers, she tasted of honey, flowers, and a hint of sweet wine. He pulled back after a moment, but she leaned into him and refused to break away. Any thoughts that weren't of her evaporated on the spot. One hand ended up in her hair, feeling through the layers of pins and silk as he pulled her in close, and the other hand slid from its spot at her back towards her waist.

He wanted her closer, wanted more. He had ever since that first night in the forest.

There were so many delicious things his mind wanted to do right now, and he'd start with—

A horn rang throughout the encampment, breaking them out of their spell.

He leaped back when one of her ladies ran into the tent.

"What is it?" Isla asked in a shaky but commanding voice.

The lady, Alynna, scrunched her face. Her princess must have looked all out of sorts leaning against the table, adjusting the pins on her hair while her guest stood awkwardly against the tent pole five feet away, probably looking extremely guilty. He shoved his hands into his pockets as if they weren't just all over Isla's silky hair seconds earlier.

No. Stop that.

Painting a forced smile as if she hadn't observed anything, Alynna smoothed out the sleeve of her dress and said, "Your brother's party has finally arrived, Your Highness. Prince Edmund is here."

Isla gasped as if Alynna had just delivered a killing blow.

Thirty-Seven

The Princess

Would he ever stop droning on?

Her brother had already kept her up half the night lecturing about the inconvenience he went through when their father called him to escort Isla the remainder of the way. Now, seeing as he had to meet with the Koliats instead of completing a campaign with his Divite legion along the eastern border, he was apparently determined to ruin her entire night with the same complaints.

What's worse is that he made her sit in this stuffy tent while he and that sour commander, along with his entire idiotic leadership team, discussed their next attack plan for his battalion after Isla was safely *handed over* to her betrothed like she was a fragile possession being passed around. Nobody bothered to include her in the discussions and waved her question off with a placating smile whenever she spoke up.

"If we move a third of your forces westward, along with those promised from Koliat, we can set up the perfect perimeter to take them unawares," Commander Skallen said to a chorus of murmured agreements. "There is a small village right on the border of Murat that we can take with ease and set up base."

Isla's heart jumped.

They wanted to enter Murat, after everything she did to make it back so this alliance could go through. She thought this marriage was to stop a pending war, not start one.

Edmund's eyes trailed along the map, darkening at some point she couldn't see. "Agreed. We need to be prepared to make the first strike. Give the men your orders and we can send them out before the week is done."

Isla opened her mouth, but Edmund tilted his head slightly to the side. *No.* Her opinion wasn't wanted.

And she had to sit and bear it all with a pleasant smile on her face like her father taught her to do. If they were so determined to exclude her, then why have her waste one of her last days of freedom in this gods-forsakened tent?

She knew the answer.

They wanted to keep an eye on her. Make sure she didn't *slip away,* again, as the commander put it. They blamed her for her own kidnapping—attempted kidnapping.

Word had spread that she ran off from camp on that first day. It didn't come from Rian, as the soldiers were determined to ignore his presence since they arrived, but a report from some of Commander Skallen's *most trusted Divites* who saw her run away without her escort.

If they saw her leave, then perhaps the commander should be mad at them for not initially reporting it and allowing only one bodyguard to follow her off into the woods, where anything could—and did—happen.

Again, no one bothered to listen when she brought that up.

Just like no one listened when she tried to tell them that Rian was the one responsible for her getting home safely. The commander immediately took all the credit for her rescue, and she was silenced by her brother while attempting to correct him.

Her time away made her forget what it was like to be important and yet invisible, like a delicate centerpiece that you forgot laid on the table for meal after boring meal.

They all wanted something from her, usually her simpering presence or approval, never anything of substance. At least Rian listened to her—in the end.

Her brother never would, and certainly not this poor excuse of a commander, who droned on about how many esteemed regiments were under his command, with his generals nodding along like a mass of puppets. It didn't look like they would be asking for her opinion any time soon, so why bother paying attention?

She touched her lips. What was her travel companion up to now?

Surely, he must be having a better time than her. Anything had to be better than this.

After Alynna announced her brother's arrival in the encampment, Rian slipped away, and she hadn't seen him for the rest of the night or the next day either. She kept her eye out but had a feeling he had been keeping to the Pedite camp, and she wasn't allowed anywhere near that section.

The spot he touched on her cheek still burned, and that feeling of her stomach dropping through the air had yet to disappear... and she didn't think she wanted it to. She could still taste him on her lips and craved more.

Both her ladies remained silent while fixing her hair before her brother's arrival. There may have been a questioning glance or two but if there was one thing she could trust, it was their discretion.

Perhaps she could slip out before this was all over. No. That wouldn't work. Even though he hadn't called on her, Edmund's eyes kept flickering toward her, as if making sure she hadn't snuck off again to cause any more delays to his precious campaign.

When it seemed the commander was finished with his long-winded story and the group began to disperse, Isla attempted to make her getaway.

Before she stepped foot outside the commander's newly erected tent—nowhere near as obtuse and ornate as the one he gave to her—a hand grabbed her elbow.

There was no need to ask who it was. Edmund.

No one else would dare touch her.

A blush filled her cheeks.

Almost no one.

Resplendent in a silver tunic with black flames woven into the thick cloth, her brother easily stuck out from the soldiers. A silver crown of flames rested on his dark hair, more ornate than her old circlet, but not as resplendent as their father's double-tiered crown. A double row of dark buttons along his torso and at the cuffs of his sleeve held the look together for Velotia's heir.

Their father's favorite.

He didn't even hug her when they were reunited—an action, apparently, still beneath him.

Edmund stared down at her with thin eyes. Some days she hated those eyes. Every time she looked at him, all she could see was her father's disappointment staring back at her. "Come dine with me, sister."

With a hint of desperation, she looked around for aid. Alynna and Susanna both stood to the side and sent encouraging nods, while nobody else paid her any attention.

A sigh escaped as she placed her hand on top of his forearm. "It would be my pleasure."

It was decided—by Edmund—that it was best to dine in her borrowed, musky-smelling tent that only brought back memories of last night's more pleasant meal. The difference in company on both nights was astounding.

All her brother wanted to do was cycle between talking about his campaign and how she had inconvenienced him so. She stabbed at the fire-roasted fowl on her plate, all hunger having evaporated long ago.

At least it was easy to pretend to listen. All that she had to do was nod every few minutes and scatter in a few *uh-huh*s or *hm*s when he paused. Her appetite had disappeared but her throat was parched for a glass of wine, which she downed far too easily.

The only thing that finally snapped her attention into place was the mention of Prince Brenner. At the name of her future husband, she felt the little food she had eaten turn to ice in her stomach.

"What was that, Edmund?"

"I said that he'll be meeting up with us before Bluemoon Bay now. His father dispatched several squads to aid in your search and they'll escort the prince to meet with us in three days' ride."

Three days? The grip on her fork tightened, turning her knuckles white. She was not prepared to meet him so soon.

"Not happy with that?" he asked, reading her expression easily. He took another stab filled with carrots and fowl into his mouth. "I don't blame you."

"What do you mean?" she asked sharply.

They'd never discussed her soon-to-be-husband in detail before. Nothing beyond who he was and when she was expected to meet him.

"We've been in contact since your disappearance." Edmund rolled his eyes. "He's been pestering me daily with missives demanding updates. He seems like a *lovely* man. I don't think his men have much pleasant to say about him either."

With that, he took a sip of his wine, before slicing open the bird's chest to get to its steaming innards.

"Why are you coming with us?" Isla tore her eyes away from the sight and placed her fork back on the table. "I thought you planned to send men into Murat. Won't that make things worse with the Muratians?"

"Things are already worse, no thanks to you. We have to prepare for the worst-case scenario. The alliance with Koliat is absolutely necessary to ensure Velotia comes out on top if war crosses the border, no matter the cost. That's our priority now."

Something in her heart dried up and turned to ash at his words. No matter the cost to *her*, was the part he didn't say out loud. She clenched her hands into fists to keep the anger from spilling out as she watched him eat his meal as if nothing was wrong. As if nothing he said would be upsetting to hear.

But everything was wrong. Nobody seemed to care about her or what she wanted. It was like she was screaming into a void that only echoed despair her way. Everything wanted to collapse in on her.

Edmund paused mid-chew and jerked his chin. "Why aren't you eating? The fowl is a touch dry but it's edible, Isla. You look like you need a good meal. What were they feeding you there?"

The thread of anger snapped and spilled over.

"I was on the run," she said, her voice rising with every word. "Nobody was feeding me. I was barely getting by—no thanks to you."

The fork clattered to his plate. Her brother's face screwed up, and his eyes were blazing. "Well, it wasn't easy cleaning up the mess you left behind either. You know there were talks that you ran off on purpose. If it wasn't for those dead bodies, I would have believed it to be true. The goddess Slin knows you put up a fight before we sent you off from Aurial."

Isla did not need any reminders about the massive fit she pitched when her father told her about her upcoming nuptials with barely a month's notice. It wasn't her finest moment.

"Sorry that my traumatic kidnapping and near murder was such an inconvenience for you. You haven't even bothered to ask if I'm alright. All that you seem to care about is what a *rough time* you've had," she finished in simpering, mocking tones.

A laugh rose from his chest. "You really are a piece of work. No wonder father was eager to marry you off so quickly. Especially before any of your unpleasant characteristics came to light." His eyes trailed to her hands which were strangely steadfast. "And you know, what? You deserve everything you're going to get coming to you with Prince Brenner."

A sharp intake of breath as his words hit her.

Panic flooded his face. Even he must have realized he had taken it too far. "I didn't mean it like that." He ran a hand through his hair. "These things are never meant for love. Look at me and Alam, I don't know her. Not really. We barely speak to each other, but we fulfill our duty. All that I meant—"

"I know exactly what you meant." Not having the heart to bear more talk about how she deserved everything coming to her, she pushed away from the table and brushed past him.

The steadiness of her hands didn't last for long—her entire body was shaking now. *Keep it together, Isla.*

Heart racing, she went off in search of a distraction, anything to keep her mind off what would happen in three days' time. She was seething and needed an outlet that didn't involve murdering her brother and half the Divite contingent—although the thought was dangerously tempting at this moment.

She spent a while searching the rows of tiny Pedite tents, which were all the same boring color and hard to tell apart. How did any of them manage to find their tents in this place?

There was a celebration tonight, leaving most of the soldiers roaring drunk and stumbling over themselves. She passed a campfire packed with soldiers dancing and singing, then another fiery pit where a dozen half-dressed men played a rambunctious game of liar's dice.

The chaos allowed her to pass through unnoticed. Just another party-goer amongst the many partakers. And none saw when she had to double back after passing the same firepit twice. This was the first time she'd ever been to this section of the camp before, it was easy to get lost in the sea of beige.

At the edge of camp, she found a small group of soldiers sitting by a nearly-burned-out fire. This group hadn't joined the festivities, and Isla wasn't sure if that was by their choice or if they were unwelcome even amongst their own soldiers.

A woman with braided blond hair pinned in dual loops and a chipped axe at her side sat at the edge. That must be Freya. The other man with shaggy blond hair she didn't recognize, but seemed to be friendly with Rian, as were the two tawny-haired soldiers who had similar enough features that they must be brothers.

The blond soldier spotted her first. She jumped to her feet and tossed her cup to the ground. "Princess Isla," she said in a cracked voice.

The rest scrambled to their feet after her. Rian, the absolute oaf, took his time as he lazily dusted his pants before standing. He jerked his head at her in greeting.

Idiot.

The black and silver Velotian uniform looked foreign after seeing him in blue for weeks. It made him look different. More mature.

That glass of wine was clearly affecting her.

At least he'd been given his Pedite badge again. The sword and hammer badge looked newly stitched to his uniform.

Boisterous shouts and hollers floated in from a noisy party just a few tent rows away.

They all looked at her expectantly and it was the woman who spoke again, head tilting to the side. "Is there anything we can help you with, princess?"

"No," Isla spoke briskly. "I need a word with your captain here."

The blond swiveled her head as if expecting to see someone other than Rian standing next to her. Her mouth hung open in a half-formed question.

"In private," Isla added pointedly.

Rian's brow furrowed as he searched her face.

The shaggy-haired soldier snorted, hiding it behind his elbow. Freya kicked his shin and Isla instantly knew she would like the fierce-looking soldier.

"Of course, my lady." Freya dipped her head and pulled the other soldier away by his shoulder. The tawny-haired brothers followed with matching looks of bemusement on their faces.

Rian stuffed his hands into his pockets. "You look like you need a drink." He jerked his shoulder at a beige tent. His gray eyes filled with a mixture of emotions. Worry, exhaustion, and... relief?

Isla knew she should decline. She knew what her brother would say, what any of the others would say, of a Velotian princess entering a soldier's tent unescorted. After everything she heard today, she didn't care. She wanted to spend her last free night with someone who didn't think she was a monster or a spoiled brat—well, some-one who didn't think that *anymore*.

"Desperately," she breathed. The sound of the party drums picked up.

He held the beige flap open and she ducked under the short doorway. The inside was surprisingly clean and spacious. There was a trunk against one side, with a spare black and silver uniform drying above it. On the other side was a simple cot, which looked comfier than any forest bed she'd slept on.

Unlike her massive tent, there was no room for chairs or a dining table. He probably ate outside with the rest of the soldiers—those that would have him in their circle.

After snooping around in a couple of jars and opening a box containing a new pair of boots, Isla settled on the edge of the bed. Rian threw a faded black overcoat and the Muratian satchel to the side, before digging through the trunk to brandish an amber bottle and two wood cups.

"Commander Skallen gave me this bottle in gratitude for services to the throne," he said with a lazy half-smile that made the skin at the back of her neck prickle. "He didn't seem happy to part with it, but the generals were watching." He tilted amber liquid into both cups and pushed one under her nose. "Princesses first."

She raised an eyebrow as she brought the cup to her lips, pausing just before the first sip. "From the commander?"

"True. It may be poisoned," he said dramatically. "Best leave it all to me."

Before he could snatch her glass away, she knocked back a swig of the liquid. It burned the entire way down and it took everything in her not to spit it back up. She'd never hear the end of it if she did.

So, this was whiskey? It was not as amazing as her brother had made it out to be, not that she'd complain or Rian would take it back.

The cot dipped as another body pressed into it. They both sat staring at the trunk ahead, their knees touching comfortably.

"Why didn't I see you today?" she asked, dragging the cup back to her lips. It didn't burn as much the second time and she swore that she could already feel her toes starting to tingle—though she wasn't certain it was from the drink.

He shrugged. "I didn't think you'd want to see me now that we're back and you have the commander and his generals to entertain. Plus, your—"

"My brother can turn right back to Aurial at first dawn and throw himself from the highest tower as far as I'm concerned," she finished for him, focusing on the divots carved into the old trunk. "I wanted to see you."

"Did you miss me?" he said in a mocking voice.

She elbowed the arm pressed against hers. "I missed your annoying attitude."

He took another swig of his drink, already down to half of his glass in the time it took her to take a few sips. "I missed you too," he said quietly.

A chunk was missing out of the corner of his trunk, with signs of it having been worn down long ago. She placed the free hand closest to him on her knee, palm up.

Without any hesitation, he placed his calloused hand on top of hers, covering it in a blanket of warmth. Isla nearly forgot about the reason her hands were shaking an hour ago.

"When do you leave?" he asked.

"The day after tomorrow," she said, failing to keep her voice steady. He ran his thumb along the ridge of her palm. "We'll meet the Koliats along the way. Is your squad coming with us?" She closed her eyes, already knowing the answer that would come.

"No."

"Hm." As there was no table or chair, she placed her cup on the floor and turned her knees to face him fully, still tightly holding his hand.

For the second time since being rescued, he was closed off to her. His expression was hard to read, hidden behind furrowed brows and darkened eyes. Eyes that she once thought were bland and devoid of color but in reality, had flecks of gold, green, and blue scattered throughout.

This feeling. It had snuck up on her, starting as a small weed she kept snuffing out, but it refused to die. She now realized it wasn't a weed at all but a blossoming flower.

Wishing she could know what he was thinking, she raised her hand and brushed the hair back from his forehead—he was in desperate need of a cut—and ran a finger down the side of his face.

A shudder ran through his body that she was certain had nothing to do with the cold. How could it be when her insides burned like the sun? Instinctively, she leaned in.

He jerked back and turned his knees away.

"You should probably leave before someone notices," he said, refusing to look at her.

Rejection—crisp and hard rejection washed through her while her lungs threatened to collapse on themselves. The cot shifted and cold filled his spot beside her.

"Why?" There were a hundred different meanings behind that question, and she hoped he understood them all.

"You know why," he said in a heavy voice, still refusing to look at her. He stood at the door as if he meant for her to go through it.

No. She didn't want to leave one of the only places she didn't feel like an outsider stuck in a crystal prison. Refused to say goodbye because that would mean tomorrow was all too near.

Isla stood. She was done being told what to do.

Thirty-Eight
The Princess

Any remnant of noise from the outside party was drowned by the pounding of the blood that rushed against her ears, nearly as loud as a war drum. She stood by the bed, clutching her hands to the side to stop the shaking—though this time it was caused by a completely unrelated reason.

Every drop of blood was alive and pumping through her body as if it was the first time through each vessel. Her skin felt as if someone had lit a fire underneath it.

When Rian finally dragged his eyes to her, she was certain that she couldn't leave. It was hard to know when was the last time someone looked at her like that—if ever.

He didn't look at her as if she was an annoyance to be removed or a pawn to be played. He didn't look at her as if he'd only seen nothing but her face for weeks already. Rian looked at her like it was the first time and the last time. He looked at her like he could never get enough.

She understood that look, as she felt the same underneath her shell of stone.

Perhaps it was thanks to the half glass of whiskey running through her veins, but every inch of her was on fire—and not in the burn-everything-to-the-ground type of way—but in a way that yearned to be drowned in relief. This was new territory for her, so she did the only thing that her limbs could do and closed the distance between them. Rian met her in the middle, pausing an inch away.

His fingers stroked the side of her face, delicately tracing the curve of her cheeks as if checking how fragile she was. As if afraid to break her. Then he pulled her in and crashed his lips onto hers. It was rough and more primal than the first kiss, and her skin burned even more under his touch. It was like being set ablaze yet she knew there were no visible marks.

Rian pressed against her with a hunger that she equally matched. His hands cupped her face and then moved to her hair. She didn't know what to do with hers so she allowed them to roam his hard chest. The same one she'd been tempted to explore every night in that forest.

The butterflies in her stomach turned into tight knots that spread further down her body, stoking that inferno within her. He must feel the same judging by the hardness between them.

As soon as it had started, he pulled away, leaving a frosty space between them. She looked up at him, breathless with worry gnawing at her brain.

Had she done something wrong?

Their eyes met in the middle and it wasn't anger she saw in them. His gray eyes were darkened, nearly black, and he was staring at her hungrily.

"We can't," he said. The rough edge of his voice twisted her chest and sent a jolt through her fingertips.

That insatiable fire rippled through her and any rational thoughts evaporated. She stood on her toes, desperately trying to capture his lips in hers, but his hands jumped to either side of her face, holding her inches away.

"*You* can't," he said firmly, as if that clarified anything to her singularly focused brain.

Her mouth dropped into a frown and he traced the lines of her lips with his thumb. That did nothing to quell the fiery storm within.

"Tell me to leave," he said.

"It's your tent." She couldn't tear her eyes from him. War waged within those flecks of color.

Then she understood. Some misplaced part of him was worried about her honor. She didn't care about what it would mean. All that she cared about—all that she craved—was him, and all the consequences in the world could be damned to Rallion's care.

Leaning in close, she whispered against his soft lips. "It's fine. It's okay."

Another quick kiss, but he still held back.

"I want this," she said. Infectious desire that begged to be released laced every syllable. She looped her hands around his neck and pulled his head closer. His body was stiff—*every inch of it*. "I want you. All of you."

He groaned. She took the opportunity to snatch his bottom lip in her teeth and tugged. That seemed to do the trick and snapped the thin thread of restraint he had been holding onto.

This time he tilted her head back and when her lips parted in a sigh, his tongue slid in, greedily searching every part of her mouth. She'd never been kissed like this before. It was *everything*, and she'd never stop wanting this, wanting more.

His kisses tasted like honey and his skin smelled like the early morning, at that exact moment the sun burst above the horizon and encompassed everything in its warm embrace.

While his hands returned to the back of her head, they now worked their way through every strand of hair, pulling out the pins her ladies had so delicately placed in there. With each ivory-boned pin, he pulled a piece of her apart and placed it back reforged.

She feathered her fingers along his collarbone and broad shoulders, then inspected the thick muscles on his arms that she had caught herself staring at several times before. She found an opening at the top of his uniform and dragged her nails along the few inches of chest she could reach, raising another guttural groan out of Rian that dropped her stomach to the floor.

The back of her legs hit the edge of the bed and she fell into the cot with strong hands guiding her. The weight of his body pressed in on hers, not stifling, but comforting like a hot flame over icy waters.

His lips returned to hers, and the heat in his eyes could have reduced her bones to cinder. He captured one last sweet kiss before sliding across her jawline. His arm slid down to her waist and heat exploded in her core when he kissed his way down her neck and to her collarbone, taking care to press a small kiss to each new inch of skin he discovered.

"You're perfect," he murmured, and for once, she actually believed the words.

The hand at her side pressed in, to the point of bruising the skin, but she wanted more—every part of her craved more. Her hips thrust upwards in an attempt to close the gap and he chuckled against her skin. His other hand must have left her hair at some point as it was now trailing at the hem of her shirt. His hand was warm against her skin, and his calloused fingers traced a circular pattern along her stomach that sent her into another wave of primal need.

The sounds coming from her were almost embarrassing at this point, but it only encouraged him further.

That lovely hand retreated from under her shirt and that pesky space between them returned. He backed off, kneeling between her legs—so close to where she needed him.

He looked at her expectantly.

Right.

Stupid honor.

He was giving her one last chance to back out. The swelling of his lips and flush in his cheeks was enough to know that she could never stop. Her body and brain would never forgive her if she stopped now, and she was fairly certain she'd burst and destroy everything.

There was too much space between them. She sat up, and her hands grabbed the edge of his tunic, pulling it up to fully expose that dreamy, muscled chest. She tugged it over his head and tossed it away, allowing her hands to run over every hard divot and tug on his chest hair. The heat beneath her fingertips was intoxicating and she needed more. She grabbed the back of his head and pulled him in for a kiss, falling back to the cot together.

A leg tangled in his, pressed at the spot in between them to feel his hardness build up. Her core rumbled with enough ferocity to bring down a mountain. His kisses grew more urgent, more demanding while her hands were shaking, but not from nerves or anxiety.

All control had been turned over to her body and heart, and they took over gleefully, knowing what to do.

He left her lips again. Before she could utter a complaint, his tongue was running down her neck. The buttons on her tunic and the laces of her undergarments were expertly taken care of, exposing her chest to his hungry mouth.

"Isla," he groaned.

The sound of her name was like a sweet bird's song on the wind, sending another wave of needy pleasure through her body. Did he know how he affected her? Every touch felt like it was the first time her skin knew how to feel and she was slowly being torn apart and smashed back together.

He must have known the effect he had on her for he chanted her name, repeating it like a prayer to one of the goddesses. She *was* a goddess right now.

Curious, she allowed the hand on his chest to slide downwards, searching, memorizing him. Past the outline of his muscled abdomen to where a trail of hair led past the loose hem of his pants.

Rian hissed when her fingers played at the edge of his pants and he rested his forehead on her chest. She withdrew her hands like a child caught sneaking a treat at night.

"So impatient," he murmured against her hot skin. The caress of his breath against her electrified outsides sent her into another tailspin. The beige canvas above swirled like a sandstorm.

They locked eyes and she nearly drowned in that dark gray sky. "More. I need more," she whispered, frantically pawing at him.

"Patience, princess." Mischief glinted in his eyes and she shuddered. "I'm in charge, remember?"

Yes. Yes! She meant to say but her response came out as a moan when his hands resumed their search, feeling over every inch of her scorching body. They were everywhere—he was everywhere—and yet it wasn't enough.

She didn't know it could feel like this, she didn't know a pleasure like this existed. Too frenzied to form words, she caught his face in between her hands and nodded. She was his, fully and completely.

If he wanted to take his time to drive her to the brink of sanity and desire, she was his to do with as he pleased. The outside world didn't exist. He was the only thing in existence right now and she craved more.

Rian returned to explore her mouth with his tongue while a hand slowly massaged her breast, teasing and playing and pinching to keep that fire lit. Taking time to savor each movement of his tongue and the way his lips crushed against hers while she lazily danced her hands through his hair.

Then the hand on her chest trailed its way down her stomach, his fingers lightly tapping her already heated skin as it moved. Deft hands quickly undid the ties on her pants and she sucked in a breath when the hand slipped past the final barrier of her clothes.

Rian lifted his head, his eyes searching hers. He watched her writhe with his first touch and studied her face as if she'd somehow grown a new one overnight.

His fingers trailed to her peak and stroked a spot that sent stars splattering before her eyes. Her back arched off the mattress, her body trying to get closer, trying to get more. Any spot they weren't connected felt too far away, and that had to be remedied right now. He pressed his forehead against hers as his hands continued pulling her to the edge.

He smirked, confirming that he knew exactly how crazy he was driving her with his attention to that bundle of pleasure.

A cry escaped her lips when he pressed his thumb right on the perfect spot. Her eyelids fluttered like a flock of birds, but he didn't stop there. The rest of his fingers curled up next to her entrance. She clutched his arm to keep from floating away.

More.

More.

She needed more and said so. She may have even begged.

He was more than happy to oblige her and his fingers were everywhere. All over her. Inside her. *Everywhere.*

Just as she was about to fall off a ledge into an abyss of pleasure, that sweetness was gone. Her insides were throbbing and she was on the edge of bursting. Rian shifted off her, leaving a cold, darkness in his place. A thud sounded as garments hit the dirt floor before he helped her shimmy out of hers.

Then his weight was back on top of her, one hand on either side of her with his head hovering above hers. He stroked his thumb along her cheek and shifted so that he was pressed at her entrance. She nodded frantically, digging her fingers into his arm and clutching him firmly, as if that contact could anchor her and keep the fire from spreading.

He pressed a kiss to her temple and slowly pushed in. There was a tightening squeeze that lasted a moment, and once that brief memory of pain passed there was nothing but him.

If she didn't remind herself to breathe, she would have passed out. She could feel every inch of him, filling her so completely. He flickered inside of her when she raked her nails along his back. A hunger pooled inside her and it needed to be satiated, now.

"Are you okay?" he asked, every word coming out as barely more than a grunt.

"Don't stop," she breathed. "Don't ever stop."

As if those were the words he was waiting for, something shifted. Raw hunger flitted across his eyes, and he pulled himself nearly all of the way out, before crashing back and burying himself in her. She cried out, not in pain but in pleasure, in unyielding, unrelenting, and desperate pleasure.

"That's it," he whispered. "That's my princess."

She couldn't form any words. Couldn't make her mouth work except to kiss him.

He continued pressing kisses to her jawline, her nose, and her temple, all while murmuring praises against her skin.

With each new motion a piece of her turned inside out and transformed into pure bliss. She met his thrusts with her hips, begging to take him in deeper. He repeated her name over and over, and each syllable felt as familiar as the sun's rays against her skin and as comforting as home.

The waves of intensity grew and grew until an entire ocean of pleasure came crashing down on her and a thousand suns exploded in her vision. Heat spread from her core to her stomach and all the way to her fingertips, nearly burning her hands, at the same time that Rian's release came and sent him over the edge.

It felt like she was created anew from the ashes.

When it was all over and they laid there together for an eternity, staring at the beige canopy above. She rolled over and traced the lines of his body, determined to memorize every freckle, every inch.

Only when her breathing steadied and the stars disappeared from her vision did she finally notice the handprint she'd burned into his arm.

Thirty-Nine
Mira

It was easy to convince Devlin to bring her back to the mountain. Mira made excuses about not wanting either of them to get into trouble and being worried about whatever awful sounds crept along the forest. While he looked disappointed, he escorted her back without further question. He made sure to hold her hand in his hot grip the entire way, as if afraid she'd run off again.

Thanks to some semblance of patience passed her way from Hierel, Mira managed to stay by his side with a simpering smile plastered on her face. Her heart was racing and surely, he could feel the sweat from their interlocked hands, but she prayed to the goddess that he assumed it was from heart-rendering jitters, and not because her body wanted to burst out of its shell. It begged her to get as far away from here—and as far away from him as possible.

She dropped his hand with a fleeting smile—similar to one she'd seen Beretta use on the guards to get extra rations—before they crossed the threshold back into the camp. The bodies were thankfully hidden behind one of the aging mess halls. The soldiers that were missing before were now in abundance, running around the place as if the mountain had collapsed or something equally sinister.

A glance at the mine entrance reassured her that nothing was amiss with the other dredgers. Something else must have sent them into a panic.

One of the guards stopped mid-run when he spotted her and frantically waved Devlin over—another fruitful sign from Hierel. With a dramatic sigh, the private told her to go back to her room and promised to find her soon.

Mira turned on her heel and headed straight for the barrack she knew Beretta would be waiting at, refusing to look behind or falter in her confident steps.

New recesses of her mind were alive as questions fluttered around inside. So, Devlin was a wielder? A healer at that.

And he somehow thought they were alike—or opposites, as he put it—in every equal way. The notion was ridiculous. She'd never kill innocents—well, almost innocents if you didn't count their attempted murder of her. It was always a mystery what Crag or the Wasp did to get themselves sentenced here in the first place so they may have been innocent. Now, she'd never know.

Because of Devlin.

Any of those butterflies that she had felt by that tree disappeared at the thought of those pikes. Her stomach roiled again.

That made up her mind. Now, Hierel willing, she just needed to retrieve the only thing in this cursed mountain that mattered to her before leaving it behind for good.

"What do you mean we're leaving?" Beretta asked in a hushed whisper, eyes darting around the small room as if worried the wood panels could hear. Mere mention of escape meant death. And Mira shuddered to think of Devlin's anger when he discovered her plans to betray his trust.

She couldn't stay in this prison. Not even for him.

Mira sat on the bed and patted the spot next to her. Beretta put down the chipped tea kettle she was tending to and sat down slowly, as if expecting the bed to spring a trap. She never removed her blue eyes from Mira's gaze, as if afraid to break the spell.

"Before we get sent back down," Mira said. "I refuse to go back there, and you shouldn't either."

Beretta's eyes grew wide as she started to understand Mira's words. "You mean to escape?" she said in hushed tones. "They'd kill us before we step foot outside this building."

"No." Mira shook her head, twisting her hands in her lap. "They called Devlin for a meeting. Something is happening out past the nearby woods—I heard what they said. They're distracted and planning to send guards out."

"Mira—"

"This is our only chance." She grabbed Beretta's clammy hands in her own and tried to muster the courage in her heart to pass to her friend. "And I'm not leaving you behind to die in this place. You can't ask that of me."

Devlin was certain she was the same as him—that her powers were exemplified with the appearance of Rallion's comet—and yet her heart was in turmoil. Her mind was confused and uncertain which path to take. She only knew with every fiber of her being that she had to leave this place. There was something else out there for her besides the mines and rocks and digging.

There had to be.

Beretta pursed her lips. For an awful moment in which all the blood angrily rushed to Mira's head, it seemed like she would resist. It seemed like she would stay behind and the thought was too frightening to consider.

Then she nodded and squeezed Mira's hand, her eyes blazing. "Okay," she said slowly. "Okay, we're doing this, then." Beretta jumped up and poured two glasses of steaming tea, shakily holding one out to Mira.

"Great," Mira said happily. She grabbed the cup before Beretta spilled it everywhere. The two made a hushed cheers and Mira pretended to sip before placing it back on the table. Honey and lavender filled her senses, but she was too excited to keep anything down. "I think we should make our move while everyone is scattered with preparations—"

Beretta held up a hand. "I love your enthusiasm, and you know I will follow you anywhere. I want you to know that I think you're insane and this won't work. But I'll be with you every step of the way, as I have been since arriving."

Mira rolled her eyes. Always with the dramatics. "We do this together," she said, crossing one leg over the first. "Let me tell you my plan."

After arguing for an hour about the best route to sneak out and timing the patrols as much as they could, they didn't have to grab much—or anything really—on their way out. They had no belongings or sentimental pieces from before their time in the mines. Mira assumed that was all taken away when they came here long ago.

The only important thing was getting themselves and the little bit of food they managed to stuff in their tunics—in case things went right—out for good.

And Mira planned on things going right.

There was no other option, and this would be it for them if they were caught. Even Devlin, with all his charm and influence, wouldn't be able to talk them out of whatever punishment waited if they failed—if he even wanted to at that point. Given what she saw on those pikes, he may very well lead the sanctions himself.

A guard came to get the one posted outside their room. He sent her and Beretta a threatening glare, stating that he would be back in minutes and that they'd join the others on a pike if they tried anything.

At his threat, Beretta whimpered, but Mira squeezed her shoulder subtly, but reassuringly. Beretta always had her back and had stuck by her side since that first day. Without her, Mira surely would be dead or broken. What Beretta lacked in confidence, Mira had to spare.

This day, she would be brave enough for both of them.

They waited until a blue group ran past the room, squinting through the small crack of window not covered by the dirty curtain.

"You sure about this?" her friend asked, one last time. "No going back once we leave."

Mira came to terms with that the moment she saw those pikes. She nodded and grabbed her friend's hand, feeling a wave of nausea threaten to overtake her. The nerves in her body tried to split her head in two.

No. She forced down the bile that had made its way up her throat. "C'mon B."

Pushing open the door, she pulled her friend behind her. She clutched that hand as if it were a lifeline that could keep them invisible, keep them safe. If they could only make it to the forest line together, then it would all be over.

Nobody would be looking for them for hours, and the one-eyed goddess would surely grace them with swift passage. The goddess of mountains and the forest owed them that much.

They crept along the side of the building, keeping to the shadows as much as they could, and prayed to Halia that no one would hear them.

The guards were gathering supplies for some sort of a mission and wouldn't be looking for wayward dredgers who were stupid enough to attempt escape. No, something else had their attention and she wasn't certain how long that would last for.

This was their only chance.

Their only shot.

They ducked behind a broken wagon that was half-decayed and yet still being used for storage. They passed another series of buildings which Mira had never seen—she'd never been to this half of the above-ground camp before. The buildings here were in even worse condition than the ones she'd seen. Row after row of dilapidated buildings and moss-covered walls. Half were torn apart or crumbling in on themselves.

Something was off. This part of the camp looked like it hadn't seen any miners in years. *Years.*

Now that she thought about it, the buildings in the other half, the parts past the main walk looked as if they were only recently restored. Most of this place had been untouched for far too long... and the habitable parts were poorly put-together, as if they had been made ready with little notice.

This mining operation hadn't been around for a while, not as long as she was led to believe.

When Mira stumbled, Beretta kept her steady, still clutching her hand. The throbbing in her head grew. Her friend's sharp eyes shone in the moonlight, searching her face and asking what the delay was.

They'd been here for what felt like forever—though time was hard to tell beneath the mountains. If they'd been in the mines for such a long time then why wasn't the rest of the camp rebuilt? They were supposed to have been here for longer. Beretta herself said she'd been here for years before Mira came, and the others—the others—she wasn't sure.

The other dredgers barely spoke to her unless it was to curse her presence or to spit in her food. She never knew how long they had been here as none of them would *talk* to her. They avoided her. Everyone did.

Everything was wrong.

This was all wrong. How had she never noticed it before?

Forty
The Captain

"I told you, it doesn't hurt." Rian pulled Isla's hand towards him. She snapped it away and scowled in a way she must have thought was intimidating but only made her nose wrinkle cutely.

It didn't help that she'd shoved her tunic on inside out, and he didn't have the heart to point it out when she was already on the verge of tears. A stark contrast to the ethereal bliss he was basking in only moments before.

This wasn't his first time. Rian had been with other women, but this—what happened between them—was different. It was as if Hierel herself tore open the skies to shower her approval in a rain of starfall. Surely, Isla felt the same. Surely?

The disgruntled look on her face made his heart sink into the back of its cage. He hoped that wasn't regret flitting behind the pools of brown in her eyes.

She grabbed his shoulder and turned him to the side, studying the mark so close that he could feel the warm tickle of her breath against his skin. "Why didn't you say something earlier?"

The truth was he didn't know exactly when that happened. Every inch of his skin that she touched felt like the inside of a sparking coal. He didn't realize at what point that heat materialized into something physical, as there was no pain at the time.

The mark didn't feel any different from the rest of him. Right now, it looked like a year-old burn, slightly darkened and shiny. It was no concern on a body already marred by dozens of scars.

He grabbed her chin and forced her to look at him, all that prior radiance had turned into a gloomy storm. "It's fine. Don't worry. And you know I've had worse."

Judging by the anger that flashed in her eyes, that was the wrong thing to say.

She grumbled under her breath, grabbed her outer jacket, and shoved it on. Worry settled in the pit of his stomach, replacing the elation that had previously flowed through his entire being.

"Did I do something?" He didn't care if his voice was shaky and he sounded needy. He didn't care about any of that.

"No," she said, throwing her arms at her side, finally pausing to look at him. It was hard to read the mix of emotions that seemed to war with themselves. "It's not you. It's just—it's just—argh—never mind."

She ran a hand through her hair and tugged. It had fallen out of its updo, and all the fancy pins were now strewn across his tent floor. She twisted it into a quick bun and tucked it on top of her head.

"Isla. Just wait. I'm sorry." Panic started to rise from his stomach, blocking his throat. This was not the direction he envisioned their night ending.

"It's not you," she said, shoulders slumping. "I didn't mean to—it wasn't on purpose. I didn't mean to burn you or whatever *that* is." She pointed at the scar.

Relief spread through his limbs. "Is that what this is about?" He pointed at the mark on his arm. "I'm sure it'll fade. Plus, I'm always wearing a uniform so no one will see."

"It's not about the uniform," she blurted. Rian froze, hoping for an explanation. "I thought that I—I just—I need—"

She mouthed silently, running a hand through the bun she had just tied on her head and nearly pulling it apart.

"What do you need?" Anything. Everything. He would give it all to her. "Nothing you did hurt me. You could never hurt me and I would never be afraid of you. Do you understand?"

Isla shook her head.

A commotion outside sounded through the tent. Someone was shouting, and it wasn't from the party that still roared through the camp. It was Freya.

Isla cocked her head to the side to listen. "No way," she muttered angrily. "Hierel give me strength." She shoved aside the tent flap and stormed out.

Rian grabbed his doublet and threw it on, making sure to do up all the buttons before following. Freya stood outside, looking extremely guilty, while Malin seemed to be enjoying the spectacle and was hiding his mouth behind his hand.

In front of his tent, looking absolutely furious, was the crown Prince of Velotia. He had *impeccable* timing.

Isla was already striding up to her brother, stopping inches away from his face with her finger pointed at his chest. "Not now," she said.

Even Freya recoiled at the heat in her voice.

Her brother, apparently, was not fazed by the princess's anger. "What in Luriel's name are you doing here, Isla?" He held up a hand and snapped before she could open her mouth. "No. I actually don't want to hear it. Do not say it. Get. Back. To. Your. Tent."

"I'm not going anywhere with you," she said, curling her fists into tiny balls of fury. Rian edged around her.

"You are making a scene," Prince Edmund said, looking around at the small crowd that had wandered in from the evening festivities. Isla dropped her fist and adjusted the mess atop her head.

The prince lowered his voice, "Go back to your tent and we shall talk later. Without an audience. *Go.*"

Something in his words must have gotten through to Isla. She let out a scream of frustration, before shoving her brother out of the way and storming off. She didn't even look behind to say goodbye.

Edmund watched her go, then turned to glare at Rian. His eyes took in his doublet and the noticeably missing tunic underneath, before moving to his newly repatched Pedite Captain's badge.

"*You*," the prince said in a low growl that brought back terrible memories. "I'll deal with you later, Pedite Cordrai." He sent one last scathing look before storming off, muttering to himself.

Freya and Malin still stood awkwardly to the side, having been no help at all. Freya held her fingers over her mouth to hide the smirk and Malin's shoulders shook with suppressed laughter.

A few Pedite soldiers were muttering amongst themselves, confusion written on their faces. The tawny haired brothers Elon and Cain watched with hawk-like attention. They could formulate whatever stories they wanted, they all could. At least no one except his friends had seen the princess going into a captain's tent, only to emerge hours later—unkempt and barely dressed—for a screaming match with her royal brother.

Frustration, anger, and confusion filled every fiber of his being. He couldn't stand the way the others looked at him. He jerked his head at his friends and they followed into his tent.

"What did you do, Rian?" Freya asked. Her eyes trailed from his rumpled bed sheet to the discarded ivory pins on the floor. When they returned to him, it was clear she knew exactly what he had done.

"You are so dead," Malin said, his shoulders shaking with suppressed mirth. "More dead than when they thought you kidnapped the princess."

At least it didn't take long to find out how much trouble he really was in.

Just past noon—after finishing his newly assigned cleaning duties that sent him to the far end of the Pedite camp, but before he could scarf down his pitiful rations for the day—that is when they came for him. The commander had sent three of his top Divites to retrieve Rian. They didn't speak to him besides relaying the orders that he was summoned to the prince's tent.

It was easy to spot his tent, given that it was twice the size of Isla's overly-large, pavilion with several black and silver flags peeking out from the top—an easy target for any ambushing army. There were even more Divite guards positioned around this one. They gave him the same stony glare, all grabbing the pommel of their swords as he approached.

Rian ignored the way his breath hitched when they whispered that name, just as he'd always done, and entered the pavilion that held his judgment.

The inside was just as ostentatious. A giant oak desk that must have been carted in stood to the side, overflowing with parchment and maps. A four poster bed with lavish furs and layers of silk lay on the opposite end with an equally impressive wardrobe that must have taken two horses to carry was swung open to reveal an array of black-and-silver uniforms, and crisp velvet capes suited for the heir of Velotia.

In the room stood Commander Skallen, hungrily surveying him; Prince Edmund, who wore a poorly concealed smirk on his face; Private Tres, who was holding something covered by a mauve blanket and looking immensely pleased with himself; and two other generals he couldn't name. Isla stood next to her brother wearing a flowing dress of white and silver stripes fastened below the waist by a bright blue belt. One of her ladies had helped fix her hair into something more presentable.

Isla's expression was unreadable—and he had grown quite good at reading her over the weeks—and she wouldn't meet his eye.

The commander spoke in silky tones that lacked an ounce of actual warmth. "Thanks for joining us, *captain*." He jerked his cleft chin at Private Tres. "We have something we wanted to show the prince and princess."

Rian's eyes finally left Isla's face and trailed back to Private Tres, who peeled back the blanket with a flourish to reveal a fine gold circlet. *Isla's circlet*.

Everything in Rian's body stopped working except for the vicious churning of his stomach. The tip of his fingers turned colder than that plunge into the icy river.

So, they had searched his belongings. He should have known.

Isla's eyes widened as she took in the leaf-filled circlet that she discarded in the ashes of the Black Forest weeks ago.

Once again, he tried to meet her eyes. He still couldn't understand that unreadable expression she wore and he hated it.

The gruff commander looked positively delighted, and her brother's lips were set in a smug grin.

"I believe this is yours, Princess Isla." Tres handed the circlet over.

Isla took it wearily and studied it closely, still unable to take her eyes off the headpiece.

A thin line formed between her brows. She must be putting together the pieces of how it happened. She wasn't stupid—no matter how many times he called her that in the past weeks—there was only one way the circlet made it back if she didn't carry it.

At the time she didn't want it.

She had left it behind.

She would have never noticed and had been driving him crazy at the time, so he thought nothing of taking it. It was easy enough to slip into his satchel and he had every intention of selling it to pay down his family's debts—no one would be the wiser.

She left it behind in the ash.

But then things changed. *A lot* changed and he needed the chance to explain it to her.

There was heavy silence while the princess examined her royal circlet, then, for the first time since arriving in the stuffy pavilion, her brown eyes met his. If only they could have a minute alone for him to tell his reasons and she'd surely understand.

From the way the prince glowered at him from Isla's side, they would not get that time again—he was a disgraced Pedite soldier and she was a princess.

"It is hers," Prince Edmund supplied, peering over his sister's shoulder.

Commander Skallen was terrible at hiding his glee. "Clearly the captain stole it," he said with silky ice wrapped around every syllable. "We shall have him dishonorably discharged and arrange for lashes immediately."

"No."

All heads turned toward Isla. The prince's eyes turned to slits.

"No, Princess Isla?" the commander repeated.

In a cold voice he hadn't heard in forever she said, "I gave it to my guard for safekeeping. I must have forgotten to retrieve it. Thank you for returning it, *soldier*."

The tone in which she addressed him was like a dagger plunging into his chest.

Disappointment and anger flashed in Edmund's eyes, quickly replaced by haughty indignation.

"Are you certain?" the commander asked. His neck turned blotchy as he struggled to contain his anger.

"Yes," was her quiet reply.

Tres's eyes widened and the blood rushed out of his face. "But—but he had it hidden, my lady. Hidden amongst his belongings. You must be mistaken."

"Are you calling the princess a liar?" Prince Edmund snapped, placing a hand on his sister's shoulder. Clearly his plot had backfired, but the way his eyes blazed at him, Rian knew this was far from over.

"Of course not," Tres stammered. "I was merely pointing out—"

"Leave it, private," Commander Skallen said.

"This matter is over. You are dismissed, soldiers," Isla said. "Leave. All of you."

"As you wish, Your Highness." A red-faced Commander Skallen grabbed Tres' elbow and led the gaping soldier out of the tent. The others followed while Rian tried to catch Isla's eye again.

She had to hear him out.

Isla took a seat in a fur-covered plush chair and pulled a stack of papers toward her, completely ignoring his presence. That damned circlet lay discarded in front of her. Flecks of black and red that he'd never seen before now danced in the tent light.

"You too, Cordrai." The prince walked over and clasped the back of Isla's chair. He gestured toward the door with a smirk, believing that he had won.

It didn't matter that Skallen didn't get his glorious punishment or to ream Rian out in front of Velotian royalty. The damage had been done.

Rian pretended that Edmund was no more than an annoying fly on the forest floor and ignored him. A brazen move to make against the crown prince, but Isla had to know *why* he took it.

"Isla, look—"

"Don't you dare address her so improperly," Edmund snapped. "She is a Princess of Velotia."

Rian waved him off. "Princess, I can explain—"

"Explain?" the prince snarled. "She doesn't want to hear your explanation. Unless you want to tell her the entire truth, and not just the gambling debts." Isla's head whipped up at this, her brown eyes blazing in the candlelight. "Did he tell you everything, sister?"

"I am trying to tell—"

361

"When he was in the regiments he amassed a mountain of debt from gambling, combined with his departed father's. Even his family's household had been seized to help pay off some of it. But you have more, still, right?"

Rian clamped his mouth closed.

"You told me it was your father's debts only," Isla said, the hurt beyond her eyes filtered through for a brief moment. It was worse than when she saw the circlet he took.

The prince laughed coldly.

"My father used to take me with him sometimes, and I guess I developed a liking for it—but that was a different me." The cold truth he was ashamed of—that he had hidden from her—felt bitter on his tongue. "I've worked hard not to become that person again, but yes, some of it was mine. I didn't want you to think any less of me."

As a child, it was hard not to be enthralled by the roar of the crowd, and the glowing warmth that filled him when he was on a streak. He kept up the terrible habit after his father passed, hoping to claw his way out of the hole which only continued widening. He only stopped after everything fell apart in Liopen.

"He clearly stole your circlet with the plan to sell it off," Edmund said. "Probably to pay off his debts or to incur further ones."

Isla's eyes snapped back to him, waiting for his rebuttal of Edmund's claim. When none came, she shook her head.

The prince's smile grew. "Just like with Liopen," Edmund said. "He abandoned his post at the first prospect of ill-gotten coin, and he's the reason we're in this mess to begin with."

"Don't—" Rian began but was cut across by Isla.

"What do you mean?" Her head pivoted between her brother and Rian, demanding an answer. "*What do you mean, Edmund?*"

"Oh." The prince laughed gleefully while Rian's fists curled into tight balls at his side. "You didn't want to tell her who was in that

Muratian party your group slaughtered—not even bothering to check who was a part of it?"

Rian felt hot all over. Hot and trapped. "We had no way of knowing—"

"Besides a royal insignia or his uniform?" Edmund said.

Rian turned to Isla, pleading for understanding. "We didn't know it was him. We didn't know what it would cause."

"No," Isla said slowly.

"The crown prince of Murat," Edmund supplied when it became clear that Rian couldn't say the words out loud. "They killed him and started this war in the first place. You can probably thank him for your capture too. Undoubtedly, it was meant as some form of message—retribution for the son taken."

Isla was silent for a moment. Her hands twisted a roll of faded parchment. "Why didn't you tell me—after *everything*?"

"I didn't know how to," Rian said stupidly.

The truth was that he was a coward. Perhaps the name had always been more fitting than he thought.

He tried taking a step toward her but the prince moved in between them. "Thank you for your efforts escorting the princess back—we are eternally grateful—but your services are no longer needed, Cordrai."

One last attempt at pleading his case. "Isla—Princess—Can we please talk? *Alone*."

"After last night? No way," Edmund said. "You may leave. You are dismissed, and you should thank the goddess that your dismissal is nothing more permanent."

Rian opened his mouth and nothing came out. Isla kept looking between him and her brother with wide pupils.

"Sister," Prince Edmund implored as she clutched the paper tightly, no sign of shaking anywhere. "He's a disgrace to the royal corps. He took advantage of the situation and he took advantage of you—in more ways than one, apparently," he finished with haughty disdain.

Rian sucked in a breath and felt his face light up in a mixture of rage and frustration. For the prince to even insinuate that anything that happened between them was planned and calculated—it was ridiculous at the very least.

"Isla, please—"

"Just go," Isla said. Her voice had lost that coldness and any prior spark. She stared at the circlet in front of her. "I appreciate everything you have done for me, but it's time for you to leave. I must prepare for my journey."

Looking between the stony resolution on Isla's face, and the dreadful glee on her brother's, Rian knew it was already a lost battle.

Forty-One
The Princess

Loneliness was always her friend. Solitude her constant state of being since she was young, and even more so as she became an adult in the palace. Why did it feel so overwhelming now? So all-encompassing and overbearing, like the weight of an entire mountain placed on top of her chest.

Edmund unbuttoned the cuffs of his doublet and rolled back his sleeves, looking pleased with himself as the last of their *guests* left.

"Glad that's over," he said, cracking his neck. "For a moment, I thought that Pedite wouldn't leave, and I'd have to call the guards."

Isla's head snapped up. She picked up the circlet to examine it for the hundredth time for surely it had to be some sort of a trick. *Surely*.

Yet, Rian hadn't denied it.

In the depths of her ash-filled heart, she knew it was true. There was no other explanation. She clenched the circlet so hard it left marks on her palm. The pain that pulsed through her skin was more than welcomed.

Edmund jerked his head. "Something wrong, sister?"

She stared, truly seeing him for the first time. "You really are an asshole somedays."

"Oh, Isla," he said condescendingly. He sat on one of the high-backed plush chairs they had lugged in just for him. "You cannot be serious. I know you covered for that soldier but surely you can see that he used you from the start. He lied to you and got what he wanted, and now he has no need for you. It's for the best."

"For the best?" The circlet dropped to her lap and her hands started trembling.

"Careful." His eyes focused on her shaking hands, a shadow darkening across them. "I thought you had better control than that. Don't get so emotional."

"It's hard when I have an insensitive troll for a brother."

"Better get yourself under control before we reach the Koliats. I doubt Prince Brenner will care for any outbursts. Speaking of, I'm not even certain about their stance on wielders. I don't think father let them know about your condition in advance, so you'll have to find the proper way to break the news. Personally, I'd do it after the marriage is consummated and the scars are burned. No going back after that." He rubbed his wrists where his own marriage scars shone brightly.

Isla clutched her hands together, focusing on deep breaths.

Edmund, apparently, didn't notice any shift in her mood. Or he was just dense enough to not care. "Does that soldier know what you are?"

"He didn't care. He didn't think I was a monster."

"I guess *he* wouldn't, considering what he's done. But that doesn't change anything," Edmund said calmly. "We all have a duty to uphold and yours is to marry the prince."

Isla stared at him.

"He lied to you—about everything. I'd be surprised if he didn't arrange the entire kidnapping to try to claw his way back into the army's good graces. Did you ever get a good look at the Muratians?"

"Of course I did. And I'm not stupid. He had nothing to do with it."

Edmund scoffed.

All she wanted was to wipe that annoying smirk off his face. She wanted him to feel some of the pain that was tearing her apart.

"I fucked him," Isla said, enjoying the way his face turned deep purple. "Hope that your precious Prince Brenner doesn't mind used goods."

This time he closed the distance between them, and pulled her chair so she was face to face with him. He looked too much like their father in the candlelight. The thought sent a chill down her back.

"Don't you ever let those words escape your lips again," he said quietly. "I don't care. Brenner is never going to know. You're going to marry him, or father will have our heads. You're going to do your job and maybe you'll finally be able to contribute one good thing to this family since killing our mother."

The moment the words escaped his lips, Edmund sucked in a deep breath. He backed off with his gaze glued to her hands as if expecting her to lose it at any moment—for her to explode.

But she was oddly calm. On the outside at least.

It felt like one of the strings leading to her heart had snapped. She focused on a large vase that Alynna filled with flowers to mask the *intense masculine energy* in this camp, it was out of place in her brother's gloomy tent. The yellow daisies had just begun to bloom, spreading their petals and nearly overtaking the entire bouquet.

"I've known," she said, desperately trying to hold back her tears. She refused to let him see any weakness. "I've known that you've hated me for a while—and all for something I had no control over. You probably have since the moment I was born."

She tilted her head up but he now refused to look at her. The wrinkles on his forehead were prominent in the candlelight.

Could he not even bear the sight of her anymore?

"I am sorry, truly, for killing *your* mother. I didn't get a chance to know her, but maybe things would have turned out differently if she'd been alive. Maybe then you could stand to be in the same room as me instead of treating me like your enemy all the time."

"Look, I know it wasn't your fault—"

"It was," she cut across. "We both know if I hadn't been born then she would still be here. Father would be different, and so would you. You'd be happy. I think about what I took from you all the time. Most days I wish it were me that died. And lately, I really wished that I threw myself into that river like I'd planned."

His eyes jumped to hers. "What do you—?"

"It doesn't matter." She rose from her chair on strangely sturdy legs. "I'm sorry for ruining your life. I'm sorry for everything. I wish you got to have your mother. I wish so badly that I got to grow up with a mother—our mother. The same way I always wished I had a brother."

"You—you do." He didn't meet her eyes. "I don't *hate* you, Isla. Things are just complicated right now."

Neither of them believed that lie. At least now there was nothing to hide. The truth was finally spoken out loud, and all Isla could feel was relief.

Sweet, freeing, relief. No matter how terrible the truth was.

"We could have been a unit. Us against him, instead of being stranded on our own deserted islands. But we aren't, and it's fine. You know that I'll do my duty—it's the least I can do after taking her from you. Then, we won't have to see each other again, if that's what you wish. I'll make a new home for myself in Koliat, as our father wants."

When he looked up, she was shocked to see a shimmer in his eyes. He swallowed and heaved a deep breath. "I know that father will be pleased."

All she could do was nod. "May I take my leave now? I am tired and have to pack."

Edmund looked like he wanted to say no, like there was more pain to layer onto her already shattered heart. He'd already torn it to pieces and burned each morsel to nothing but ash. So had Rian.

Instead, Edmund merely nodded.

Good. It was settled.

She was exhausted beyond measure, and she had a long journey ahead.

~

Isla stifled a yawn behind her palm and wondered if she'd finally, truly lost it. For why else would she be standing in front of this cursed tent again, waiting for more ways to torment her crumpled soul?

She'd been up all night writing and rewriting until wrinkled papers replaced the plush carpet of her tent. After the circlet, and then the fight with her brother, her brain couldn't formulate the proper words. She didn't even know what words wanted to come out. So, she tried and tried until the ink ran out. Sleep refused to find her.

So, here she was, in the crisp air before the sun had even peeked over the horizon, standing in front of Rian's tent. He was already outside, whittling again. When he saw her, he dropped whatever stupid carving he was working on—some sort of flower. From the dark smudges under his eyes and the rumpled tunic he wore, she knew that sleep avoided him too.

Good.

He deserved to lose all the sleep in the world for his lies.

Gods. Why did she even come here?

"I didn't think I'd see you again," Rian breathed.

That made two of them.

The doublet of his uniform hung loosely off his slouched shoulders and he looked miserable. More miserable than he was that night he drank too much beer and woke up with a splitting headache. The worry lines on his face cut deep and she refused to feel any guilt for causing them.

"I'm sorry," he added, rubbing the back of his neck.

"For what?" she bit out. It was harsher than she expected, but then again, she didn't even know why she was here or what she was feeling. All that she knew was she had to see him again, before the end. It was a good thing the Pedite camp was nearly empty at this ungodly hour. "For lying to me? For *stealing* from me?"

"To be fair, you had thrown it away, and I wouldn't necessarily call..." he trailed off with one scathing look from her. "Yes, I stole from you. But I wanted to give it back to you, I really did. I just didn't know how to do it without—"

"Incriminating yourself?"

"Yes." His eyes dropped to the ground at her feet. "I was a coward."

"You were—you are." He winced but she ignored him and kicked a turned over log. "I don't want any more lies. I've had more than enough for two lifetimes now."

"I wasn't thinking when I took it, but I did have somewhat good intentions. After what happened at Liopen, it changed me, and I wanted to make amends in every way possible. It's been so hard to move on while I have this massive debt looming over me and my family. My younger siblings are in line for the conscription because of it. I wanted to stop that. You of all people can understand how I've been trying to become a better person."

"You could have come to me if you needed money." She liked to think she would have helped, in the end at least. She liked to think she wouldn't have judged him for all his other deeds too.

"I didn't want to use you like that. I honestly thought you'd never find out."

Well, now she knew. Laughter—mirthless and void of any humor—escaped her lips. She'd done some terrible things too, things he knew about. And yet he still lied to her in the end.

"I didn't know how to tell you about the Muratian Prince. We truly didn't know it was him, he wasn't wearing a special uniform, and when we saw what his soldiers did to the villagers, rage blinded everything... I have—deep regrets about that, and every life that is lost in this war weighs on my shoulders. I know it."

"That was my mother's crown." She sighed and sat on a stump, he sat across from her. Hints of sunlight peeked from beyond the horizon. There wasn't much time left. "I only had a few things of hers, and I thought it was lost. I suppose I should thank you, but you don't deserve that."

"I don't."

"You saw the worst of me, and I thought I knew the worst of you. I guess I was wrong."

It hurt that he lied to her. It hurt that the entire time she had known him, he was only using her. Yet a part of her—a part she deeply resented—longed to understand and forgive. She was too stubborn for that.

"I wanted to—"

She held up her hand. There wasn't much time and Commander Skallen would be looking for her, likely thinking she'd run off again. "Save it. It doesn't matter anymore."

"I am sorry, even if it means nothing now. I want you to know that. I also want you to know I'd never use you, not like that."

"I don't need your apologies," she said. "None of it matters anymore."

"I know. I hope you find happiness over there."

She frowned. What lay beyond for her was uncertain, and her stupid heart ached and spasmed. It didn't want her to leave. "I've always managed to survive and besides." She smirked. "It's much easier to survive when you're waking up in a four-post bed covered with the most luxurious furs the Koliats can supply instead of a dirty forest floor, no matter how comfortable the sleeping partner."

A smile ghosted across his lips. "I bet it is. But at least the cot is pretty comfortable."

Isla fought the blush that wanted to fill her cheeks. "It doesn't change the fact that you lied to me. Nothing changes that."

"I know." There was a strange sadness hidden in his eyes. "There's no point wishing that things were another way when the path is already set."

Exactly. Her path was set. As was Rian's.

There was no escaping their duty. Their destiny.

Some movement over her shoulder caught Rian's eye and he jumped to his feet, rubbing his arm in the spot she knew the scar was burned into.

"Commander Skallen," he said, backing away so there was more space—proper space—between the two of them.

Right. Her heart thumped loudly. He was always worried about his position. About getting back in the commander's good graces. Nothing had ever changed.

The gruff commander was resplendent in his travel wears, with shining silver badges taking up half of his left jacket breast. No wonder he was so full of himself.

"Princess Isla," he said breathlessly. "Our party is ready to leave. I'll be personally escorting you until we convene with the Koliats." The commander's eyes trailed over to Rian. "Prince Edmund wishes for me to keep the party small for your safety."

Isla's stomach dropped. "Will my brother be joining us?"

The commander scratched the back of his wrist and refused to meet her eyes. "No. Prince Edmund has instructed us to go on ahead. He received an urgent message and will be heading back to Aurial mid-day." He hesitated, shifting from foot to foot. "The prince also mentioned there was no need to wait before our departure as he will not be seeing us off."

That was it, then. He wouldn't even say goodbye. He must really hate her. At least now, he would be rid of her forever.

There were other ways of dying besides your heart simply refusing to beat or your lungs no longer working. This—this felt like one of them. Yet, she could still feel the blood surging through her veins as if it hadn't caught up to the fact that her heart should be nothing more than withered coal.

As she had trained herself to do since she could walk, she forced a smile on her face, ignoring the disparaging look the commander sent Rian's way. "Thank you, commander. Please ready my horse." She turned to Rian. "Thank you, captain, for everything you've done for me."

Never taking his eyes off hers, Rian ignored the commander's disgruntled look, grabbed her hand and pressed his lips to the back. "It was my honor, princess."

He made to turn but paused. He reached into his wrinkled jacket and passed her a small blade with a faded bell on it. The one she had named Shadow Death. "In case any branches try to attack you."

The commander muttered indignantly, but Isla took that piece of him he offered. She toyed with the blade between her fingers while Skallen watch on grumpily. She'd find a safe place to keep it, though a part of her wanted that place to be right in the middle of Rian's stupid chest.

The goddess scriptures said that if the body was the pathway to the promised heavens, then the eyes were the rocks in which that path was carved. Words could be conveyed without having to open your mouth or lift a finger to write prose to parchment.

In those gray eyes, she understood many things. But she wasn't ready to forgive yet, so she left without another word.

Minutes later, Isla was assisted to the back of a spotted white mare with silky, flowing hair. A sturdy beast, but it wasn't hers.

May as well get used to it. Everything she owned and everything she was would soon be torn from her. Best to accept her destiny now.

With one final look at the encampment, including her hilariously large red tent, her brother's even bigger black one, and the rows upon rows of beige Pedite tents where she could still pick out Rian's, she gave the signal to Commander Skallen that she was ready to leave.

Forty-Two
The Captain

The prince found him just past mid-day, right in the middle of packing what little belongings he had before finally heading home for a much-needed leave. Freya expressed a desire to meet her sister at one of the nearby ports before parting, but Rian wanted time alone with his thoughts. As much as he appreciated the offer from a friend that would have once shunned his presence, he planned on making the two-week trip back home the way he came here—entirely alone.

That was what he deserved.

The year of the trickster goddess was not to be taken lightly and he'd discovered exactly why firsthand. She relished in tormenting him at every available opportunity. Perhaps the next year will bring better order to things. What was it again—Kiemp, the goddess of the oceans and rivers or was it the mountain goddess?

Not that it mattered. Anything had to be better than this.

Their parting had not gone the way he wanted. None of this went the way he wanted. He wanted more time to explain himself better. To make sure that she *knew* there was nothing premeditated about what happened between them. Nothing.

Now, the chance was lost forever.

It was stupid of him to think he even deserved a proper goodbye after all he'd done. In a way, it was rather fitting. Mannop's justice taking a round on the pendulum only to come back to shatter him with her full wrath.

At least he could see his family soon and bring back his commissions, slowly paying off his debts to right everything he'd failed on. That was the only thing keeping him going.

But for some reason, that impertinent prince decided he hadn't suffered enough and wanted to talk. Seeing as he wanted to keep what little commissions and honor he had left, Rian had no choice but to indulge him.

That's how Edmund came to be sitting in his small, barely furnished tent, on the second of two chairs that a fumbling General Xavier found for them. Apparently, Pedite generals weren't often in the company of Velotian royalty.

Annoyed by the delay to his departure, Rian refused to entertain any pleasantries with Isla's royal pain of a brother. He refused to meet his eyes, where the sea of brown that reminded him so much of *her* would be staring back at him.

The prince took great interest in Rian's tent and his belongings. His eyes traveled over the small cot and worn trunk with haughty disdain. If he was a good host, Rian would have offered him a drink of that aged whiskey he and Isla didn't finish, but he didn't want this man lingering a second longer than he had to.

Edmund frowned and refused to be the first to speak. He donned a velvet jacket with shining silver buttons, and his ornate crown rested firmly atop his head as a reminder of his elevated status.

That arrogant stillness ran in the family and Rian was certain both of them would die here before the prince deigned to break the awkward silence.

"You know," Rian said. "I really must be off soon, so unless there is a reason—"

"Apologies if my presence here bores you," the prince cut across.

"Bores isn't exactly the word I'd use," Rian replied with equal disdain.

The prince rubbed his temple and crossed one foot over the next. He looked exhausted. Good. "I've been up all night thinking." That made two of them. "And I want to try to right some of my wrongs. My sister *is* going to go through with the wedding as planned. Prince Brenner can actually take care of her, unlike a low-life disgraced captain."

Rian clenched his jaw. "I wasn't expecting anything else." And the insinuation that Rian thought elsewise was insulting.

"Nobody is to know about you two. *Nobody.*"

Rian nodded.

Nobody except for Freya and Malin, and any of his fellow Pedite soldiers that witnessed that sibling fight outside his tent. But nobody knew for certain what had transpired. None of them would––and not for Edmund's sake, but for Isla's.

"*And.*" The prince leaned in, lowering his voice dramatically even though no one was around. "I know that you know about her—ahem—*talents.* I spoke with General Xavier and Commander Skallen, and for your troubles in Murat and for your silence on some delicate matters, you are being promoted to general. The papers have already been sent off. General Xavier is still in charge of the Pedite contingent, yours is nothing more than a sham title along with half the appropriate salary."

Promoted.

Promoted?

Is that what they called it now?

They were buying his silence. That had to be it. The thought tasted bitter on his tongue and made him want to jump out of his skin.

The prince held up a hand. "Before you object, remember that I know about your history. Everyone does. I know you need the commissions that come with this, so ask yourself if you can really afford to decline such a generous offer. It would be a grave offense and there won't be another chance like this again. I also couldn't guarantee what would happen to you without it, as the commander seems to hold quite the disdain for you."

Rian clenched his jaw at the threat. All he could bring himself to do was nod.

Coward.

"Now." Prince Edmund slapped his knees and rose, he extended a hand which Rian loathingly took, both squeezing as hard as they could until Edmund tugged his away. "I have a long journey ahead of me, an extremely cross sister to try to make amends with, and an obnoxious Koliat prince to prepare myself for, so you'll excuse me if I don't stay to offer any further congratulations on the new role, *general*."

General.

The name—that position—it sounded odd to his ears. Foreign. Strange. Like it was meant for another.

It also seemed a bit—

"Wait. Koliat?" Rian froze. "I thought you were headed back to the capital."

It was the prince's turn to look confused. "Why would I go to Aurial when I'm escorting Isla to meet with Prince Brenner? The goddess Dia knows that I can't trust any of you lot anymore."

Rian's brows furrowed. "You're a bit late then, aren't you? The party left this morning."

"No," Prince Edmund said, speaking slowly as if he thought Rian was an invalid. "I just saw General Kolan. He and I are leaving with Isla this afternoon so we can make camp at the village Saval tonight. Where is she, by the way? I assumed she'd be sulking in this run-down camp and I need to speak with her."

His eyes searched Rian's tent as if expecting his sister to pop out from behind his dented trunk.

"Isla left," Rian repeated stupidly. "She left this morning with Commander Skallen. Commander Skallen said you were called back to the capital."

"I received no such message," he said stiffly. "I'm to escort her the rest of the way as planned. We have things to discuss."

The words hit him harder than that hammerboar in the forest. "What?" he said, his voice oddly hollow. Perhaps it was the mixture of fear and bile that was stuck in his throat that made his voice sound like a stranger's. "They already left."

The prince's voice turned low and deathly steady. "This morning with Commander Skallen, you said?"

"Yes." It was like being swallowed by one of those sinking mud pits Isla could never spot. Somehow, it was already too late.

Commander Skallen was the one who assigned Rian, an easy scapegoat with a dodgy past, as Isla's personal guard—all as a punishment or so he'd said. The same commander who had been in charge of the shift changes with Isla's guard that day of the attack, ensuring no one else was around to aid. That commander had taken her early this morning, without her brother as an escort, as was apparently planned.

The realization took his breath away.

Around the same time, the prince seemed to come to the same, terrible conclusion. His eyes widened when he asked, "Which way did they go?"

Forty-Three
The Princess

Saying that this boisterous commander loved hearing his own voice was a gross under-exaggeration. He never stopped talking, even if his travel partner was slightly less loquacious than a stone wall.

He sat rigid atop his black war-mount with all his badges glistening in the harsh sunlight—the perfect picture of her father's favorite commander. And that made her hate him all the more.

"We should make excellent timing, Your Highness," he droned on. "Then we can put all this nasty war business behind us. I believe you'll find the accommodations at Vaner suitable to your liking. Better than the paltry conditions back at the camp, I'm certain, or that dingy village in—"

The commander stopped his tirade, and wisely so, before mentioning her time lost in Murat.

At least he was smart enough to avoid that rather cumbersome topic. It didn't mean she was spared from his constant drabbling, though, as he picked back up describing one of the recent campaigns he led near the Hattien swamplands border, waving his free hand dramatically as he spoke. She was surprised his horse didn't buck him off with all that movement.

That exasperating Commander Skallen had stuck to her side all morning, barely giving her a reprieve to think. He was worried that she would "wander off" again, as he put it. At least it'd all be over in a few days as she constantly reminded herself.

Her old life would be over and she'd soon enter a twisted one of new beginnings. Then she could forget all this business ever happened and put it behind her once and for all, as the commander constantly said.

Except she didn't want to forget, even if she thought she could. That was like asking to discard a newly formed part of her. She'd changed over the past weeks, and she liked to think it was for the better. Her heart had been carved out and forged anew, along with the rest of her.

Even though it had come at a terrible cost, she learned to be more accepting of her gifts instead of being afraid of them. Fear was much worse. It took control over everything and removed destiny from her hands.

Now, she had a semblance of control over her life and her powers. It could only get better from here. There was no lower she could go. No further digging could reach the lowest depths where her heart lay burnt and raw.

Perhaps the Koliats would be more accepting of wielders than her father was.

Maybe they wouldn't be afraid.

"Did you hear what I said, princess?"

She blinked and adjusted the circlet atop her brow. It felt heavier today for some reason. "What was that, commander?"

Commander Skallen scowled, then quickly corrected his face to hide his annoyance. "I was saying there is a lovely grove just beyond that ridge where we should rest the horses."

Isla frowned.

It was awfully close to the towering forests, whose long branches seemed to reach toward her, beckoning her back in. How had they managed to wander so close to this place?

"Are you certain we can't find another area to stop?" She'd rather not spend one of her last free meals staring at a reminder of what she'd lost.

"I am in charge here, after all. And your safety is my responsibility, Your Highness." He raised a fist over his medaled chest. "Let me handle this."

She nodded, having no energy or will left to fight him on this. She'd lost all that spark when she'd seen that circlet.

It didn't matter where they rested.

None of it really mattered except the end of the destination, and her new life.

Forty-Four

The General

"When we are done with this, I am *so* having my father throw you in the dungeons," the prince grumbled angrily. "Forever!" He ran a hand through his brown hair and twisted around in circles in the middle of Rian's tent for the fifth time.

"Just tell your men to have horses ready to leave in five minutes," Rian muttered, throwing on his graying uniform jacket and tucking a pair of daggers safely underneath––his favorite one noticeably missing as it was now in Isla's care. He prayed to the goddess that she didn't have to use it before they got there.

"How long ago did you say they left?" Freya asked, tucking Bone Breaker into her belt. Rian caught the chipped longsword that Malin threw his way, ignoring the pain in his barely healed side. He really should have found a wielder to finish healing it.

There was no time now.

The useless prince still had yet to contribute anything to the preparation besides muttering a mixture of insults and threats. His jibes and promises of a swift death washed over Rian, who was focused on the task ahead.

Commander Skallen had betrayed them. He practically handed Isla over to the Muratians that day in the forest and clearly had plans to finish the job again. They were all too stupid to see it.

Now the commander had hours on them at this point. They'd have to travel swiftly, once the prince could stop rambling like a fucking headless cock and get his men together.

He should have stopped them. He should have questioned Skallen further, but he was too lost in his own problems at the time. He failed her.

"Hey!" Freya grabbed his elbow. "No point in feeling any of that right now. We need to leave if we have any chance of catching them."

"You said they left this morning?" Malin asked, strapping a pair of longswords to his back.

"Just after dawn," Rian said quietly.

"And you didn't think to question it?" Edmund said angrily. He paused his frantic circling to get in Rian's face. "You just thought 'Oh, why don't I let our Velotian Princess, my sister, go off on her own—'"

"With his commander in charge," Freya seethed, stepping between the two of them and jabbing her finger into the prince's chest.

Edmund scrambled backwards.

Rian didn't blame him as Freya could be a force to be reckoned with, and she looked as if she was currently planning several ways to dispose of the prince's body.

Freya closed the gap, refusing to let the prince escape so easily. "Why should he question our highly-decorated commander who your own *father* appointed and you clearly had no suspicions of either?" She turned away and scoffed. "I thought princes were supposed to be smart."

Malin's smile was positively devilish when Prince Edmund's face turned a deep shade of purple, and he stuttered incoherent nonsense.

"Guess not," Freya said with a half-smirk, answering her own question before turning to Rian. "Is this one *actually* coming with us? I don't want him slowing us down."

The prince straightened his collar and sputtered. "I am the crown Prince of Velotia and in charge of the rescue operation, of course I'm coming."

Freya shoved the pommel of a sword into his gut, and the prince wheezed. "You'll need an actual sword then, my prince, and not that delicate thing I've seen you wave around spasmodically."

The prince had an overly bejeweled broadsword, that Rian had seen him sparring with around camp. It was made of much too delicate material and purely for showmanship. Someone like him would have never seen real battle or hardship in his privileged life. He'd be a liability out there.

Same as Isla before that day in the forest. The thought sent a pulsating pang from his arm all the way to his heart. He nearly dropped his broadsword.

What was that?

"Stop that. Unhand me now!"

Rian whipped around.

Freya had placed Edmund into a firm headlock. She hooked a thumb under Edmund's thick crown and forcibly removed it. It landed silently on Rian's bed.

She smirked. "Another one for your collection, Rian. And take that godsdamned jacket off." She pointed at Edmund's luxurious overcoat. "We don't need any easy targets, especially not a *royal* target."

The prince started another slew of silent curses but quickly unbuttoned his pristine coat when Freya took a step towards him. It was discarded on top of the fiery crown. "Those better still be here when this is all over," Edmund said, rounding on Rian.

All Rian could do was laugh at the prince, something that made him even angrier. Let him think what he wanted, he was the least of Rian's concerns right now.

Freya froze and cocked her head to the side. "Do you hear that?"

Before anyone could answer, she was outside of the tent. Rian and Malin sheathed their swords and were close on her heels with the prince stumbling behind, still muttering incoherently.

He hadn't even made it ten feet away from his tent when a colossal force shuddered across the camp. Swords that were once resting against a makeshift fence fell to the ground in a clatter, several poorly constructed tents slid off their wooden poles, and horses bucked at the commotion.

Rian grabbed Edmund's collar, forcing the prince into the dirt, and holding him there for several seconds until—whatever it was—had passed. He only released his grip on Edmund when the dust finally settled and the last of the weapons were in a heap on the ground.

"What in Rallion's name was that?" the prince stuttered. He picked himself up from the ground and dusted his tunic. He sent another scowl Rian's way as if he was solely responsible for the ruckus.

An explosion—somewhere near the Divite camp by the sounds of it.

Freya and Malin's head turned west as a new sound met their ears. Chaos erupted all around as a roar approached, followed by a wall of blue, all brandishing steel.

The Muratians had found them. There must have been at least a hundred judging by the thunderous footsteps that followed.

Edmund still sputtered, "What in the…"

A spear of ice flew past a beige Pedite tent, impaling a large chestnut. The horse screamed and fell to the dirt. It withered and whined until Malin approached it and slit its throat, putting the poor beast out of its misery.

Icewielders.

They had wielders with them, and who knew what others lingered beyond the blue waves.

This couldn't be happening.

Not now.

They had no time for this. They weren't prepared for this.

Rian whipped around, searching for a safe exit among the invading blue soldiers. His fellow black and silver-clad men were shouting at each other, racing for their own weapons. The way the camp was set up, the Pedites were always in the most vulnerable position. So naturally, their camp would be hit the worst.

General Xavier was already yelling orders at a group of Pedites, shouting at them to get to the other end of camp where the explosion hit.

There was no time. He *had* to get to Isla.

"Rian!" Freya yelled, grabbing him. She turned him around, clutching both his uniform and the sleeve of Edmund's light blue tunic. "He's the *crown prince*. We need to get him to safety."

Rian froze. Intensely aware of Malin's scrutiny and Freya's heated glare. Every second they waited was precious time they didn't have to waste, and the waves of blue grew ever closer.

"Are you planning on leaving, *general*?" Freya's tones contained no ounce of forgiveness or give.

Every part of him warred within himself. His sense of honor—of duty—versus the thought of Isla. He'd made a foolish decision before and it had cost dearly. He'd already spent two years trying to make up for it. Duty said he had to stay and protect the prince while his heart—his soul—screamed at him to leave.

He thumbed the chipped hilt of Dark End, ignoring the chaotic thumping of his heart. The sound now matched the beat of boots against ground, edging ever close.

The sight of Edmund's scrunched face, the fear he couldn't contain behind his eyes, and the nervous way he rubbed his hands together made up Rian's mind for him. Isla could be far away by now, but Edmund was here in front of him, and Rian knew his duty--as much as his heart felt like it was impaled by the same ice arrows dancing through their camp.

He turned from the opening in the tents. Turned away from the quickest exit he could have used to sneak out, to sneak away, and sent a silent prayer to Hierel, to Slin, to Rallion—to all the goddesses—that Isla would not be harmed.

When the first blue-clad soldier crossed the threshold into their opening, he pulled his broadsword from its scabbard, hearing similar noises echoed from Freya and Malin.

Freya called over Elin and Cain, the tawny-haired brothers that wielded double rapiers. They'd served with both many times before.

"Help protect your prince," Freya said with a glare.

The brothers' eyes widened as they took in the sight of Edmund without his crown or jacket, standing out of place next to Rian. Probably wondering what trouble the wayward captain—now general—had gotten up to now. Likely curious what their prince was doing all the way in the Pedite camp without his guards or his Divite contingent.

There was no time for explanation, for the line of Muratian soldiers was fully upon the Pedite camp. A cloaked wielder was visible, lingering at the back of the group.

Arrows blocked out the sun as they rained upon the camp. Rian and Freya each grabbed one of Edmund's arms and hid under her shield. The arrows gushed against the shield in a fury, sounding like a storm's rain against a paned window.

When the torrent stopped, Rian was the first on his feet. His broadsword was at the ready for he knew these types of soldiers would give them no reprieve and would certainly show no mercy.

He'd been in battles before—with Freya and Malin at his side, along with other friends he once had. This was not orchestrated. It wasn't planned. And they'd never been attacked in the middle of their own camp like this.

It was brutal and chaotic. Plus, they had a virtually useless royal to keep alive. It was bodyguard duty all over again. But a million times worse.

Freya was a fierce figure with Bone Breaker cutting through blue and gold like it was nothing, all while keeping one hand on the back of Edmund's tunic and throwing him around like a toy—avoiding any shiny blades as she did.

Together, they formed a misshapen circle with the prince at the center. Backs inward, swords up. Facing the enemy as one.

It was like the courses his father made for them. Working together with his brother, solving the problem, and putting one foot in front of the other. There were no wooden sticks used as swords though. And the scarecrows he dressed as enemies were very real.

This time, he didn't want to pretend he was playing on his father's course, cutting down a stuffed enemy. This time, they were real foes who had tried to kill him. And they had taken from him. The mark on his arm pulsed as if spurring him on, encouraging him.

His sword sliced through soldier after soldier as if they were nothing. It was easier this time to cast out everything that would distract him from focusing on each new blue-clad soldier in front of him. He didn't look at their faces. Refused to look at them and see that split second of unfiltered terror that flashed before he made his final cut.

If he stopped to think about it, he'd be dead. Then he'd never make it to her.

So, he cut again and again. Parrying and defending as needed.

"Aargh."

Rian whipped around to see Edmund on the ground, clutching his arm as Freya pulled out a long white—something—spraying blood everywhere. A ripple of chills ran up his spine as he realized what it was.

An icicle.

The icewielder had found them, and he was eyeing up the prince.

Forty-Five

Mira

"What's wrong?" Beretta asked. Her eyes studied her closely, seemingly unsure as to why Mira froze without warning. Her grip on Mira's hand was firm—tight even.

Mira's mind couldn't process everything that was going through it, as the hidden depths of her memories struggled to claw to the surface. Memories of a black comet, a raging glacier river, dark mines that went on and on forever, and those decaying bodies on the pikes.

Then she was back in the mining camp, surrounded by dusty buildings that didn't belong. Harsh moonlight shone down on them, nearly as bright as the morning sun.

Another cloud of sickness came over her and sent a hammer pounding against her skull. Her body wouldn't move even though it felt like she was screaming from atop the mountain peak. Everything was wrong and yet she was the only one who noticed—or hadn't noticed before.

Why were the buildings not set up as they should be for a camp that had been here at least two years? Why did it look like they were set no more than mere months ago?

The storm in her brain pooled and swirled, on the verge of making her stomach upend itself. She tugged her hand out of Beretta's grip and everything stopped. Clarity settled again.

Mira stepped back from her friend, her back hitting the wall of a dusty building which shuddered behind her.

"Don't be mad," Beretta said in a strange voice. Unusual worry clouded her blue eyes. Fear. Fear that she didn't think her headstrong friend was capable of showing. "I did everything I could to talk her out of it. I tried to stop her."

Wait. What?

To stop *her.*

Mira looked behind but there was only the wall at her back. The confusion lasted for a moment until she realized that Beretta was not talking to her. She was speaking to someone else.

Mira whipped back around to see a figure emerge from the shadows of the next building. She'd recognize the shine of those boots and the shimmer of his pristine uniform anywhere.

Devlin.

Her fingertips felt like icicles and her heart didn't know if it wanted to stop altogether or rage like a vicious waterfall—it made all the blood swarm to her chest and she swayed, feeling lightheaded.

Devlin was not alone. He had a dozen other blue-clad guards with him.

What was he doing here? He was supposed to have been sent away with the others.

Perfectly polished boots kicked up dust as he sauntered over to her, his hands behind his back as if he were taking a leisurely stroll through the woods. The soldiers behind him kept their hands on their pommels, eyeing Mira wearily.

"Confused?" Devlin asked, scratching the scar along his chin. Those dark blue eyes danced hauntingly as he approached. A solider grabbed Mira, holding her in a painful grip. "I didn't think this would happen so quickly. I'll have to admit we weren't quite prepared after they attacked you, and we had to bring you up for healing."

Beretta snorted. Devlin shot her a deep glare and she straightened her back.

Mira's head pounded again. "I don't—I don't—"

"Not surprised the confusion is still there—the fog," Devlin said. He tilted his head and a smile curved along his lips. "It was a lot of effort to get you this way."

Beretta stepped around Mira, dragging her feet so each foot step seemed to take minutes. Step after step until she stood beside Devlin.

No. No. No.

"Do you know how long it took to break you?" Beretta kicked a rock which bounced off the frail building with an echoing clang.

It was as if she was back beneath that mountain with the walls closing in on her. Even the air was thin and hard to take in.

Beretta.

"She was out for days after working on you," Devlin said, an over exaggerated pout shaping his lips. He placed his hands on B's shoulders. "I don't think she'll be as nice next time."

Her *friend's* eyes flashed. Mira remembered seeing that danger in those blue irises before. Always glad it was directed at someone else, usually another dredger. Now—now she didn't recognize her friend with that loathing focused on her.

Something dark pooled inside of her, itching to get out. Begging to be released.

Beretta.

She was her closest friend. They'd never left each other's side throughout it all. And yet, it felt as if they were separated by the exact mountain looming behind them.

"*Next time*," Beretta hissed. Her head snapped back to Devlin. "I can't do that it again, I'm not suicidal."

"You will do as commanded, soldier," Devlin said in a calm voice. There was no overt threat, no angry shouting, but for some reason Beretta shrunk into herself.

The grip on Mira's shoulder flexed but remained firm. Several of the blue-clad guards shifted uneasily. All of them refused to meet Devlin's heated gaze.

"I don't understand," Mira repeated, feeling incredibly dull. It felt like everyone was invited to a meal that she was meant to observe from a dusty window.

Everyone knew something that she didn't.

"Remember what you were mining?" Devlin asked.

"The firestone..." Mira started, not even sure what question she wanted to ask.

"It does wonders at muting powerful wielder gifts," Devlin said happily. "And it's even more amazing at hiding a valuable wielder when there are multiple trackers looking for them."

Something knocked against the recesses of her mind, like a long forgotten memory that was desperate to escape.

"Obviously, we had some hiccups along the way," Devlin said. "Isn't that right, Beretta?"

"I didn't know they were going to attack her. I just needed a break." Beretta flexed her hands, the scars of her recent lashes reflecting in the moonlight. Mira thought she got them for trying to save her, she would have never suspected they were as punishment for leaving her alone.

"Really? After everything she did to them. Think better, commander. You almost ruined everything."

Commander? Commander?

"I did?" Beretta raised a sharp eyebrow indignantly. "Bodies. On pikes. *Really?*"

"Watch who you're talking to." He didn't bother to look sheepish and stood with that straight backed confidence that oozed power. "I thought it was a romantic touch, someone like you would have appreciated it."

Beretta jerked her head. "I wouldn't have minded. Not the typical gesture you want—or that most girls want," she added quickly. "Just—think about it. Something better for the next time—if I really must."

Mira stood there, dumbfounded.

The way they spoke to one another was familiar, like old friends. How could she have missed it before?

Devlin stepped toward Mira with a blazing look in his eyes. It wasn't fury that she saw in there. They were almost begging—pleading for understanding.

"Everything I said was true—about what I want. You don't remember, but Hierel's comet showed up right when we first met. Even the goddesses shower you in their power and glory. Think of what we could do together. I wanted to help you with your gifts instead of forcing you to hide them, to hate them, like you have all your life."

Mira opened her mouth, about to tell him exactly what she thought of his proposal when a commotion by the mouth of the mines stole her attention.

A group of the miners—dirty, bruised, and frightened—were brought up in chains. The guards shoved and kicked them into a neat line in front of Mira.

Over twenty accusatory eyes found their way to her face. Exhaustion lined their faces. Exhaustion, fear, and hate.

How had she never noticed the pure vitriol in their eyes before? It was like a fog had been lifted from her sight and mind.

A fog that was somehow connected to Beretta.

"Do you remember these villagers?" Devlin asked calmly. "Do you remember what you did to them?"

Their faces—they were faintly recognizable, but she'd worked with them for months. Yet, there was something more familiar about them—as covered in dirt and grime as they were. She'd seen them before—outside of the mines.

"Remember why they hate you?" Beretta asked. Mira was shocked at how cold and lifeless her voice was. How had she never noticed that beneath the mask Beretta had worn all this time? This person who stood in front of her, she was nothing more than a stranger.

Mira shook her head.

Beretta gestured at one of the far guards, who carried a brown bag over his shoulder. He dumped the contents over Mira's boots. Several of the miners gasped, and one of the women started sobbing at the powdery substance.

Mira bent down and rubbed some of the ash between her fingers. Black ash.

She turned her head toward Devlin and whispered in horror, "What did you do?"

Devlin laughed. He laughed at this. Even Beretta's cold mask was broken with a glowing smile. "What did *I* do?" he repeated. "This wasn't me. It was all you, dearest."

Mira couldn't tear her eyes from the ash still on her fingers. "The Wasp?"

"He had another name before," Beretta added. "Not that I ever bothered to learn it. But you probably knew, once. If you didn't think it was beneath you."

Mira looked questioningly at Beretta, trying desperately to wipe the ash—the Wasp—off her fingers.

"I think you took someone from him," Beretta said in a bored voice. "He really had it out for you. They all did, after what you did to their village—to their loved ones. So, the Wasp waited," Beretta added. "Waited for the perfect opportunity when you were on your own. That was my mistake." She dipped her head. "I didn't think their hatred for you would overtake their own self-preservation, as they knew what would happen if they touched you. We made certain of it."

Gummy looked at her with hollow eyes. She remembered those green eyes once before. If he still had his hair and weight around the belly, he would almost be familiar. They'd pulled his teeth out—possibly as a warning when they were first taking down here. But he was so jovial when she met him at the inn.

Devlin jerked his head at the row of guards behind the miners—the villagers—and before anyone could utter a syllable, hot steel burst through the chests of every single one of them.

Forty-Six
The General

Every inch of skin, every drop of blood—every ounce of him—screamed at him to run.

The Muratian icewielder was less than ten feet away, another jagged spear already conjured and ready. The tip of the ice blade glistened like precious jewels in the sunlight.

The wielder's hood fell back to reveal dark eyes, and two long scars dragging down his cheeks. The scars were nearly opaque, oddly resembling a layer of thin ice over a mountain stream.

Edmund was thrown to the ground when two thick-necked soldiers attacked Freya. At least no Muratians had yet to notice the Velotian Prince was in their midst. If they did, he'd be swarmed.

Rian frantically dug into his breast pocket, but the usual blade he wore wasn't there. The one from his father.

Right. It was Isla's now.

He slid his hand over to the other pocket and pulled out another dagger—the same one he'd taken from the dead Muratian wielder that day in the forest.

He flipped it in his hand and it slid off his fingers like butter, aiming true for its target. Before it could connect with the wielder's heart, a wall of ice went up and the blade scattered to the side.

Rian groaned.

Fucking wielders.

"Icewielder!" he warned the others, having no chance to stop and see if his words reached them. It was hard to focus on anything besides the clatter of steel against steel and the grunts and cries from soldiers all around.

He kept his eyes on the wielder before he could take out the lot of them. He just needed to keep the wielder's focus on him. Anything so the wielder didn't turn and realize exactly who was in their small group.

A well-trained wielder could do as much damage as fifty soldiers... some types could do even more, he thought as the mark on his arm panged. If this one got past, he could do untold damage to those Rian cared about.

Sliding to the side, he raised Dark End, ready for whatever this wielder may send his way. He'd been to Rallion's first gate and back again, he could handle anything.

The blue-cloaked soldier raised a hairless eyebrow. A smirk jumped to his face and silent laughter rolled off him. Rian's blood curdled at the sight.

The wielder twisted his hand—still keeping his eyes locked on Rian's—and a white, crystalline longsword materialized in it. Puffs of deadly cold air mixed against the warm breeze.

He was fast. Faster than Rian had expected. Wielders were known to have augmented physical strengths, especially ones that had worked their gift for years—which this wielder clearly had been doing—but this seemed different.

Every beat of his heart was matched by a movement from the wielder. In two swift heartbeats, he was upon him, his ice blade meeting Rian's metal blade in a frightful crash that sent waves down his arm. He pushed back, barely managing to move the wielder an inch, but it was enough to pull back and strike again.

Once again, their blades met in the middle, crushing against each other. Despite being made of what Rian assumed was delicate ice, the blade was as formidable as if wrought in the toughest iron.

To his side, Freya and Cain tangled with a nearly seven-foot-tall soldier. Edmund had finally found his blade and was using it to make some pitiful attempts at sparring in the midst of the chaos, but Freya kept him close, always pivoting back so the prince was within arm's reach.

Rian and his friends had seen enough battles to know how each other moved. They knew what to expect. So, when Rian pulled back to make a second go at the wielder, Malin appeared, stepping in his place and blocking a side hit that would have made it through.

With a flourish and cocky wink, Malin slithered away and blocked a similar blow for Freya. He always kept to the shadows and out-skirts, coming in at just the perfect timing.

Malin bought him just enough time to gather his strength and catch the wielder off-guard. Rian's dark blade hit the middle of the ice-sword, right in the perfect spot, and it shattered.

The wielder bared his teeth and growled. Frost sparked at his fingertips and a slim sword appeared in each hand.

Rian grimaced—the only emotion he'd allowed himself to show. Of course, the wielder had to go for two blades. Slin hated him, and Rallion was clearly in her corner.

If Sister Death was determined to drag him back to the first gate herself, the least he could do was put up a fight. A damned good one, if the goddess was willing.

Rian closed the distance again so the wielder couldn't get a decent swing.

The ice-wielder's face contorted into one of pure rage, and frosty webs danced up his neck. He parried with his left hand, sneaking the other knife in for a side-strike while Rian was busy with the first. Luckily, Rian managed to duck just in time, feinting to the side and blocking the next strike.

The wielder attacked again and again. Forcing Rian away from the others, who were occupied with a new group of Muratian soldiers. He had to hold faith in his friends. They'd see to it the prince was kept safe. Isla would kill them if not—kill *him*.

When he charged, the wielder crossed both blades and blocked him, barely holding him at bay.

At this closeness, he could practically hear the wielder's heartbeat. Coldness leaked off him in droves and the frost spread up his fingertips.

Interesting.

He slid Dark End and twisted the first ice blade of the wielder's hand. With a roar, he charged but a blast of cold air shot him back ten feet. Before Rian could get up, the wielder held out his hand and sent a large ball flying toward a group of black and silver soldiers. It landed and splintered like a thousand small knives, cutting through leather and skin while all Rian could do was scream.

He needed to finish the wielder before more damage could be done—he needed to do something—but Dark End lay nearly twenty feet away.

The wielder jumped and was at his side in an instant, Rian had nothing to defend himself with except his hands and feet—and he was still on the ground. He curled his feet into himself, lifting his hands in surrender, and when the wielder was close enough, he focused all his force and kicked. He heard a popping sound—the wielder's kneecap—followed by a strangled scream.

The wielder stumbled back, panting. But then that stupid smile returned. He placed his hand on his leg and an ice-brace formed, curling around his broken knee.

Rian cursed. Godsdamned wielders.

At least he bought himself enough time to make it back to his shaky legs. He wiped the blood that had started dribbling down his nose and raised his fists as if hoping to sway the wielder to fight in hand-to-hand combat. Not that he would fare much better.

The wielder laughed, contorting the scars on his face. He was coming to the same terrible conclusion as Rian already had. Rian was outmatched, and there was no way the wielder would even the odds.

His bruised ribs screamed at him and his arm continued throbbing for some reason.

Usually, imagining that he was young and back on that course his father built helped him get through battles like this, it brought him back to the basics. But today he didn't want to pretend, he wanted to make them pay for what they'd done to Isla. And he couldn't let any more of his friends suffer because of him.

Cain bounded into view, blocking the wielder with his double rapier. The wielder snarled and sent crushing blow after blow his way. When a sword broke, another icy one was in his hands in seconds, ready to strike with vicious accuracy.

A flash of blue light and Cain was on the ground, his eyes open and a sharp icicle sticking in the side of his neck. Crimson gushed everywhere.

His brother, Elin, roared and charged the wielder, his eyes too flooded with rage to see the ice-arrow sent his way. He ended up on the ground next to his brother, neither moving.

No. Not again.

This couldn't be happening again.

Red filled his vision, focused entirely on the laughing icewielder. As Rian's hand brushed his side, he remembered that he still had one small, simple blade. He pulled it out, knowing it would be useless against his double-sworded foe.

The wielder was upon him, hitting the side of his head with the back of his sword. Stars and circles burst into his vision once again and Rian spat a mouthful of blood. He was on his knees—clutching the small blade, but with no real plan on what to do—when the wielder kicked his arm, sending it, and his last hope of a defense, sliding into the dirt.

The wielder threw his second ice sword to the side and used both hands to lift the thicker one for a killing strike.

Rian's heart battered his chest as if trying to escape before its inevitable end. At least it would be quick.

As the sword came down, a terrible, jarring pain shot from his arm and reached into his chest. It jolted him to the side and the ice-knife missed his head, skimming the side of his hair.

The wielder's eyes widened for a second, shocked that he had so clearly missed his mark. Ice started to claw its way up the soldier's hand, and a cold draft hit Rian.

Not again.

The throbbing pulled at his arm and he rolled to the side, grabbing the discarded sword, his fingers sticking to the cold ice weapon and protesting against the bite of the frosty hilt.

Before the wielder could turn, Rian swiped the sword—hitting his mark.

A row of blood splattered over him as the wielder's throat split open, cutting deep past blood and bone. The surprise was still frozen on his cruel face as the wielder dropped. Finally dead.

Rian crumpled to his knees. He didn't know how long he stayed there, staring at the wielder's body, at the bodies of his friends, and at the unmoving Pedite soldiers among the blue and gold Muratian ones. At some point his hand started throbbing from the cold sword, so he dropped it, allowing it to shatter against the dirt and gravel.

The battle was nearing an end, and a quick look around told him they won—though the black and silver bodies may disagree. This attack was not meant to destroy them or kill their prince. If it was, they would have sent more.

No, Rian realized with a sickening feeling, it was a distraction.

The Muratian soldiers were sent with no intention of winning this battle. They weren't meant to come home.

Rian's head snapped back to the spot where he had left his friends, and a shaky breath bubbled its way up when he saw Edmund on the ground, still clutching his shoulder. Freya towered over him with her bloodied battle axe still in her hand, as if worried more Muratian soldiers hid behind a decimated tent.

Malin was helping another injured Pedite when he locked eyes with Rian. His silver hair band somehow miraculously stayed in place throughout the battle. He shook his head and pointed next to a mass of bodies next to a black tent.

Their General—General Xavier lay dead underneath his horse.

"This was all your fault," Edmund punched his shoulder, then cried and fell to the ground, clutching his own where the ice blade had broken skin.

"You're fine," Rian said disdainfully; his heart still thundered dangerously loud. "Stop being a baby and get up. Get your men together and make yourself useful for once in your life."

"Don't you dare speak to me like that." Edmund struggled to his feet with a huff, his good arm swinging widely.

"I'll speak to you exactly how you deserve," Rian said, wincing at the venom that flowed from his voice. "Just like you spoke to your sister, who we'll never reach in time now thanks to saving you—you poor excuse of a prince." He pointed at the pile of bodies. "It should have been you lying on the ground."

Edmund recoiled.

"Idiot." Rian sent him a withering glare before turning his gaze to his bloodied friends. "We need to prepare those that can leave as soon as possible."

"What about the injured?" Freya asked.

"We'll leave them behind with enough supplies and able men. It's not them that they are after."

"Right," Malin said, nodding softly. Blood dripped from a thin cut that trailed from his temple to his ear.

Other Pedite soldiers gathered, shifting from foot to foot as if waiting for something, waiting for orders. What were they waiting for?

Freya nodded at him.

Rian cursed.

Oh gods.

Oh no. Oh no. No. No. No.

With General Xavier dead, he was now, apparently, the leading commander of this Pedite battalion. The memory of what happened the last time he was in charge roiled through him like a hot coal.

But he promised himself never again. Taking a deep breath—a steadying breath in which he tried to draw power from the sky goddess herself—he turned to the other Pedites and gave the order to pack up everything they could, trying not to feel like the fraud he was inside.

After the group dispersed, Rian turned back to his tent and stumbled.

They'd never make it there in time now.

As the truth settled in, his heart skipped as if it didn't remember how to beat properly anymore. As if a chunk had been carved out by a flaming knife and taken from him. A part of him had been taken.

A cloud passed overhead, casting a fitting shadow that mirrored the darkness he felt in his heart.

"Rian," Freya said sharply.

He whipped around at the worry in her voice and found her and the prince staring above. Edmund pointed stupidly at something in the sky.

The sight above could have turned the blood pumping through his body to ash if it hadn't already evaporated in a fit of rage and loss and desperation. The skin on his arm felt as if it were lit on fire. He didn't need to look down to know it was the spot where Isla had marked him.

When he looked to the prince, laying there and clutching his shoulder all while whimpering pathetically and staring at the dark omen in the skies—*Rallion's comet*—it was then he knew he had to find her or die trying.

After Freya yelled at him to pull himself together, Edmund made his way to his feet with his eyes piercing through Rian's. A shaky thread of understanding passed between the two of them. It likely wouldn't last for long.

Edmund jerked his head and clenched his teeth. "What is our next move, then, *general*?"

Forty-Seven
The Princess

"Are you certain you don't want some wine, Princess Isla? It's imported from southern Shiaarl and has the most amazing hints of cherry and oak."

Isla eyed the wineskin the commander threw in her face with disgust, but after thinking about the certainly yawn-inducing droll the commander was about to spew her way while they ate, she grabbed the skin and drank directly from the spout. Before he could ask for its return, she turned her back and walked away. She couldn't look at that annoying commander or the dreadful forest anymore.

The wine was decent, but she'd had better. Much better. This once had a cloying taste and was likely going bad. What would the Koliat wines taste like? Would they be overly dry and oaky or offer anything sweet and fruitful—just as she preferred? It wouldn't take long to find out once they met up with the prince's party tomorrow.

It didn't matter that her brother refused to come with her—she was done trying to piece together a bridge to a relationship that he clearly didn't want. It didn't matter that Rian had used her—she'd never see him again anyway. Soon, it would all be behind her and she was determined to start her new life with a fresh mind.

Maybe Prince Brenner wasn't as bad as everyone said?

Isla snorted at the absurdity of the thought. Of course, he'd be as terrible as the rumors, and she shouldn't expect anything less.

At least the Koliats had money, so she wouldn't be wanting for anything. And she'd have far better wine than this sludge, Isla threw the wineskin to the ground and climbed to the top of a nearby hill to sulk.

The mid-day sun's rays stretched far, covering the grassy lands ahead in a dull golden hue. A field of purple wildflowers swayed in the wind, while an unseen brook bubbled in the distance.

The sight would be beautiful, if Isla didn't feel dead on the inside. But she was resigned to her fate, to seal the alliance and prevent more unnecessary deaths. That had to count for something, right?

A shuffle behind her.

Commander Skallen sidled up next to her and tucked his hands behind his back. "It's a shame, this entire business of war with the Muratians."

"Yes. Yes, it is." Why wouldn't that persistent commander leave her alone? She had half a mind to run straight into the Black Forests at this point, even if it felt like a part of her never left.

"I don't think I ever properly apologized for what happened in the forest that day," Skallen said. "We should have had you more properly guarded."

"It's nothing." She waved her hand, hoping he'd get the hint to leave her alone.

Her head was starting to fog over. Exhaustion from the hard day's ride settled in as Skallen had barely let them stop for a break, insisting they had a schedule to keep to. Even her circlet, which had felt extra heavy the entire ride, now seemed to want to drag her entire head down.

"Well." He rubbed his hands together. "At least the matter will be all settled soon, won't it?"

"Yes." That was one way to refer to her forced marriage to Prince Brenner. Isla rubbed the back of her neck, feeling a cool breeze start to settle in.

Skallen looked over his shoulder, not towards the men who were preparing a light lunch for them, but towards the forest in the distance. Towards the swaying branches and deep shadows that Isla had spent days in, only emerging after she had been turned completely inside out.

"As I said, it'll soon be settled as it should have been in the first place." He shifted from foot to foot.

The wine in her stomach pooled and churned. as if curdling into something rancid. All that riding had made her queasy. A pang shot through her. She dropped to her knees, doubling over and placing her palms on her knees in an attempt to keep her stomach from turning out.

The circlet slipped from its spot on her brow and landed on the lush grass in front of her. She couldn't move to grab it.

"Not feeling well, are you?" Skallen asked lightly. "I'm sure it'll pass."

One of the horses whinnied, and she was reminded of sweet River, with his light temperament and constant need for affection. What had happened to the beast?

"The others say that the goddesses smile upon you. Though it sounds like you have obtained favor by Sister Death herself instead of being blessed by Hierel."

In between the deep breaths she took to try to calm her stomach, Isla frowned.

"Not that it matters. A debt will be paid, the way it should have been done from the start. A child for a child. Repayment for the son taken. Then it can all be over with. No need for any more unnecessary bloodshed. I'm just sorry we weren't able to hand over the one responsible for it as planned, but hopefully, this will be enough. I think it should be. Yes, it should be."

Her breaths came in giant gasps as if her lungs had shrunk and couldn't fit any more air. A bead of sweat dripped down the back of her neck.

No. No.

"It shouldn't have been dragged out so, but we weren't aware of the skills of that *soldier*, or your gifts, as I said. A shame we were kept in the dark."

The commander's shadow moved, blocking out the sun entirely.

There were shouts from the soldiers down below, and the commander cursed. Something was happening, but all Isla could do was grip the coarse grass in her hands and try to keep from landing face-first in it.

Metal unsheathed from leather, ringing oddly in her ears. Her heart pounded frantically, but she couldn't stand, let alone run away. She could barely think thanks to whatever was in that godsdamned wine. Rian would be cursing at her right now.

Commander Skallen moved behind her, surely readying for that final blow.

At least the war would be over.

At least her death would mean something.

Isla clamped her eyes shut and waited for the darkness to take her. It didn't come.

Something hurtled through the air and there was a small thud, followed by an even louder thump as Commander Skallen fell to his knees beside her.

Isla opened her eyes to see a gold dagger lodged in the commander's chest, pools of scarlet already spilling out as he sputtered a blood-soaked cry. Boots thundered up behind them, and for a glorious second Isla's heart soared. *Rian was here.*

Then a wielder grabbed the commander by his hair, tilting his head back so she could split his neck in two.

When the light went out of Skallen's eyes, the blue-cloaked wielder tossed him to the side with a disparaging noise.

"Filthy traitor to his own kingdom," the wielder mumbled in that ice-cold voice that raked its claws along Isla's spine.

"Get her up," a deep voice commanded. A pair of hands were under her shoulders and tugged her to her unsteady feet. A hand rested on her shoulder—a warning. If she had more than half a brain working, Isla would be insulted that they didn't think she was enough of a threat to warrant restraints.

That's because she wasn't.

The small part of her brain that still functioned understood that the shakes were gone. That strange pull of darkness and feeling of instability meant that her powers were smothered, shoved deep inside to a part that she couldn't remember.

As Isla stared at the blue clad soldiers in front of her, she couldn't help but think how smart they were... and how dumb she was.

One broke through the ranks, wearing a dark blue uniform that had not a single speck of blood or dust—even on his tall, shiny boots. He had the same rusty brown hair that Isla had seen in portraits of the Muratian Queen and bright blue eyes that were devoid of all emotion. Matching gold straps ran across his broad shoulders with a crest in the middle of each. A series of medals covered his left breast pocket, each more extravagant than the last. He was definitely royalty, and from the way he spoke, was the same one hunting them since that day in the river.

Their prince. Isla wasn't certain exactly which one, though she knew the oldest was dead. Abrax. The one Rian had killed.

The wielder strode towards the prince, whipping back the hood of her cloak and Isla finally got her first look at the one who had haunted her nightmares.

At first all she could see was red. Fiery red hair that cascaded everywhere, framing a freckled face and light blue eyes that sparkled with haunting glee.

"The rest are dead," the wielder said, a cruel smile curving at the corner of her lips. "That witless commander helped us more than he realized, spiking all their drinks like he did."

Isla clutched her hands so tight it was painful. They were all dead?

The prince stepped closer to Isla, the wielder mirroring his every move as if she was his bodyguard–or something more?

"You were quite difficult to hunt down, did you know that? Something interfered with our trackers."

Isla clenched her jaw. She'd always hated her powers and the destruction that came with it. This day, for the first time in her life, she found herself craving that feel of death coursing through her veins. She'd never wished to unleash it on another as much as she did now.

Nothing stirred, no matter how hard she tried.

He tilted his head toward her. "Don't feel like talking? That's fine." He circled her, studying her. "Your people killed my brother and nearly drove my mother insane—well, more insane than usual." His left eye twitched. "Granted, my brother went off on his own to neutralize a threat to the crown, but still... your death *should* be the key that fixes everything. Even so, I'm not here to kill you. As much as that witless commander thought that was the deal he struck."

Isla twisted her head, too late to hide the surprise that filled her face.

"He thought he was handing over the key to fixing this war. The key to peace. But it was never about that. My brother's death was merely the catalyst—a perfect reason to begin the invasions. You are much more important than you realize. I know you don't see it now, but in time you will understand."

"I'm not coming with you," Isla spat out. "I'd rather you killed me now than drag it out."

"You will come willingly." The prince placed his hands on the wielder's shoulders before stepping around her, closer to Isla. "My friend here has quite the way of convincing people. You'd be shocked at what she can do with even the toughest mind."

The wielder's face practically glowed. The sight churned Isla's insides.

What Isla wouldn't give to wipe that grin off her face. If Rian were here, that smile—along with her head—would already be removed.

Darkness from a passing cloud covered everything and the prince's head shot upwards.

Knowing it would surely get her killed, Isla's hand found its way to the dagger Rian had given her, tucked beneath the layers of her travel leathers. Shadow Death. She'd kept it on her despite Skallen's protests that it wasn't becoming of a lady to be armed so. Thank the goddess she didn't listen.

Perhaps they hadn't expected her to be armed—or so stupid—as no one was able to stop her in time. She took a swipe for the prince, channeling all her energy and aiming for the neck.

The red-headed wielder grabbed his shoulder at the last second, and Shadow Death only ended up nicking his jawline. His blue eyes widened in shock and he cursed, then something hit her and all she saw was blackness and stars.

She was face-first in the grass, stunned from the blow to her head, and struggling from the efforts to keep her stomach contents inside her body.

Someone pulled her hair and wrenched her to her knees.

The wielder.

A strange glow pulsed from her hands, and blinding pain erupted in Isla's brain. It crashed against the sides of her skull and felt like a dagger was being dragged through every inch of her head, turning it inside out.

"Stop!" The prince clutched his neck, trails of crimson dripping between his fingers. "I told you that I don't want her dead." His blue eyes trailed along Isla's face, sending a shudder down her spine. "It's only a scratch. It hurt like a bitch because it's infused with firestone. Where'd she get a Muratian blade from?"

The red-haired woman released her hair and Isla fell panting to her hands and knees next to the discarded circlet.

She was a mindweaver. A powerful and dangerous one who seemed to relish in others' pain.

Isla didn't know the Muratians had one in their armies, as mindweavers were supposed to be carefully watched across the kingdoms due to the damage they could cause. Diving into a person's mind to cut and twist and bend until there was nothing left was not something to be taken lightly. Clearly there was much the Muratians were hiding.

Why didn't they just kill her and get it over with? Perhaps she would be made to suffer as atonement for her kingdom's transgressions.

The prince pointed at the still-darkened sky. "Look."

Shaking from toe to fingertip, Isla blinked and looked up. The darkness hadn't come from a cloud like she thought. It was something else.

Something terrible.

A black ball of fire was making its way across the skies, its tail stretching behind like death's swooping hand.

"Rallion's comet," the woman whispered. "Just like you said."

"You never should have doubted me." The prince didn't take his eyes off the sign from the heavens. "My mother was right. She was right about it all... do it."

Before Isla could pause to understand or ask what that meant, the woman's hands were on her head, and that invisible dagger was back with heated venom. She was paralyzed with pain.

It took its time carving her insides into nothing. It relished in her pain and dug deeper any time she screamed.

That dagger took her memories, turned them inside out, and lit them on fire. It was hard to remember who she was. All she could remember was the blind, all-encompassing pain that clung to every fiber of her being and wouldn't release her from its clutches.

The world was torn away from under her. Ripped apart and made anew in her mind. Replacing everything.

She wasn't certain if it had been seconds or minutes or days. When she emerged from the pain everything was replaced by dark stone and cold and loneliness. She did not know anything else, not even her name.

Hands still kept a tight grip on her mind and the female asked in a hollow cold voice, "What do you want to do with her? They'll come right away. They'll track her."

"I *know*, Beretta."

"Her powers? She could kill us all once that potion wears off."

"I know they'll come for her and I know she's dangerous. I don't care." A pair of boots approached, stopping in front of her and crouching so she could stare into his eyes. A terrible and vicious sea of blue. "I have the perfect place, and you're going to *love* it."

Untold waves of pain upon pain slammed into her as everything was shredded away.

Forty-Eight
The Princess

PRESENT DAY

Red flooded her vision.

Thick crimson rained onto the dirty ground and pooled into muddy puddles of death, refusing to stop. The miners—they were dead.

No, not miners. She knew them from before. They were villagers. And they'd done nothing wrong to deserve what had happened to them.

This was her fault. It was all because of her. All because they had stayed for the night. The trickster Slin truly was a cruel goddess; she'd thrown everything in her life out of sorts.

She was on her hands and knees, sobbing and trying to keep everything from spilling out. It was like she forgot how to breathe—how to think—how to *be*.

A rough hand pulled her up by her hair, nearly tearing her scalp off.

"Oh, come on now," Beretta chided, towering over her like death's shadow. "Stop that. They tried to *kill* you. They wanted you dead—do you get that? Don't waste your tears on them."

"They knew the price of touching you," Devlin added. "They all did. And they still chose to act."

The sight of his smirk curdled her stomach. It needed to be removed from his face. How could she have ever trusted him? He didn't care about the lives he took. He didn't care about any of it.

Going off some obscene instinct, she lunged for him, not really certain what she was hoping to accomplish with nothing but her hands and nails. She thrashed, trying to get any inch she could get her hands on before splitting pain erupted against the back of her skull and rough hands pulled her away.

One of the guards held her in a death grip, his rancid breath heating the back of her neck.

"I *told* you to be careful with her," Beretta said exasperatedly, releasing her hold on the prince's shirt. She'd pulled him away to safety, out of reach.

Devlin rubbed his scratched cheek, heated anger flashing through his eyes. "Don't. Do. That. Again."

"Those people—you—you killed them—you killed Crag and the Wasp—"

"Oh, no, no, no." He wagged a finger in front of her face. "I didn't kill the Wasp." He gestured at the black dust on the ground, a small stream of blood had reached it. "You did."

The sob about to release stopped in her chest and lodged itself there, clinging to her lungs, her heart, to everything.

"What?"

"That was all you," Beretta said. "I guess your powers were able to break through the hold of the firestone in order to save you. By the time we got there, he was nothing more than bones and ash. You almost made me proud."

She felt sick to her stomach—and this time it had nothing to do with Beretta touching her. Pain and anger filled her. Hatred like nothing she'd experienced before filled her limbs, reaching all the way down to her shaking fingertips.

"They were already sentenced down here for letting you escape from their village," Devlin said. "And we needed someplace to hide you, to keep you from hurting yourself, or us, and it seemed a bit..." he trailed off, scratching his chin.

"Poetic?" Beretta supplied helpfully. "A delicious taste of Slin's sweet trickster justice?" She narrowed her eyes. "Or Rallion's wrathful retribution."

Isla thought she was going to be sick. What's more, she thought her outsides were going to explode. The soldier holding her relaxed his grip and kept a warning hand on her shoulder only, as if she was no more a threat than a tree mouse.

Why weren't they worried about her?

The tea.

The tea Beretta gave her before leaving.

It was laced with something... but she didn't actually drink it. Not because she didn't trust Beretta—though that thought twisted her stomach into knots—she was too excited at the prospect of escaping, a futile attempt she now realized was always failed to doom. They'd never let their prisoner out of sight. They hadn't for even one second since she was brought here, for Beretta never left her side... not even when she slept.

She stood amongst the ruins with nothing but the sight of red and the coppery stench of blood mixed with ash and dirt, and felt unimaginable loss and pain. It was too much.

Beretta laughed when hot tears started pouring down her face.

They did this.

All this death and destruction for what—some fairy tale following of a long ago departed goddess and the vague promise of power? They were crazy and vicious and uncaring for anything but their own convoluted purpose.

They were blinded by the thin prospect of might in a cruel world.

Isla finally understood. She was no longer afraid of this power coursing through her veins. No longer afraid of the destruction and chaos it brought. She didn't care if she burned herself out doing it.

If she was truly blessed by Sister Death, then it was time to show them exactly why death should be feared. She should be feared.

But hatred wasn't enough though. It pooled at the edge of her fingers and lingered there, waning. It was never about being angry.

Instead, she focused on that feel of morning sunshine and the way it felt on her skin—on her lips. That feeling pulled from something deep within her like an ember exposed to hot air, traveling up her spine. It burst forward, clawing against the grip on her shoulder and pulling all that energy away.

It rippled outwards and reached into every terrible living thing within its grasp.

Devlin shouted something but the guards were too slow to run. He grabbed Beretta as a wave of darkness pulled everything into her in a burst of black and ash. This time—she welcomed the destruction.

This time, it was exactly what she wanted.

The guards around her withered into nothing as ash blew about, blocking all else.

It took a moment for the ash to disappear, when she turned to leave, feeling triumphant in her victory. But when the final specs of dust floated down, two people were still standing.

Forty-Nine
The Princess

Was this what being stuck under a cave-in was like?

Unable to move, unable to breathe or think. An invisible boulder was shoved onto her chest, stealing the air from her lungs and making her body incredibly heavy. She had dug too deep and was on the verge of losing herself under the weight of her powers.

"I wouldn't try that again," Devlin said angrily. This was the first time he'd lost that finely crafted composure. "Not unless you want to kill yourself." He kicked a thin sword out of the way. "And I have plenty more men where those ones came from."

Behind him, Beretta still crouched with her hands up. Her mouth moved silently as she surveyed the pile of ash all around.

"How?" she asked. They should have been killed like the others.

"I told you before." Devlin opened the lapel of his blue jacket to pull out a dagger fashioned from rock. She recognized that dagger. "Firestone has many amazing properties, and it looks like it can protect from an unstable ashfeeder."

She stepped back, nearly tripping over a sword and scabbard.

"I recognized the make of this one. You came to us with it, in case you forgot." Devlin stepped closer to her, his eyes sparkling in the moonlight. "You also forgot that we're the same, you and I."

He grabbed her hand and agony erupted from her side.

It felt like she was being split open fresh and raw. Like being stabbed with the sharp end of a pick, but a thousand times worse. Over and over again.

She cried out, her body begging for a reprieve. But she couldn't break his fierce grip, no matter how she wiggled and pulled. She was on her knees now; her legs had turned to mush—as had the rest of her body.

One look at her torso showed crimson exploding from her freshly re-opened wound. It may have even grown in size. Surely, it would swallow her whole.

Once he determined that she'd had enough, he released her. Everything kept spinning even though she was on her hands and knees, trying to regain precious breaths that had evaded her. And every cursed wheeze of air was tainted with the smell of blood from the villagers.

"But you—you're a healer," she said stupidly, staring at her blood-soaked palm.

He hooked a thumb into the belt of his pristine uniform. Behind him, Beretta had finally gotten to her feet and dusted herself off as if nothing had happened. Devlin didn't so much as glance her way.

"Healing is rather boring, don't you think?" he said, flexing his spare hand and staring at it as if it were Hierel's own. "My mother adheres to the teachings of Rallion's followers, and they strive to push wielders beyond what we once thought were their limits. I've learned how to develop my powers, to expand them. Since Rallion's comet, those limits seem to be endless."

She continued to stare at the blood pooling on her brown tunic. Her hands started to shake and the darkness at her fingertips still hadn't fully retreated. She was empty.

Drained.

If she tried to use her powers again, it would take all she had.

Devlin's eyes followed hers. "I can help you with your powers. You'd be unstoppable—we'd be unstoppable."

"It won't work," Beretta chided from behind him, exasperation lacing every syllable. "I *told* you this."

Devlin shrugged off her words. "I know you're on your own and didn't think you'd fight that hard to hold on to your old life. What's holding you back, Isla?"

Isla. Isla. The name felt foreign yet familiar to her. That was her name once.

Beretta kicked a pile of dirt into her face. "No one's coming to save you this time. I know you think you have others out there looking for you, but they'll never be able to find you. Not with all the firestone around."

Devlin's eyes narrowed. "What was that name you said she called out in her sleep?"

"Can't remember," Beretta said casually. A cruel smile teased her lips. "He won't be able to find her either, not if we keep her below *like we planned*."

Devlin brushed Beretta off like an annoying tree mouse.

He took to one knee and stared into Isla's eyes. "There's nothing and nobody left for you back home. Let me help you. Think about what we could achieve together."

Beretta sighed, louder this time.

"Why would I side with you? You're nothing but monsters—both of you."

Devlin clutched his chest. "You wound me." He pointed at the pools of blood and the ash piles where there should be bodies. "Look around. I'm not the only monster here, princess. Not only did your soldiers kill my brother and start this whole thing, but it turns out that you are no better than the rest of us."

Isla shakily rose to her feet. Beretta was next to Devlin, pulling him back so they were no longer face to face, so he wasn't within reach again.

"I'm sorry about your brother, but it doesn't have to be this way."

"We want the same thing. We both want to put an end to this war. Our methods may be a bit different." Devlin's eyes darkened. "The stories I told you about Rallion's followers were true. They believed that Rallion would be rebirthed one day and herald a new age for wielders like us." He pointed between himself, Beretta, and her.

Beretta narrowed her eyes and added, "We'd never have to hide our powers or worry about kings or queens tearing us from our homes again to fight in their wars."

"From *your* war, you mean?" she bit back.

Devlin reached beneath his blue coat and something gold scattered to the ground in front of her. The delicate circlet sung to her. Called to her.

She plucked her circlet from the ashes, brushing away the soot and grime to reveal thin filigree leaves. Familiar, yet somehow foreign after all this time. Again, her head throbbed and pulsed. The faint light shone upon the leaves and pearls, one of them fully rubbed clear of its gold casing. Only now could she see the flecks that were woven into the small orbs. Black and red.

Firestone.

"Think about what you are going back to," Devlin said. "Did you ever ask yourself why your mother had this particular circlet? Why she favored it so much and insisted it was gifted down to you?"

She shook her head.

"That's not a Velotian crown," he said quietly.

Did this mean—could this possibly mean what he suggested? Her mother's line likely carried the magic that cursed Isla, but she would have known if her mother was a wielder. Someone would have told her.

Her father hated wielders. He never would have married one. Unless... unless he didn't know. Unless nobody knew.

"It was always in your blood." Devlin took a small shuffle towards her, still closely shadowed by Beretta. "Think about it. Think about what you could help accomplish, Isla."

Her?

"Rallion's followers predicted that the same magic would come from the old High King's line and be reborn anew. They followed the lines closely, especially down the royal lines. It took a long time to figure out that the old tales never referred to the powers passed down through the king's sons."

She shuffled back. Her heel hit a longsword, still buried in ash.

"Why do you think her followers burned their skin for a mere chance to be graced by a kiss from the goddess?" He pointed to the ash blowing around their feet. "Some of those devotees may have been a bit too rabid in their offerings but they *understood*. Ashfeeders are blessed by Sister Death herself."

No. No. No.

Blood pooled at her feet. Too much of it.

If she didn't close this wound, she'd bleed out. It was now or never. She had to escape.

A part of her knew if she made it to the forest then she'd somehow be safe. She just had to make it to the forest.

But they'd never let her get that far. Not after everything they'd done to keep her here.

Devlin shook his head. "I thought we'd be able to get through to you. I see now that we need more time." He swiveled his head to Beretta and nodded.

Beretta swallowed and stepped carefully toward Isla. Anger burned in her eyes. Then a brief flash of fear and uncertainty, but it was gone as quickly as it came. Now the woman in front of her—the soldier, the wielder—had nothing but stoney resolve in her face. If words could be conveyed between the two, then it was clear this time would not be like the last. She'd be made to suffer far worse.

"Do try to make it stronger this time," Devlin added.

With her back to Devlin, only Isla saw the grimace that crossed Beretta's face.

Isla slumped her shoulders and knelt to the ground, head bowed as if in acceptance of her fate. But the thought of being sent back under that terrible mountain was too much. She'd rather die out here, breathing the fresh forest air before setting another foot in that rotten mine shaft, Rallion be damned to all hells. She couldn't let her—

Pain. A terrible pain crept from the back of her head and down her spine, flinging her head back against the sharp knife digging at her skull. Vine-line tendrils crept along her mind, pulling and picking apart memories without care for the pain it caused.

It slunk around her mind, to the parts she had long forgotten, and squeezed. The pain was so much this time, she knew it meant to take those ones away forever.

No!

Isla was lying in the cold dirt, gasping for breath. She wasn't the only one.

Beretta was feet away, equally breathless, with her hands on her knees and staring at Isla with fear.

"Again," his cold voice rang out. "I said to make it stronger."

Beretta brushed sweaty strands of that fiery hair off her forehead, and slowly nodded. Her jaw was locked as she stepped toward Isla.

Another sharp breath tore its way through her lungs. She couldn't go back. She couldn't go through that again without being torn to so many pieces that no one could ever hope to stitch her together again.

She grasped around in the dirt to try to lift herself up. Her fingers touched the edge of a cool blade, discarded from that soldier. She squeezed around the steel, ignoring as it cut through her flesh, and sliced the end through the air.

Beretta screeched as the tip of the blade cut across her chest and up her neck. Isla pushed in with everything she had left, splitting her open from blood to bone.

Devlin roared and was at her side before Isla could get a second killing strike in. She hadn't expected him to move so fast. That firestone dagger was in his hand one second, then cutting into her arm the next.

Pain split her in two—different and deeper than before. The dagger skimmed her skin but seemed to cut *past her*. Blood pulsed at the open spot and scattered in fear. It felt like she was on fire and burning out.

He lifted the dagger again and instinct told her she wouldn't survive another slice. She grabbed his wrist and the two toppled to the ground. Isla used her spare hand to scratch and claw at his, making sure the blade didn't touch her skin.

The tip nicked Devlin's shoulder and he screamed. He pushed her off and her head made contact with a broken wagon. Grasping his shoulder, Devlin crawled away from her, towards Beretta who lay covered in deep crimson.

With stars blocking half her vision, Isla used the cart to pull herself to her feet, gasping for whatever breath she could steal.

Devlin was bent over Beretta, drops of blood spilling onto her white face.

This was her chance. Without looking back, Isla launched herself off the cart and ran the opposite way. Devlin shouted but was still crouched over Beretta.

She stumbled into the side of a building with peeled paint, pushing herself to keep going. The wound at her side was gushing blood and the cut from that blade had turned ice cold now, sending tendrils of pain up her arm.

But she had to keep going.

One foot in front of the other.

Then another shaky step.

She tripped over a pile of ropes, unable to spot them in the dim light, but pushed herself up and started again. Devlin and the others were still not in sight but would be upon her soon.

Somehow, she managed a brief sprint, still clutching that dagger in her hand. Running and running with her eyes on the tree line, highlighted by the moonlight which now glimmered with an extra ferociousness.

If she could only make it to the forest, she'd be safe.

Seconds dragged on for eternity and every movement of her limbs brought fresh waves of pain that threatened to overwhelm her. Lights in the back part of the camp flickered and brightened, while new shouts in the distance started.

Devlin must have found new soldiers to aid him. But she had precious minutes on them.

Finally, she took a step into the dark forest and relief and victory seemed to replace that pain. Fresh pine air no longer tainted by blood and stone filled her lungs and she took the first real breath she had in months.

Now, each step she took was with purpose. She didn't know what she ran towards, she only knew that something called to her in the forest.

Fifty
Prince Edmund of Velotia

It was a miracle no one had spotted him yet, hiding under the blue cloak of his poor excuse of a wielder disguise that still felt foreign upon his body. He should probably pray to the goddess that the general was so distracted now that they crossed back into Murat for their final attempt.

Three months.

It had been three months since Commander Skallen's betrayal, and the only hint of solace they'd seen from Slin was the fact that the disgraced commander's body had been found with the rest of their men at the ambush outside of Vaner.

And yet here he was, still trudging through the edge of the Muratian Black Forests, disguised as a lowly wielder in the Agicae corps. While he hated the disguise, it was perfect at keeping him far away from that insufferable Pedite *general*.

To this day, he viciously regretted that promotion he gave him. It seemed like the right thing to do to ensure his silence on all matters relating to Isla. He never would have thought it'd give that godsdamned Pedite oversight over her second rescue mission when there were no others available.

Edmund should have had him killed after Isla was abducted for the second time, and if it weren't for the fact that he had extensive knowledge about this part of Muratian lands, along with a way to track Isla that Edmund still didn't understand, then he would have done away with him long ago.

He still hadn't made up his mind about what to do with him once they found her. Though, that seemed like a problem for when they returned to safer lands. He still needed him until they got her back to the safety of Velotia.

Everyone was on edge since—whatever it was—passed them by in the forest. Freya whispered that it could have been an elemental or another godly spirit sent to smite them. Edmund was just glad it passed without returning to see who intruded in its forest.

The general, Rian, or whatever his name was, sat close to his respite spot, talking to his soldiers, Freya among them. Edmund tipped his head at the Pedite, hiding further under the safety of his cloak's hood.

Freya'd already had to trail back to help when he and another soldier got their boots stuck in a sinking pit—*again*. She nearly made good on her promise to remove a limb if it weren't for the others who watched them. She still kept quiet about his secret and he somehow managed to keep his hood on throughout the entire ordeal in the mud pit—which the general seemed to find amusing for some reason.

Edmund thanked the one-eyed goddess that the general hadn't come to help himself. Then everything would have been ruined.

After all the rows they'd gotten into, he was certain Rian would throw him back to Velotia immediately, probably using his lingering icewielder injury as an excuse.

Now, he was stuck here with wet boots and a severely injured pride as he couldn't ask anyone for help, and Freya'd already refused. He wished someone was here who could make a tent for him instead of having to sleep on the forest floor. *In the dirt.*

Edmund knew that Freya watched him closely—as much as she could without giving him away—even as she spoke to the general about their plans for tomorrow. Edmund listened in, curious to know their next steps.

"Are you certain this is the correct way?" Freya whispered, loud enough for Edmund to hear, which he greatly appreciated.

"Yes," came the gruff reply.

Edmund bristled. Whatever happened between the general and his sister had thus far remained a secret. Freya seemed to know—or at least have guessed at what happened—and kept what she saw to herself.

At least that made this Rian equally as determined to stay here until they succeeded.

As Edmund listened in, the two spoke at length about the rest of their travel, Rian confident in the direction they headed, though he was quiet about where that confidence came from, considering only a few days ago he'd been wrought with indecision for some unknown reason. They brought another wielder with them, a tracker, and yet Rian seemed to have a better idea where Isla was than the tracker.

How was that possible?

"The red mountains?" the other soldier, Malin, asked. "Are you certain?"

The general rubbed his arm, staring into a thicket of bushes. "Absolutely."

Edmund shook his head. He still thought they were close and would have to move quickly, but Edmund knew it was complete lunacy. It had to be.

What did that make of him then, still following this lunatic because he had no better option?

Desperate.

Fifty-One
The Princess

It was hard to tell how long she ran, but it wasn't without stumbling over a lumpy patch of dirt or running into a spiky branch or two. It was so dark now, with nothing but the faint moon and stars peeking through the forest brush to guide her way.

The same vision of an unnaturally darkened sky flashed through her mind, along with other hazy faces and places. She knew blood still poured from her side but the smell of fresh pine and earth helped keep it at bay. The cold from the wound in her arm started to spread like a sickly insect crawling on the inside of her skin.

Once she could take it no more, she stopped for a breath. Doubled over and panting as if her lungs hadn't breathed properly in months—which they probably hadn't—she finally paused to think of what next. She knew her name, her real name now. At least she thought she did.

Everything else still lingered just out of reach. No matter how hard she tried, nothing came up except faded blurs that were no more than a whisper in the night sky.

Something scuttled behind a small oak. She jumped up, that thin dagger still clutched in her hands as if she had any energy left to fight. Every part of her body threatened to collapse on itself, and the pain sent constant ripples through her body that nearly toppled her with each movement.

This was it.

They'd found her and would take her back. Down below.

The thought of those mines raged through her body like a shock of lightning.

No! She refused to go back. She'd never go back.

Her resolve held strong. With a shaky hand, she lifted the dagger, holding it above the spot in her chest where she hoped her heart was. There would only be one shot at this, and she had to meet her mark.

The corners of her eyes burned as she imagined that canopy of sand swaying above her, as she tried to imagine the feel of warm morning sun caressing her skin one last time. She blinked away the weak tears and released one last breath before they came, waiting to get a view of Devlin. In a twisted sense, she wanted him to know she chose death over him.

It wasn't the sounds of soldier's footsteps that greeted her, but a horse whinnying. The sound disarmed her and she loosened the slack on her grip as the creature cantered into the clearing.

At first, she thought it came from the mining camp but there was no rider on its back. There was no saddle or reins attached to the beast either, so it couldn't have come from the Muratians.

The chestnut came to a stop in front of her and pawed at the ground, shaking its head. Its brown hair was in tangles, indicating it had been out here for weeks or months. It wasn't wild or it would have run at the sight of her and seemed far too calm in the presence of an intruder in this forest.

Another pause while she listened to the song of the forest. There wasn't anyone or anything else nearby, thank the goddess.

She tucked the blade into her pants and reached a shaky hand, feeling its hot breath on her palm. Its dark eyes stared into hers and she finally realized that it was missing an ear. A one-eared horse. Surely a jest from the one-eyed forest goddess, Halia.

"Can you take me home?"

The horse whinnied and stomped its hoof, as if to answer her question.

Without fully understanding the pull she felt in her core, she knew she could trust the creature. She knew it would do her no harm. It may even be a friend.

Like Beretta.

A *friend*.

That word felt foreign on her tongue after everything. She didn't know the meaning of it anymore. Couldn't trust her own mind.

The horse grunted, eager to get moving—as if it too, couldn't stand being in this forest any longer than necessary. She ran a hand along its long nose and past its missing ear, getting her fingers stuck in the tangles of its flowing mane. The horse would let her on, that was another thing she was certain of.

When she ran her hand along its back, it bowed its head and knelt on its forelegs.

With the last bit of strength she had, she grabbed the horse's hair and pulled herself to its back, nearly falling off the other side.

"Sorry," she mumbled, even though the horse wouldn't understand.

She didn't remember riding many horses prior but assumed it would have been with a saddle, not bare back like this.

The horse snorted and shook its head one last time before getting up, nearly unseating her.

Once she found her balance, she let her mind and body finally relax without allowing the darkness to pull her in.

The horse would know where to go, even if she couldn't direct it. Even if she couldn't fully ask. Even if she didn't know where it was anymore.

It was taking her home.

THE END

The goddess years

The Star-Years of the Goddesses:
Leto: Overseer of harvests
Neme: Goddess of birth and fertility
Halia: The one-eyed watcher of mountains and forests
Insmia: The fire goddess
Poron: Goddess of health and healing
Slin: The trickster goddess of chaos
Kiemp: Goddess of the oceans and rivers
Wallienne: Goddess of sin and lies
Laian: Warden of wrath and retribution
Imoten: Guardian of fortune
Mannop: Deliverer of justice
Kheppi: The morning sun goddess
Dia: Watcher of the unknown

The sister goddess years, as foretold by Rallion's comet:
Hierel: The star goddess
Rallion (Sister Death): Goddess of the gates

About the author

Cadence is a Canadian author who enjoys reading any Science Fiction and Fantasy novels she can get her hands on, and has loved disappearing into a great book ever since she learned to read. She loves writing new characters and getting to explore new worlds and creatures. In her spare time she tries to get outdoors as much as she can and spends time cuddling her cat, who is the world's worst assistant!

www.ingramcontent.com/pod-product-compliance
Lightning Source LLC
Chambersburg PA
CBHW030920120726
47906CB00002B/416